Praise for *New York Times* bestselling author Maisey Yates

"Fans of Robyn Carr and RaeAnne Thayne will enjoy [Yates's] small-town romance."
—*Booklist* on *Part Time Cowboy*

"Passionate, energetic and jam-packed with personality."
—*USATODAY.com*'s *Happy Ever After* blog on *Part Time Cowboy*

"Yates writes a story with emotional depth, intense heartache and love that is hard fought for and eventually won in the second Copper Ridge installment... This is a book readers will be telling their friends about."
—*RT Book Reviews* on *Brokedown Cowboy*

"Wraps up nicely, leaving readers with a desire to read more about the feisty duo."
—*Publishers Weekly* on *Bad News Cowboy*

"The setting is vivid, the secondary characters charming, and the plot has depth and interesting twists. But it is the hero and heroine who truly drive this story."
—*BookPage* on *Bad News Cowboy*

D0043079

**In Copper Ridge, Oregon, lasting love
with a cowboy is only a happily-ever-after away.
Don't miss any of Maisey Yates's
Copper Ridge tales, available now!**

From HQN Books

Shoulda Been a Cowboy (prequel novella)
Part Time Cowboy
Brokedown Cowboy
Bad News Cowboy
A Copper Ridge Christmas (ebook novella)
The Cowboy Way
Hometown Heartbreaker (ebook novella)
One Night Charmer
Tough Luck Hero
Last Chance Rebel

From Harlequin Desire

Take Me, Cowboy

Look for more Copper Ridge

Hold Me, Cowboy (Harlequin Desire)

For more books by Maisey Yates,
visit www.maiseyyates.com.

MAISEY YATES

Last Chance
Rebel

HQN™

If you purchased this book without a cover you should be aware
that this book is stolen property. It was reported as "unsold and
destroyed" to the publisher, and neither the author nor the
publisher has received any payment for this "stripped book."

ISBN-13: 978-0-373-78982-5

Last Chance Rebel

Copyright © 2016 by Maisey Yates

Recycling programs
for this product may
not exist in your area.

All rights reserved. Except for use in any review, the reproduction or
utilization of this work in whole or in part in any form by any electronic,
mechanical or other means, now known or hereinafter invented, including
xerography, photocopying and recording, or in any information storage
or retrieval system, is forbidden without the written permission of the
publisher, HQN Books, 225 Duncan Mill Road, Don Mills, Ontario
M3B 3K9, Canada.

This is a work of fiction. Names, characters, places and incidents are
either the product of the author's imagination or are used fictitiously,
and any resemblance to actual persons, living or dead, business
establishments, events or locales is entirely coincidental.

This edition published by arrangement with Harlequin Books S.A.

For questions and comments about the quality of this book,
please contact us at CustomerService@Harlequin.com.

® and TM are trademarks of Harlequin Enterprises Limited or its
corporate affiliates. Trademarks indicated with ® are registered in the
United States Patent and Trademark Office, the Canadian Intellectual
Property Office and in other countries.

www.HQNBooks.com

Printed in U.S.A.

Last Chance
Rebel

CHAPTER ONE

REBECCA BEAR FINISHED putting the last of the Christmas decorations onto the shelf and took a step back, smiling at her work.

Changing seasons was always her favorite thing to do at the Trading Post. Getting the new stock in and arranging it on her antique furniture, adding appropriate garlands and just the right scented candle to evoke the mood. It was the kind of thing she could never do in her own house, since all of her money was poured straight back into the business. So she got it out of her system here.

The air was filled with pine, apples and cinnamon spice. She inhaled deeply, a sweet sense of satisfaction washing over her.

Her store was tiny. Rent on Main Street, Copper Ridge, Oregon, was most definitely at a premium. Which was likely why every decent building on the block was owned by the richest family in town.

But she liked her modest space, stacked from floor to ceiling with knickknacks of all varieties. From the cheesy driftwood sort tourists were always after when they came to the coast, to art and furniture handcrafted by locals.

Beyond that, she tended to collect anything that she found interesting. She turned, facing the bright blue sideboard that was up against one of the walls. That was her bird display. Little ceramic birds, teaspoons with birds engraved on the handles, mugs with birds and frivolous little statues made of pinecones and driftwood to be placed anywhere in your home. All of them arranged over a beautiful handmade doily from one of the older women in town.

She kept that display all year round, and it always made her feel cheerful. She supposed that was because it was easy to identify with birds. They could fly anywhere, but they always came back home.

The bell above her door tinkled, and she turned around, a strange, twisting sensation hitting her hard in the stomach as a man ducked his head and walked inside.

His face was obscured by a dark cowboy hat. His shoulders were broad, and so was his chest. In spite of the cold weather he was wearing nothing but a tight black T-shirt, exposing muscular arms and forearms, and a dark band tattooed on his skin.

He straightened, tilting his hat backward, revealing a face that was arresting. It really was the only word. It stopped her in her tracks, stopped her breath in her lungs.

She had never seen him before. And yet, there was something familiar about him. Like she had seen those blue eyes before in a slightly different shape. Like she had seen that square jaw, darkened with stubble in a different context.

It was so strange. She wondered for a moment if maybe he were famous and it was just such a shock seeing him in her store and not in pictures that she couldn't place him. He was definitely good-looking enough to be a celebrity. A male model. Maybe a really hot baseball player.

"The place looks good," he said.

"Thank you," she responded, trying to sound polite and not weirded out.

She wasn't used to fielding random compliments on the look of her store from men who towered over her by at least a foot. Occasionally, little old ladies complimented her on that sort of thing. But not men like him.

"You do pretty good business," he said, and it wasn't a question.

"Yes," she said, taking a step backward, toward the counter. Her cellphone was over there, and while she doubted this guy was a psychopath, she didn't take chances with much of anything.

"I've been looking over some of your financial information, and I'm pretty impressed."

Her stomach turned to ice. "I...why have you been looking at my financial...anything? How do you have access to that information?"

"It's part of the rental agreement you have with Nathan West. He's the owner of your building."

She knew perfectly well who the owner of her building was. It felt a lot like making a deal with the devil to rent from Nathan West, but he owned the vacant part of Main, and she'd done her best to separate her personal issues from the man who potentially held her financial future in his hands.

Anyway, she'd figured that if she didn't rent from him—if she found a place off the beaten path—and took a financial hit for it, then she was allowing the West family to continue to damage her.

So she'd swallowed all her pride—which was spiky, injured and difficult at the best of times—and had agreed to rent the building from him.

Also, it wasn't Nathan West she had cause to hate. Not really.

It was his son.

Suddenly, she felt rocked. Rocked by the blue eyes of the man standing in front of her. She knew why they looked familiar now. But it couldn't be. Gage West had taken off years ago, after he'd ruined her life, and no one had ever seen him again.

He couldn't be back now. It wasn't possible.

Well, it was unless he was dead, but it wasn't fair.

She drew in a breath. "I reserve the right to refuse service to anyone. I've never cashed that chip in before, but I think today I just might."

"Rebecca," he said, his voice low, intense. "We need to talk."

"No, we don't," she said, her throat getting tight. "Not if you're who I think you are. *We* don't need to do anything. *You* need to get the ever-loving hell out of my store before I grab the shotgun I keep under the counter."

"Gage West," he said, as though she hadn't spoken. As though she hadn't *threatened* him. "I'm acting as my father's executor. I don't know if you heard, but he had a stroke a couple of days ago and is still recovering in the hospital."

"I hadn't heard," she said, not quite able to bring herself to say she was sorry. She wasn't all that surprised the news hadn't reached her; gossip tended to travel quickly in a town the size of Copper Ridge, but she'd all but been hibernating in her store while preparing for the holiday season. "I don't need to do any business with you, though."

"That's not the case."

"Yes, it absolutely is. I've managed to rent this building from your father for seven years. And in all that time I saw him face-to-face only a couple of times, otherwise we went through a property manager. I don't see why it has to be any different now."

"Because things are different now."

"Okay. Do you want to talk about things being different? I assume you know who I am." Her voice was vibrating with rage, and she resented him. Resented him for walking into this little slice of the world that she had carved out for herself. This beautiful, serene place that was supposed to be hers and only hers. And in had walked her own personal demon in cowboy boots.

"I know who you are," he said, his tone rough.

"Then you know I'm not kidding about the shotgun."

"Look, Rebecca—"

"No, you look. The only thing I know about you is that you were driving a car on a rainy night seventeen years ago and caused an accident that destroyed my life. I assume that's all you know about me too. My name.

Maybe my age. Maybe how much my mother was paid to keep the whole thing quiet."

Those blue eyes burned into hers for a moment. "I don't know the exact amount, but my father made it clear that he paid to take care of my mistakes. And yes, I know about you too."

"Then why are you in my store? You shouldn't be able to look me in the eye, much less stand here and talk to me like you don't know exactly what you did."

He just stood there, looking a lot like a fighter resigned to taking blows. He didn't look defeated, nor did he look properly ashamed. And it seemed as though her jabs were glancing off of him.

"I'm here because I wanted to make sure that you knew the details of the situation."

"I'm informed," she said, hearing the weariness in her tone. "Thank you for stopping by. Feel free to let the door hit you on the way out."

"I'm going to buy the building." He continued on as though she hadn't spoken.

She felt like she had been hit by a car he was driving all over again. "You what?"

"I've been back in town for two days, and in that time, I've been going over the financial situation my family find themselves in."

"Filthy rich with silver spoons up their asses?"

"Much less rich than my father would have people believe." He crossed his arms over his broad chest. "And like it or not, it's my job to fix it. From my point of view the only option he has is to start lightening the load, so to speak. It's a sinking ship. And that means we have to throw cargo off. That means these little buildings that he owns here on Main are the first thing that need to go, from my perspective."

She struggled to keep her voice calm even as the world reeled around her. The Almighty Nathan West wasn't swimming in money? And her store—her safe haven—was about to be sold out from under her, just like that? "Wait a second. You think you're qualified to make decisions like this? Where exactly did you get your degree?"

"Some online program. I printed the actual degree out at a Motel 6 in a shit town in Idaho I was passing through a few years ago."

If it had been someone else under other circumstances, she might have appreciated his quick wit. "Which just serves as reminder that you've been gone from Copper Ridge for years. So why exactly do you think you're qualified to make this decision? A decision that affects me, and the other people who are currently tenants in your father's little fiefdom here."

He lifted a shoulder, maddeningly calm, as he had been from the moment he had walked in. "I don't suppose I could ask you to trust me on that."

"I don't suppose you could."

"That's too bad, but unfortunately it doesn't change anything. I'm not here to put you out, but we can't hold on to any assets that are going to damage the West family finances."

"But you said that you're buying the building. Aren't *you* the West family and its finances?"

"No," he said, another infuriatingly opaque answer.

She narrowed her eyes. "If you're going to hand out an eviction notice, why don't you do it now? There's a nice symmetry to it. Just give me one more problem to put on your shoulders, Gage West. I don't mind. I'm happy to let you carry around my suffering."

"I don't want your suffering," he said, studying her from those impenetrable eyes. "But I would like to give you the building."

GAGE HALF EXPECTED her to go for the shotgun now. Not that he could blame her. He couldn't blame her for any of this. For her anger, for her threats. He deserved every single thing that she lobbed at him. And more. But he had never pretended he wasn't guilty.

He was guilty. Straight down to the center of his soul, if he even had one left. He wasn't looking for atonement, wasn't searching for absolution. It wasn't to be had.

He simply wanted to fix what he could. It was why he was here.

"Get out."

That wasn't the response he had expected. He had at least expected curiosity. But from the moment he had walked into the store, it had been apparent that Rebecca Bear wasn't quite what he had bargained for.

He hadn't pictured her being this hard, for one thing. He hadn't exactly pictured her as a woman either, in spite of the fact that he knew she had been running her own business here on Main Street for the past seven years. He was well aware of that because he had financed it in the first place. Not that she knew that. If she did, she would probably make good on her threats.

Still, it had been a shock to walk through the door and see her standing there, her chestnut hair cascading down past her shoulders, a smooth silky river, the petite but generous figure perfectly designed to draw a man's eye to all of the relevant dips and swells. Then there were her eyes, dark, sharp.

But what stopped him short was her smooth golden skin. Smooth golden skin that then transformed into a rough landscape midway down one side of her face, extending down her neck and beneath the collar of her shirt.

His most enduring gift to her.

"Not until you hear me out."

"I'll call Sheriff Garrett."

"I own the building. Or, my family does."

"Eli won't care." He could tell by the determined glitter in her eyes that even if she was bluffing, she was prepared to take her chances. Well, so was he. And the threat of having the police called was not exactly a deterrent to a man like him.

"I want to give you the building," he repeated.

She looked as though she had been slapped. "I don't want your charity."

"It isn't charity. Consider it payment."

"Payment?" The word was nearly a feral growl. "Compensation for everything that's behind door number one?" She waved her hand over the left half of her body as she said that. "Thanks, but I'm going to take a hard pass on your blood money."

He had expected a lot of things. That she would be angry, of course. That she would be justifiably upset at his presence. But he had not expected her to reject his offer to give her the building her business was in outright.

"It isn't blood money. I owe you."

"Yeah, you're damn right you do. But you couldn't repay me, not in this lifetime. There are things money can't fix, and I know that since you're a West that's a difficult concept for you to wrap your brain around, but it's the truth. And it's a truth people like me have known for years. Because we can't just throw money at things to make our problems go away. To cover them up. We actually have to deal with them."

"You think I've been off somewhere living the high life all this time?" His conscience, so seared he had thought perhaps it had no more feeling left in it, burned slightly. Regardless of what he had actually been doing or the means within which he had been living, he'd had access to a lot of money.

"I think however you've been living, you have the mindset of someone who was born with money. Which is why you ever thought it was all right for you to behave in a way that put you beyond the rules. And when people like you do that, people like me suffer. That's the end of the story. I am the cautionary tale of your excess."

She wasn't saying anything he hadn't already said to himself, every day for the past seventeen years. It was why he'd tattooed the reminder on his arm. It was why he had left. Why this was the first time he had set foot in Copper Ridge since that night he'd walked out of his father's office for the last time.

"Trust me. I know."

Her lip curled. "You don't know anything."

"Unfortunately, I do."

"*Unfortunately.* Of course it all feels unfortunate to you. To realize that your actions have far-reaching consequences that you can't control." She took a deep breath. "But I can't just call it unfortunate. This is *my life*. Now get out of my store."

Well, Gage hadn't had a positive greeting from anyone in town so far. So he couldn't really blame the woman he had permanently scarred for being the least enthused of all upon his return.

"Okay. I'll go. But I'm going to be back, and we're going to talk when you're able to be rational."

She planted her hands on the counter, staring him down. "Oh, I haven't begun to be *rational* with you. If you overstay your welcome, I might be tempted to *rationalize* a whole lot of things. Such as taking advantage of certain home-invasion laws and twisting them to include my business."

If there was one thing Gage had learned over the years, it was the value of retreat. He tipped his hat in a gesture he hoped she'd take as polite and not cocky. "I'll take that as my cue. But I will be back, Rebecca."

Then he turned and walked out of the store. Back on Main Street, he let out a hard breath, his chest loosening, a tension he hadn't realized he'd been carrying easing slightly.

Dealing with Rebecca was never going to be simple. He'd known that going in. But he was here to deal with his responsibilities.

If there was one thing he'd learned, it was that you

couldn't run from your demons. They'd spent years nipping at his heels as he'd moved from place to place, before they'd caught right up to him and possessed him outright.

He was here to perform a damn exorcism. And although she had every right to hate him, Rebecca Bear's pride wasn't going to get in the way of that.

He'd been close when he'd gotten the call about his dad. Closer than he usually let himself come to his hometown. Typically, he avoided Oregon altogether. But he'd been down near Roseburg doing some temporary work clearing brush and burning it while it was wet, to keep things safer during fire season. Dirty work that kept his mind clear.

The fact he'd been just a couple of hours away would seem like a sign, if he believed in those.

When his lawyer had called, he'd been shocked to hear about his father's stroke. And to learn that he was the executor of the estate if Nathan West was ever incapacitated.

It had felt...well, it had felt far more damned significant than it should.

It also didn't escape his notice that his family hadn't called. Clearly his father's attorney had been able to get in touch with Gage's, so that meant someone knew how to contact him. But of course it hadn't been his brother. Or his mother.

It had been made abundantly clear when he'd gone to the hospital a few days earlier that his siblings were shocked anyone knew of his whereabouts. Shocked he'd returned.

Hell, in some ways, so was he.

He paused, looking up and down the street at the place he'd called home for the first eighteen years of his life. The place he'd been absent from almost as long.

There was a near distressing sameness to Copper Ridge's Main Street. It had changed shape in many ways, more businesses open than he recalled, a new sort of vitality injected into the local economy.

But it smelled the same. The air unrelenting in its sharpness. Pine mixing with salt and brine as the wind crossed down from the mountains and mingled with the sea. It settled over his skin, the cool dampness wrapping itself around him.

Most days, a thick gray mist hung low, making the sky seem like it was something you could reach up and touch. Today, it was great enough that it blanketed the tops of the buildings, swirling over the red brick detail, blotting out the big American flag that flew proudly just behind the chamber of commerce.

There was an espresso shop across the street, the kind of place that served coffee with more milk than actual substance. He never thought he'd see the day when something that trendy hit Copper Ridge.

Though he supposed it was a little less unexpected than it would have been if they'd gotten in one of those big chains. Copper Ridge just wasn't a chain kind of place. Mostly because they didn't have the population to support them.

That had been the bane of his, and his friends', existence growing up. He supposed it was what made it an attractive tourist destination now.

Funnily enough, when he left he hadn't sought out a bigger city. Hadn't cared at all about chains or entertainment. Instead, he'd stuck to the back roads, spending his time in various small towns in different parts of the country.

But nothing was quite like this.

Somehow there was no comfort in that for him. The town brought back too many old memories. In fact, he resented the fact that it was so distinct. He had been to enough places that everything started to blur together eventually. Nothing was unique.

Except Copper Ridge. And that felt like adding insult to damn injury.

He took a deep breath, daring the air to feel familiar. Daring it to push him down that rabbit hole of memories he didn't want to have.

Gage West was home. And he would rather be anywhere else.

CHAPTER TWO

REBECCA FELT BOTH exhausted and emotionally scarred by the time she turned her open sign around. She needed to get home. She needed to figure out how to deal with the fact that Gage West was apparently back in town and intent on forcing his guilt on her.

No, guilt might make her feel good about herself. She didn't believe for one second he felt guilty. Not in any real, contrite sense.

Not that she would care either way. His guilt, his overall contrition, didn't matter. It never had. It didn't change a damn thing.

She turned, walking back toward the register, feeling weary down to her bones.

The bell sounded behind her and she turned again, about to let whoever it was know that she was closed. But it wasn't a customer. It was Alison, carrying two boxes that Rebecca knew would be filled with pie. And following closely behind her was Lane, two bottles of wine in her hand. The door closed behind them and opened again as Cassie walked through also carrying a pastry box.

She had managed to forget entirely. Tonight was the

weekly girls' night, and the Trading Post was hosting this week.

"Hi," she said, feeling even more tired. She wasn't sure she had it in her to do the socializing thing tonight. The little group of friends, comprised of the female business owners on Main, had become an important source of companionship in her life over the past few years. But there were some things she had always felt most comfortable dealing with on her own.

Or not dealing with at all as she hid away in her mountain cabin. Whatever. It was her drama, her prerogative.

"Hello," Cassie said, her voice chipper. "God bless Jake. He's up to his neck in diapers and is at least *pretending* to be completely cheerful about it."

Of the group, Cassie was the only one with a husband and children. The rest of them had become pretty confirmed bachelorettes. But if anyone could entice Rebecca into thinking that maybe a husband and kids wasn't the worst idea, it was Cassie. She was always disgustingly happy.

"What's the plan for tonight?" Alison asked, walking to the back of the store and setting her box of pies down by the register. "We are not watching another male stripper movie," she said, directing this comment at Lane.

"I incurred the entire rental expense for that atrocity," Lane said.

"But *my life*, Lane. I want my life back."

"It was two hours," Lane said. "Calm down."

"Two hours when I could have done anything else."

"And yet, I notice you didn't get up and leave during the movie," Lane replied.

"I was waiting for the payoff. I assumed that at some point someone would get naked. Instead, there was so much talking," Alison groused.

"Well, whatever we decide to do, there are snacks," Cassie said, lifting the tops of the boxes Alison had brought, and also the box she'd brought, and revealing two different pies and an assortment of pastries.

"Snacks are good," Rebecca said. "Of course, I haven't had dinner."

"This is dinner," Cassie said, advancing on the pie.

"I need a drink," Lane said, going back behind the counter and rummaging until she produced the wine glasses that Rebecca kept back there for these occasions. "You, Rebecca?"

"I'll just make some coffee. I have to drive back home after this, and I don't think I can stay long enough to wait for the buzz to wear off."

"Rough day?" This question came from Alison.

"Just tired." She was a liar. A cagey liar.

Her friends knew about her accident. She found that until she divulged the source of her scars it was just a weird eight-hundred-pound gorilla in the room. But nobody knew who was responsible. In fact, she kept the details as private as possible.

She kept it simple. She had been in a bad car accident when she was eleven, and it had left permanent scarring. The end.

"Are you sure?" Cassie asked, busying herself starting to brew coffee.

"Yes," she said, "I'm sure. Also, Cassie, you don't need to make me coffee. That's what you do all day."

"I'm well aware of what I do all day, Rebecca. But I don't want to drink the swill that you call coffee. I'm a connoisseur. An artisan."

"I'm not going to argue," Alison said. "Mostly because I just want you to make the coffee."

"Well, you spent all day making pie. So I suppose I'll allow it," Rebecca said.

"Nobody *allows* me to do anything," Cassie said. "I'm independent and free. I do what I want."

"Right," Lane said. "I imagine if Jake gave you some orders you might take them."

Cassie wiggled her eyebrows. "Depends on the orders."

Rebecca always felt a little bit uneasy when the conversation took this kind of turn. Lane and Alison were currently single, but Alison had been married before, and Rebecca couldn't imagine Lane was as pathetic as she was. Rebecca had no experience with men. And it wasn't something she ever felt like discussing.

That meant a lot of smiling and nodding was required of her at moments like these.

Right now, she was all out of smile and nod. She just felt depleted. Alison seemed to notice.

"Okay, Rebecca. What's really going on? You're being supernaturally quiet."

"I'm contemplative," Rebecca said.

"No. You really aren't," Lane said.

She let out a long slow breath, using the opportunity to try and think of a very vague way to disclose what had happened today without giving too much away. "I just had kind of an unexpected brush with the past."

Lane snorted. "There's small towns for you. Your past is basically your present because nobody ever leaves."

"Thank God my past left town to keep Sheriff Garrett from breathing down his neck," Alison said, referencing her hideous ex.

"Not *that* kind of past." Though Rebecca thought as soon as she spoke those words that she probably should have let the group think it was an ex.

Alison arched a brow. "Intriguing."

"No, it isn't. I... I had an encounter with the man who caused my accident when I was a kid." There, that wasn't so bad. She'd said it.

Then she began to reevaluate her "not so bad" assessment. Her three friends were looking at her with very wide eyes.

"He came into the store."

"You actually *know* who caused your accident?" Alison asked.

"Yes," she responded.

All her friends knew was that she had been in a bad accident that had left scars. And of course, that was bad enough. But there was more to it. More that she had never really wanted to talk about with anyone else. And, now was no exception.

"What did you do?" Lane asked.

"I kicked his ass out," Rebecca responded.

"Did you call Jonathan?" Cassie asked.

"No. And I'm not going to tell him, because the last

thing I need is for my older brother to end up in jail because he killed someone. And trust me, if Jonathan had any idea that this guy was back in town, he would get himself locked up for homicide." Rebecca was only a little bit sure she was exaggerating.

"Do you want me to call Finn? He can come down and hang out by the store. Look menacing or whatever," Lane said, referencing her friend Finn Donnelly.

Though, she wasn't entirely sure the cranky rancher would refer to Lane as a friend. Actually, Rebecca wasn't entirely certain what Lane and Finn's deal was.

"Thanks for offering the use of Finn without his permission," Rebecca said. "But I'm fine."

"What does he…want?" Alison asked. "Did he just want to check in with you? After all these years?"

Rebecca lifted a shoulder. "I don't know. And I really don't care. As far as I'm concerned he can jump off a bridge. I don't really want his apologies. Or his pity. Or his anything." And she certainly didn't want him to seize control of her building. She didn't want him to give it to her. She didn't want him to have his hands on anything that she touched.

"Well, I'm all for holding grudges," Lane said. "I think it's healthy. Good for your pores."

"And, often keeps you safe. Forgiveness is for chumps," Alison added.

"I would be the first to say that some people are just better off out of your life. Or, off the planet." Rebecca knew that Cassie was thinking of her ex-husband, the total dud she'd been with before meeting Jake, the love of her life.

"Yes," Lane said, nodding, taking a sip of wine.

"Some people really don't need forgiveness. And, I imagine the man that left you with permanent physical scars is one of them. He was… He was driving recklessly, wasn't he?"

He had been. And the ensuing cover-up had meant that he had never been charged. And that no one ever knew. But even if he had been, it would not have solved what happened next. Because that one event was the breakdown of the rest of her life as she'd known it then.

"Yes. I just… It wasn't really something that I wanted to deal with. I've dealt with it, really."

If dealing with it meant growing yet more bitter by the year, then she most certainly had.

"Well, if he comes back during the workday, you know you can always call me," Lane said.

"Me too," said Cassie.

"Obviously, I will also show up with a weapon of some kind," Alison said.

"I appreciate that. You have no idea how much your willingness to appear with weaponry means to me. But, I think it will be fine."

"It's just so desperately random that he showed up," Lane commented.

It wasn't quite as random as Lane thought. But, Rebecca didn't want to get into it. Legally, Rebecca wasn't allowed to get into it. But then, since none of the payoff money from Nathan West had ever made it into her possession, she wondered if the agreement applied to her. Her mother had taken off with it a long time ago.

The money had never been for her pain and suffering. It had been her mom's getaway fund.

"I guess assholes who are prone to driving recklessly are also prone to random appearances?" she suggested.

"I guess so," Alison said, watching her a little bit too closely. Almost as if she sensed there was more to the story. Well, Alison was going to have to keep sensing. Because she was not going to get any more out of her. Alison had a past she didn't like to talk about. She should understand.

"I don't want to talk about the asshole anymore. I just want to eat some pie."

"I respect that." Lane took a piece of pie out of the box and set it on a paper plate. "Eat your feelings. I bet they're delicious."

"Of course her feelings are delicious," Alison said. "They're going to be consumed in a vehicle that I baked. And everything I bake is delicious."

"Hear, hear," Cassie agreed.

Rebecca was just going to try and put Gage out of her mind. With any luck, he would give up. He had disappeared very effectively for the past seventeen years, and she didn't really see why he would suddenly be persistent with her now. Hopefully, he had done what he needed to do, and that would be the end of it.

She just wanted to keep sending her checks to the rental company and not dealing directly with Wests.

Yes, not dealing with all of this was definitely her preferred method.

Hopefully, Gage would do the very best thing he actually could do to try and make up for what had happened seventeen years ago. Hopefully, he would leave her alone.

"WHAT THE HELL are you doing here?"

Gage wasn't terribly surprised to receive that greeting from his younger brother. He was standing on Colton's porch, his hands stuffed in his pockets, more or less expecting to be punched in the face.

Surprisingly, Colton made no move to attack him physically. He did not, however, allow him in. That was not surprising.

"I suppose you wouldn't believe it if I told you I was here to catch up on every Christmas dinner we have ever missed."

"No. And I would tell you that it's way too early to be talking about Christmas. We just had Thanksgiving."

"The stores put the decorations out earlier and earlier every year. Corporate greed I guess."

Colton looked at him hard. "I don't suppose you came by to get philosophical about the morality of retail stores."

He shook his head. "No. I didn't. But, we do need to discuss the ranch."

"The ranch that I imagine is one fatted calf short now that you've come home?"

Gage examined his younger brother, the lines on his face making his stomach tightened in a strange way. When he had left home Colton had been sixteen. A boy. He hadn't carried around the burdens of their family, certainly not carved into his skin.

There wasn't much that made Gage feel like a complete ass these days. But that did it.

"There was no fatted-calf slaughter," Gage said. "So you can calm down. I'm not the prodigal son. I'm not any kind of son, and we both know that. But I have been looking at all of Dad's records and I have concerns."

"Concerns about what?" Colton asked, dragging his hand beneath his chin.

"Dad is broke."

"What?" Colton lowered his arm, as though he had given up on being gatekeeper between Gage and the house.

"That's what I'm saying. I've been going over all of his assets, all of his debt. He and Mom don't have any money. What they have is property. Lucky for them they own most of it outright."

"That doesn't make any sense. How could they not have money? The equestrian facility is doing well."

"Yes. But he's been diverting those funds. It looks to me like it's probably gambling debts. At best. At worst he's deeply involved in a very sketchy ring of high-priced hookers."

Colton shook his head. "Or, he has more bastard children."

Gage gritted his teeth. "You know about him, do you? I mean, do we know about the *same* one? I wouldn't be surprised if the Oregon coastline were littered with secret Wests."

Colton's expression went slack. "I only know about the one. Jack Monaghan?"

"Yeah. That's the one."

"When did you find out?" Colton crossed his arms across his broad chest, and this time Gage put a little bit of thought to the fact that it was entirely possible his younger brother could take him in a fight. Well, depending on what sort of fight Gage treated him to. He was never going to fight his little brother the way he'd learned to fight on the rodeo circuits, and in the bars. He didn't want to kill him, after all.

It wasn't just years that stood between them. It was experience. Colton might have earned some facial lines here in Copper Ridge, but Gage had earned scars all across the country.

"I've known." He could remember clearly being introduced intimately to the shady underworld of their father's empire. Finding out who the man beneath the façade was. It was clear that his father had taken a similar approach to indoctrinating Colton into his world as he'd taken with Gage. And that made him think a little bit differently about his brother.

"Interesting," Colton said.

"Why is it interesting? *You* clearly know."

"Oh, I found out on accident. We've all known about Jack for about a year now."

Just like that, he found himself reevaluating again. "So Dad didn't tell you?"

"No." Colton frowned. "Did he tell you?"

"It was one of the payments I needed to understand. Before I left he was priming me to take over the business. You know that."

"I don't see what that has to do with his dirty secrets. He didn't tell me."

Gage lifted his shoulder. "Yeah, I imagine he figured he wouldn't make the same mistake twice."

"What's that supposed to mean?"

"Well, seeing as I took off after I found out what a

gigantic prick he was, I imagine he figured he wouldn't let you in on the secret. Losing one heir is a problem. Losing two just starts to look careless."

"That's why you took off? Because you found out what a terrible person Dad was?"

It was damn sure close enough. "Yes. I was poised to become king of his trash heap. And it wasn't what I wanted."

"And you think it is what I want? Did you think for one second what kind of position it would put me in? Mom?"

"No," he said. It was honest. When he had taken off he had been eighteen years old, full of self-loathing and anger. All that had mattered was his pain. It had been unique to him, of course. And nothing anyone else could possibly understand. Because he had been eighteen. So, he had been a dick.

"Yeah, I didn't think you did." He took a deep breath. "Thanks for not lying about it, though."

"There's no point. I didn't come back here to be the hero of the story. But I did come back here to take care of what I was asked to. Dad's lawyer contacted me and said that I'm still the person Dad has written down to be the executor in case he was incapacitated."

Colton shook his head. "I've been the one here taking care of things."

"I didn't say it wasn't messed up. I'm just telling you how it is."

"So, now you're going to step up?"

"Yes."

"And that's it? Whether I think you should be here or not?"

Gage pushed his hat back on his head. "Look. Nobody asked you. And I can understand why you're not happy about it, but that doesn't change anything. I have some things to take care of here, and I damn sure intend to take care of them."

"What will that entail? Are you going to deal with Mom's emotional fallout when she finds out that she's destitute?" Colton took a step forward. "That's what I've been dealing with. The fact that Mom is always one major incident away from a complete emotional meltdown. And Sierra is pregnant."

"I know. I mean, I noticed at the hospital."

"She's a woman. When you left she was a kid."

Gage's face heated. He felt like a fire had started in his chest and spread outward. Anger, pouring through him like molten metal. "I know."

"Madison… You have no idea what she's been through. The things they say about her… She could have used you here. I could have."

"What happened to Madison?"

"She's going to have to tell you about it. You don't get to come in and learn all of our secrets right off the bat. We've been here. Taking care of Mom, taking care of each other. All you took care of was yourself, Gage. So forgive me if I can't just accept the fact that you're here. And that you think you have a right to step in and start handling family business."

Gage pressed his hand against one of the supports on the deck. "This isn't about rights. It's about responsibility."

"You haven't cared about responsibility at all in more than a decade. Why are you starting now?"

"Because I was asked to."

Colton didn't say anything to that. Instead, he rocked back on his heels, looking toward the inside of the house.

"That woman is your wife?" Gage asked, suddenly realizing that he didn't know much of anything about his siblings. Beyond Sierra's very obvious pregnancy.

"Lydia," Colton said. "And yes. She is."

"It doesn't seem right that you're married. I remember you being sixteen."

"Hate to break it to you, but time marched on while you were gone."

Gage suddenly felt hideously old. And a little bit like something that might be found on the bottom of his boot. But then, he imagined that that was Colton's goal. He couldn't say he didn't deserve it.

"Yeah, I guess it did."

"What exactly are you going to do? About that debt?"

"I'm going to sell off as much as I can. My goal is to preserve the business and the ranch. I assume you're good with that."

He could tell Colton was good with it, and more than a little annoyed that he couldn't disagree. "Yes. I mean, that's what I would do."

"I don't have a sinister agenda, here. All I want to do is what I was asked to. And then, I'll get right back out of your life."

"I don't feel like Mom is going to be very impacted. Unless she goes through and counts all the assets."

"I guarantee you the only thing she goes through and counts is her pills."

His brother's stark words hit him hard. He'd known their mother was fragile. He'd always known. But this... this hurt. "That bad?"

Colton shook his head, his expression suddenly softening. "She does her best. But, Dad was bad enough that you left. I don't know what you've been out doing, but whatever, you had the skills to do it. Can you imagine being stuck with him? There's nothing else for her."

Horror streaked down his spine. "He doesn't... He's never laid a hand on her, has he?"

"It isn't like that. But she's stuck. She's completely dependent. And he's... He doesn't care about anyone but himself. You know that. Everything is justifiable as long as Nathan West is comfortable. We found out about Jack this past year." Gage had a feeling his mother had known a lot longer than that, but he didn't see the point in correcting Colton on that score. "We all found out," Colton continued. "Now her husband, who I think she hates as much as she loves, has had a stroke. And you're back."

"She doesn't know that yet, does she?"

"No," Colton said. "Stay away until we're ready to deal with it."

Gage took a step back. This command from Colton was more convenient than he'd like it to be. The edict to stay away from his mother, from his father, for a while suited him more than he'd like to admit. "You have my word on that."

If there was one thing he was good at, it was staying away.

CHAPTER THREE

REBECCA WALKED OUT of her bedroom door and onto the deck, wrapping her fingers more tightly around her cup as she stared out at the lake. It was chilly this morning, mist hovering over the water and on her breath.

She shifted her grip on her mug, grabbing hold of the edges of her blanket and wrapping it more tightly around her as she settled into the wicker chair she had placed in just the right spot so that she could watch the sun rising higher over the mountains, illuminating the low-hanging clouds and throwing gold dust onto the lake's surface.

She had a humble house, but there was nothing humble about the location. Nestled in the middle of the trees, way out of town, it was her own private sanctuary. She didn't mind the rustic nature of the cabin, anyway. It was perfect for her. After working days in the store, it was important for her to have a retreat. And days off. She had finally graduated to where she could pay a couple of employees, and that meant two days off a week like a human person.

Today, she fully intended to revel in the time off. She could take her kayak out on the lake. She preferred riding to paddling, but since the shop had left her so busy for the past few years, owning a horse had been impractical.

Of course, for the past few years running a shop had not been compatible with having a life of any kind. But, things were getting better. She had leisure time today. And she felt leisurely.

She inhaled deeply, feeling the need to soak her coffee in through every sense. The warmth of the cup on her hands, the smell and the strong, bitter taste that burned all the way down.

The sound of an engine spoiled her solace. She leaned forward, pushing herself into a standing position and trumping down the side steps on her deck, rounding to the front of the house just in time to see a black truck barreling down her driveway.

Usually when someone random drove down to her house, they were just looking for a place to turn around. The road up to the lake was narrow and windy, and if you happened to miss a turnoff, finding a way to make it right was often difficult.

She felt compelled to stand there, and keep an eye on her unexpected guest.

But, the truck didn't turn around. Instead, it stopped. And the driver killed the engine before getting out and revealing a man she herself would like to kill.

"What are you doing here?" she asked as Gage walked toward her. He was wearing the same thing he'd had on the last time she'd seen him. Cowboy hat, tight black T-shirt and snug, well-worn denim. Again, her eyes fell to the tattoo on his forearm.

Then she forced herself to look at his face. It was

grim. His mouth set into a firm line, his dark brows drawn tightly together.

"I wanted to talk to you about the shop," he said. "And to see about getting a welcome to the neighborhood."

"It's not really a neighborhood, *per se*. Mostly, you're in my driveway, and I need you to not be in it."

"I just bought the place across the lake."

Rebecca was certain she blacked out. Her rage was an epic creature, rising up from the depths inside of her and threatening to consume them both. "You what?"

"It's a coincidence that we're so close to each other."

"Sure it is, Edward Cullen."

"What?"

"If you start watching me when I sleep, I'm going to shut your dick in the open window."

"I have no interest in watching you sleep," he said.

"Then what is this? What is all of this? If you're interested in using me to appease your conscience, then you're shit out of luck. Because I'm not going to provide balm for your wounded soul. I'm not going to stand here and tell you that I forgave you years ago when I didn't. And I'm not going to suddenly grant you absolution now."

He paused for a moment, looking past her, his eyes fixed on the lake. "That isn't what I'm here for. I think you need a soul to be forgiven. I think you need a conscience in order to soothe it. I don't have either. Not anymore. I'm here to make things right, though."

"You can't. So, you might as well stop trying." She crossed her arms, staring him down. She didn't owe him anything. Not reassurance, not some kind of absolution. Because, whatever he said, he must be after that.

"Let me finish what I started."

"No problem. Right after you return full range of motion to my arm. My scar tissue is a little bit thick… makes it difficult to straighten completely."

He didn't flinch. And in that moment, she had to wonder if he was right. If he didn't have a soul or conscience. But if that were the case, why was he back at all?

Of course, if he had either of those things, why had it taken him seventeen years to come back?

"You're too proud to take help from me? Is that it?"

"Yes. I am too proud. I'm too *a lot* of damn things, Gage West. Everybody has monsters in their closet when they're little. You were mine. You are the reason I was in physical therapy. The reason I endured months of recovery. The reason that I had to have more than one surgery to try and restore the skin on parts of my body."

He tilted his head back, as though her words were physical blows. "I know."

"And it doesn't matter," she continued, her voice shaking, "that it was an accident. It was an accident that could have been prevented if you would have just used a measure of common sense. If you weren't driving too fast. If you hadn't been horsing around with your friends, or whatever you were doing. And maybe it's something that all teenage boys do, but when you did it, you crashed into me. And congratulations, you got to walk away. You got to walk right out of town and

never look back. But I had to stay. I had to live in this
body, and exist in your consequences."

His eyes darkened, her words touching him for the
first time. "You think I wasn't affected? I changed my
entire life because of that accident. You're right. I was
a spoiled, entitled, selfish ass who didn't think of anyone but himself. I didn't have respect for consequences.
I didn't think for one second what my behavior might
do. I've spent every day since then thinking about it."
He looked down, brushing his fingertips over his forearm, over the dark band that was inked there. "This is
a reminder."

Rebecca was shaking. Rage all but consuming her.
"That's lovely," she spat. "You got a tattoo. So that you
would be permanently scarred by all of this too. Well,
here's a news flash for you: I didn't get to choose a de-
signer scar. I'm marked by it even if I don't want to be.
Even if I *want* to forget, I can't. I'm so very glad that
my suffering has become a monument to your change
and betterment."

"Would you prefer that I didn't change at all?"

"I would prefer that I didn't know a damn thing about
you. I would prefer that I had no idea if you felt guilty,
if you had changed or if you had drunk yourself into
oblivion. Because I don't want your life touching mine.
Not again."

If he had been human, he would have been reduced
to ash by her rant. She was breathing fire. Instead, he
simply lifted a shoulder. "I can understand that. But
that isn't the way things are working out. I'm back. I'm
dealing with my parents' property, and your building

happens to fall under that umbrella. This is the situation. You can self-destruct because you hate me, or you can accept my help."

She gritted her teeth, refusing to back down. "Where's that self-destruct button? I'll hit it now."

"You haven't had any trouble spending my money for the past ten years—I don't know why you need to stand on principle now."

A line of frost bloomed down her spine, leaving a painful prickling sensation on her skin. "I've never taken anything from you. And if you're talking about that payoff from your father—"

"I'm not. When you were eighteen you received settlement money."

"From the insurance company. From your insurance company. That was what the letter from the lawyer said."

"Yeah. That's because he lied to you. I sent you the check."

"And the adjustments after that?"

"Also from me."

Her knees wobbled, threatening to give out beneath her. She turned sideways, leaning up against the rough-hewn side of her house, trying to keep from collapsing onto the ground. She was such an idiot. But she had no idea how insurance worked. She had no idea how any of this worked. Not beyond the way it had worked for her.

She had gotten a letter from a lawyer claiming to work for the West family, along with a check for an obscene amount of money that had allowed her to cover the start-up of her store. Those payments had given her the livelihood she had, especially in the beginning. Without it, she would have nothing.

That meant that Gage West owned her business. He owned her. In every way that mattered.

Is it any different than if it were insurance money? Isn't it all money off of your suffering?

It felt different then. Different when it was an arbitrary sum of money that Gage had decided to bestow upon her. Different when it had seemed like an insurance company had decided it was official damages, or something to do with her hospital bills.

Why did everything always come back to him? Why was everything so tangled up in the West family so that she couldn't escape?

"No."

"You can say no—it doesn't make it different."

"Why are you telling me all of this? Why are you here? What are you doing? I just… I don't understand why you thought it would be a fun thing to come in and completely mess up my life again."

"I'm not trying to mess your life up. I'm trying to give you something."

"Do I look like somebody that accepts gifts?" She flung her hand backward, indicating her house. "I work for what I have. I always have. My brother and I… It's a point of pride. When life got hard, my mother just sat down and took it, and Jonathan and I refuse to do that. We always have."

Jonathan had always told her they couldn't depend on other people to help them out. That no one cared what happened to a couple of poor kids, so they had to make their own way.

So they had. And they'd survived because of it. Not only that, they'd become successful in their own right.

Needing people…that would only leave you crippled when they walked away. And people always walked away.

"It doesn't make any sense to me. What good is pride if you don't have what you worked for?"

"It doesn't have to make sense to you. It makes sense to me. You haven't been in my life for all of this time, and you don't have any right to walk in now and pass judgment on the way I've been living."

"I'm going to sell off my father's assets. It's something that I have to do to save the ranch. I have to do that for my mother. While I was doing it, I wanted to help you. Instead of leaving you completely screwed in case somebody buys out your building and doesn't want to give you any kind of fair terms."

"It's a little bit too late to worry about my well-being, don't you think?"

He took a step toward her, and she pressed herself even more firmly against the side of the house. "You don't need to be so stubborn."

"Yes," she said, peeling herself away from the wood. Because why the hell was she shrinking away from him as though she should be afraid of him? She wasn't. She shouldn't be. He had been a monster in her closet when she was a girl, but right now, he was just a man. And she was going to treat him like any man who was on her property when he shouldn't be. "I have to be damn stubborn. Sometimes my stubbornness is the only thing that has gotten me through life. And I'll be damned if I back down just because you showed up and told me to."

"That's where you have yourself a problem. Because I'm not exactly known for my easy disposition and temperament."

"Are you actually fighting to give me something? I don't understand you."

"You don't have to understand, just be reasonable," he said.

"No. I don't know how to be reasonable. I only know how to be right." This, this right here, her inability to give on anything had gotten her in trouble more than one time over the years. But life was hard, so she had to make herself harder. She didn't regret it. She didn't regret learning to insulate herself from hardship. It was a necessity.

"You don't want to be in debt to me, that's your main issue. But the way I see it, you already are."

"Get off my property."

For once, he complied. Turning away from her and heading toward his truck. She watched him get in, watched him drive away. And then, her knees did give out. She slid down the side of the house, shaking, feeling every inch like the little wimp she was.

The fact that she wasn't stronger than this was a blow. At least she had held her own when he was here.

Her head was spinning. She was trying to work out exactly what all this new information meant. Gage West was her benefactor. The man she attributed the ruination of her life to was actually responsible for the way that she lived now. He was the reason she had a business. He was the reason she had a house. He was the reason that she had enough money to hire employees and was now indulging in a completely ruined day off.

It all started with him. Even though her business was completely self-sufficient now, without that injection of cash, she wouldn't have any of it. And yes, whether it should or not, it mattered that it was from him and not from the insurance company.

Like the monster had reached out of the closet to offer a piece of candy for everything he'd put her through. She didn't want that. She didn't want to be bound to him. Didn't want to be tied to him completely.

There was only one option. Only one option that was acceptable to her, anyway.

She dumped tepid coffee out into what would be flowers, if she ever bothered to plant any. Then she took a deep breath. She was going to get dressed, and then she and Gage West were going to meet on her terms.

GAGE HAD BEEN going over paperwork for hours. The text on the page was starting to wiggle, numbers beginning to reverse themselves. He was not a paperwork guy. He had a brilliant understanding of numbers and how investments worked. It was the reason he had any money to call his own. And he had quite a lot of it.

But, having a good head for business often meant knowing exactly which tasks you needed to farm out to other people. And that was another area he was expert in.

He had people to take care of the actual act of investing, people who managed his finances. Meanwhile, he continued to work with his hands whenever he could. Most people who had come into contact with him over the past few years probably imagined that he was destitute. And, he couldn't really blame them. He tended to live in motels; he traveled from place to place; his truck wasn't anything to write home about.

Of course, he'd owned this property on the lake for years. But no one knew that. He bought everything through a shell company and had his attorney handle all of his business. Finding caretakers for the place and everything else. He bought the house about a decade ago but had never actually lived in it.

It was the kind of place his father would find far beneath West family standards, but to Gage it was much better than the places he'd been staying while on the road.

It was rustic, but spacious. The property had a couple of outbuildings on it, including a barn that was housing horses for an older couple who weren't in town half the year. His caretaker had taken care of them while he'd been gone, but he wouldn't mind a chance to handle horses while he was in town.

Of all the things he'd done while he'd been wandering the country, rodeo and ranch work had been his favorite. And staying mobile had been a great way to keep ahead of his demons.

He wasn't entirely certain what had prompted him to buy a place in Copper Ridge. Only that some part of him wanted to own a piece of it. Wanted to have a foot in it.

It was a difficult place to let go of, even when you

were desperate to do it. But, it was all working out now. In that way that shit shows could work out. Which was definitely what this was.

He pushed his fingers through his hair and walked over to the kitchen window, looking out at the lake, barely able to glimpse Rebecca Bear's house where it was nestled in the trees across the water.

He could totally understand why she felt like she was being stalked. In some ways, he kind of was stalking her. In order to get her to stop being so pigheaded and take the store. He supposed he could sign it over to her, and then there wouldn't be much she could do about it. Except maybe refuse to sign her part of the deed. And then shoot him in the face.

His doorbell rang, and he could not for the life of him figure out who it might be. Maybe a neighbor with cookies. A neighbor who had no idea who he was. Because it sure as hell wasn't a member of his family, or anyone else who had a clue that he was the disgraced Gage West.

His father had done a damn good job covering up what had happened the night of Rebecca's accident. Nobody knew that he had been racing some friends on a back road and hit a car carrying a woman and her daughter. But, they did know that he had abandoned his family. They knew that he had left his fragile mother and a father who was endlessly generous to the community.

Gage West was nobody's favorite. And he knew it.

He crossed the kitchen, heading into the entryway,

jerking the door open without bothering to look out the window and see who was standing there.

When he saw his dark-haired, petite visitor, he felt like he'd been kicked in the chest by a bull. "What are you doing here?"

Rebecca frowned. "I thought you might like to see what it's like to have somebody show up uninvited at your place."

"I'm not nearly as disturbed by it as you were. But, I am curious."

"I don't want to owe you," she said.

"Okay."

"I see you have a working ranch here."

"Nothing major. Just a few horses."

"Well, someone has to take care of them. Someone has to ride them. And there are bound to be other things that can be done around the property."

"Are you offering to do manual labor in exchange for the multiple thousands of dollars that I gave you?" He was being an ass now, and he knew it. But then, he was often an ass, so he didn't see why he should change it now.

"I know, it's barely going to put a dent in it. But I'm going to do my best to work off my debt to you. And then, I will damn well buy that building from you. But I'm not going to owe you. The way I see it is this—I'm going to work, you're going to knock some numbers off of the debt. And then, when all is said and done, whatever else I owe you can put into the cost of the building."

He rocked back on his heels. "That isn't quite how I saw it going."

"Too bad. I don't know what you expected to come back and find. I imagine you pictured some broken, fragile girl who was just going to get on her knees and weep at your unexpected charity. But that isn't me. I'm not a crier. I'm a worker. And my life is my own. So, at the end of the day, I don't want to owe you a damn thing, Gage West. At the end of this, we part ways, and neither of us owes the other a thing."

He stared at her for a moment, his stomach twisting. This angry, strong woman, who was completely different than what he had imagined she might be, was offering him absolution in a way he had never considered.

Ultimately, he imagined that he was beyond forgiveness. And he stood by that. But she was right. This clean break could mean neither of them would owe anything to the other—it was the only way they could fully extricate themselves from each other's lives.

He had never met her before. Not before this week. And yet, Rebecca Bear was the person who had affected his life more than any other. The reason he had made almost every choice he made in the past seventeen years.

And he could see that he was tied up in hers too.

So this could be the end. This could be the clean break. He would be a fool not to take it.

"You've got yourself a deal, Rebecca. I'm going to be here for as long as it takes. And in that time you can work on my ranch and assist me with other things that might come up as I organize my father's assets. Then in the end, we'll draw up an agreement for the building, and I'll sell it to you, and we will filter all payments through a bank."

He stuck out his hand, and she just looked at it as though it were a snake. He watched as she curled her fingers into fists, but she did not lift her hand. He let his own drop back to his side.

She tilted her chin up, her dark eyes glittering. "Then, it's a deal."

CHAPTER FOUR

"YOU AGREED TO WHAT?"

Rebecca rolled her eyes and shifted the phone so that she could hold it between her ear and shoulder while she finished spreading jam on a piece of toast. "Calm down, Lane. If I wanted hysterics, I would have told Jonathan."

The idea of talking to her brother about Gage being back in town—living near her—and enlisting her services to help on his little ranch spread made her cringe. Well, especially because she had enlisted herself, not the other way around.

"I'm not being hysterical, but I am questioning your sanity. This guy rolls back into your life…"

"He did not *roll back into my life*. That implies that he was part of my life prior to leaving town. He wasn't. We ran into each other once or twice. Literally, in the most notable case."

"That's not funny," Lane said.

"It's actually hilarious. Don't police my humor. But, it's a whole big complicated situation, and I just wanted to let you know that I was going over to his house to do some work this morning so that in case I went missing you would know that I was finally finished off by the man who started killing me seventeen years ago."

Lane growled. "Again, not funny."

"Lighten up," Rebecca said, lifting her thumb to her lips and licking a bit of errant jam from her skin. "I'm just doing what I have to."

"Sure. But in a cagey fashion. You haven't exactly explained to me how all this works."

She took a bite of her toast. "It just does."

"Rebecca, I often find your unwillingness to share the details about your life slightly charming. You're kind of a little lockbox, kind of mysterious and that makes you interesting. However, in this case I'm a little bit frustrated with the fact that you are associating with this man without fully explaining everything."

She took another bite and spoke around the bread. "I don't have time to explain this morning. I have to get to work."

"You don't have time to do this," Lane continued, protesting sharply in Rebecca's ear. "You barely have any time off as it is."

"I have an overprotective older sibling, Lane. The position is filled, there's no need for you to apply."

"Sure," Lane said, "except you haven't told Jonathan. So, seeing as your overprotective sibling has not been informed, and is therefore not able to comment..."

"Because his comment would be vulgar at best, potentially homicidal at worst."

"Because you're being crazy."

Rebecca shoved the last piece of her breakfast into her mouth and grabbed her thermos full of coffee off of the counter. "I'm not being crazy. I'm making the most of a bad situation." Claiming her business for herself, trying to regain some kind of control in this situation.

She hated being out of control. She hated being needy. After the accident she felt like she'd been existing in a period of extended victimhood. Her body hadn't done what she wanted it to do, she hadn't had any decision-making power when it had come to submitting herself to another surgery, to another excrutiating recovery.

To being cared for by other people.

And, once their mother left, Jonathan had gone into overprotective older brother mode, and even though all of his decision making came from a good place, it was still overbearing.

"Fine. We'll discuss this later. See you tonight at Ace's?"

"Maybe," Rebecca said, shrugging her jacket on and zipping it up all the way to her throat.

"At least text me so I know you aren't dead."

"Promise."

She hung up the phone before heading out the door. She closed it tightly behind her, not bothering to lock it. Usually, she just kept it locked when she was home. If anyone wanted to steal her crap while she was gone, they were welcome to it.

She was more concerned about somebody assaulting her person while she was in residence.

Curling her fingers tightly around her thermos, she began to walk down her driveway. It would be much faster to drive over to Gage's place, but she wasn't exactly in a hurry to get there. Anyway, a little bit of time in her own head before she had to deal with him would be helpful.

She took a deep breath of the morning air, letting it sear her throat. Then, she took a sip of her coffee, letting out a long slow breath that turned into a cloud and drifted past her as she continued to walk quickly down her dirt driveway.

Wind rustled through the pines and the oaks, a few brown leaves fluttering down to the ground in front of her. She stepped on one, satisfied with the slight crunch that it made beneath her boot.

She found a simple kind of clarity in mornings like this. In her surroundings. It was one reason she liked living so far out of town. Too many people, too much noise and her brain ended up feeling cluttered. She had to have time to sweep it all clean again.

She looked up at the gray sky, at the pale yellow shadow of the sun trying to break through. She imagined it would all burn off around noon, treating them to a clear fall day, which was as rare as it was enjoyed by the people in this part of the world.

You had to cultivate a bit of enjoyment for gray and mist if you were going to live on the Oregon coast. Rebecca had always felt like it was part of her blood. She had been born here in Copper Ridge and had never felt the inclination to leave.

She kicked at a pile of leaves as she turned that thought over. She supposed that in some ways her life might have been easier if she had left. She wouldn't spend her time tripping over as many ghosts. But then, she supposed that all went back to control.

Why should she be the one to go? Why should she run away from her home because some teenage asshole had scarred her for life—more literally than emotionally.

Her conclusion had been that she shouldn't. And anyway, Gage had been the one to leave.

"But he's back," she said quietly, the words floating away on another cloud of her breath.

She reached the main highway and walked on the narrow shoulder, keeping an eye out for any cars that might be driving on the road. She doubted she would see anyone. It was still pretty early and unless people lived here, they didn't really have a reason to be driving out this way.

She looked down, focusing on the white line painted onto the black asphalt, watching as one boot landed perfectly in the center, then the other, with each footstep.

She paused when she arrived at his driveway, taking another deep breath, relishing the scent of the lake, cool and damp, and the overriding sharp tang of the ocean that permeated everything, a constant reminder that it was there, even when it wasn't in view.

Yes. This was her home. The Trading Post was hers, because she was the one who had built it up from nothing. If it had really been left up to Nathan West, it would be nothing. It would be nothing but a hollow shell. She was the one who had given it life. She was the one who was entitled to it.

She would be damned if Gage got to come in and make her feel like it wasn't hers. She would be damned if she would be chased off. She had made that decision early on. Even while she endured somewhat pitying stares from the townspeople, those who remembered the circumstances surrounding her accident, and the general indifference of men that had forced her to cultivate a shell that was so hard she didn't think anyone could get through it now. Even if she wanted to let them.

Feeling fortified, she continued on down the driveway, feeling gradually less fortified the moment his house came into view.

She loved her house, and she was proud of it. It was rustic and cozy and entirely perfect for one woman who lived by herself. But his place... Well, it was something spectacular. She had rarely had occasion to see the house up close, even though it was visible across the lake from her back deck. She'd known that it was impressive, she just hadn't realized quite how much.

It was one of those fancy, two-story cabins with logs that shone like honey and a green tin roof that pitched at sharp angles, following the expansive sprawl of the house itself. There were large windows at the front that reflected the scene around her, and herself, in their shining surfaces.

She looked determinedly at the door, and not at the reflection of herself. The reflection that looked very small and ineffective in the vast open surroundings.

She was *not* ineffective. She was a warrior.

She repeated that mentally with her every step up the front porch and to the door. Then, she knocked sharply, twice, before wrapping both hands back around her thermos. Clinging to it as though it might offer some source of power. Her own little caffeinated talisman.

She waited. And then, at a certain point, she decided that he was making her wait. That made her grit her teeth in frustration. As if all of this wasn't irritating enough, the man was playing power games with her.

Too bad for him, that kind of thing didn't work on her. She had lived through hell. Nothing scared her anymore. Least of all monsters under the bed, in the closet or in the spectacular log cabin.

Just when she was about to knock again, the door swung open and her heart, stomach and every other organ in her torso plummeted down toward her toes, leaving her hollowed out and breathless. He was…well, he was shirtless.

And while she considered herself impossible to intimidate, she was, apparently, easy enough to shock.

She swallowed hard, doing her very best not to stare at that broad expanse of bare chest. At the dark hair that covered his well-defined muscles, thinning out as it reached his incredibly cut abs.

He was wearing jeans that were disconcertingly low, revealing chiseled lines that acted as an arrow, directing the feminine gaze down to the rather prominent bulge at the apex of his well-muscled thighs.

She imagined that this moment, this moment that seemed horrifically extended, was actually over quickly. That she wasn't really standing there gaping at his body for a recognizable or measurable portion of time. She imagined that in actuality things were just moving slow on a scale of relativity at the moment. At least, she hoped so, because if not, she had just made a complete and total ass of herself.

Still, she found herself looking at that perfect body again. All hard lines and gorgeous skin and…not one single scar.

Unlike her own skin. Which was a guide to every injury, every surgery…

How was it fair that he looked like this and she looked like she did?

She forced her gaze up to his face and found it no less disturbing. Monsters, she decided, should be hideous. They should not be lean, finely honed examples of masculine perfection complete with an utterly offensive yet compelling tattoo on an equally compelling forearm.

They should not have sharp, hot blue eyes and curved sensual lips that put a woman in the kind of mind that began to wonder about how they might feel beneath her own.

But it occurred to her then, that maybe that was what made a monster like him so terrifying. He wasn't repellent. He was the embodiment of all of her nightmares, and she should hate looking at him. But she didn't.

Yeah, she wasn't easy to scare. But that was damn scary.

"You took all that time to answer the door and you couldn't find a shirt?" she asked, keeping her tone as hard and arid as possible.

"I took the time to find pants."

"Allow me to thank you formally. Are you… Heading out soon?"

"No," he said, offering no explanation beyond that.

"I thought that I was handling your ranch stuff because you were busy."

"I am. But this morning I'm concerning myself with my own personal business, and that is all work that I can do in my home office."

"Okay," she said, feeling a little bit like she'd been punched in the head. "I can figure out all the stuff out here." She waved her hand somewhat wildly, as if he needed the gesture to understand that she meant all of the tasks spread about across the property.

"Don't be ridiculous, I'll show you around. But I do need a shirt before I go outside." He turned away from her slightly, then back. "Come in?"

"I'm good," she said resolutely. She pressed her weight more firmly down toward the soles of her feet, completely determined to stay right where she was standing.

He said nothing. Instead, he turned away, closing the door behind him, leaving her standing there alone.

What exactly had she gotten herself into? Maybe she was crazy. Maybe Lane was right.

No. You're reclaiming. It's important. Essential.

Yes, it was. Protecting the part of the world that she had carved out for herself was the most important thing. Her home, her shop. And dammit all, her pride. She hated that she had accepted handouts from him without knowing it. She just needed to... Well, much like she needed to wipe her brain clean at the end of the day, she felt like she needed to wipe the slate too. Or she would never be free of it.

It would loom. And so would he. The monster she would never be able to vanquish.

She was here. She was vanquishing.

The door opened again, and this time, thankfully, he was wearing a tight black T-shirt and a black coat. "All right," he said, "come this way."

She followed him down the steps, down along a dirt road that led around back of the house. She wasn't really sure if she was supposed to make conversation with him. Then, she decided she really shouldn't care what she was supposed to do. There wasn't a protocol for the situation. And it wasn't on her to make him comfortable.

Of course, it would be nice if she could make herself comfortable, but that might be a step too ambitious.

"The horses are down this way," he said, gesturing toward a stable that was clearly visible. "If you wouldn't mind feeding them and taking care of the stalls, that would be helpful."

"I'd like to come by in the evenings and ride too," she said. "To make sure that they're getting some exercise."

"How often do you work your store?"

"Five days a week," she said.

"And you want to come here every day and do some work?"

"I was working in the store seven days a week until recently. The fact that I get time off at all is kind of a strange new situation."

"It seems like a lot."

"Are you concerned for my well-being?" If he said yes, she was going to kill him.

"No," he responded, hard and fast. "Just don't want you to drop dead on my property."

"Your concern is touching. With my last gasping

breath I'll send a text to one of my friends and have them drag me over the property line, would that help?"

"Yeah, if it makes you feel better."

"I don't know how to do this," she said.

"You don't know how to do ranch work? Because that presents a problem for our arrangement."

"No, I don't know how to talk to you like there isn't something huge hanging between us. I don't know how to talk to you like you're a person."

"You just do it, I guess."

"Or," she said, "I don't. We could always pursue that avenue. One where I just get to work and you go do your work and we don't have to try and communicate."

"Works for me. How long are you planning on staying today?"

She shrugged a shoulder. "I don't have to work today. So I figured I would feed them, clean them and take them out for a ride. So, I imagine I'll be done around one or two."

"Okay."

Then, he turned and walked away from her, leaving her standing there in the middle of the muddy drive all by herself.

Well, that was what she wanted anyway. Now, she could get to work.

GAGE HUNG UP with his business manager and leaned back in his chair. It was strange to be in a house like this. Someplace permanent. He was accustomed to motels that catered as much to roaches as they did to their guests. He was also accustomed to doing a little bit more hard labor than this.

Letting Rebecca handle anything on his property went directly against his usual mode of operation. He needed physical labor to deal with his shit. Otherwise, he started to go stir-crazy. He had a good head for investments and money management, but it was boring as fuck.

It had also made him rich, so he supposed he couldn't complain.

He heard a knock on the door downstairs and he abandoned his desk, taking the steps two at a time as he headed to the front entry. He half expected it to be Rebecca, so when he opened it and saw his sister Madison standing there, the shock hit him like a bucket of cold water over his head.

"What are you doing here?" he asked.

"Hello to you too, jackass," she said, pushing past him and walking straight inside. "Nice place," she said, looking around. "Colton didn't mention that. I imagine his general rage and anger at you prevented him from saying anything nice at all."

"He's mad at me, huh?"

She snorted. "Do bears poop in the woods?"

"I assume."

"Then assume he's pretty mad."

"Everyone else?" he asked, crossing his arms over his chest and rocking back on his heels.

"Sierra is young. She's also much nicer than I am. Colton is... Well, he's as decent as cornfields and apple pie. Mom is as emotionally compromised as she ever was, and I think she's...shocked. Yes, she's surprised you came back."

So Colton had decided to fill her in, Gage assumed. But she wasn't asking to see him. He couldn't blame her.

He was as surprised as anyone that he'd come back. But when he'd gotten that phone call, he'd known there was no other choice. Because he already knew there was no end to the running.

He'd been doing it for long enough that if there was an end, he would have found it. So he'd decided that maybe the only way to fix it...the only way to end that gnawing, desperate ache in him, was to go back.

So here he was.

"And you?" he asked. "How do you feel about me being back?"

"I'm reserving judgment." She took another step, looking around the room, her eyes sharp, the same blue as his own. He remembered Madison as a little girl, and he could see nothing of the little girl in her now. "I didn't exactly make it to this point unscathed. And believe me, there was a point in time when I really wanted to run away. Sadly, I couldn't, because you already had. You realize, it puts a lot of pressure on the remaining children to stay put when someone else has already scampered off."

"I imagine," he said. He also imagined that whatever Madison had been through, it wasn't exactly his situation.

"But, even saying that, I get it. I get why you left. I don't know what happened, but I understand that sometimes things are just too hard. That this place—this place where everybody knows you—is just oppressive sometimes. I was seventeen, and I got involved with my dressage trainer. When I say *involved*, I mean I was having a relationship with his penis."

Those words, so flippant and hard, had been chosen carefully, he could tell. To distance her, to distance him.

"Sure," he said, keeping his voice as neutral as hers. "Those kinds of relationships make the world go round."

"Indeed they do. And, when you're a woman, they can make things stop altogether. He was married. Which, I knew, but of course I bought into that tried-and-true line about how he was going to get divorced, and she didn't love him and she didn't understand him like I did." She laughed, but the sound didn't contain any humor. "The only reason it's even remotely forgivable is that I was so young I didn't realize what a cliché it was. Anyway, I came out of it with a big scarlet letter, and he ended up doing just fine. In fact, he even stayed married. So, I was clearly the villain."

"How old was he?"

"He was almost forty," she said. "It's entirely likely I have daddy issues."

"That fucker is lucky I wasn't here," he said, meaning that down to his soul.

"But you weren't. Anyway, the point is I have my own stuff, and my own reasons for doing the things that I do. That means that I'm probably your best bet as an ally in this family."

"You said Sierra was nicer than you."

"She is. And she'll forgive you. Trust me. She'll probably even hug you. But she's not going to understand you. I have a feeling you and I were created out of the same end of the gene pool." She looked at him, her expression expectant. And he wondered if she was waiting for him to pour out his heart. To confess all. To say exactly what he'd been up to for the past seventeen years, and what had sent him running in the first place.

Yeah, that wasn't going to happen. Not today.

"How is Dad?" he asked.

"The same. Still in the hospital."

"I've been going over the finances." He watched her expression closely, and it remained smooth, impassive.

"We're broke."

"You aren't," he said. "Your business is doing very well. In fact, most everything that centers directly around the ranch, around what you and Sierra do, works very well. It's just that overall the family is in a lot of debt. And if I want to save the ranch, I have to manage all of that as best I can."

"Right," she said. "But I don't understand why you have to do it. I don't understand why not Colton, or me. Not Sierra, because she's about to produce progeny. But the rest of us. Why aren't we doing it?"

"Because I'm done running. This is my responsibility, and I'm going to see it done."

She swallowed hard, nodding slowly. "And after that?"

"Well, then I start running again."

"That particular brand of denial is probably good for your quads, anyway," Madison said.

"Well, that's good to know." He cleared his throat, a

strange uncomfortable sensation filtering through his chest. "I'll walk you out."

Madison's pale eyebrows shot upward. "Wow. Direct. I suppose I had better let you get back to all that brooding you seem to be so fond of doing."

"Do you have anything else to say?"

"I always have something else to say, Gage. It's best not to leave that door open." Then, Maddy turned and walked out of the house. He followed after her, standing on the porch and watching her as she walked toward her sporty little car.

"No truck?"

"Do I look like I would drive a truck?" she asked.

"Colton and Sierra do, don't they?" He recalled that from the hospital when he'd been there visiting his Dad.

"One of these things is not like the others. But I thought that maybe we might be." She squinted. "I'm not entirely convinced we aren't." Then, she got into her car and backed out of the driveway. He watched her until she was gone.

Having his family around was…strange. It did weird things to his mind and his body. Leaving him feeling stretched and brittle.

There was always a vague sense of something pressing at the back of his mind. A part of himself that he had left behind in Copper Ridge. It was inescapable. It had proven to be so in all his years of wandering. It was one reason he was back now. One reason he was so determined to settle everything once and for all.

But this… This was different. Now, his family was real, not just a vague impression of a thing left behind.

His siblings were right in front of him, the adults they had grown into and not the children they'd been when he'd gone.

And some jackass had taken advantage of Madison.

That made his chest feel tight, the sensation spreading up to his throat. He hated that. Hated the thought of her feeling alone. Feeling broken because someone had treated her carelessly.

Yeah, he'd always had that sense that part of him was still here in Copper Ridge, but in his head, those parts of him were young and innocent, and still under the protection of his parents. For all their father was flawed, he took care of his children, even if it was only to prevent scandal from spreading.

At least, he took care of his legitimate children.

Even when they didn't deserve it.

He gritted his teeth, curling his fingers into a fist and slamming the side of it against the support post on the porch.

It didn't take much to remind him exactly why he had spent so long avoiding this place. It was easy to be a martyr in isolation. To self-flagellate without the consequences of your abandonment staring right at you.

Hell, there was nothing he could do about it now. What was done was done. All he could do now was fix it, and then get the hell out of Dodge.

He looked toward the barn, toward where Rebecca Bear was currently working to pay off debt that in his mind she didn't have. She didn't owe him anything. But she was stubborn, and she had pride. He had taken enough from her. He wasn't going to take that too.

He had left a hell of a mess in this town. He wasn't sure it was possible to clean it up.

But, if he died trying, at least it wouldn't be his problem anymore.

CHAPTER FIVE

SHE HURT EVERYWHERE. There was nothing like a day of manual labor to remind her that she had once shattered her kneecap. And broken her femur. And that doing too much seemed to tighten her muscles up around the bone and make everyplace that had ever been fractured ache.

She had never hated Gage West more than she did in this moment. Actually, that was a lie, she had hated Gage West plenty of times over the years. Too many to list.

But, she could clearly picture him while she hated him now. She hobbled over to the bar, leaning against it, trying to get as much weight as she could off of her leg.

"Beer me, Ace," she said, pressing her hand to her forehead.

The bar was crowded. It was Sunday night, and no one was looking forward to going back to work tomorrow. So, instead of getting a good night's sleep, they were obviously out playing darts and riding on the mechanical bull that Ace had installed about a year ago.

Recently, Ace had opened a more upscale place, but he could still often be found here at everyone's favorite dive. The fact that he wasn't here some of the time was strange though. Copper Ridge was a constant. A small, slow-moving community that didn't often see change. But the last few years had brought quite a bit of it. Tourism was beginning to become a major industry, and while she was definitely grateful for that, it was also changing her beloved landscape.

Just a year ago Ace had been single, and flirting with everything that moved. Now, he was married and about to be a father. Not that it bothered her. She had never been interested in Ace that way. It was just… Watching other people, people like him who had never even seemed interested in such a thing moving on with their lives and finding a companion made her feel hollow. Unsatisfied in a way she rarely was.

The fact he had married a West made her feel even weirder. Because the Wests made her feel weird in general. It was like they were infiltrating everything.

Not that she held anything that had happened to her against Sierra, Ace's wife. Sierra was at least five years younger than Rebecca and wouldn't remember anything about the accident, much less have any culpability in the events surrounding it.

Still. It was the whole thing.

"You feeling okay, Rebecca?" Ace asked, setting her preferred brew down in front of her. She hadn't even had to specify what she wanted. He knew.

"Just worked too hard," she said.

"I'm not sure I've ever talked to anybody who suffered from that affliction before," he said, winking.

"What can I say?" she responded. "I'm a glutton for punishment." As she said it, she had to wonder if it was true. She nodded once, picking up the beer and lifting it to her lips as she turned away from the bar and headed toward the table where Lane and Alison were already sitting.

"Is Cassie coming?" she asked, sitting down at the table slowly, her muscles screaming at her.

"No," Alison said. "Something about date night."

"As if that sexy mechanic she's married to is better company than we are," Lane said, grabbing hold of the toothpick in her drink and lifting it to her lips, plucking one of the impaled cherries from it and eating it.

"That's a fancy drink," Rebecca said, looking down at her beer. "What's the occasion?"

"Wanting to feel fancy."

Rebecca doubted a cosmopolitan with an entire handful of cherries could make her feel fancy after today. "Well, I guess that's fair enough."

"You're limping," Alison said, her expression concerned. "Are you okay?"

She was annoyed that they'd noticed. "I'm fine."

"Except this is probably related to the work you were doing today?" Lane asked.

"Maybe." She looked resolutely at her drink and not at Lane.

"What did he have you do? Were you riding the horses or bench-pressing them?"

Rebecca scowled. "There was just more lifting than I anticipated."

"What's happening?" Alison asked.

Rebecca shook her head, and Lane shot her a sharp look, then spoke anyway. "Rebecca is working for the guy who caused her accident."

"You're what?" Alison asked.

Rebecca reached across the table and grabbed hold of the remaining cherry on Lane's toothpick, then took the unnaturally red fruit and popped it into her mouth.

"Hey!" Lane groused. "Cherry-stealing bitch."

"Loudmouth."

"What is going on?" Alison asked, clearly unamused by all of the antics.

"Exactly what I said," Lane said. "Rebecca has decided to work for the guy who caused her accident, and clearly she has put herself under physical duress doing it."

"Why?" Alison asked. "Rebecca, do you need money? If you need money, you can ask us. I would much rather give you some. Or, put you to work mixing frosting."

"I don't need money," she said, feeling like a cat that had been backed up against the wall. "There's a specific thing that I have to work out. And it requires working for him."

"Could you possibly be more cagey?" Lane asked.

"If I tried," Rebecca said, her tone deadpan, "I suppose I could be."

"I just don't get it."

"It's complicated. I owe him money."

"How do you owe him money?"

"It's complicated!" A prickling sensation assaulted the back of Rebecca's neck, and she looked up just in time to see Gage walking through the door of the bar. "Oh, great," she muttered.

"What?" Alison asked.

"Nothing," Rebecca responded. She stood up, taking a long drink of the last of her beer. "I need another drink."

She made her way back over to the bar, too late remembering that everything hurt and walking across the space was an assault. "More beer," she said to Ace, setting the glass on the countertop.

"What happened?"

She turned around, her heart thundering hard against her chest as her gaze clashed with Gage's stormy blue eyes. "Nothing," she bit out.

"Then why are you limping?"

Rage poured down through her like an acid rain. "Oh, I have a little bit of a problem sometimes with my joints. My bones ache. Not because I'm old, mind you. But because I sustained a pretty serious injury to my leg and sometimes after I work, the muscles tighten up and everything goes a little bit nuts." She gritted her teeth. "I feel like you might know something about that."

"The work is too much for you," he said, his voice flat.

Ace came back over to the bar and set the glass down in front of Rebecca.

"Put that on my tab, Ace," Gage said.

She grabbed hold of the beer, her heart hammering hard. "Don't do that, Ace."

"Don't listen to her," Gage said.

"I'm going to pay for the beer if you can't figure it out," Ace said, turning away from them and going to help another customer.

"I'm trying to work off my debt to you," she said, "not accrue more."

"I can't buy you a beer?"

"I'm confused about why you're talking to me."

"I don't like you limping like this. I don't like that the work hurt you."

"I didn't ask for your charity." She scowled. "In fact, I think I've made it pretty clear I want to blot your charity from the record."

"You're not doing the work anymore. That's it. Not going to have you limping around town because you're trying to repay something I didn't want you to pay for in the first place."

He was just so large, hard and imposing, looming over her, his face a whole thunderstorm. He made her feel small and vulnerable. Like she was out of control. And she hated it.

"It isn't your decision," she said, her voice hard. "I have some say."

He shook his head, and she found her eyes drawn to the grim line of his mouth. She was fascinated by it. By the deep grooves around it that proved this firm, uncompromising set was the typical expression for him. She wondered what he had to be uncompromising about.

She shouldn't wonder. She shouldn't wonder any damn thing about him.

"Sorry to say," he said, not sounding sorry at all, "But you don't."

"I don't understand why you're doing this," she said, keeping her voice low. The last thing she wanted to do was draw attention to them. They probably already were drawing attention. Pathetic, scarred-up Rebecca Bear talking to the tallest, hottest guy in the room. People were probably pitying her. Or wondering if he was asking for directions.

Heat washed over her skin, leaving a prickling sensation behind. Humiliation. Anger.

"You don't think I feel bad about this? Do you think you're the only person who lost sleep over it?"

"Well, I know I lost sleep. Recovery is a bitch."

"I want to fix it. I want to make it right."

"You can see the way that I'm walking today, can't you? There is no making it right, Gage. There's no fixing it. You can't just make it like it didn't happen. I'm not something you can just walk into town and put back together. I'm broken. That's the beginning and end of it. And it's my burden to bear, it isn't yours. It isn't fair. To wander around acting like you've been shouldering some of this for the past seventeen years when you just haven't been."

"The hell I haven't," he said, reaching out, wrapping his fingers around her arm and drawing her in closer to him.

His touch burned her, scorched her from the inside out. Her mind was blank, except for one thought. How long had it been since a man touched her? Anyone? She couldn't remember.

"You can't buy me," she said, her voice low, shaking. And she wasn't really sure if it was from rage, or because of the way he touched her. So firm and sure and completely unexpected. "You can't throw money at this and expect it to go away."

"Hey." Rebecca turned and saw Ace standing behind

the counter right next to them, his expression hard. "Is he bothering you?"

Of course Ace knew who Gage was. Ace was his brother-in-law. She wasn't sure if anyone else in town recognized Gage West yet. And even if they did, they didn't know the connection she had with him.

She doubted Ace knew either. But then, she couldn't really be sure of what Gage had told his family, and what he hadn't.

She pulled away from Gage, taking a step back. "It's fine," she said. She treated Ace to a hard look that expressed her to desire to have him go away.

She didn't want him white knighting. She didn't want anyone else enmeshed in this at all.

When he was out of earshot, Gage turned to her, leaning in slightly. "I've lived with it for the past seventeen years too," he said. "Whether you want to listen to that or not, it's true. Whether you think it's fair or not, it's true."

"So, it sounds like you're a big fan of being punished for your mistakes, then. Enjoy me withholding forgiveness."

She didn't even know what this fight was. Hating him for caring. Hating him for feeling some kind of responsibility for it. She shouldn't know any of it, that was the problem. What she'd said to him earlier was the God's honest truth.

She didn't want to know his life. She didn't want to know if guilt kept him awake. Didn't want to know if he felt good, bad or indifferent.

This belonged to her. It was her pain. Her own personal tragedy. It had shaped everything she was, had disrupted her entire life in ways no one knew. In ways Gage West certainly couldn't know.

Him feeling guilty...well, that seemed selfish. He wasn't scarred up. His body was beautiful. Women didn't look at him with pitying glances the way men looked at her. He didn't have to deal with a terrible limp after a long day of physical labor. What right did he have to co-opt any of the suffering?

She should probably tell Jonathan what was going on. At least he could tell Gage to back the hell off. Except, she knew that she wouldn't. Mostly because she wanted to handle all of this herself. It felt unwieldy and more than a little out of control, but she still didn't want anyone else getting involved. Because her feelings were too raw. Too confusing. She didn't know what to do with them.

She didn't want to talk to Lane. She didn't want to talk to Alison. She didn't want to talk to anybody. She wanted to pick up a chair and break it over the back of Gage's head.

Except she was too sore to do that. Because of him. Which made her want to hit him even more.

"I'll be at your place tomorrow," she said. "By six. Because I have to go in and work at the store afterward."

"You damn well won't be there."

"I damn well will be, and if you stiff me out of my pay, I'll make your life hell."

"We haven't even settled on a wage."

"Make it a fair one!" She turned on her heel and hobbled back to her table, her heart pounding hard. She had no idea where all that had come from. All of that anger, all of that effortless rage. She wanted to stand there and scream at him forever.

She remembered her dreams then. She'd had all kinds of dreams after the accident. Some of them were about pain, and about more surgery. But then, after those dreams had faded had come the other dreams. Dreams of standing in an empty room, in front of a man whose face was hidden in shadow. And she would scream at him. Yell at him and hit him until all of her anger had quieted.

She would shout every detail of everything he had done to her. Emptying all of the toxic pain from her chest and pouring it into him.

She wasn't going to do that in Ace's bar. But she had a feeling she had it in her.

"Who was that?" Lane asked when Rebecca sat back down at the table. She had sort of forgotten that her friends were an audience for that encounter.

"That was him," Alison said, "wasn't it?"

"I don't want to talk about it." She was starting to feel a little bit like a broken record. And like a terrible friend. She had never confided everything with them. She had never really confided everything with anyone. She didn't like anyone knowing she was vulnerable. Didn't like anyone to know that she was affected by what had happened all those years ago.

It was important that Jonathan not know how badly her injury still hurt sometimes, because he was already too protective for her sanity. It was important that her friends not realize what a ridiculous sad virgin she was.

It was just as important that everyone stayed a good distance away from the black hole of horrific nonsense that was the epicenter of her life.

"It was him." Lane frowned. "He's younger than I thought he would be."

"How old did you think he was?" Rebecca asked.

"I don't know. I just didn't expect…that."

Rebecca knew exactly what she meant. The tall, broad-shouldered, hard-bodiedness of him that just didn't seem to be right or fair.

"It's always the handsome ones," Alison said, her tone decidedly bitter. "If evil men looked like the trolls they were inside, it would be much easier to avoid them."

"I don't know if he's evil," Rebecca said, not sure why she'd said it. He might as well be. What he'd done had changed her life forever. Ruined her life. If that wasn't evil, she wasn't entirely sure what was. Still, he wasn't evil in the way Alison's ex-husband was, and she couldn't even pretend he was. "But, not exactly a nice guy."

"Just be careful," Alison said. "I know a little something about getting drawn into unhealthy relationships."

"We don't have a relationship. In fact, that's why I'm working for him. I told you I owe him money. Apparently, some of the payout that I thought was from insurance came directly from him. I'm not comfortable with it. I want to make sure that I don't have any kind of debt to him, and he doesn't feel like he gave anything to me." She was going to go ahead and leave off the complication of the store and the fact that he wanted to give it to her.

"That makes sense," Lane said, frowning as though it absolutely didn't.

"It does to *me*," Rebecca said.

"I guess that's what matters." Lane looked down at her drink. "You owe me a cherry."

Rebecca looked back over at where Gage was, leaning against the wall and brooding. He lifted a bottle of beer to his lips, and she felt the long slow sip inside of her. For the life of her, she couldn't figure out why.

"That's all that matters," she said, trying to convince herself.

She was going to show up at six o'clock tomorrow morning and she was going to work her ass off.

And nothing Gage West said or did was going to stop her.

CHAPTER SIX

JUST AS SHE'D said she would, Rebecca walked around the side of his house and toward the stable at exactly six in the morning. Gage was already out there, chopping wood and ready to jump into whatever work she thought she was going to do.

If she insisted on doing this, then she was going to have assistance. Whether she wanted it or not.

And you think this is the best way to mend fences?

It didn't matter. He wasn't exactly here to mend fences. Just to make the scales balance. Rebecca was never going to like him, and he wasn't going to lose any sleep over that. There were a lot of people who were never going to like him. He hadn't earned it.

"Good morning," he said, swinging the ax down so that the head was resting on the ground and leaning his weight on it.

Rebecca startled, jerking backward and looking up, her eyes clashing with his. "What are you doing out here?"

"Chopping wood."

"Clearly. But, why are you out here now doing it?"

"I'm going to help you with your work."

She scowled, her expression turning feral. "The hell

you are." She grabbed hold of her long dark braid and whipped it over her shoulder. "You seem to misunderstand the point of what I'm doing here. This is not leisure time for me, neither is it some kind of therapeutic thing where I put myself in the path of the one person that I can stand the least. I can't owe you."

"Or," he said, taking a step toward her, "you just want to be pissed."

"Yes," she said, her tone dry, "I live to be angry. And I certainly enjoy investing all of my thought and energy into you."

"Then why won't you just take it? I could get out of your life a hell of a lot faster if you would just accept my help."

"I'm not going to," she said, breezing past him and heading toward the stable.

"Are you always this stubborn?"

"Yes," she said without turning around.

"Why is that?"

"It may surprise you to learn that I have dealt with a little bit of adversity in my life."

"I'd like to ease that."

She stopped, whipping around. "Not your privilege."

"Does standing on principle ever get uncomfortable?"

"Standing in general is uncomfortable, asshole. Why is that?" She turned away again, her words hitting their target even as she continued on toward hers.

She disappeared into the stable, and by the time he entered behind her she was already holding a pitchfork.

"Are you going to stab me with that or are you going to start cleaning stalls?"

"It's up for debate."

He grabbed a hold of his own pitchfork, heading to a stall at the opposite end. "I'm still going to help. You have to get to work, and so do I. This is my property, and if you're going to work for me, then you're going to help me in a way that makes sense to me."

She nodded once, her expression fierce. She seemed much more able to take orders than she was able to take charity. Even though, in his estimation, it would never be charity.

How could it be?

"Does Ace know?"

The sound of her voice on the other side of the stall surprised him. He pushed the pitchfork down into the shavings. "Does he know what?"

"Does he know that you caused my accident?"

"Nobody does." The words fell flat in the mostly quiet room. The only sound was the horses swishing and flicking their tails and nickering softly.

That response made him feel…well, more ashamed than he had imagined it could. Everyone knew what she'd been through, more or less. She wore the evidence of that time all those years ago on her skin. He didn't. And sure, he had left town, had left his family, but if he didn't want anyone to know, then they wouldn't know.

Rebecca didn't have that luxury.

Her response surprised him more than his own did. "Good."

"What you mean?"

"I don't like to talk about it. I don't really want anyone knowing my business. At first, I didn't talk about it because of the hush money your dad paid. But, at this point, I'm just more comfortable with people not knowing the particulars."

"Why is that?" He was genuinely curious. Curious as to what she got out of hiding the details. She could point at him, scream at him and have him strung up in the town square if she wanted to. And yet, she seemed to have no interest in it.

Well, she seemed to have an interest in screaming at him, but mostly in private.

"Maybe I don't have a choice about whether or not people know I was in an accident. It's pretty obvious. But I don't need people to know everything about me. I don't need them all up in that."

"Distance," he said. "I get that."

"It's hard to get privacy in this damn town."

"Why are you here then?" He looked up, his eyes connecting with the wall that separated them.

"Because it's my home. Why should I leave just because people are difficult? Or because you made things hard for me?"

She really was stubborn. And angry. He couldn't blame her for either. "I suppose you shouldn't have to."

"I love it here," she said, stubborn. "And I'm proud of everything I've accomplished. People like me… We're not supposed to be able to end up owning businesses."

"People like you?"

"Poor people." Her answer was simple and to the point.

"Who says that?"

"Everyone. Though, sometimes especially other poor people. It seems like people don't want you to get too far ahead of yourself sometimes. Don't want you to be too ambitious. They say it's because you'll only be disappointed, but sometimes I think it's just because they're afraid of being left behind."

She was more comfortable with this. A discussion that wasn't focused specifically on her.

"But you did it anyway."

She laughed. "Well, I'm not exactly rich. But my business supports itself, and I have a house. I don't know what else you really need."

"A fancier house? Fancy car, vacations to tropical islands."

"I live alone, I own a truck and can you imagine me on a tropical island? It's not like I'm going to wander around in a bikini." There was that bitter edge to her voice again.

"So you're content. That's pretty unusual."

There was a long silence. "Yeah," she said finally, "I guess I am. More content than a lot of people."

"But also sort of angry."

"I've earned that."

He finished up with the stall and walked out into the main part of the stable at the same time Rebecca did.

"All right," he said, "why don't I help you get the first one saddled up?"

She glared at him. "I don't need help with tack, thank you."

"Well, since you don't have a lot of time, what if I

go ahead and get Deuce ready and we'll go on a ride together."

He could tell that she had no interest in that whatsoever, but that she also couldn't figure out a position from which to argue. She didn't have that much time, and she wanted both of the horses ridden, so she might as well accept his help. He could see all of that in the slight contortions of her facial muscles, her dark brows snapping together, the corners of her lips tugging down in a frown. That frown pulled at the scar tissue on one side of her face and he felt an answering pull inside of himself.

"It's settled then," he said, knowing that in Rebecca's estimation it was far from settled, but that she wasn't going to argue.

They got the horses ready to go and he watched as she got herself into the saddle effortlessly. She had been sore yesterday, but she seemed much better today, which was a relief to him. Watching her limp, knowing that he was the cause of it… Well, it really was no more than he deserved. And in this instance, he was the cause of it in more than one way. But she was also refusing to do this a different way.

"Where did you ride yesterday?" he asked, bringing his horse alongside hers as they headed up on the trail that went behind his house.

"I just went up this way," she said, gesturing ahead. "I like the view. And… I like to ride. I don't have a horse right now so…so this is nice."

He could tell those words nearly choked her, so he

didn't acknowledge them. "How long have you lived up here?"

"I bought my house about a year ago. Before that, I lived with my brother, Jonathan."

"What about your mom?" He wondered about her, because she had been the other person in the accident. Though, he knew she hadn't been injured. At least, not to the degree that Rebecca had been.

"She's not around," Rebecca said, the words short and clipped, and clearly not an invitation for investigation.

"Sorry about that," he said.

"I'm not." He could tell that she was. But hey, he knew all about complicated relationships with family.

The trail wound upward, going through a grove of evergreen trees, narrowing slightly and getting rockier. He hadn't ridden out this way before, since he'd only just moved here. He missed being outdoors. It was the only therapy he'd ever gotten, and it had been more effective than talking to some doctor ever could have been.

When he'd first left Copper Ridge he'd had half a mind to work himself to death. And then, he'd more or less tried to ride himself to death in amateur rodeo events. Getting on the backs of bulls he had no business getting near, participating in a down and dirty, unregulated version of the sport.

It had never been about the money. It had just been about daring fate. It was what he'd been doing ever since he'd left. But he hadn't found an answer there, and he sure as hell hadn't found peace. So here he was in plan B. And he wasn't really finding this all that much better.

Right now was okay.

"You like to ride," he said, not a question, because it was clear from her ease on the horse and from the mildly more serene set of her shoulders that she was enjoying herself.

"People are terrible. They judge you based on how you look, they leave you, broken and bloody in some cases. Horses don't. Horses are forever."

"Oh, come on now, Rebecca. The horse would happily leave you broken and bloody in the right circumstances."

"Maybe they'd leave *you*. Horses are excellent judges of character."

"Is that so?"

"I've gotten a lot more scars from people than I've gotten from horses."

He let that go. Let the barb hit. He had no call to be defensive, or to protest. Instead, he kept his eyes fixed on the trail ahead. He moved easily with the horse's gait as he picked up the pace to get up the side of a rocky hill that spilled them out of the trees and into a clearing.

The view in front of them was endless, a patchwork of mountains that wove together, creating an endless tapestry of green. Clouds hung low around them, the mist the only thing that blunted some of the deep color. And beyond that was the gray, endless sea.

It made him feel small. Made him conscious of all the history that was contained in this land, more than just his own. He dismounted, leaving the horse standing as he walked toward the edge of the mountainside, letting the thick silence close in around him.

He heard the sound of feet hitting the ground behind him, and turned to see Rebecca moving toward him. "Going to shove me off?" he asked.

"No. That would be stupid. Then who would end up owning my business? Better the devil you are already dancing with, right?"

"Better to not be dancing with the devil at all, I expect."

She shrugged. "Sure. But that's the kind of option I've never been afforded."

"What are your options, then?"

"Deal with the devil, figure it will cost you your soul. But maybe you'll get something in return. Otherwise, just keep living in hell without getting anything in return. There's really no decision to be made if you think about it."

"There's another option."

"What's that?"

"Don't care about anything. Doesn't matter if you're in hell then, or if you get anything in return."

"You don't care about anything?"

There was no good answer to that. Not one he liked. He wished he didn't give a damn. The problem was he gave too many.

He looked out at the expanse of scenery, avoiding looking at her. At her face that bore the marks of his actions. It was a complicated question. If he didn't care at all, he supposed all the things he'd left behind wouldn't feel so heavy.

"I don't have very many connections," he said, because that much was true.

Just a bunch of people he used to know, people who had been in his life and weren't anymore. He had never maintained a connection. When he moved on, he moved on. Whether it was from old coworkers, friendships or women.

He didn't look back. He never had. He never went back to a place he'd been before either. The country was vast, and if you were willing to work with your hands you could do just about anything. And then, there was the financial stuff on top of it. He supposed he had the longest term relationships with his accountant and his lawyer.

"What have you been doing all these years?" The question was asked with more hostility than curiosity, and he had a feeling she was more annoyed with herself than with him in that moment. That she wanted to know anything about him at all.

"Everything. Construction work. Ranch work. Rodeo stuff."

She nodded once, then turned away from him sharply, taking a step back toward her horse. Then, she pitched forwards, losing her balance and stumbling. He reached out, grabbing hold of her arm and spinning her as he tugged her back, bringing her up against his chest.

Soft breasts pressed against the hard wall of his muscles and when he looked down at her face he didn't see her scars. Instead he saw luminous, dark eyes and full, tempting lips.

And as quickly as that heat overtook him, shame

rushed behind it in an icy chill, cooling the instant, inappropriate attraction.

He moved her back slowly, making sure she was steady. "I imagine we better get back," he said.

She nodded, her expression blank. "Yes," she said.

They both got back on their horses, and on the way back, they didn't make conversation. Instead, Gage spent the entire ride trying to convince himself that the burning sensation in his palm was all in his head. It certainly wasn't from touching her.

If he needed to get laid, he could hit up any woman here. Except for this one. She was the last woman he should ever touch. He was here to sever ties, not make new ones. Here to clean up messes, not make things worse.

The biggest problem with that was, he didn't exactly have the best track record when it came to fixing things.

In fact, all he'd ever done in his life was leave things broken.

But he'd be damned if he broke Rebecca Bear any further.

CHAPTER SEVEN

SHE HAD STOPPED shaking by the time she got to her store, but only just. He had touched her again. That was the second time in the space of twenty-four hours. And it wouldn't be so bad, except that she could still feel it. Not just the touch from earlier today, but the one from last night.

Her skin burned. Her entire body burned. It wasn't… It wasn't normal. And it was about ten kinds of messed up.

Talking to him today had probably been a mistake. But she had really needed to know how much of the story his family knew. The fact that he was the only one… It was strange. They shared a secret, in spite of the fact that they had never had a conversation until last week.

But then, that about summed up her entire relationship with Gage West. He had loomed large over her entire existence in spite of the fact that they had never come face-to-face.

It was strange and comforting to realize she had also been in his.

The front door to her store opened, the little bell above the door signaling the entry of a patron. She looked up, and was immediately flooded with guilty heat.

"Jonathan," she said, as her half brother made his way into the building.

He looked… Well, about as pleasant as he ever did. Which wasn't very. His dark hair was tied back in a low ponytail, his dark eyes, very similar to her own, glittered with irritation.

"Good to see you. I haven't heard from you in a few days."

"I've been busy."

"Why have you been busy? Because I'm tempted to think that you've been avoiding me."

She loved her brother. She loved him more than anyone else in her life. That didn't mean her relationship with him wasn't difficult. Jonathan had stepped up and taken care of her after their mother had left when she'd been eleven.

She was well aware that not very many twenty-one-year-old boys would want to take care of their half sister. But he had. He had worked two and three jobs to make sure she was well taken care of and that child services wouldn't take her away.

But, the problem with Jonathan was that he had yet to realize that she had grown up, and that she didn't need him to direct everything anymore.

"I'm not avoiding you, you paranoid weirdo." Except that she was. And now that she had phrased it that way, he was probably absolutely certain of that fact.

"That's so weird, because you haven't been answering my phone calls."

"Not on purpose. I've just been busy. Store. I'm a homeowner now, so that's some responsibility. Which you should know something about." Jonathan's construction business had been particularly successful over the past couple of years. He did most of his business outside of Copper Ridge, seeing as his chosen profession put him in direct competition with one of the town's favorite sons, Colton West. It was always Wests.

"I'm never too busy to talk to you," he said.

She rolled her eyes. "You need a girlfriend."

"I don't have girlfriends."

She put her hands up. "I don't judge."

"You know that isn't what I meant. I meant I don't do long-term relationships."

She frowned. "That, I judge a little bit."

"Well, we both know you don't date at all. So maybe reserve judgment."

She scowled. And, this was why she hadn't wanted to talk to her brother. He always got under her skin. And when that skin was still burning from the touch of the last man on earth she should have ever let put a hand on her, it was extra obnoxious.

"I don't think I asked for your commentary," she retorted.

"I know I didn't ask for yours."

"But you walked into my store. Had I gone to your work site, then I would've had to put up with you. But, you're the one who came into my house."

"I just wanted to make sure you were okay. And, don't think I don't notice that you're limping."

Her scowl deepened. "I'm fine. Jonathan, you have to stop treating me like I'm a kid. And you have to stop treating me like I'm an invalid."

His face looked like it had been carved from stone. "In fairness to me, for most of the time I raised you, you were both a kid and kind of an invalid."

"Thanks."

"I'm not trying to offend you. I'm just saying. I'm used to protecting you. And I'm used to looking out for you."

"But look at this," she said, indicating the store. "Look at everything I have. This place. Look what we've built. Nobody expected us to be successful, and you know that. And we both are. But I didn't make it here without you. I appreciate everything you've done, Jonathan. But you have to stop worrying so much." Those words tasted bitter on her lips, because she knew if he had any idea why she was limping, he would cheerfully commit murder.

"Fine. I just wanted to stop in on my way out to Tolowa."

"I appreciate it. Everything is fine. Completely fine."

Finally, she was able to usher her brother out of the store. As soon as he was gone, she let out a long sigh of relief. She always felt like he could tell when she was lying. Not that she often lied. She had never really had anywhere to sneak out to when she was a teenager, and she hadn't ever dated back then either.

The lies she had always told him were that her leg didn't hurt. Or that she didn't really want anything for Christmas. That she hadn't remembered it was Mother's Day either, and she was definitely not thinking about their mother. Little lies here and there to try to ease his stress. Because he had always done the best he could.

To protect her. To take care of her. Those little lies were the way she gave back.

She didn't want to ask more of him on top of all the other things he did. Didn't want him to know when she was in pain. Or when she was lonely. It wasn't his job to take care of all that mess too.

The door opened again and she turned, her heart tumbling down into her feet when she saw Gage come in, wearing his typical uniform of skintight T-shirt and well-fitted jeans. When she thought of how closely he had come just now to encountering Jonathan, her mouth dried, anger spiking through her.

"What are you doing here?"

"I thought we should talk about the kind of work you're doing."

"I think we should talk a lot less."

"I think you should help me with some of the paperwork I'm going through. And, help me make some decisions about the properties here downtown."

"What?"

"My dad owns a lot of property here on the main street, which you probably already know. More than just your store. I'm trying to decide what I should personally acquire, and what I should sell off."

"Wait a second. You made it sound like you've been a drifter for the past seventeen years, but drifters don't burst in and buy prime real estate by the ocean."

"I got into investing. I'm very good at it."

"Right, so all that crap about you not living a life of luxury?"

"I've had access to a lot of money, I haven't used it.

I didn't lie to you when I said I've spent a lot of time living in shitty motels."

She gritted her teeth. "It may surprise you to hear this, but I don't actually care if you lied to me or not. I'm not invested in trusting you."

He took a step further into the store, and she retreated behind the counter. He smelled good. He had gotten close enough for her to catch a little bit of that clean, masculine scent cutting through the heavy fragrance of the spicy candle that lingered in the air. There was rough-looking stubble on his jaw, and for some reason, she found herself wondering what it might feel like beneath her hand.

She could only figure she had imagined that because she had felt his hands on her before. So it seemed like maybe someday she might have hers on him.

She blinked. That was ridiculous. She wasn't making sense.

The door swung open and three older women walked into the shop, talking and laughing. Rebecca let out a long sigh of relief.

"Welcome to the Trading Post," she said, "I'm Rebecca—if you need anything just ask."

"That's very nice, dear," said one of the women, smiling brightly, before turning back to her friends and continuing to talk.

"You did not greet me like that when I walked into your store."

"Yes, well, I don't hate them."

He moved over to the counter, leaning over the surface, and suddenly, it no longer felt like a safe haven back there. No, instead, she felt trapped. He was so very...tall. And broad. He filled up the space so completely, not just with his frame, but with his presence.

"I figure you know a lot of the people who have shops on this street. You might be able to advise me on how I should move forward."

"A fire sale on all West properties? Everything must go?"

"I could definitely offer that up, though not everybody is going to be able to get a loan. And I'm not entirely sure I want to own anything here in Copper Ridge."

"It wouldn't be an issue for you at all if you had somebody managing the properties. Anyway, most of the people that are in their shops on Main Street have been in them for a few years. Everything kind of runs like a well-oiled machine, and none of the businesses are going anywhere."

"And some of them are empty."

She knew that he meant the small block of buildings on the very back end of the street, curving around to face the ocean and the wharf. "Yes, those have been empty for a long time."

"I could sell those or, if I was interested in keeping investment properties, I could rent them out. What kinds of businesses aren't represented here yet?"

"Why, are you thinking of starting one?"

"Just curious."

"My friend Lane runs the mercantile, and she has specialty foods."

He nodded once. "I know. We own that building."

"My friend Alison has a bakery, there's a second-hand store…"

"Alison owns the bakery, I believe, but the West family owns the thrift shop."

"And you own empty buildings."

He nodded. "Do you have any ideas about what they could be used for?"

"Something that you don't have to stay around to oversee?"

A smile curved the left side of his mouth, and she wondered if she'd ever seen him smile before. She didn't think she had. It was strange what it did to his face. Lightened everything up a little bit, like a cloud break in the middle of a storm.

"Okay, noted. You want to get rid of me."

"Lane might really appreciate the opportunity to buy her building," Rebecca said. Lane's business had been extremely successful since the tourism in town had started picking up, so Rebecca imagined her friend had the financial ability to buy the building if she wanted to.

"Then I'll have to have a talk with Lane. Maybe you could facilitate that?"

"Are you… Are you making busy work for me to do?"

He shrugged slightly. "Not necessarily."

"You are. You're making busy work for me to do so that you can pretend that I am working off what I owe you, when we all know that as it is I'm barely going to be able to do it without you allowing me to charge you an exorbitant sum for every hour I'm in your presence."

"You want the impossible, Rebecca," he said, his

voice suddenly rough. "You want to be able to run your store and work enough for me so you're going to somehow be able to pay back the thousands of dollars that I gave to you. You want to be able to do it without your physical limitations getting in the way. But, you want it to all be fair. You want to make sure that you're not taking any kind of charity, and I'm not being easy on you, when we both damn well know you need me to be easy on you."

Stupidly, horrifically, she felt tears stinging her eyes. Because it all felt so impossible. And her pride felt so small, and silly. But she didn't cry. Crying was useless. It didn't fix anything. All it did was show people that you were weak. That you were hurt. She refused to do that.

She gritted her teeth, planting her hands on the counter. It brought her closer to him, made her very aware of his size, his strength and the heat coming off of his body. But she did her best to ignore it. "You're right," she said, lowering her voice. "I do wish the impossible. I wish that your car had been the one to swerve. I wish *you* had hit the tree. I wish I was fine, and that I had never had occasion to know your name. I just wish…" She swallowed hard. "I wish I didn't care. If I can't fix it, I wish I just didn't care."

She hadn't meant to say that. She didn't want him to know that she was hurt. Yelling at him was one thing, but revealing emotion was quite another.

"Just these," one of the women said, coming up to the counter, looking at Gage out of the corner of her eyes. A small smile tugged at the corner of her lips. "Very handsome friend you have," she said, putting an array of ceramic birds on the countertop.

Rebecca forced a smile in return and began to scan the barcodes on the birds, getting them all tallied up in the register before wrapping them in plain paper. "Sure, when he's not getting in the way," Rebecca responded finally, when she found a way to make her mouth work.

Her head was swimming, and her eyes stung. Her chest felt heavy, and her arm still burned where he had touched her. She wanted to go throw herself down onto her bed and weep for a solid hour. She wanted to yell at Gage some more. She wanted to let him sign the store over to her and pretend that it didn't matter to her that she had accepted his pity and his charity.

She wanted to be stubborn forever, if only to make him miserable, so that he couldn't feel like he'd won.

She wanted to feel normal.

She wanted a whole lot of things she wasn't sure were actually possible.

Fishing a canvas bag with her store logo on it from beneath the counter, she gently put the ceramic birds inside and handed them to the woman. "Thank you for coming in," she said, surprised at how normal her voice sounded when her insides were a screaming legion.

When the women exited, she was left alone with Gage again, who was still standing resolutely at the counter.

"She liked me," he said.

"She doesn't know you."

"Neither do you," he pointed out.

She gritted her teeth. "And, I'm never going to. Fine.

I'll help you with this. I'll help with whatever. And then we'll call the money you gave me even. And you can carry the loan on the store and I'll continue to pay you monthly what I already pay in rent. I won't fight you. Or work myself to death." The words exited her mouth in a rush, and she knew that she was probably going to regret it.

"Works for me," he said, his dark brows lifting in clear surprise.

"What?" she asked, bristling. "What's that face?"

"I'm just surprised that you agreed to anything without fighting me." He lifted a shoulder. "Although, I suppose that isn't entirely accurate since you've been fighting me every step of the way. I guess I'm just surprised you stopped."

"I'm not fighting you for the sake of it."

"Yes," he said, "you are. But I get the feeling that's what you do with everybody."

"How dare you? How dare you come in and comment on how I do anything? The way that I conduct my relationships is my business. And, largely formed—"

"Around that big chip on your shoulder."

"Who put it there?" she shot back.

"Maybe I did. But, everyone else in your life didn't. So if you're going to try and pretend that you only act this way with me, and it's because I deserve it, go ahead. But I watched you with your friends back at Ace's."

She snarled. "What did I say about acting the part of the creepy teenage vampire?" She moved from behind the counter, stomping across the narrow store to one of her seasonal displays, fiddling with a garland of autumn leaves and blowing out one of the candles she'd lit upon entry. She moved it, bringing out a candle that was in the cabinet that housed the display and lighting it. "I was doing just fine without you here. Everything in my life was going well. Yeah, I have to kind of grit my teeth to pay your dad, but it isn't as bad as dealing with you."

"Why is it so bad to pay my dad?" She could tell the question was leading, and she found that obnoxious.

"Because you're all awful. Don't think I don't know that. Don't think it doesn't bother me that your dad gave my family a massive payoff to keep our mouths shut. Because protecting you was so important, but screw everyone else."

He laughed, a hollow, humorless sound. "It was never about protecting me, Rebecca. It had everything to do with protecting himself. He's a master at that. He always has been."

"Next you're going to tell me that you're not bad, you're just misunderstood. Because you have daddy issues." She gritted her teeth, resolutely adjusting a small display of scarecrows.

Suddenly, she found herself being hauled backward, pushed until her back was pressed against the wall. And in front of her, six foot plus of hard, angry man. She wasn't afraid. Instead, she felt exhilarated. This was what she wanted. She wanted a fight. She wanted the chance—the excuse—to haul off and hit him.

Tension swirled inside her chest, begging for release. Physical release. She just wanted to throw herself at him. To fling herself against the hard wall that was

Gage West and inflict as much damage as she possibly could. To make him bleed, like she had done. She wanted him to feel even a fraction of the uncertainty, the pain, that she had spent the past seventeen years dealing with.

"Is this what you do with everyone? You push them away with your bad attitude, and then you blame everyone else for the fact that you don't feel like you can get close to people? Is it my fault that you're like this? Or is that just what you tell yourself?"

She planted her hands on his chest, momentarily shocked into immobility by the feel of his hard muscles beneath her palms. But then she shoved him back. When he didn't budge, she was infuriated.

"You don't get to come in here and comment on my life."

"What would happen if you stopped fighting for a second, Rebecca? What would happen if you used a little bit of common sense and accepted some help?"

She didn't like that question. She didn't like it at all. And it had nothing to do with the fact that she thought he was terrible, and that he had no right to know anything about her life—though, those things were true. No, it had everything to do with the fact that it scratched at the door that she kept locked tight, concealing all of the strange and terrible vulnerable things deep inside.

"I can accept help," she lied. "I just don't want to accept it from you."

"We went from an agreement to this pretty quickly."

"Oh, you mean to you manhandling me again?"

As soon as she said the words, she became incredibly

conscious of the fact that her hands were still planted on his chest, that he was still so close to her she could feel the heat radiating from his body. That she could feel his breath fanning over her cheek, and that it wasn't off-putting or disgusting in any way.

How long had it been since she'd been close to some-one? Anyone? Gage. It had been Gage these last few days. Why was it that this man seemed to just crash through all the walls that she had put up around her-self? Everyone else respected them. Leave it to him to knock them down. To get right up in her face, where no one else ever dared to get.

He didn't pity her. That was the weird thing. He should. Of all the people in Copper Ridge, Gage should pity her. It was his fault. All of it was. From her scars, which he was directly at fault for, to the abandonment of her and Jonathan's mother after all of the hush money from his father had gone through to their bank account, which he was indirectly responsible for.

But that look on his face wasn't pity. It was hard as granite, uncompromising and anything but sympa-thetic. She had gotten pretty good at keeping people from being invasive. Either through her prickly behav-ior or the way she relied on them not wanting to retrau-matize her by pressing for anything.

Gage didn't seem to mind retraumatizing her at all. Jackass.

But, right in that moment, the anger inside her turned like an hourglass, the sand suddenly running an entirely different direction. The flip side seemed to be no less intense, but certainly less sensible.

She couldn't stop staring at the hard lines of his face. The deep grooves on either side of his mouth, the sharp, hard angle his jaw created, emphasized when he was like this, all tense and angry with her. As if he had any right to those emotions. She tried to remind herself who he was, why she was justified and he wasn't.

Her throat was dry, though, and her heart was pounding so hard she was afraid it was going to drill a hole straight through the front of her chest and tumble out onto the floor, right in front of him. So he could see just how he was affecting her.

She didn't even know how he was affecting her— how could he see it? She didn't know what this was. This gathering ball of tension at the center of her chest that wasn't comfortable, wasn't pleasant or easy to identify at all.

Of course, her feelings rarely were. Which was why she didn't particularly like having them. There was no choice now. Like he had torn layers off of her and exposed her without even trying.

"I haven't manhandled you," he said, his voice rough. "This?"

He had his hands braced on the wall on either side of her face, his body pressed so near hers that only her hands on his chest kept him from making intimate chest-to-toe contact with her. "Not manhandling," he said, leaning a little bit closer.

Her entire world felt like it was pitched to the side then, everything she thought, everything she knew about herself, everything she had learned about self-protection over the years, had been burned straight through, and now he was burning through her too.

She found herself swaying forward slightly and she still didn't know why. Until, it hit her. Exactly what she had been about to do. Exactly what this mounting tension inside of her was. If it wasn't rage, and she knew that it wasn't, not right at this moment, then it could only be one other thing.

And oh, sweet Lord, there was no way he was thinking the same thing. If he didn't pity her before, he would if he'd realized exactly what she had been about to do.

So she shoved him again, and this time, he lost his footing, going back a couple of steps. "Close enough," she said. "Anyway, I agreed to help you, I didn't agree to accept commentary on the way that I handle things, talk about things or engage in my actual relationships. We—" she gestured between them "—don't have a relationship."

"I never said we did."

"Sticking your nose in other people's business is just kind of your thing?"

"Actually, I don't normally get involved in anyone's business. Because I don't get involved with them at all."

"So, I'm special?" She bit those words out, hard, hoping that they would hit him and sting.

"Yes. Whether or not you want to be, you are." He didn't seem any happier saying it than she was to hear it. "You're one of the things that I need to fix. I don't give a damn about much, Rebecca—you have to believe that."

"But you care about me?"

He shook his head, his mouth pressed into a firm,

grim line. "I don't care about you. But I care about what happened. I care about dropping a little bit of the burden that I've been carrying around for over the past decade and a half. My motives aren't exactly pure, and it would do you well to remember that. I'm not asking you to trust me, not completely. But I am asking for you to stop snapping at me every time I come within a few feet of you."

There was something about those words that deflated her. Which was silly. It shouldn't deflate her to hear him speak the truth. If he had said that he cared about her, she would have hit him anyway. She didn't want him to care about her. Still, hearing him say all this, unvarnished, completely honest—she knew it was honest—wasn't exactly heartwarming.

"Fine. What do you want me to do?"

"My house. Tomorrow night after you close."

A vague sense of disquiet overtook her, and she shoved it down immediately. She was the one who had almost done something crazy. She was the one who was being slightly psychotic around him. She hated him. Absolutely hated him. Had without even knowing him for the better part of her life. The fact that she had thought, even for a moment, about closing the distance between their mouths…that just proved that she was under some kind of psychological duress brought about by his presence, no doubt.

There was no reason to feel disquieted. He wasn't going to do anything. He looked at her like some kind of score he had to settle. That was it. He didn't see her as a human, much less as a woman. This all had to do with some vague idea about soothing a conscience that she imagined was way too damaged to ever truly be soothed. But, that part wasn't her problem. Her problem was getting him out of her life, and getting final ownership of the store.

"Fine," she said through her teeth.

"I'll see you tomorrow night then."

He walked out, just as another customer walked in, and it didn't even give her a moment to breathe a sigh of relief over his absence. Didn't give her a moment to recalibrate, which was why—she told herself—she spent the rest of the day with her head churning. She had a steady stream of customers, and it kept her just distracted enough that she didn't brood, but wasn't quite able to ever calm down.

She felt restless, edgy, for the rest of the day, a strange kind of energy shooting through her veins that she couldn't quite put a name to.

By the time she got home, she just wanted to collapse. And she very guiltily ignored a couple of texts from the girls. Because she didn't want to go out, and she didn't want to talk to anybody. She didn't want to tell them about what had happened with Gage, but she had a terrible feeling that if she talked to any of them, she would end up spilling the beans.

She wanted to keep all of the dark, confusing feelings from earlier today locked up inside, but they were beating at the door, desperate to get out. She was confused, and she was restless. Those things were a very bad combination.

She was pretty accustomed to keeping her feelings and thoughts to herself when it suited her.

But she could tell this was not a well-behaved feeling. It was not going to sit in the corner until she told it it could be done. It was going to burst out of her at an inopportune moment unless she got a handle on it.

She wandered to the fridge, reaching inside and taking out a piece of pie that was left over from Alison's shop the other day. She hummed as she took a bite of the lemon meringue, wandering over to her couch and taking a seat with her feet folded underneath her.

She grabbed the remote that was next to her and turned the TV on, flicking it to a network that usually replayed old comedies. She didn't watch TV often enough to keep up with any shows, not because she didn't like it, but because her schedule was too haphazard.

But reruns were always a good bet.

It was an episode of a show that she liked, so she settled into the couch, taking another bite of pie. This was good. A little clarity. A little pie.

Except, the comedy took a slightly emotional turn as two of the main characters started fighting about their relationship. And then, when things hit a peak and the woman unlocked the door to the coffee place, letting the man back in so that they could kiss passionately, Rebecca's mind went completely blank of everything except what it would be like to kiss Gage like that.

What would've happened if she had leaned forward, closing that distance? If she had grabbed hold of his face and pressed her lips to his, pressed her breasts to his hard chest…

She set her pie plate down on the couch and jumped up, walking back behind the couch and trying to do something with the restless energy inside of her. She should not be thinking of him this way. She really shouldn't be thinking of anyone this way, and typically, she didn't. She had all that stuff under control. Her life moved in a series of predictable patterns and she liked it that way.

What she didn't like was this. This longing that worked in direct opposition to reality. She didn't… There were a lot of reasons that she had never been with a man. Valid reasons. The last time she'd gone out with a guy, he had assumed that because of her scars she should be grateful for the attention. He had assumed that she would be easy.

She wasn't going to be anyone's pity lay, ever. That guy, at least, had been something of a difference in contrast with a couple of the other men she had tried to date who had treated her like she was made of glass. They had treated her like an invalid, like there was something wrong with her. And that really wasn't any more appealing to her than being treated like a sexual charity case.

Plus, whenever she went on a date with a guy, he was always asking questions about her. And she didn't like that either. Basically, she hated dating. But, dammit all, she liked men. Their bodies, anyway. At least, she was pretty sure she did. Would like a chance to explore that a little more.

She growled, reaching down and taking hold of the

remote, turning the TV off. She didn't need to watch other people make out when all she could think of was making out with the last man on earth she should ever want to touch.

This just made her hate him even more. The fact that this man who had already had such a profound, indelible effect on her body was reaching inside of her and changing her yet again.

She grabbed her pie, holding it close to her chest and marching back into the kitchen. She stood at the counter and finished it, not taking any more chances with the TV.

When she finished, she walked into the bathroom, stripping her clothes off as she went. She started to run water in the tub, turning and looking at herself in the mirror as she waited for it to fill. She pinned her hair up slowly, examining the woman looking back at her. She was... Well, she was used to her reflection. To the patches of skin that were puckered on her face, that tugged at the corner of her mouth and made her smile asymmetrical. To the little crease by her left eye that pulled it tight and made it slightly more catlike than the right.

To the large depression of skin by her rib cage, and the patch that had been surgically removed from her stomach to be placed on her leg, where it had been most badly damaged.

It was her body. She didn't know it any other way. She had been young enough when it had happened— barely pubescent—that her body hadn't really begun to change into a woman's shape yet. So, along with her curves, these scars were a signal of growth and change.

It was just her.

It wasn't beautiful, but it was all she knew.

She sighed heavily, turning in the small space and walking across the stone floor to the claw-foot tub in the corner. She stepped inside, her muscles relaxing as she sank into the warm water. Finally she felt some of the day's tension begin to fade.

She closed her eyes, letting her head fall back, and something about resting her head against the hard surface brought her thoughts back to that moment in her shop earlier today. When she had been braced against the hard wall with Gage in front of her, so unyielding, uncompromising.

So hot. And so very masculine.

Her breath hitched, her breasts rising up out of the water, the cold air making contact with her wet skin, causing her nipples to tighten. At least, that's why she told herself her nipples tightened. It couldn't have anything to do with him. Certainly not.

Except, the memory of what she had just seen on TV superimposed itself over the memory of what had actually happened today, and she was powerless to stop herself from imagining what his face would feel like beneath her fingertips. Rough, from the dark stubble, hot like the rest of him.

Her heart was thundering in her chest, so hard and so loud she was almost sure she could hear it echoing in the small space. For just a moment, she forgot that it was a bad idea to let herself think of him like that. For just a moment, she forgot everything except for how wonderfully compelling his face was.

He wasn't beautiful. He was too hard for that. Too uncompromising. But that was what made him so fascinating, at least for her. He was so raw, so undeniably male, and that was outside of her sphere of experience.

What would have happened if she had leaned in? If she had touched the tip of her tongue to his bottom lip. What would he taste like? What would he sound like?

Her heart rate quickened even more and an answering pulse began to beat at the apex of her thighs. She was tempted then, so tempted to slip her hand between them, to try and ease the ache that was building there.

She closed her eyes, biting her lip as she let herself do it. Just for a moment. Her fingertips grazing her sensitized flesh as she gave herself over to the image of his lips pressing against hers.

"Gage," she gasped.

And it was that, his name, that hard slap of reality, that saw her removing her hand and launching herself straight out of the tub.

No. This was too much. There was crazy—which, agreeing to work for him to pay off the debt she hadn't even wanted, possibly was—and then there was just insanity. Fantasizing about the man who had caused her accident, who was responsible for each and every scar on her body was insanity.

She looked at herself in the mirror again, allowed her fingertips to trace the ruined skin, rather than that lying, treacherous part of herself that was so needy for a man it would even allow her to fantasize about the man who had harmed her. This was what she needed to remember. That he was responsible for this pain. Not just the scars, but everything that had come after it.

Her mother leaving. Jonathan being put in the position where he had to assume the responsibility of raising her.

He had come in and accused her of being guarded. Of pushing people away.

She did it because of these. These scars. She moved her fingertips over a particularly ugly one just beneath her breast. That did it. It cooled her arousal.

She wouldn't think of him like that again. And if he ever laid a hand on her again, she would remove it.

She grabbed a towel and wrapped it around her body, nodding once at her reflection and walking out of the bathroom. Gage West was already far too big in her existence. She would not allow him to loom any larger.

CHAPTER EIGHT

IT WAS STARTING to get dark outside, and Gage entertained the momentary thought of sending a search party out for Rebecca. Then, he imagined the indignity that she would feel if he did. The idea made him smile.

A little bit perverse, sure, but Rebecca Bear was a hellcat. It kind of amused him. He had definitely expected her to be slightly more downtrodden than she was. But she was all fight. Which, in the grand scheme of things, wasn't the best thing for her. In his opinion, she would be better served fighting against actual enemies, instead of just being angry. Particularly at people who were trying to help.

Just as he was seriously thinking he was going to have to make sure she was okay, he heard footsteps on his porch. Followed by a knock that was incredibly surly.

There she was.

He crossed the expansive space and went to the door, pulling it open and looking at the small, indignant woman standing there. Her arms were crossed tightly across her midsection, her dark eyebrows lowered, her lips set into a frown.

"Hi," he said, standing to the side.

She glowered, not offering him a greeting in return, as she walked into the house. She unzipped her jacket, taking it off and holding it out. He took it from her, hanging it on the peg that was just behind her.

He didn't see any point in commenting on her bad attitude. First of all, because it was kind of funny to watch her behave like an unhappy teenager. Second of all, because she was more than entitled.

"Why don't you come upstairs with me," he said, turning and heading toward the staircase. He did not hear her footsteps behind him. He turned slightly. "I'm not going to bite you."

Her lip curled and she arched her neck to the side, dragging a fingertip over a perforated line of flesh. "Too late."

His stomach tightened. "Fair enough."

He walked up the stairs, and this time, he heard her following behind. He paused at the top, looking down at her, part way up the stairs, and at the view of the rest of the house. It was nothing like his childhood home, not glossy or marbled in the least. But, it was also completely different to the motels he had spent the past seventeen years inhabiting.

The high ceilings, large windows that overlooked the view of the lake and the natural wood beams were a happy marriage between the moneyed lifestyle he had grown up in, and the more rustic accommodation he had grown accustomed to.

He pushed open the door to his office, a slight smile curving his lips as he realized that this one room, containing a computer, a desk, a chair and a couch had more space than the entirety of his typical living situation.

"Have a seat," he said, gesturing to the couch.

She gave him a sharp bit of side eye, clearly considering defying him for the sake of it. But, seeing as there was nowhere else for her to sit, she clearly decided against it. Instead, she took up a position on the couch that managed to look both furious and inconvenienced.

Her shoulders were stiff, her hands folded tightly in her lap, her knees locked together.

"That's a very comfortable couch," he said. "And yet, you seem determined to make it feel very uncomfortable."

"I couldn't be comfortable in your house no matter how I sat. That's like trying to be comfortable in a bear's den."

He lifted his lip, touching his tongue to the bottom of one of his canine teeth. "My teeth aren't quite that sharp."

He watched as the color rose in her cheeks, as her body tensed even further, a feat he wouldn't have imagined was possible, since she was already wound so tight he figured a stiff breeze could snap her in half.

"Let's just get to the work farce," she said, her tone hard, brittle.

"There's nothing farcical about the amount of work I have to do. Sadly."

He reached over to the desk, pulling a large stack of papers off of it and depositing it on the couch next to her.

"Go ahead," he said, "have a look."

She looked at him skeptically. "Why are you letting me look at your family finances?"

He shrugged, sitting down in the office chair, leaning back and clasping his hands behind his head. "We already know each other's secrets, what's a few more?"

Her eyes narrowed. "Okay," she said, sounding completely unconvinced. She started to leaf through the papers. "I'm not a financial analyst by any stretch of the imagination but even I can see that there are negative numbers where you would rather have positive ones."

"True."

"So, what is this?" She set one of the papers aside. "Your version of a white flag? Show me the soft underbelly of your family and… What? Do you want me to tell everybody? Do you want me to stab you with a broadsword?"

"I'd rather you didn't do either of those things. But, now you see what I'm contending with."

"And you want my input on…what to do with the stores?" She looked back at of the papers. "You need to sell off everything you can."

"The thing is, I don't want to destroy the main street. I don't want someone to take ownership of those buildings who doesn't care about the town. For all of my father's sins he does seem to love Copper Ridge. I'm not sure he much loves anything else. But this town has been his kingdom for a long damn time, so if he has ever protected anything, it's this place."

"Like I said before, Lane will buy from you happily."

"I think I want to put some covert feelers out for

people who might be interested in the empty block of buildings at the end of the street."

"You suddenly care about the town?"

His chest tightened. "For once I just want to leave a place a little bit better than when I first got there, instead of a little bit worse."

She didn't say anything to that. "Well, I'm not completely against what you're saying. And as somebody who has an investment in the businesses on Main Street I prefer this to just selling to a big property management company or something."

"You haven't mentioned anything about eliminating your competition or making sure that another knick-knack store doesn't open up."

"Frankly, whatever brings people to Copper Ridge is good. In a small town it doesn't benefit us to look at each other as competition. At least, not from my point of view. We want people to know they have options, to know there's a reason to walk down Main Street. Ample reason. That means that I want every business on that street healthy, and every building full."

"Not very many people would feel that way. Most people prefer to cut the throat out of their competition."

She lifted her shoulder. "People aren't going to come to town once. They aren't going to buy one thing. They're going to want to eat at more than one restaurant, make sure that they have exhausted the full selection of driftwood-based paraphernalia."

He smiled, enjoying this more animated version of her that wasn't simply glaring daggers at him. "Your store is a lot more than driftwood paraphernalia. I mean, granted, scented candles and ceramic woodland animals aren't exactly to my taste, but I imagine it appeals to a lot of people."

"It gives me an excuse to buy endless seasonal decorations for the shop. And I can constantly refresh them."

He shook his head. "To each his own."

"Well, I was mostly raised by my brother. It isn't like I ever had anything pretty in my house." Her tone was light, but he could tell that the moment she said that, she regretted it. That she was irritated with herself for saying anything to him that wasn't hostile.

"What happened to your mother?" She had referenced being without her a few times now, and he was curious. It wasn't fair, the way that all of the shitty things in life seemed to happen in concentrated doses right above certain people. But, it seemed to be the way life worked.

"She left. She took that big fat payoff from your dad and she left."

Her words settled hard in the room. "How long after?"

"About a year," she responded, her tone flat. "Honestly, I guess it wasn't very appealing to take care of a daughter who was in and out of different reconstructive surgeries."

"She left you? She left you when you were going through all that?" Pressure built in his chest, rage, hot and completely inappropriate roaring inside of him. He had caused this, he had no right to be angry about the fallout. He had left—how could he be angry about what she'd been subjected to when he'd never made a move to protect her?

He had never had the right.

He didn't have the right now. But that wasn't what this was about. This was just about giving her something. But he hadn't fully realized everything that he owed her. Just how impossible it would be to make a dent in this mess.

"She was never going to win an award for being the world's greatest mother, Gage," Rebecca continued. "Really, she thought of us as a burden most of the time before the accident. But after that? Yeah, after that any maternal instinct really seemed to go out the window." She looked away from him, her eyes unfocused as she stared at the back wall. "Hell, if I could have escaped my body I would have. Too damn bad I was stuck with it. But, feeling that way, it makes it difficult to be all that angry. Who wants to deal with that? Nobody." She looked back at him, her dark eyes glittering. "I was a burden before, but I was a damaged burden after that."

"Bullshit."

"What?"

"Bullshit," he repeated, harder, louder.

"Right. Because you know. Because you would have treated someone in your life differently? Because you really would have been there for your family."

He gritted his teeth, her words hitting their target. They broke through his skin, burning beneath the muscle, painful in their accuracy. "I wouldn't have left a child alone in a hospital."

"But you did," she said. "You left me. You damaged me and then you left me. You left me in a state my own mother didn't want to deal with." She stood, her voice rising as she did. "You know everybody feels sorry for me. Just desperately sad for everything I might have been. I could have been beautiful, at least that's what I've been told. But I'm not."

"That's not true," he said, his voice rough. And as soon as he said that, he realized that she was beautiful. She really was.

Her long, dark hair was perfect for a man to wrap around his hand so he could draw her forward. Her lips were full and dusky. Captivating.

And, looking at her like she was a woman was a step too far. He had done enough. He didn't need to be a perverted asshat on top of it.

"That's all you have to say?" She took a step toward him, challenge lighting her dark eyes. "You wanted to share secrets. So, you show me your horrible family finances, and I show you what my scars really mean to me. Or is that a little bit too real for you? Did you want to come back and lift the downtrodden, artfully damaged princess from the muck you left her in? Has it been terribly confronting for you to come back and see that you left behind a bulletproof bitch that doesn't need you to come in and fix her?"

"If you don't need to be fixed, then why are you so angry?"

She launched herself at him then, one small fist pounding against his chest. "You can't fix it. The fact you're even here trying is insulting. Everything I've been through. I hate you." She hit him again, harder this time. "Everything in my life was going fine. At least, it went in a routine. And then you came back. And you're just here, acting like you could be some kind of benevolent savior, but you never asked if I wanted to be saved."

She hit him again, just for good measure, he had a feeling. And he grabbed hold of her elbows, holding her steady, not doing anything to keep her from beating on him. She wrenched herself partly away, pounding against him again. "How dare you?" she asked. "How dare you change things, again? I was fine. Everything was going well. You just… You came here for you. It's for you, because it sure as hell isn't for me."

"I wanted to give you the shop and then leave."

"You could take my pride with you. Forgive me, but it's in short supply, and I'm not handing bits and pieces of it out at random."

"Then maybe stop running your mouth at me." He felt something in his chest, something more than anger. Something that felt raw and wounded. Just plain bad. And he didn't like it. Didn't like that growing sense of tenderness that was just plain painful, not to mention misplaced. He tightened his hold on her, looking down into her molten brown eyes. "The way I see it, you either take the handout or you stop fighting me every step of the way. The simple fact is, our lives have collided again. And there's no sense pretending they didn't in the past. That we don't have a connection. Whether you like it or not, we do. Whether you think it's fair that I was affected by this or not, I was. But you can't have it both ways. You can have me be absent and eternally punish me. You can't want nothing from me, but need something that I own. It doesn't work that way."

Something in her expression changed, the light in

her eyes sharpening, turning feral. "You want to make things right? You want to get back something that was taken from me?"

"I already told you that I'm here to fix things. As best as I can."

There was only a breath between those words and what happened next, and he didn't have time to react. She leaned forward, using the hold he had on her to her advantage, pressing her lips against his.

And they ignited.

REBECCA HAD NO idea what she was doing. In about every way that phrase could be applied, she had no idea what she was doing. She had been kissed before, but it hadn't felt like this. Maybe it had to do with all of the anger that was coursing through her veins. She could honestly say she'd never kissed a man whom she also wanted to kill.

But, then, added to that fact, she had no idea how she had gone from yelling at him to tasting him. Yet she was. And, the realization that it was completely insane didn't find her scrambling back to safety.

The first touch of his lips was like a taste of water after years in the desert. She hadn't realized how thirsty she was. And, no matter that it was a terrible idea, the only thing was the thirst. It was all that mattered. Satisfying it, quenching it. A few moments ago, she hadn't known that it existed. Now, it was the only thing inside her. Bigger—at least in this moment—than her anger. Bigger than her scars. Bigger than who he was.

His grip on her arms was punishing, bruising as he held her steady, letting her continue her wanton attack of his mouth with hers. He was just standing there, as impassive as ever, as if he was merely allowing this kiss, and not participating in it.

That made her even angrier. It shouldn't. It should be the jolt of sanity that she needed, but she wasn't feeling particularly sane.

She wrenched her arms free, wrapping them around his neck and leaning forward, her breasts pressing against the hard wall of his chest as she tilted her head, all the better to breach his defenses.

He was like iron. Cold, impenetrable. But she was hot enough to melt him, she was sure of that. She was made entirely of rage, and need, a red, molten thing inside of her that couldn't be contained anymore. It was too big for her, and too destructive.

So, he was going to have to have some of it. He was going to have to carry some of it inside of him, so he could be burned just as she was. Why should she be the only one?

She parted her lips, tracing the seam of his mouth with her tongue. And that did it. On a growl, he wrapped his arms around her, the shock of being surrounded by him, overtaken by him, momentarily immobilizing her.

It was all he needed to assume control. And assume it he did. He slid one hand up her back, pressing his palm between her shoulder blades, the hold possessive and intense. A shockwave rolled over her as she tried to reconcile the years spent with so little touch, broken by this force of contact that rivaled anything she had ever felt before in her life.

His stubble was rough, his cheek scraping against

hers as he took the lead, changing the angle yet again, forcing her lips apart even further, his tongue sliding against hers in a sensual echo of the verbal sparring they had just been engaged in.

He was so hot, so big and hard, the extreme of absolutely everything. The epitome of masculinity, making her feel tiny and delicate and a whole host of things that she would normally hate to feel. Somehow, he made it all seem okay. He made it seem right.

Somehow, he made her savor that feeling. Being small, being held. Being helpless to do anything but submit to the power of his touch, the absolute and complete dominance of his kiss.

He pulled back from her for a moment, then returned, cupping her face, holding her head steady as he tasted her deeper, taking the kiss to a place that was so hard, so hot, she thought it might destroy her completely.

Her knees went weak, and she started shaking, a hollow sensation beginning to expand deep and low in her stomach. She ached. All the way down. And she needed… She just needed.

She arched against him, and he stood firm, as unyielding as granite. But she liked that. Very few people stood firm against her. For fear of breaking her, or for fear that she might break them. But he did. He stayed hard, and he gave her something to launch herself at, and she had no idea how much she needed that until now. Had had no idea just how much she needed to go up against the side of a mountain.

Gage West was most definitely her Everest. And

right now, she wanted to climb him all the way to the summit.

He growled, his teeth scraping against her bottom lip before he went back again, and again, tasting her deeper and deeper with each pass of his mouth over hers. And she was lost in it. Completely consumed. And why not? She had been lost in the fog that he'd caused for so many years. Why shouldn't she get lost in this one?

Suddenly, he pulled back, pushing her away as he did, releasing his hold on her completely. He stood there, his chest rising and falling sharply, his eyes hard, his dark brows locked together. "What the hell are you doing?"

"Don't you mean what the hell were we doing?" She would be damned if she accepted his anger for this.

"What the hell do you want?" he continued, as though she hadn't spoken.

"I thought—" she cleared her throat "—well, I thought that maybe you could at least treat me like a woman. Since nobody else does. And it's your fault."

"Is that what you want? You want to trade for sex?"

His words were like a slap. They were also her fault. Because she was the one who had led the conversation, hell, the entire interaction, down this road.

"Don't," she said.

"You said I owe you. I owe you sex?"

Anger made her mean. "Sure. Why not? Or is that a step too far for you? You'll give me a building, but you're not going to pity fuck the girl you scarred for life?"

"No," he said.

She shouldn't be sad he was turning her down, be-

cause she wouldn't take him up on it anyway. She didn't
want his pity. And she didn't want to sleep with him.
She hated him. She had never been with a man before,
and he was hardly going to be the first one. That would
be… It didn't make any sense. Still, she didn't want him
to turn her down. But it was another blow to her already
fragile self-esteem.

"I guess your sense of justice really only extends
so far."

"You don't even want to take a building for me. I'm
not going to pay you in sex. Mostly because that isn't
really what you want."

"Oh, so now you're an expert on what I want?" She
moved past him, dodging him neatly when he attempted
to reach out and grab her. "Don't."

"Is this the part where you tell me you're not going
to speak to me anymore? And you're going to refuse to
have anything to do with me?"

"No," she said, the word vibrating inside of her, the
denial filled with rage and conviction. "I care about
Main Street, and from where I'm sitting you have way
too much power. I want to make sure that whatever happens is something that helps shape the town that I love.
So, I'm going to take this opportunity. But it doesn't
mean I don't hate you." That last part was a little bit
childish, and she wished that she had been able to play
it a little bit cooler. Wished that she weren't quite so
transparent.

Wished that she weren't made entirely of wounded
female ego, busted up pride and frustrated lust.

Because no matter that it was a terrible idea, no matter that she was infuriated at him, she was still trembling with desire for him. She had never felt like this before. She had never felt so desperate, so needy, after a kiss. Or, ever, really.

She was so angry at him. Angry, because he was the one to bring all of these feelings up, and it really did only seem fair that he be the one to satisfy them. Angry because she should never have been attracted to him in the first place. Angry more at herself than at him, which made her even angrier.

She continued on out of his house, stopping as soon as she got outside the front door, leaning up against it, trying to stop her hands from shaking. She should go home. She should go home with her tail between her legs and hide. Forget this ever happened. Forget that she had ever wanted any of these things, most especially with him.

But that's what you always do. You hide when it gets hard.

He was right. That was the part that was so damned irritating. He was right about her. About the way she pushed people away, about the tools she used to do it.

But she didn't have to. She was going to go home, but only for a few minutes. Then she was going to get dressed in something other than this. And she was going to finish what they had started upstairs. Not with him. Never with him. But she was going to stop allowing Gage West to have so much control of her life.

CHAPTER NINE

IT HAD ONLY taken a moment's hesitation for Rebecca to leave the house wearing a short dress and a pair of knee-high leather boots. Her hair was loose and more than a little bit disheveled from spending the day partly caught up in a twist.

She didn't often bother with makeup, but she had done her best to enhance her eyes and her lips, not bothering with the rest since, unless she was really going to use foundation like spackle, she always felt like it tended to exacerbate the appearance of her scars rather than obscure them.

It had taken another moment's hesitation once she had gotten to Ace's for her to get out of the car. And then, another moment's hesitation still to go from the parking lot to inside.

Finally, she pulled the door open and walked inside, immediately enveloped by the warmth and the noise of the atmosphere. She glanced behind the counter, relieved to see that Ace wasn't in residence. This would all be much easier without him being misguidedly paternal, or whatever his deal was.

She was also thankful to see that her friends weren't here. Because they would likely stage an intervention, which, she maybe needed. But, she had managed to cling to her arousal and her rage the entire time she had gotten ready to go out. She'd had a whole hour to simmer down, and she hadn't done it yet, so she doubted she was going to until she completed her mission.

It was necessary. Actually, she was just angry it had taken Gage's appearance in town to push her to this point. It was easy for her to fling accusations at him, to say that her life was ticking along just fine and he had come and disrupted it. But, she had to admit—at least to herself—that even when he wasn't here, he had control over what she did. Because she allowed the scars to control what she did.

She was over it. And she wasn't going to wait for someone special, or some other crap. She wasn't in the market for a relationship. She never had been. Which was a huge part of why she'd never slept with a guy. Because, even though she knew that it wasn't like it had to mean anything or be special, it had always kind of seemed like it should. But, she had also never really wanted anything special. Depending on another human being was her worst nightmare. Needing someone— when there was no guarantee at all that they would stay—just wasn't something she'd ever wanted. That put relationships low on her list of priorities.

But sex had suddenly been bumped higher on the list. She wasn't going to be a virgin for the rest of her life—that meant that she was going to have to rip off the Band-Aid at some point. So, virginity Band-Aid was going. Now.

Though, based on things she had heard over the

years, unlike taking a Band-Aid off, she doubted that doing it quickly would make it hurt less.

She gritted her teeth, scanning the bar. She should have stopped for condoms. She was making assumptions that the guy that she decided on would have them. Actually, she probably didn't want to choose a guy that didn't have them, because that would imply a lack of sex preparedness. If she were looking for a relationship, she might want the kind of guy who didn't carry protection around. But she wasn't looking for a relationship, she was looking for a guy who knew what he was doing.

A guy that made her feel even a fraction of what Gage had made her feel. A guy who could, at least, keep the fire going, even if he hadn't started it himself.

She looked across the room, her heart doing a strange dip and twist when she spotted Finn Donnelly. He was hot, there was no doubt about that. Tall, broad and well muscled from days spent working on his family ranch.

Not the most approachable guy, but sexy. So that was a bonus.

She chewed her bottom lip. He also knew her, and was very good friends with Lane. Lane insisted that there was nothing between them, nothing romantic at all. Finn was just the guy who changed her lightbulbs so that she didn't have to get up on a ladder, the guy who fixed up her place if there were any issues.

In fact, when pressed, Lane always looked mortally offended by the assertion that she might have latent Finn feelings.

Rebecca bit her lip, crossing the room to where Finn was standing. "Hi," she said.

He looked up from his beer, a dark brow raised, the left side of his lips quirked upward. "Hi, Rebecca. Are you here with Lane?"

"No," she said.

"Oh," he said. He lifted his beer, taking a sip of it, and Rebecca wondered if she had miscalculated. She wondered if maybe he had some feelings for Lane, regardless of what Lane said about him.

She cleared her throat, bouncing uncomfortably on the balls of her feet, not knowing what to say next. Finn was hot, but she didn't exactly want to touch him or anything. And she didn't know if that was because of the specter of her friend looming over them, or the potential consequences because of his close relationship to her friend, or what. Maybe it was just chemistry, and the cruelty thereof.

Because Finn was not the kind of guy to do serious relationships, so he would be perfect for her purposes, if not for all the other entanglements. Small-town ridiculousness.

"You can have a seat if you want," he said, gesturing to the empty chair across from him.

"No," she said. "I mean, are you waiting for someone?"

Something shifted in his expression, his lip quirking at a slightly different angle, the light in his whiskey-colored eyes flickering. "No."

The air stretched between them, and she was suddenly fighting to catch her breath. She sensed that this was her moment. To either put her cards on the table or walk away. It was a weird thing, the fact that he seemed to understand what she was thinking, and that he hadn't run the other direction.

Maybe, if she wanted to, she could have Finn Donnelly.

There was nothing to be pitied about that. He looked… Strong, and capable. And he had very big hands. That was supposed to be a good thing. She was pretty sure. Really, regardless of what it was indicative of, his hands were nice.

She sat down. Still, she felt anything but decisive. "Let me buy you a drink," he said.

She crawled her hands into fists, resting them on the tabletop. "Okay. That would be great."

He stood up, crossing the space and moving over to the bar. She pressed her hand against her forehead, wondering exactly what she was doing. Well, she knew what she was doing. She was hoping to pick up a guy. And she had of course ended up sitting with the guy that she knew. Though, they didn't know each other that well.

A bottle of beer appeared on the table in front of her and she looked up, her eyes clashing with Finn's. "Thank you," she said.

He lifted a shoulder. "Sure." He sat down across from her, his gaze assessing.

Every other time she had ever put herself in a position similar to this with a guy, she had carefully set it up to fail. To trap him into saying something that would make it so it was easy to send him packing. She usually went out of her way to find something wrong with him. Something wrong with what he said, what he did.

But…

But, in theory she wanted this to succeed. To go to its final conclusion. Oh Lord. Did she actually want to have sex with Finn? An image of Gage superimposed itself over the picture she was trying to create of herself kissing Finn.

"How about we dance?" She was surprised by that offer, in part because Finn didn't exactly seem like the kind of guy who danced, but maybe that was just because she had never seen him pick a woman up.

Was he picking her up? Was this actually happening? She swallowed hard. "Okay."

He reached out, taking hold of her hand, and she followed his lead, allowing him to take her to the middle of the uncluttered area of the bar that acted as a dance floor. The jukebox was playing midtempo country music, and Finn pulled her up against his hard body. For the second time that night, she found herself in a man's arms. After going so long without being touched, it was especially strange.

She let out a slow, shaking breath, resting her forehead against his shoulder as he took hold of her hand and held it up, bracing it against his chest.

"We don't know each other that well," he said, his voice low in her ear. "Strange, since we're around each other enough."

"We don't have to talk," she said.

She raised her head, examining his expression. He looked surprised, but amused. "Suit yourself."

"Sorry. I didn't mean to be horrible. I just… You don't have to play like you're interested in what I have to say suddenly just because…you know."

He nodded slowly. "I appreciate the honesty. Are you okay, though? Because from what I know of you, this isn't exactly typical behavior."

She forced a smile. "What do you care if you get laid?"

To his credit, he didn't look shocked. "I guess I don't."

"As long as this doesn't…as long as it doesn't cause any problems with Lane."

His jaw tensed, almost imperceptibly. But she was so close she could see the slight shift, and he was holding her against his body, so she could feel the tension rise inside of him. "It wouldn't. It won't."

"Good."

So weird. So strange to have this conversation when they hadn't even kissed. Suddenly, he moved his hand on her back, the hold becoming more all-encompassing, and she could sense that he was about to remedy the kiss situation.

She let her eyes flutter closed, tilting her face up, showing him that she was ready. She did her best to push back on the intruding images of Gage. She wasn't going to think about him. Or the kiss they had shared just an hour and a half ago. Wasn't going to think about the fact that when she thought about kissing, it was him that she wanted. That it was him her body was electrified for even now, readying itself for.

"I had a feeling I would find you here."

That voice, gravelly, rough and most definitely not belonging to Finn, broke into the moment. Her eyes flew open and she turned, turned to see Gage standing there. And he was, regrettably, not a hallucination.

"What are you doing here?" she asked, still holding on to Finn, who looked more amused than angry.

"I came looking for you. Since you took off from my place like a bat out of hell."

"You were at his place?" Finn asked.

"It's not like that," she said.

"You wanted it to be."

She all but snarled at Gage. "What? You hadn't humiliated me enough? So, you figured you would come down here and finish me off?"

"I figured I would come make sure you weren't doing anything stupid."

Finn shrugged. "She hasn't done anything stupid yet, but I have a feeling she's about to."

She wasn't even sure which of them he meant, all she knew was that it was really annoying to be in between two posturing alpha males. Annoying, because they were acting like she wasn't even there. And annoying, because part of her actually got some kind of strange satisfaction out of the deal.

"Stop it," she said, extricating herself from Finn's hold. If there was one thing she knew for certain, it was that the mood was dead.

There was never a mood. And you know it.

There should have been. Because seriously, any woman should be excited by the attentions of a man like Finn. He was ridiculously good-looking. And yet, she was staring down her enemy, anger and arousal pouring through her blood in equal measure, and she could feel inevitability pounding between them like a drum.

"Why don't we have a talk, Rebecca?" Gage asked, his tone even, conciliatory even. She wasn't fooled.

"It may have escaped your notice, but I wasn't looking for a conversation."

"You're coming with me," he said, his tone hard. "If I have to carry you out of this bar, then I will."

"I don't think that's going to happen," Finn said, taking a step back from her and crossing his arms over his broad chest. "I'm not letting you carry her out of here."

She really was grateful to Finn, because he had to be aware that sex was completely off the table at this point, and he was still playing the part of protector.

"Rebecca and I have unfinished business," Gage said.

"It's finished if she wants it to be," Finn responded.

Gage turned to her. "You want this jackass fighting on your behalf? Or are you gonna come deal with me yourself? I didn't think you were a coward."

She bristled, but still, she took a step back. Because she wasn't stupid enough to think that if she went with him this was going to end in another fight. She knew exactly where this was headed. She could stay here with Finn, and whatever happened happened. Maybe she would go to bed with him, maybe she would finally lose her virginity. Or maybe they would just dance. But it wouldn't shake up her life either way. It wouldn't rattle her down to her very core.

But if she went with Gage, she knew exactly what would happen. She could see it. In the heat in his eyes, and she could feel it in the answering heat in her own body.

Rebecca had always been practical. It was the hazard of growing up with just enough. And sometimes not enough. You made do with what you had, and you learned very quickly what you could do without. You knew what necessity was, and what it wasn't.

Gage was a necessity. She knew it. Looking at him, she knew. If it wasn't him, it would never be quite right. It didn't matter if he was first, but it would be him eventually. And if it wasn't... She would always feel it. Feel a bit of unfinished business deep inside of her, an itch that would never be scratched.

And it was all tangled up. In her scars, in his part in them. In her anger at him, and in the way that anger had always driven her. Had always driven her to chase people out of her life, to keep men at an arm's length. It was so many things. Just so many things.

Settling it with Finn really was just a Band-Aid, like she'd been thinking earlier. But, different than she'd been thinking. It would be covering the wound up, not taking any steps to get rid of it.

It occurred to her then that if Gage was going to be here, if he was going to be in her business, well, then he owed her this. He really did. Whether it was pity or not. It shouldn't matter to her. The only thing that mattered was getting what she wanted. What she needed.

So, he needed to feel like he was giving her something, like he was taking steps toward atoning for his sins, whatever. She needed to put the monster to bed. She needed to start untangling the ways in which this had affected her life.

This seemed like a pretty good start.

"It's fine, Finn," she said. "I don't need you to punch anyone out today."

She couldn't tell if the look on his face was brought about by skepticism, or by the fact that she was rejecting him. "Give me a call if you need anything," he said, backing away from her and Gage.

"He's not your boyfriend, is he?" Gage asked.

"If he were my boyfriend and that's all he did to keep me from leaving with another man, I would break up with him. Let's go."

She stalked through the bar, doing her best to avoid looking at anyone. By tomorrow, she was going to be the subject of gossip, she just knew it. It was unavoidable. She had burst into the bar wearing an outfit that was advertising her intentions, then danced all up on Finn Donnelly, before leaving with another man.

Oh well. At least she was making a scandal, and the whispers behind their hands wouldn't just be about how poor and sad she was. About how beautiful she would be if she weren't damaged. About how tragic it was that her mother had left her. And how very brave she was to persevere in the face of it. Yeah, she would rather be the subject of this kind of gossip. At least it was interesting.

The night air bit into her skin, the cold coastal mist that settled over her face, sinking right in and chilling her down to her bones. But, she wasn't cold for long.

Gage grabbed hold of her, hauling her into his arms and kissing her, deep and long. She lost herself in it, in him. And she let her mind go blank. Of everything. Let herself forget that any time had passed between the moment he had held her at his house, that first moment his lips had touched hers, and this moment.

She wanted to forget all about Finn. Wanted to forget about what she had almost done. That she had even for one moment entertained the idea of being with another man when Gage was the one who she wanted. It didn't make sense. None of it did. And maybe it was all anger. Anger getting bound up in this hang-up that she had that was so big it was impossible to ignore. Really, it was impossible to separate them from each other.

Because what she hadn't done, and what she had done, were largely dictated by the accident. And so, it was tied up in him.

Her body rebelled at that idea, forcing the thoughts out of her mind. And yeah, maybe it was best she didn't think of it. Maybe it was best that she just pretended that she wanted him. That he was a stranger. And she was just a woman who needed a man very badly. Maybe that was the key. The way to cling to the tiniest sliver of sanity she could find.

If there was any sanity to be found in this.

She shivered, feeling hot all over by the time he released her. "You drunk?" he asked.

"Why?" She answered his question with a question mostly because she couldn't really remember if she was drunk or not. She felt sluggish, a little bit dizzy. But it had nothing to do with the single sip of beer she'd had, and everything to do with the kiss that she'd shared with Gage just now.

"First of all, if you're drunk, you're not driving. Second of all, if you're drunk, we're not doing this. Well, depending on how drunk."

"I'm not drunk," she said.

"Then get in my truck."

CHAPTER TEN

IF GAGE'S SPOT weren't already reserved in hell, he might be more concerned for his eternal soul. But the fact of the matter was, he was going to burn already. He might as well burn for this.

"I'm not drunk. I can drive." Rebecca didn't seem quite as intense as she often did. At least, not quite as ready to engage him in battle.

"I'm going to drive you. Your truck will be fine here for the night."

"Except that everybody's going to know that I left it here. And everybody is going to assume that I went home with someone."

"Is that such a bad thing?"

He watched her face, studied the nuance of her expression. "I guess not."

He wanted her—that was true. He had wanted her ever since he'd first backed her up against the wall in her shop. It wasn't right. It wasn't simple. But she was beautiful, and it had been a good while since he'd been with a woman.

Yeah, it was pretty terrible behavior to get involved with the woman he had already made so many terrible mistakes with. But she wanted it. She wanted him. As little sense as that made, it was clear. Made even more clear by the fact that she had gone straight to Ace's bar, as he had suspected she might, to go and pick up someone else.

That was all frustrated longing and anger at being turned down. And he recognized it, because he had been considering doing the same thing. But, he had also been pretty sure that he was going to find her there. And he'd been right.

So, it had worked out better than he'd imagined. Worst case scenario, he'd figured he could get some random woman to go to bed with him. But, that wasn't what he wanted. He wanted Rebecca.

He let that play over in his mind again, slowly, as he watched her climb up inside his pickup truck. He wanted Rebecca Bear.

There was nothing honorable in that. He couldn't even pretend. It was easy to tell himself that he was doing something that she wanted, that it was all a part of his attempt to make things right. But what he felt for her in this moment was completely separate from their history.

This was just about him, about her. About her being a woman he wanted with a particular kind of fire. Strange, because he wasn't usually one for difficult hookups. He didn't do relationships—he tended to gravitate toward women with empty heads and full bras who just wanted what he did. A little bit of mindless sex, an easy orgasm. That was all he was good for.

Rebecca wasn't that. She never could be. She was challenging, she was angry and she wasn't after his body simply because she thought he was hot. There was something else happening here, and he knew it. But he also didn't want to press.

He had too much on his plate as it was. But this was the kind of distraction that he needed. Actually, fighting with Rebecca in general was a welcome distraction. Otherwise, all he was left with was his family. Family that had become a group of strangers.

Yeah, he'd rather fight with Rebecca any day of the week.

He let out a long sigh as she closed the door, then he got into the truck, starting up the engine and putting it in Reverse.

Rebecca was quiet as they drove onto the highway, quiet as they continued on down the road.

He didn't like this. This pause before the action. It gave him too much time to think. He was afraid it might be giving her too much time to think. He should want her to change her mind, to turn back. Because he knew beyond a shadow of a doubt that this wasn't going to end well. Still, he was looking forward to the getting there.

He was that simple. Apparently.

It was a bit of a drive from town up to the lake and the silence began to expand until it was bigger than the cab of the truck. Talking to Rebecca would be a mistake, though. It inevitably was. They didn't have much of anything to say to each other that didn't end in a fight. He was much more fond of the way they interacted physically than the way they interacted verbally.

"What changed your mind?" It was Rebecca who broke the silence.

"My dick." He gritted his teeth, tightening his hold on the steering wheel. If that put her off because it was crass, it was probably for the best.

"I'm not sure if I should be flattered by that or not."

"Not," he said. "In fact, you should probably let that offend you real good. You should probably go ahead and run the other way."

"There you go getting cold feet again," she said, shaking her head. She planted her boot-clad foot up on the dash of the truck and his body turned to granite.

He looked at her out of the corner of his eye. She was bathed in the pale moonlight shining through the windshield, casting her skin in an otherworldly glow. He could see a tempting expanse of side, revealed from where her boot ended just at her knee, and ending at the short hem of her dress, which had ridden up thanks to the position she was sitting in.

"Me? I don't have cold feet. Honey, I've had more hookups than I can count. In fact, I purposely stopped counting at a certain point because I gotta say, it's not something I'm particularly proud of. This is just one more. But, I am giving you a chance to back out."

She was silent for a moment, and he snuck another glance, took in the mutinous set of her jaw. "Thanks for letting me know," she said, her tone casual. "I'll make sure I don't fall in love with you."

"I don't think there's any danger of you falling in love with me, but you might get addicted to me."

She laughed. "Wow, that's quite an ego you have there."

"My ego isn't the most impressive thing I've got,

honey. That may be a problem for you." He hated himself right now. Hated the cocky, stupid words coming out of his mouth. He was trying to put her off, even while he hoped that she wouldn't ask to be taken home.

He couldn't do a damn thing he set his mind to. Not when it came to making decisions that were better for other people, rather than for himself. He had made it a point to do one thing. To stay away from Rebecca. To try and fix some of her circumstances rather than breaking her down even more.

He held his jaw so tight it hurt. Yeah, he was doing a stellar job.

"Don't worry about my feelings," she said. "Just this once, okay?"

She sounded so much softer than he'd ever heard her sound, and he wasn't sure he liked it. It was easier when she fought him. Easier when she threw herself against him and he could just kind of take it. Take all that anger and let her pour it into him. He was comfortable with that. Part of him even liked it. This… This meant he had to maybe do something. Reach out, comfort her.

He didn't know how to do that. He could be her punching bag forever and a day. But anything else? Yeah, that was a little bit beyond him.

But, she wasn't asking for anything much. He might not be able to offer comfort, but he could make her come. He figured that was good enough.

Actually, maybe he was the one being stupid thinking of sex as something that would damage her. Clearly, she had no issue going out and getting it if she wanted it. She was a strong woman. Who knew what she wanted?

Maybe it would be best for both of them. Break a little bit of tension.

Because God knew there was tension.

"I won't worry about it," he said.

He turned the truck off the main highway and onto the narrower, windier road that led up to his place.

He pulled into the driveway, his body filled with tension as he turned the engine off and turned to face Rebecca. She was staring straight ahead, through the windshield still, her posture stiff.

"Rebecca," he said, "are you having second thoughts?"

He hated himself for asking that question, mostly because he was afraid that she would say that she was having second thoughts and she wanted to go home instead of to his bed. But, this was the last time he was going to ask. After this, he wasn't going to be able to stop. If he touched her again, it was over. That meant he had to take this moment, this pause, to make absolutely certain.

She didn't say anything. Instead, she reached across the space between them and wrapped her arms around his neck, launching herself at him as she claimed his lips with her own. He grabbed hold of the back of her head, lacing his fingers through her hair and holding her tight as he staked his claim on her mouth. He tasted her, deep and long, and he let himself forget everything except how much he wanted her. Let his body drain completely of all the tension that he'd been carrying inside from the moment he'd come back to town.

There was no room for it. He was too filled with her. With how much he wanted her. How much he needed her. Ironic, that it was Rebecca who was finally making him feel at home. Like something other than a puzzle piece shoved into the wrong puzzle, trying to fit when he belonged anywhere else.

Rebecca tasted like home. Like the ocean and the pine trees, like regret and a raw, aching need that he knew would never go away no matter how many places he went to, no matter how long he stayed. He would always miss Copper Ridge as it was when he was younger. As it could be in a memory only, or in a strange moment that seemed to stand outside of time. A heartbeat that existed outside her body, when things still seemed simple and beautiful.

Before everything had been ruined by reality. Before he had ruined it for himself. For himself, for his family, for Rebecca.

This was like a little slice of that feeling. That feeling that had been lost to him for so many years. The sun filtering through the trees, a glimmer on the waves and a sense of endless possibility that had long since been drained out of him.

He growled, changing the momentum of the kiss, pressing her against the passenger door of the truck. He stripped his jacket off, flinging it to the side, wrapping his arms around her and pressing her breasts firmly against his chest as he settled between her thighs. The gearshift dug into his ribs, but he didn't care. He kept on kissing her. She slipped her hands up around his neck, then let her fingertips drift to his face, holding him steady as she returned his kiss with all the ferocity that he poured out into her.

He slid one hand down her back, all the way down to the curve of her ass, urging her to press herself against him, to arch the cradle of her thighs against his cock. He growled, swearing into her mouth as that gentle pressure of her body on him sent a lightning bolt of sensation straight through him.

He shoved his other hand up underneath her dress, his fingertips skimming over soft skin, resting his palm on her hip, teasing her by pushing one finger, then another, beneath the elastic waistband of her panties.

She gasped, wrenching her mouth away from his. "Inside?"

"Maybe in a minute," he said, kissing her again, sliding his tongue against hers and groaning at the slick friction.

"Please?"

He looked down at her, trying to catch his breath, trying to get a hold of his racing heart. He was tempted to tell her he didn't have a second to waste. That he had a condom in his wallet and he needed to use it now.

"Sure," he said, his voice a rasp of need.

He released his hold on her, pressing his hands against the bench seat of the truck and pushing himself up. He was shaking. Dammit, he couldn't remember the last time that had happened. Probably not since he was a sixteen-year-old virgin making out in his truck for the first time.

He opened up the driver side, getting out on unsteady legs before making his way around to the passenger side. He opened the door slowly, and Rebecca tilted partway out, still lying down in the seat, looking up at him from her strange position.

In spite of himself, he laughed. "Are you coming?"

"Oh, I hope so," she said, rolling to the side, ending up on her knees on the floorboard of the truck, before sliding out onto the ground.

He reached down, grabbing hold of her hand and tugging her up, then against him. He kissed her nose, and she giggled. Which was basically the last sound he had ever expected to come out of her. "You're sure you're not drunk?"

"Just… I'm so turned on. We have to go inside."

A rush of air escaped his body, and he swept her up into his arms, grabbing her like he was a villain in an old movie, which he basically was. Then, he strode across the driveway, up the steps and into the house.

He continued on through the living area, and up the stairs, heading straight to his bedroom. He set her down, right in front of the bed, and when he looked at her face, her eyes were huge, glittering.

"Full-service," he said, leaning forward, kissing her lightly on the lips, then again on the chin, and down her neck. "I aim to please."

"I—I…" She seemed completely incapable of speech. Which was fine with him. If she could still talk, he wasn't doing his job. He didn't want conversation. Not now.

"Quiet," he said, biting her lower lip. She complied. Then, he returned to the business of making love to her mouth, taking her deeper and deeper with each pass of his lips over hers.

He continued to kiss her until she went limp, pliant. He imagined this was as docile as Rebecca Bear got.

"Turn the…" She let out a long breath. "Turn the lights off?"

Her words were like a punch to the gut. Because, whatever her reasons were for turning the lights off, it reminded him of her scars. And it reminded him of the fact that when he saw her naked, he would be confronted with the full extent of her injuries. Injuries he had caused. He felt like he was a bastard complying, but he did anyway. Mostly because he wasn't sure he wanted to confront all that right now. He wasn't sure he ever did.

That made him an ass. Or, maybe he did it because he was an ass. Because it was easier to shroud them both in darkness and pretend there was nothing hard or impossible between them.

Her scars would spoil the illusion, not because they would turn him off. That wasn't the problem. They would spoil the illusion that they were just a man and a woman looking for a way to pass the time. Looking for a way to blow off a little steam. Her scars carried all their history. Those years that they'd spent never talking to each other, never seeing each other and yet living with each other. Her every step weighted down by him, no matter that he had never spent a minute in her company.

He couldn't bring that to this. Not now. He would never have been the one to ask that the lights go off, but since she had, he was willing to take that easy out.

Now all he could see was her silhouette, nothing in

detail, and as much as he mourned not getting a chance to take a look at that beautiful body of hers, he welcomed what it would conceal.

He grabbed hold of the flowing hemline of her dress, tugging it up over her head and running his hands over her bare curves. Then he dispensed with her bra, pushing her panties down her thighs, and taking a step back.

He could see the silhouette of her figure, and those long legs—long in proportion in spite of her diminutive height—still partly covered by those high boots.

"Damn," he said, his curse almost reverent, "you're sexy."

He saw her breasts pitch with her sharp intake of breath. "Really?"

He moved forward, grabbing hold of her arm and tugging her toward him, placing her palm right over his cock. "What does that feel like to you?"

"I… I… I guess…"

He chuckled, bringing her in even closer, pressing his lips to her ear. "I want you. I'm so hard for you I'm about ready to burst through the front of these jeans. I want to bury myself so deep inside you I won't be able to feel anything else."

She trembled in his arms. Honest to God trembled. She didn't say anything in return, and he wasn't sure how he felt about that. He supposed he should be happy that she wasn't talking, that she finally wasn't fighting him. At least not now.

He separated from her for a moment, tugging his shirt up over his head, then moving to his belt, jeans, underwear and boots. Then, he pulled her back up against his body, letting out a sigh of relief when her skin was pressed against his. Every inch of her, against every inch of him.

He kissed her again, moving his hand between her thighs, finding her wet and needy for him. His breath hissed through his teeth and he drew his fingertips through her damp flesh, teasing the entrance of her body before drawing her moisture out to that sensitive bundle of nerves, moving his thumb in a circle until a short, shocked cry escaped her lips.

"Tell me what you want," he said, his voice like gravel, his dick so hard he thought it was going to break.

He wanted her so much. In spite of everything between them. Hell, maybe it was even because of everything between them. Maybe he was just that sick. Maybe he was just that destructive.

Maybe he was just his father. He'd run for a lot of years, and yet here he was. Back at the scene of the crime.

He gritted his teeth, pushing back at that thought.

"Tell me," he coaxed, "I want to know exactly what you want me to do to you."

"I don't know," she said, a shiver lacing her words. "I don't know. I've never... I don't know what I'm doing."

"Rebecca?" he asked, that one word a demand for clarification.

"I'm a virgin."

CHAPTER ELEVEN

SHE WASN'T SURE why she'd told him. Maybe because she knew there was no way she'd be able to hide it. Because she knew that there was no way she could possibly appear to be experienced when she was shaking inside and out. When she needed someone to take her hand and lead her through it, to show her exactly what was supposed to happen.

Or maybe, it was because she was still hoping he would back out. Because some part of her wanted to be completely, totally absolved of the decision. He would either turn back now, or move forward, but that admission had put the ball back in his court. She was a virgin, she was inexperienced and that meant all of this was his domain, and he had to know it.

The virgin could hardly be held responsible for her actions, right? She didn't know if it was a big decision or not. If it was actually possible to have sex and not form a connection, if this was actually what she wanted, because she couldn't really know the consequences of sex.

Yeah, basically, she had admitted it not because she was brave, but because she was scared. She hated that. She hated that she was that much of a trembling little coward. But she was a trembling, turned-on little coward, so she didn't want to turn back… Exactly. But, she also wanted to wash her hands of the decision making yet further.

That was actually kind of understandable. She was about to make love with the man who was supposed to be her mortal enemy. The monster in her closet, as she had told him before. And he was the man who wanted to make love to her even knowing that. She didn't know which of them was more messed up.

Maybe they just both were. Maybe because of each other, or because of that one event that connected them. Maybe because of something else entirely.

She wasn't really sure of anything right now. And she was very much uncertain about what the intense expression on his face meant. He was just standing there, his eyes glittering in the darkness, his large, muscular frame held taut and stiff in front of her.

She was grateful for the darkness, even as she wished that she could see him better, she was grateful he couldn't see her. That as obscured as he was, she was equally hidden.

She'd had this dream before. Standing with a man in the dark. But she didn't want to scream at him, not now. She wanted something else entirely.

Something a whole lot scarier than screaming.

"What do you mean by that?" he asked.

"Is there more than one application for that word?"

"Do you mean as an expression? Like, it's been so long since you've been with somebody you might as well be?"

"No, I mean the literal application," she said, shrinking back, wrapping her arms around her midsection.

"But you've... You have experience. Some experience," he said, his tone intense.

She shook her head, then realized he might not be able to see the gesture. "No. Not really. I mean, I've kissed a couple of guys. But that's it. It's never gone very far. I've never seen a naked man before... No man has ever seen me naked before... Although, you aren't really seeing me, because we turned the lights off." She swallowed hard, aware that she needed to stop rambling like an idiot.

He didn't say anything. He just stood there, still naked, she knew, even though she couldn't make out the fine details of his body. She wished that he would do something. Wished that he would close the distance between them, or walk away. Of course, she was at his house, so she was probably the one who would have to walk away. But she wished that he would at least say something definitive.

She felt...she felt completely unguarded. Stripped bare. It had nothing to do with being naked. She didn't like it. It made her want to hit him, to yell at him again, to get into another fight, because it was easier than this.

She opened her mouth, ready to say something confrontational, but he overrode her. "This is what you want?"

She wished that he wasn't asking her. She wished that his voice weren't so enticing, so masculine and husky, thick with his desire for her. She wished that he didn't sound so tender. She wished that he were angry. Because that would make this easy.

He seemed intent on making it anything but easy.

"I said it was what I wanted. You're the one that's surprised by the virgin news, not me." She despised the sound of her voice. Tremulous and uncertain, rather than sharp and clear the way she would prefer. But she was in over her head. Drowning. She needed him to reach down and pull her out, to show her what to do, to dictate what happened next. She was dependent on him. It was nothing like she had thought it would be.

She had thought to find some kind of power in this. To reclaim something. But she didn't feel it. Not now. She just felt hollow and vulnerable. She felt like any other woman, and yet at the same time so painfully aware that she wasn't. Because she was twenty-eight, and she was a virgin. Because her skin was scarred and most people would never be able to call it beautiful.

She just wanted him the way a woman wanted a man. But it wasn't that. It couldn't be. It could never be. Because of her, because of him. Her teeth chattered, and suddenly he reached out, cupping her cheek, his warmth enveloping her, sending sweet, warm honey through her veins. It slowed her blood, slowed her heartbeat, slowed everything down until all she could do was focus on him.

On where his skin made contact with hers. On his breathing. On the way it matched with the steady beating of her heart.

"I want you," he said.

The words were simple, but they were everything.

They were the only thing that mattered. Because they stripped all that other stuff away, and they left behind the things she wished she could be. So maybe, for tonight, just for tonight, here in the dark, she could be brave. Beautiful. Sensual.

She didn't say anything. She didn't have anything to say, which was a miracle in and of itself. Instead, she swayed forward, pressing her lips to his. His thumb skimmed over her cheek and she melted into his touch, resting against the strength of his hand.

Her stomach turned over, something about that simple display of strength, that encompassing heat made her feel safe in a way that nothing else had.

How could she feel safe in his hands?

She blinked back a sudden, unexpected sheen of tears. She wished that she could see him, and she was glad that she couldn't. Those two thoughts, those two desires, fought with each other as she gave herself over to their kiss. As she allowed him to pull her completely up against his body, so that she was pressed against him, from breast all the way down to her toes.

His arousal was hot and hard against her stomach, big and overwhelming, and something she couldn't quite bring herself to think about. She was much happier wrapped in this kind of gauzy prelude that wasn't overly realistic just yet. She was cocooned in darkness. In a deep, emotional hunger that made her feel so hollow she was desperate to be filled, and it all seemed limitless and endless. When she began to apply it to the physical, to reality, it seemed a little bit more impossible.

But he was sure, and he was certain, and she took a lit-

tle bit of pleasure in the fact that she had been right about
the kind of man she wanted to do this job. His hands were
firm, knowing, as they slid over her curves, as he moved
them both to the bed, laying her down gently, rising up
over her, kissing the edge of her mouth, her jaw, down
to her collarbone.

She might be hesitant, but he wasn't. She might not
have any idea what was happening, what was going to
happen next, but he did. That certainty spoke loudly
through each and every touch, through every branding
kiss that landed on her skin.

He moved lower, his tongue sliding over the curve of
her breast. She gasped as he moved to the side, his lips
brushing against one of her scars. He skimmed over it
as though it weren't there. And she squeezed her eyes
tight, trying to keep tears from falling, because that
was exactly what she needed, and he seemed to know it.

He moved lower then, shattering her thoughts as he
drew one tightened nipple into his mouth, sucking hard
before lapping at her gently, then scraping her with his
teeth, a little bit rough. She squirmed, unable to keep
back the hoarse cry that broke through her lips. It was
the combination. That sweet, almost deferential touch
that paid homage to her inexperience combined with
the more challenging elements—scrapes of his teeth
against her skin, hot, roughly spoken words that made
her shiver at the erotic promise in them.

He continued to blaze a trail down her stomach, to
that tender skin just beneath her bellybutton, where he
paused, tracing a lazy circle there before dipping his

head lower, his breath hot over that bundle of nerves at the apex of her thighs.

He groaned as he nuzzled her aching body, then pressed his lips to the most intimate part of her. She arched up against him, not sure if she was trying to get closer, or get away. Knowing about something intellectually was a lot different than actually experiencing something. Exposing yourself to something so intimate was different than anything. She didn't have a single thing she could compare this to. This surrender of herself, of her inhibitions—of which she had plenty.

But with each pass of his tongue, a few more were stripped away as her arousal was wrenched up higher, impossibly so—she cared less and less about anything except what Gage could do to her with his mouth and his hands. He was holding tightly to her hips, holding her to his mouth so that he could control the pressure and the speed with which he ravished her.

Pretty soon, she wasn't worried about anything except the promised pleasure that he hinted at with each wicked taste. She found herself moving in time with him as best she could, even though he was holding her so tight it was difficult to move at all. She liked that too. Enjoyed the evidence of his strength, of how large and male he was. How different he was from her.

He released his hold on her with one hand, sliding it between her thighs and pushing one finger deep inside of her, then another as he stretched her gently, thrusting into her in time with each pass of his tongue over her clit.

Something began to fracture in her chest, breaking

her apart piece by piece. It was horrible, and wonderful, blinding and completely overwhelming. She felt herself splintering, shattering, starting near her heart and moving on down, deep and low, the resulting damage causing answering waves to begin to swell inside of her.

She tried to fight it, tried to hold herself back, digging her heels into the mattress as the pressure built and built until she could barely breathe. She was fighting a losing battle to hold the pieces of herself together, even though the damage had already been done. And when she dissolved, she wondered why she had ever tried to stay whole.

Because being broken and sobbing in Gage's arms, reaching this peak of pleasure that rivaled anything she had ever fantasized about, made her controlled, rigid existence seem so dry, so very small. Like she'd been living in one room when all she had to do was open the door to find the freedom she'd always craved.

As the aftershocks continued to shudder through her, Gage moved away, right when she needed to cling to him. He moved to the edge of the bed, opened his nightstand drawer and pulled out a box of condoms.

"Hold tight," he said, his voice strange.

"Okay," she responded, because she wasn't really sure what else to say. It wasn't like she was going to get up and run out of the room now, even if part of her wanted to. She was too… Well, she was boneless for one. For another, she wasn't going to go this far without taking it all the way.

While he took care of the protection, she closed her eyes, listening to the sound of the package tearing, fighting against the anxiety starting to chase around inside of her.

Then, he moved back to her, positioning himself between her thighs. He gripped her chin between his thumb and forefinger, turning her face and pressing a kiss to her lips. She kept her eyes closed.

He moved his hand back down between her legs, stroking her a couple of times, groaning when he found her wet.

"I'll try to go slow," he said.

She just wished he would quit talking. Because suddenly everything felt way too real, and who he was seemed impossible to ignore, and what was about to happen was so incredibly huge.

And it was Gage West.

She gritted her teeth, turning her head as he pressed the blunt head of his arousal against her entrance, sliding inside of her slowly, stretching her, filling her. It was impossible. She could hardly breathe. He was too much.

Instinctively, she grabbed hold of his shoulders, clinging to him even though part of her wanted to push him away. She held on to him so tightly her nails dug into his skin, but he didn't stop her, didn't act like he was in pain.

He made a harsh sound as he pushed into her all the way, and she started to shake. It was terrible. It hurt. He was so big she didn't think she would ever get used to the feel of him inside of her. And he was so close. Of course he was. He was in her. But, she hadn't fully appreciated what that might mean. Or maybe, she had.

Maybe that was why she'd never done this before. Because she knew how it would feel.

He was over her, around her, in her, all-encompassing in ways she had never anticipated.

He consumed her every sense. Every part of her.

How was she supposed to keep him at a distance when he was in her? How did she keep her shields up when he was so far past the walls? She should have known. And somehow, she hadn't. All that want, all that longing had been so big she'd forgotten the rest. Forgotten words like *intimacy* and *possession*.

A tear slid down her cheek, and she was thankful he couldn't see it. Thankful that it was dark, and he was lost in his own pleasure, too wrapped up in all of it to realize that she was unraveling.

He started to move. She wanted to beg him to stop. Not because it hurt, but because it began to feel good. And that was even worse.

He flexed his hips, his hard body pressing up against her clitoris, sending sparks of pleasure through her. She fought it. There was no reason for her to have an orgasm again. She'd had one already, and honestly, another one would be gratuitous. And dangerous.

But, Gage didn't seem to take note of her resistance. Or, he didn't care. He slid his hand down her back, moving to cup her butt, pulling her up hard against him with his every thrust, forcing her into deeper, harder contact with him.

He ground his hips against her every time he went in deep, making her gasp, pushing the strange surge of emotion that had overwhelmed her when he had first entered her into the background. It was still there, lingering, but the feeling, the pleasure, it was bigger now. Starting to blot out common sense, self-protection and everything that had just told her to try and hold back.

She didn't want to hold back anymore. She just wanted, more than that, needed him. Needed this. Needed satisfaction more than she could ever remember needing anything else in her entire life.

He wasn't talking now. He was just breathing, hard and fierce, broken. She liked it. Because it sounded like she felt. On the verge. Out of control.

She let her head fall back, and he kissed her throat, those hot lips and the gentle scrape of his beard sending a sensual shiver right down through her body.

Suddenly, the sensation of being overwhelmed by him wasn't bad. It wasn't too much.

It wasn't enough.

She found herself arching into him, holding on to him, pressing her body against him. Clinging to him, to this.

She wrapped her legs around his, tangling herself in him completely as he continued to drive them both harder, higher.

He gripped her face again, holding her steady as he kissed her deep, his desperation echoing through her, pushing her to the brink. She held there for a moment, suspended in space. And then she fell.

She felt him stiffen above her, heard him growl as he pulsed deep inside of her. But she was too caught up in her own release to have any more than a vague awareness for what had happened with him.

When she came back to herself, she was still cling-ing to his shoulders, and he was breathing hard, his face buried in her neck.

She blinked, realizing that there were tears on her face that she wasn't aware of having shed. He moved away from her and she rolled onto her side, curling into a ball, tucking her knees up against her chest.

She closed her eyes tightly, listened to the sound of him cross the room, going into what she assumed was a bathroom. She just lay there, counting her breaths. She had done that. She wasn't a virgin anymore.

She'd had sex with Gage West.

She sat up, breathing hard, an adrenaline surge pour-ing through her. She had to go. She had to get out of here or she was going to completely lose her mind in front of him.

She swung her feet over the side of the mattress, pressing her hand to her chest, feeling her heart raging beneath her palm.

"You don't have your truck."

She turned, seeing the vague silhouette of Gage standing in the bathroom door. "I know," she said.

"I don't think you did. You had the look of a woman about to run out on a man."

"I'll just walk home," she said, ignoring him.

"Like hell. Give me a couple of minutes and I'll drive you back if you need to leave. Or, you're welcome to spend the night here."

"No. Absolutely not."

He let out a heavy sigh, crossing the space and mov-ing to the foot of the bed, where he retrieved his jeans.

"Have it your way. I don't exactly want to go outside again, but if you need your space…"

"I need to go home. I told you. One time. That was it. It's done."

He started to pull his pants on slowly. "Right. And you were a virgin. You just…wanted to lose that really quick?"

"There was nothing quick about it. I'm twenty-eight."

"Sure. But I think you know that's not what I meant."

"Hey, could we skip the heart-to-heart, postmortem thing?"

"I haven't decided yet." Suddenly, the sound of a phone vibrating on a hard surface cut through their conversation. He crossed to the nightstand and grabbed hold of his phone, looking down at the screen. He answered it. "Hello? Yeah." He paused. "Is everything okay?"

In spite of herself, Rebecca felt tense listening to the single-sided conversation.

"I can come down there." There was another pause. "Right. All right. Some other time then." This pause wasn't longer than the others, but it felt thicker, heavier. "Tell her I said… You know what, don't tell her I said anything."

He hung up the phone, setting it slowly on the nightstand again. Then he turned, walking toward the window and bracing his hands on the windowpane.

Her breath caught as she looked at his powerful physique, outlined by the pale moonlight. She felt exposed, she still wanted to escape, but that didn't make him any less beautiful. It didn't make her any less captivated by him. Or any less concerned about what was happening, even if she shouldn't be concerned about him at all.

"What happened?"

"My little sister," he said, his voice like gravel. "She had a baby."

CHAPTER TWELVE

"Is everything okay?"

He wasn't accustomed to Rebecca looking at him with anything like compassion or concern, but she definitely showed both at the moment.

He nodded slowly, his heart thundering a dull, painful rhythm in his chest. A lot like a boulder hitting up against a bruise. He had barely recovered from what had just happened between him and Rebecca, and having this thrown over the top of it when his orgasm was still buzzing through his blood was all a little bit much.

"Yeah, everything's fine. Madison wasn't sure if Sierra would want me to come down to the hospital." And why would she? Until that first day he'd come back, he hadn't seen her since she was six years old.

Damn.

Suddenly, he felt the weight and importance of every single year he'd been absent. Sure, he'd been close enough to an adult when he'd left, but his siblings had been kids. Those years mattered. They had changed things in inestimable ways. He could never have that time back. Ever.

He had missed everything. First dates and inches grown and all the shit that Madison had gone through.

Colton was married, and in his mind his brother was still a skinny sixteen-year-old, not a man. Not someone's husband.

He had missed Sierra getting married, and now she was a mother.

All in all, he had changed the least.

His years hadn't been full of this kind of change. He had just wandered on down empty roads, rolling into towns where no one knew him and then rolling back out again when they knew him a little bit too well.

Yeah, it had all blurred together out there. By himself, the years hadn't seemed to matter so much. But back here, he could see just how essential each and every one had been. Now that it was too late.

"Why doesn't she think you should go to the hospital?"

"Probably because me being around is still a little bit of a problem. Colton is mad because I'm the one that Dad put in charge of managing his affairs if he ever became an invalid or died. I think that pisses him off because he was here being the good son, and I was off doing God knows what. That's fair enough. Except, I don't actually think he wants a front-row seat to all of this. But, I don't blame them for not trusting me." He looked at her, at the woman he had just slept with. The woman whose virginity he had just taken. She looked rumpled, warm and soft, and a hell of a lot more tempting than the problems that were laid out in front of him.

The prospect of taking Rebecca back to bed was much more appealing than walking through this field of emotions that he had a feeling was full of a hell of a lot more burrs than wildflowers.

"At a certain point you're going to have to start going," she said, her tone maddeningly matter-of-fact. As if this weren't a complicated issue.

"No," he said, "I don't. I'm not going to stay in town. Nobody wants me to. Come to that, I don't think I want to."

"Plenty of people live out of town and still stay in touch with their families. Do you honestly think that coming back for a few months and laying out ultimatums and commands is going to heal a rift? I mean, that's what you've been doing with me. Burst in and tell me how it's going to be, then expect me to thank you for it."

"You didn't mind being told what to do a few minutes ago," he said.

He couldn't read her expression in the darkness. But, he had a feeling that it wasn't a pleasant one. He was comfortable with that, though. Comfortable with her being angry with him. More comfortable with sex than he was with the complicated feelings surrounding his family, and his sister giving birth.

"How old was she when you left?" He hadn't expected that.

"Six," he replied.

He remembered her clearly. An impish little girl with wide blue eyes and almost white blond hair. And of course, he'd been a teenager, so he had found her mostly boring. He'd been so wrapped up in his own life, a life that he had been convinced the universe revolved around. What else mattered except for his own comfort? His own happiness?

He had never, not once, considered that his actions might affect other people. He had never particularly cared. The entire world—in his mind—had existed to bring him happiness.

He wished he would have cared about her then. When it would have mattered. It was all a little bit too late now.

"That must be hard," she said, speaking slowly, as though it were foreign to her to say something comforting.

"Yeah," he said, bracing himself on the window, staring out into the blackness beyond his front yard. "You could say that."

"Let's go."

"Where?" he asked, turning slightly to face her.

"To the hospital. I'm driving you. No matter what Madison says, if you don't go, they're going to hold that over you. Better to go and have them be unfriendly jackasses when you get there."

"You care whether or not they're mad at me?"

She shrugged one bare shoulder, then moved across the room, fishing around for her clothes.

"Now suddenly you don't have a comment?" he asked.

"I don't know why I care," she said, straightening, pulling her dress over her head. "Maybe because there's no chance ever that I'm going to make up with my mom? Maybe because I never even knew my dad, and also maybe because my brother is one of the most important people in the world to me? Maybe it's just the fact that your family is right there, and you could fix it. But you aren't."

"Our situations aren't that easy to compare," he said.

"Maybe. Maybe not."

"You have a lot of *maybe*s."

She growled. "I'm sorry, I'm fresh out of certainty. I just did about the craziest thing I can think of with the last person on earth I ever should have done it with. You want certainty? You should damn well be at the hospital with your little sister. No matter what. Even if she doesn't want you in the room, even if you end up cooling your heels at reception, you should be there."

"Why?" he asked, taking a step toward her, pressure building in his chest. "According to you I'm a scourge, so what good could I possibly do there?"

"You're her brother," she said, her expression furious. "Maybe that doesn't matter to you right now. Or you've lost touch with what that means, but it's a big deal."

Everything in him felt like it exploded then, a devastating thunderclap that toppled defenses, that exposed pain he hadn't even known existed.

His little sister. His little sister he'd abandoned. It was so clear then. What he'd lost. What he'd missed.

All he could think of was that he had to make it stop. That he needed something, anything. And since Rebecca was the one to rock him like that, he felt like she might be the one to fix it. He advanced on her, only stopping when she shrank back. He closed his eyes, inhaling the scent of her, so close he could reach out and touch her with ease. So close he could just pull her into his arms and kiss her and forget that Sierra was in the hospital. That she'd just given birth.

That his whole damn life was…this. Years wandering in the wilderness, building nothing except a fortune, without a single damn person to call if he had a heart attack or some shit. He had a family. That was his one tie. The only one that couldn't be severed by distance or negligence. Because it was blood.

Whatever he'd been about to say, whatever he'd been about to do…it all just sort of evaporated. Because there was nothing he could rail at, destroy or run from that would fix this. Distance would only widen the wound, and he'd had enough of that.

There was only one thing to do.

"Take me to the hospital," he said.

He should take her home. He shouldn't have her drive anywhere.

"Sure." Her voice was blank, and what he could see of her face was too.

They didn't talk as they headed out of the house to the truck. He handed her the keys when they got to the vehicle and she took them, getting inside and starting the truck while she waited for him to get in.

As soon as they were on the main highway, she started to chatter. Which was very un-Rebecca-like.

"You probably don't know the layout of the new hospital," she said. "So it's better if I drive because the birthing center is kind of hard to find. Like it's in its own little…part of the…" She trailed off.

It suited him to have her manufacture excuses for why she was coming with him. For why he was having her drive. It was true, he didn't know where the birthing center was, but he had a smartphone so he could figure it out fast enough by using the map app.

But he just wanted her with him. Whatever the fuck that meant, he wasn't in the mood to figure it out.

"I bet when you left there were hardly any shops open on the main street," she said as they drove through town. "So this must be very different."

She sounded nervous. Nothing like she normally did. He didn't like it. He would rather have her going after him with verbal knives than acting like she was nervous. He didn't want her nervous. Pissed and profane, or panting beneath him, sure. But not nervous.

"Yeah, it's pretty different," he said.

Main Street had been white noise to him when he'd been in high school. Something he'd driven by every day of his life. He'd stopped looking at it. He'd stopped looking at much of anything except for what benefitted him, what gave him a rush of adrenaline.

He'd been the heir apparent to the town in his mind, and he'd felt like it all existed for him. That was what he remembered now as they drove on the dark, rain-drenched streets. The world's quietest homecoming parade. Just him riding shotgun in his own truck as Rebecca filled the silence with talk about what business was where and for how long.

While he thought about that night he'd driven through town then sped off north. His friends were messing around. Passing on double lines, and it was his turn to pass and take the lead so, even though it wasn't safe, he did. And then he saw headlights coming his direction.

He gritted his teeth, keeping his eyes on the road. On the headlights firmly in the correct lane.

Finally they arrived at the hospital. The tiny parking lot at the birthing center was packed full, and there was only one available space. Rebecca turned into it sharply and killed the engine, then got out without waiting for him.

She scurried quickly to the automatic glass doors, dodging raindrops as they started to fall. He walked slower, not caring when the icy drops hit his bare skin, slid inside the collar of his shirt and down his back. He'd forgotten his hat. Which seemed about right since his whole world had been pitched just slightly to the left and he wasn't sure what the hell he was going to do about it.

He wasn't sure what the hell he was going to do next.

They walked into the waiting area, a small space with double doors on the opposite side of it, guarded by a man sitting at a desk positioned out front.

"Who are you here to see?" he asked.

"Sierra West." Then he remembered that wasn't her name anymore. "I mean Sierra Thompson. Sorry. I can't quite get used to that."

The man looked at the registry book in front of him, offering Gage an understanding smile as he did. "Takes a while for a name change to stick." He took two name tags and dated them, then passed them over to Gage and Rebecca to add their names. "If she's not taking visitors the nurse will stop you. She's in room three."

He nodded, missing his hat again and feeling a little like an ass.

"Come on," Rebecca said as the man at the desk pressed a button and opened the security doors.

She didn't touch him, but he still felt connected to her by some invisible thread. But that was low on his list of things to worry about. Especially when he saw Colton, his wife, Lydia—who Gage had yet to formally meet—and Maddy sitting in the waiting room.

They all stood when he walked in. Colton wrapped his arm around Lydia and drew her close. Maddy crossed her arms, holding herself close and putting obvious distance between her and himself.

"We have to stop meeting like this," he said, his lame joke doing nothing to defuse the tension in the room.

"Then, maybe don't make a habit out of showing up only when someone is hospitalized?" This came from Maddy.

"How is she?"

"Great," Colton said. "Resting."

"Everything is good with the baby?"

"Everything's fine. It's a girl," Maddy added. "If she wasn't okay, I would have told you."

"Yeah, I figured." He actually had. Madison was straight up, that much he had gathered in their limited interaction.

"You can go," Colton said.

Lydia put a hand on her husband's shoulder. "I don't think he wants to go, Colton."

"No," Gage said, "he doesn't."

"She didn't ask for you," Colton said. "Why would

she? For seventeen years you haven't been around. There would be no point in her asking for you. Why would she ask for you now?"

"I know. I'm not going to stand here and try to justify myself. Not now. That's a conversation for a different time. And it's going to take a lot more than one conversation, frankly. But right now, I want to see her. Or, I at least want her to know that I was here."

Colton frowned, looking past Gage, his eyes landing on Rebecca. "Are you with him, Rebecca?" he asked.

Gage looked down at Rebecca. Her golden cheeks darkened, pink flushing up beneath her skin. "I drove him," she said, her voice monotone.

Colton looked like he wanted to launch into an inquisition, but he refrained. "I can check and see if she wants to see you."

"I will," Maddy said, treating him to a look that would have scorched a lesser man before she walked toward the patient rooms, disappearing into one of them.

A heavy, uncomfortable silence descended over them.

"Were you all here the whole time?"

Colton nodded, and so did Lydia. "That's what we do," Colton said. "That's what I do. It's what I've done ever since you left."

"I need coffee," Lydia said, her tone firm, giving every indication that she had no need of coffee, she only wanted to remove herself from the conversation. "Rebecca, why don't you come with me?" She smiled pleasantly at Rebecca, making it very clear that it wasn't optional.

Rebecca didn't look at him. Instead, she turned and went with Lydia without giving them another glance. Probably for the best. He didn't exactly want to play up his connection with her. Both because he didn't want Colton to know about the accident just yet, and because he really didn't want his brother to know about the fact that he had slept with Rebecca.

"That was subtle," he said.

Colton lifted a shoulder. "That's Lydia. She's a politician. She gets things done one way or another, but not necessarily with subtlety."

"I'm not going to hurt her," he said, speaking of Sierra.

"I don't believe you."

He deserved that. He knew he did. But hurting Sierra was the last thing he wanted and he'd be damned if he let the accusation stand.

"Do you think that I came back to help handle Dad's affairs and cause more damage? That doesn't make any sense. I can't fix what happened in the past if fixing it means making the last seventeen years completely different. The only thing I can do is change what I'm doing now."

"And then you're going to leave."

He gritted his teeth. "Plenty of people maintain a relationship with their families while they live in different towns," he said, echoing what Rebecca had said earlier.

"Yeah, but even you have to admit your track record on that is pretty bad."

"I'm not going to deny it." Tension stretched between himself and his brother. Tension and so many years of silence bringing them to this moment. "There were things that I couldn't talk about. Things I still don't want to talk about. But I was young, and I was stupid. I did the easy thing," he said, nearly choking on the words because there hadn't been anything easy about leaving his family. "But I'm thirty-five years old, I'm not eighteen. I'm not going to handle things the same way now that I did then. It was easy for me to think that time stopped here while I was gone. That Sierra was still a little girl, that you were still a skinny kid. But now, I'm thinking I'm not the only one that's guilty of that. You think that I went away and did nothing, that I learned nothing, that I suffered nothing. I had a life. Seventeen years of it. I'm not the same person I was when I left."

Colton eyed him warily. "Sure, I hear you. But I'm not sure that I can trust the person standing in front of me any more than I could trust the person you were."

"Let's meet tomorrow. I want to talk to you about the financial situation. The best I can do is be transparent with you about this stuff. The best we can do is start, right?"

"I guess so."

Maddy reappeared then, her expression just as guarded as Colton's. "She said you can come in."

His heart dropped slightly, and he realized then that he hadn't really imagined she would let him visit her. He had expected to get turned away at the door. The fact that Colton, Maddy and Sierra were accepting him in any capacity was more than he had expected.

He had imagined resistance. Outright refusal. It was strange to wrap his head around something different.

He nodded, following Maddy to the door and stopping her just as she started to push it open. "Thank you for calling me," he said.

"I told you not to come."

"I know. But would you have listened if our situations were reversed?"

A reluctant smile tugged at her lips, and she quickly forced it back down. "No. But also, I haven't been out of Sierra's life all this time so I would punch you because you would have no right to tell me to stay away."

"You're protective of her and I get it. I respect it. But I don't want to hurt her, I promise you. I think you're right. I think we are alike. Which means I know, and I trust, that if I mess this up you'll come after me with a knife."

"I will eviscerate you with the confidence and skill of a woman who is no stranger to self-defense. On that you can trust me."

"I do."

"Good," she said, pushing the door open and indicating that he should go in without her. "Oh, and, Gage?"

He looked at her again. "What?"

"Don't hurt me either."

That small moment of vulnerability from prickly Maddy made his chest tighten. "I won't," he said, his voice gravel. And he prayed to God right then that he could keep that promise.

It had been a long damn time since anyone had asked anything of him. Since anyone had expected anything of him. Maddy made him want to try.

She gestured for him to go on, and he did, walking into the darkened room, a curtain that separated the entry from the main part of the room blocking his vision.

"Sierra?" he asked.

"Come in." He heard his sister's weary voice.

He came around the curtain and his throat tightened, so suddenly, so swiftly, that he could hardly catch his breath.

Sierra was hooked up to IVs and wires, different monitors with various displays that were representative of his sister's life, shrunk down to a pair of green lines. Her blond hair was disheveled, her hospital gown tied crooked, circles beneath her eyes were visible even in the near darkness.

Her husband, Ace, was standing at the head of the bed, his expression one of pure exhaustion and awe. There was a little bundle in Sierra's arms.

"This is Lily Jane Thompson," Sierra said, beaming as she angled the baby in her arms so that Gage could see her tiny, perfect face.

His gaze flicked to his brother-in-law who was beaming with pride even in his sleep-deprived state. He put a protective hand on Sierra's shoulder, sliding it over to the other, rubbing her gently.

Gage felt like he was having an out-of-body experience. He could see Sierra perfectly as she'd been when he left. A little blonde girl with tousled curls. And here she was, her hair just as messy as it had been back then, holding her own little girl. And she had a husband by her side. A man who was going to take care of her.

She really didn't need him. Hadn't for a long time.

And when she had, he hadn't been around. Like all of them. Like everyone he'd left behind.

"Do you want to hold her?" Sierra asked, looking up at him with bright blue eyes. He had a feeling she didn't actually want to relinquish the baby, which was fine by him since the idea of holding something that tiny and fragile scared him shitless.

"I can see her just fine from here," he said, his voice foreign to his own ears. "She looks perfect to me," he said, not sure what else you were supposed to say about a baby. Not sure at all what a person was supposed to say in this situation. To the sister you didn't know anymore.

"She is," Ace said, his tone firm.

Gage had a feeling that Ace would effectively end anyone or anything that ever threatened his wife or daughter.

He respected that. And as much as he couldn't quite believe that Sierra was a grown woman with a baby, as badly as it settled with him in general, he knew that he couldn't have picked a better man for her.

For some reason, that cast his thoughts back to Rebecca. She had an older brother. One who would probably kill him if he had any idea what had happened tonight. There was no way Rebecca's brother, or any man, would ever happily look at him and their sister and think that he was the best man she could possibly end up with.

Good thing he didn't intend on ending up with anyone.

"I just… I had to come and see you," he said.

"I'm so glad that you did." She smiled.

"Maddy was right," he responded.

"About?"

"She said that you were nicer than she was."

That made Sierra laugh. "It depends on who you ask."

"Not really," Ace said. "Sierra is nicer. Unless she's drunk and recently bucked off a mechanical bull. Then she's kind of mean."

"There's a story there, I take it."

"There is," Sierra said, sounding cheerful. "I'm going to tell it to you someday."

He believed it. And there was something in that simple promise that warmed him. Made him feel… Something a lot like hope.

"Get some rest," he said. "Thank you again. I'm glad I got to come and see her."

"Of course. You're her uncle Gage."

Those words hit him square in the chest. Now there was another person in Copper Ridge who was depending on him. Who was part of his family. His blood. A web that kept on expanding. There was no cutting ties to this damn place.

As he looked around the hospital room, he wondered why he had ever wanted to.

He nodded once, then turned and walked out of the room. It wasn't the best goodbye. But then, he wasn't very good at goodbyes in general.

When he got back into the waiting area, Rebecca and Lydia were there, holding coffee cups. Neither of them seemed to be interested in drinking them, which only served to reinforce his belief that the coffee in question had merely been decoy coffee.

"Are you ready to go?" he asked Rebecca.

"If you are," she said, sounding slightly dazed. He couldn't really blame her.

"You're just going to go?" Maddy asked.

"I saw the baby," he said. "So, yeah."

He didn't know how to do this. He didn't know how to stand around with his siblings and have a conversation that wasn't loaded. He didn't know what to do with the emotions in his chest. He didn't know how to stand there and look at Madison and not pull her into a hug. Because she was a woman now, and not the girl he remembered. Because she had been hurt, and he hadn't been here. Because it had just been so damn long. But you couldn't hug a stranger, even if she was your sister.

And he never really hugged anyone, even if he knew them. Hell, he hadn't even hugged Rebecca and he'd taken her virginity.

"I rode with Rebecca," he said. "I don't want to keep her too late."

"I'm not in a hurry," Rebecca said.

He moved nearer to her, and put his hand on her lower back. "Are you sure? I thought you had to be up tomorrow."

"You know, I should get going." Rebecca shot him a deadly glare. And he knew that it had everything to do with the fact that she was afraid of what he might do next in front of his family and Lydia.

He looked back at everyone and noticed the shock on their faces. Letting them all know he had seduced a nice girl like Rebecca would only confirm their suspicions that he was a prick. Probably ease their consciences when it came to hating him a little bit.

But that didn't sit right for some reason. Not after Maddy. Not after seeing Sierra and the baby. Still, there was nothing else to say. Nothing else to do.

So, he grabbed Rebecca's hand and led her out of the hospital.

REBECCA'S HEART WAS THUNDERING, and her head was starting to pound. She felt disoriented, confused and a little bit like she was living the world's longest day. Today, she had kissed Gage for the first time. Tonight, she'd gone to a bar and danced with one of her best friend's best friends, and come very close to propositioning him. Then, she had been hauled out of said bar by Gage, and she had lost her virginity.

Then they had talked. Really talked, with a whole lot more honesty than she liked to employ with people. Then they'd gone to the hospital, and somehow, she had thought it would be a good idea to drive him. Probably because she could sense that he needed her to, just as she could sense that he wanted to pretend he didn't.

Which suited her just fine, because she would rather pretend that he didn't need her to either.

Now, they were back in his truck, and this time he was driving.

"I'll take you back to your car now," he said, turning onto the road that would take them back to Ace's bar.

"Thank you," she said. She didn't even know what time it was now. Edging on to last call, if it wasn't closing time altogether.

She felt… Well, she didn't know what she felt. She tried to shrink the evening in her mind, compartmentalize it. She went to the stretch of time she had just spent at the hospital. That walk down the hall with Lydia had been uncomfortable. Lydia clearly suspected that something was going on between Gage and herself, but she hadn't outright asked.

She was familiar with Lydia, but they didn't really know each other, and they had certainly never discussed their dating habits, or anything of a remotely personal nature.

Lydia was mayor of Copper Ridge. And while she was perfectly cordial to Rebecca, she just wasn't the kind of person who would associate with Rebecca. Not beyond campaigning, anyway. Though, Rebecca supposed that as a small-business owner in the town, things were a little different now. But she could never quite shake off the feeling that she was nothing more than a poor, scarred girl from the wrong side of the tracks.

And then, Gage had done his level best to get her out of the hospital as quickly as possible by making physical contact with her. She hated that she had been so predictable. She knew he had only done it to get her moving. She supposed it served her right for meddling. She had no right to meddle in his family business. Moreover, she didn't know why she cared.

She didn't know how she could see him as anything other than the man who had ruined her life. But now it was complicated because he was both her own personal monster and her lover.

Really, only she could make a decision this bad.

She didn't feel better. She didn't feel fixed. She didn't feel like she had solved her problem. In some ways, she would be able to relate to her friends a little bit better. She would at least know what all the fuss was about. Because, as messed up and topsy-turvy as all of the emotions surrounding the sex were, the sex was, objectively, amazing.

She had absolutely nothing to compare it to, but orgasms she knew. She had plenty of those on her own. She was a capable, red-blooded woman, after all. But those were… They were all under her control. She had them when she wanted them and never when she didn't. There was predictability to them. To achieving it all on your own.

She had no control with Gage. And he had done things to her that… She knew things. She knew plenty about sex. But theoretical sex is not actual sex. Actually having those things done to you made them wicked and almost beyond belief rather than uncomfortable and slightly giggle-worthy.

She had definitely not been giggling during the sex.

She was overheating thinking about it, and she needed to get her mind on something else.

It didn't matter, because just then, he turned into the parking lot at Ace's. "Thank you," she said, practically leaping out of the truck before it had fully stopped. She said a prayer of thanks that she had actually remembered her purse, and that her keys were inside of it. She needed to get some distance between herself and Gage.

He got out of the truck, the driver side door closing hard, the sound echoing across the empty lot. Ace's had clearly emptied out promptly tonight. Probably because other people had left in a hurry to hook up. Just like they'd done earlier. She tried to shove that thought, that memory out of her mind.

And when she looked at him walking toward her, she tried to think of him as that monstrous villain she'd imagined him to be. But it was hard. Hard when she had been intimate with the man. When she had seen the way he had responded to the news of his sister giving birth.

Harder still when he had confided in her about some of those things. That Sierra had been six when he left. That it clearly hurt him, the passage of the years, how much he had missed.

That he wasn't some callous monster who had left town and never thought of them again. He had thought of his family. He had thought of her. It was easy to be offended about that. That he had somehow co-opted her pain and made it his own. But maybe he just had his own pain.

That thought made her feel like her chest had been cracked open for some reason. It was uncomfortable, invasive, and it seemed to demand something of her. She didn't know what.

She went to the driver side of her truck, unlocked the door and opened it, then she turned to look at Gage one last time. There was something tortured in his expression, something drawn and tired. He looked older than he had at the start of the evening, reinforcing that feeling that today had actually contained years.

Each and every one seemed to be written on that gorgeous face. She couldn't stop staring at him then.

Looking at him like it was the first time she'd seen him as he stood there illuminated by the security lights, the sharp, blue glow highlighting his cheekbones, casting the planes of his face into sharp relief.

She looked down at his forearm, exposed because the idiot wasn't wearing a jacket. At that tattoo. She had touched his body. Had touched it naked. He was muscular, hard and rough, hairy in all the right places, just like a man should be.

She wished that he were just a man. Just a man she had decided to sleep with for the first time. And it made her angry that he wasn't. That this couldn't be simple. That it couldn't just be fun. That it couldn't just feel good. That it had to be just tonight, and never again.

As if he read her mind, he let out a harsh, low sound, and crossed the space between them, taking her into his arms and pulling her up against him, claiming her mouth with his. He kissed her deep and long, sliding his fingertips down between her shoulder blades, along the line of her spine and down to cup her ass.

She whimpered, arching against him, pressing herself hard against his erection. She just wanted to hold on to him, to hold on to this. Maybe it was better that it was him. That it wasn't someone she should want, wasn't someone she would want again when she was thinking clearly. It wouldn't be awkward later, because they were never going to hang out. And when they saw each other, the feelings had never been easy anyway. So, it could hardly be worse.

She justified. She justified all those things as he pushed her back, laying her down across the bench seat of her truck. He pressed his hand between her thighs, sliding his fingertips beneath her dress, beneath the elastic of her panties.

He stroked her, where she was wet and aching for him, his thumb making tight circles over her clit.

She reached out, grabbing hold of his forearms. "Gage," she gasped, "I want… I want…"

"No," he said. "You'll be way too sore. Just take this." She hated that he had read her mind. That he knew she had been about to beg to have him again. And she hated even more that he had refused.

But not half as much as she hated that he had taken her from slightly muddled confusion to so aroused she couldn't think straight in under thirty seconds. White lightning streaked from where he touched her down deep to her core, her internal muscles pulsing. She was hungry for him, for his penetration. And she begged. Made incoherent moaning sounds as he continued to torment her, as he ratcheted her desire up hotter, higher.

And then, it completely shattered over her, like a pane of glass, glittering and sharp all around her, cutting into her. She couldn't catch her breath, didn't want to, as glittering shards of sensation worked their way beneath her skin, invading every part of her. She couldn't do anything, couldn't say anything. She could only feel.

And when it passed, she became very aware of his hard body above her, of the tight band of his arm, wrapped around her waist, holding her against him. Of those blue, endless eyes. Eyes as sharp as any blade cutting deeper than the pleasure. Leaving more pro-

YOUR PARTICIPATION IS REQUESTED!

Dear Reader,

Since you are a lover of our books – we would like to get to know you!

Inside you will find a short Reader's Survey. Sharing your answers with us will help our editorial staff understand who you are and what activities you enjoy.

To thank you for your participation, we would like to send you 2 books and 2 gifts – **ABSOLUTELY FREE!**

Enjoy your gifts with our appreciation,

Pam Powers

**SEE INSIDE
FOR READER'S
SURVEY**

For Your Reading Pleasure...

FREE!

We'll send you 2 books and 2 gifts
ABSOLUTELY FREE
just for completing our Reader's Survey!

YOURS FREE!
We'll send you two fabulous surprise
gifts absolutely FREE, just for trying
our books!

Visit us at:
www.ReaderService.com

YOUR READER'S SURVEY
"THANK YOU" FREE GIFTS INCLUDE:
- ▶ **2 FREE books**
- ▶ **2 lovely surprise gifts**

▼ DETACH AND MAIL CARD TODAY! ▼

PLEASE FILL IN THE CIRCLES COMPLETELY TO RESPOND

1) What type of fiction books do you enjoy reading? (Check all that apply)
○ Suspense/Thrillers ○ Action/Adventure ○ Modern-day Romances
○ Historical Romance ○ Humour ○ Paranormal Romance

2) What attracted you most to the last fiction book you purchased on impulse?
○ The Title ○ The Cover ○ The Author ○ The Story

3) What is usually the greatest influencer when you <u>plan</u> to buy a book?
○ Advertising ○ Referral ○ Book Review

4) How often do you access the internet?
○ Daily ○ Weekly ○ Monthly ○ Rarely or never.

5) How many NEW paperback fiction novels have you purchased in the past 3 months?
○ 0 - 2 ○ 3 - 6 ○ 7 or more

YES! I have completed the Reader's Survey. Please send me the 2 FREE books and 2 FREE gifts (gifts are worth about $10) for which I qualify. I understand that I am under no obligation to purchase any books, as explained on the back of this card.

194 MDL GJ2Z/394 MDL GJ22

FIRST NAME	LAST NAME

ADDRESS

APT.#	CITY

STATE/PROV.	ZIP/POSTAL CODE

Offer limited to one per household and not applicable to series that subscriber is currently receiving.
Your Privacy—The Reader Service is committed to protecting your privacy. Our Privacy Policy is available online at www.ReaderService.com or upon request from the Reader Service. We make a portion of our mailing list available to reputable third parties that offer products we believe may interest you. If you prefer that we not exchange your name with third parties, or if you wish to clarify or modify your communication preferences, please visit us at www.ReaderService.com/consumerchoice or write to us at Reader Service Preference Service, P.O. Box 9062, Buffalo, NY 14240-9062. Include your complete name and address.

© 2015 ENTERPRISES LIMITED ® and ™ are trademarks owned and used by the trademark owner and/or its licensee. Printed in the U.S.A.

ROM-216-SUR16

READER SERVICE—Here's how it works:

Accepting your 2 free Romance books and 2 free gifts (gifts valued at approximately $10.00) places you under no obligation to buy anything. You may keep the books and gifts and return the shipping statement marked "cancel." If you do not cancel, about a month later we'll send you 4 additional books and bill you just $6.49 each in the U.S. or $6.99 each in Canada. That is a savings of at least 19% off the cover price. It's quite a bargain! Shipping and handling is just 50¢ per book in the U.S. and 75¢ per book in Canada.* You may cancel at any time, but if you choose to continue, every month we'll send you 4 more books, which you may either purchase at the discount price or return to us and cancel your subscription. *Terms and prices subject to change without notice. Prices do not include applicable taxes. Sales tax applicable in N.Y. Canadian residents will be charged applicable taxes. Offer not valid in Quebec. Books received may not be as shown. All orders subject to approval. Credit or debit balances in a customer's account(s) may be offset by any other outstanding balance owed by or to the customer. Please allow 4 to 6 weeks for delivery. Offer available while quantities last.

◀ If offer card is missing write to: Reader Service, P.O. Box 1867, Buffalo, NY 14240-1867 or visit www.ReaderService.com ▶

BUSINESS REPLY MAIL

FIRST-CLASS MAIL   PERMIT NO. 717   BUFFALO, NY

POSTAGE WILL BE PAID BY ADDRESSEE

READER SERVICE
PO BOX 1867
BUFFALO NY 14240-9952

NO POSTAGE
NECESSARY
IF MAILED
IN THE
UNITED STATES

found scars than any that could be seen written across her skin.

She gasped, extricating herself from his hold, scooting backward, putting her hand over her face. "I… Not again," she said.

"Rebecca," he began.

"Just. Tonight."

"I didn't hurt you, did I?"

She shook her head, even though she was lying. He had hurt her seventeen years ago, and on so many other occasions since, without even being present. But she had a horrible feeling that tonight he had hurt her worse, with repercussions that would show up when she least expected it.

"It's fine. Of course you didn't… It isn't that… I wanted it," she said, because she couldn't have him believing anything else.

"You're upset."

"I'm tired. I just need to go home. I need to be alone."

She needed solitude desperately. Because the only other option was breaking open in front of him, and pouring out all of these emotions onto him. And a very large part of her felt like she would rather die. She didn't share these things with people. Not with anyone.

She certainly wasn't going to share her emotions with him, with the man who was basically the reason she was such an emotionally stunted nutcase. Much to her relief, he didn't press. Instead, he turned and got back into his truck.

She let out a sigh of relief. There was a very large part of her that wished Gage West would just drive off into the sunset, or the sunrise—which was more accurate to the moment—and disappear for another seventeen years.

She started the engine, and let out a sharp sob the moment the roar filled the cab, blotting out the sound her tears made as she pulled out of the parking lot and onto the highway. She would fall apart here, where no one would see, and then by tomorrow everything would be fine. The next time she saw Gage, she would have everything together.

Tonight had been all about letting go of baggage and liberating herself. It stood to reason that it would feel strange at first. But everything would normalize. And now, maybe so would she.

She was desperate to believe it. Because otherwise, she might just be falling apart for no good reason. She had survived too damn much to crumble now.

CHAPTER THIRTEEN

BY THE TIME Rebecca walked into Lane's Mercantile at lunchtime she had more or less convinced herself that she was in control of her emotions, her body and her feelings. Sure, she had alternately spent the night weeping and tossing and turning because she was aroused and wanted nothing more than to be touched by Gage again. Which was never going to happen, so her body needed to get over it.

She felt refreshed, and much less dire in the light of day, which was helpful.

She didn't know why everything had felt so crazy last night. Probably all of the emotions, and the climaxes. But today she felt renewed. She felt like maybe she had finally put a demon to rest.

She felt…oh crap. Clearly she had been celebrating a little bit too soon.

Because there was Finn up on a ladder looking at light fixtures in the mercantile. Being very right there, when she would rather he weren't at all.

"Hi, Rebecca," Lane said, her eyes fixed on Finn.

"I came for lunch, since you said you were sampling that new cheese that you got."

"It's from France," Lane said.

"We make cheese," Finn said, his tone hard.

"And the Laughing Irish cheese is great," Lane said, "but while local cheese is certainly a draw, I need to carry European cheeses too. So get over yourself. Your cheese is not the only cheese, Donnelly."

Clearly, Lane was ignorant about what had transpired between herself and Finn the night before, and Finn wasn't paying any attention to her, which was more typical than the interaction they'd had last night.

Still, seeing Finn reminded her of last night, which reminded her of everything that had happened after the two of them had parted.

All of the Gage things. The things that she was trying to be not completely psycho about.

"My cheese is the only cheese anyone would ever need, if they would just try it," he said, descending the ladder.

"Was that some kind of weird, cheese-based euphemism?" Lane asked.

He cocked his head to the side, his expression long-suffering. "I wouldn't waste my euphemisms on you, Lane."

She waved a hand. "Whatever, man."

Rebecca's eyes clashed with Finn's, and an electric current of awkwardness arced between them. She had a feeling that was all on her end, since Finn was infinitely more experienced with bar hookups and the like.

"Was everything okay last night?"

Finn was looking at her with far too perceptive and searching eyes.

"Yeah," she said, looking down and walking a few

steps for no particular reason except that it gave her something to do.

"Why?" Lane asked. "What happened last night?"

"Nothing," Rebecca said.

"Some guy came and dragged her out of a bar," Finn said at the same time.

"What?" Lane asked, sadly keying into what Finn had said.

"It wasn't a big deal. And," she continued, directing her words at Finn, "I'm here, so clearly I'm okay. Also, if you were so concerned maybe you shouldn't have let him drag me out of the bar."

"You said that everything was fine. You insisted. But, I did regret letting you leave."

She wasn't entirely sure what the context of that was. It made her stomach do weird things. Tighten. Turn over.

"Start at the beginning," Lane said, her voice sharp. "What happened?"

"I was dancing with Rebecca, and some dude took issue with it."

"That's not the beginning," Lane said, the color in her cheeks darkening. "You were dancing with Rebecca?"

Finn's expression hardened. "Yeah," he said, "I was."

"How did that come about?" Lane asked, her tone a little bit too casual.

Oh great, now Rebecca had the feeling she had stepped in the middle of something. But, Lane was always the first person to insist that there was nothing going on between herself and Finn. Still, she was a little bit too interested now for Rebecca to believe that was entirely the case.

"I knew him," Rebecca said. "And I wanted to dance."

Finn arched a brow. "Yeah," he said, not doing his part at all to sound convincing. Whatever he was doing right now, he really had to stop because she needed to preserve her own self and he didn't seem remotely interested in that.

"Okay," Lane said, her expression dark.

"I'm fine," Rebecca said pointedly. "Everything is fine." She began looking for something to busy herself. "I was promised cheese."

"You can't have cheese. Not until you provide me with a sufficient explanation."

Rebecca stamped, feeling more frustrated than the situation warranted because everything felt too big and too strange inside of her right now to deal with a Lane Jensen inquisition. "You cannot hold French cheese hostage, Lane. It's cruel and unusual."

"You were dragged out of a bar by a man after dancing with Finn. I think if anyone is owed an explanation, it's me."

"I'm sorry, I forgot that time you bought front-row season passes to my entire life."

"You're being impossible. Most people would just tell their friends what was going on. Actually, the biggest reason I think there's something going on is that you won't tell me. Because, if nothing had happened with the guy from the bar, why wouldn't you tell me what happened?"

Rebecca gritted her teeth. "Fine. Nothing happened with the guy from the bar."

"Who was it?" Lane pressed.

Her face heated and she knew that she was the color of a ripened raspberry. Finn was standing there, his arms crossed over his broad chest, and Rebecca was ready to kill him for bringing any of this up in the first place. The problem was, he knew exactly what had happened, because he knew why she had been at the bar in the first place.

She was pretty inexperienced when it came to men, but she knew that the two of them had been on the same page. Not that they had wanted each other extravagantly, but that they had at least been willing to take each other on as consolation prizes.

Or, if not specifically a consolation prize on his end then a little bit of casual entertainment. Either way, he knew too much. And she suddenly felt embarrassed, exposed and more than a little humiliated.

"Who was the guy?" Lane repeated.

"I just needed to have a little talk with Gage," she conceded finally.

"Gage. Gage West? The guy who is offering to sell me this building." Rebecca could see everything slowly coming together in Lane's mind, watched as the dots connected and formed to make a picture of horror on her friend's face. "Who is the guy that caused your accident. And is the guy you're working for," she said, her words coming faster and faster as she began to put all the pieces together.

"Yes. That's him. We just needed to talk about… You know, the details surrounding our agreement."

"Which is why he grabbed you like a jealous boyfriend?" Finn asked.

"Rebecca," Lane said, frowning. "Is everything okay? He owns your business, and he's completely invaded your life, and now I hear that he has dragged you out of a bar like he has some kind of claim on you."

"Nobody has a *claim* on me but me. So, you can just stop with that dramatic nonsense right now. There's nothing… This is nothing…" Suddenly, horrifically, she felt her eyes fill with tears.

She felt like all of the invisible seams from where she had once been stitched back together were beginning to tear open. And that all of her insides, all of her secrets, her fears, her *everything*, was going to spill out right here in the mercantile, in front of Lane and Finn.

If that happened…she just couldn't have them knowing. What a mess she was. What a damn freak show beneath all the *I'm fine*s.

"Excuse me," she said, rushing past Lane and heading into the bathroom, closing the door behind her and locking it. She put her hand over her mouth, trying to stifle the sob that was building inside of her. She was unsuccessful.

She wanted to tell Lane what was happening. And, she never wanted her to know. She never wanted *anyone* to know. She was ashamed and embarrassed and upset that Lane might have been hurt because Rebecca had been trying to avoid dealing with her own stuff and had brought Finn into the mix.

Finn, who Rebecca should have known was off-limits, regardless of what Lane said. Even if he wasn't a boyfriend, even if he never would be, it wasn't right for Rebecca to step in the middle of that relationship. It was too complicated to do something like that. Sure, Finn wasn't her friend, but it was still idiotic of her.

She plunked down on the closed toilet seat, resting her elbows on her legs, burying her face in her hands. She was just going to go ahead and internally berate herself for everything, even things that weren't her fault. Even the things that weren't her responsibility, like Finn and Lane's whatever-the-hell friendship. Because she felt crappy, and for some reason that compelled her to try and make herself feel crappy all the way down.

She was an idiot to have ever let Gage touch her. No, she was more than an idiot. There was something wrong with her. As if the scars he had given her ran so deep, and were so pervasive that they had screwed up everything. Even her ability to be attracted to a normal, good man who hadn't…hurt her.

It all involved him. Somehow, he was tangled up in all of it.

She couldn't even tell Lane. Because she was too ashamed. Because she didn't like telling people anything. That was his fault too. All of it, every last bit.

She wanted to cry and wail and scream a little bit too, but instead she kept it all bottled up. Kept her hand planted firmly over her mouth, and dashed each and every tear away as it fell.

Gage had messed up her life pretty bad seventeen years ago, but this part of it, all of this, was on her. She was the one who had gone after him. Well, then he had gone after her. After she had kissed him. She was the one who had made it like this. She had really, royally messed up her own life, and there was no one to cast aspersions on but herself.

She straightened, brushing her hands over the front of her clothes, then turning and looking in the mirror. Yeah, she looked like she had escaped into the bathroom to cry. There was no recovering from this. She might as well just go and brazen it out. Then there was a knock on the door.

"Rebecca?" She heard Lane's voice through the door.

"I'm fine," she said.

"I think when you storm into a bathroom and lock yourself in, you probably aren't fine. Basing that hypothesis on most of the episodes that occurred during my teenage years."

Rebecca let out a shuddering breath, then reached out and unlocked the door, turning the knob and pulling it open. "See?" she asked. "Fine."

"You aren't usually emotional," Lane said, her voice muted.

The accurate and painfully honest assessment hung between them. Rebecca didn't like it. She didn't want it. Why did Lane have to be such a good friend? Why had she let her get this close? Surface stuff was so easy. A worse friend would have just said okay after Rebecca said fine.

Lane was not a worse friend, sadly.

"I'm a little bit messed up right now," Rebecca admitted, her throat closing up.

Lane laughed, a leaden sound that did nothing to buoy the mood. "Who isn't?"

"Nothing happened with Finn," Rebecca offered.

Rebecca watched as Lane's expression went through four seasons. From hot to cold and everywhere in between. "It wouldn't matter if it had," she said finally.

It was Rebecca's turn to try and be a decent friend. To press instead of letting lies sit.

"It wouldn't? Really? You can honestly say that you are completely okay with all of that?"

Lane let out a slow, unsteady breath. "Look, I would rather if you didn't sleep with him, just because it would be weird." She tucked a lock of dark hair behind her ear. "I don't... I don't really think of him as a man."

Privately, Rebecca had to call bullshit on that, but she wasn't going to say it out loud. She had a feeling she'd reached the end of where she could push. And anyway, she was too committed to hanging on to her own bullshit, hoping that Lane wouldn't say anything to call her out directly.

But that didn't mean she couldn't push a little.

"Right," Rebecca said. "So, it would be weird if someone that you were close to thought of him as one."

A crease appeared between Lane's eyebrows. "Do you? I mean, do you think of him as a man?"

"Yes," Lane said, honestly. "He's...he's really good-looking."

"But nothing happened," Lane said again.

"Nothing. And, nothing is going to."

"But...it was," Lane insisted, her tone strangely flat. "It was going to happen, wasn't it?"

"No," Rebecca said, and the minute that she spoke the word, she knew it was true. She would never have been able to do with Finn what she had done with Gage. She would have gotten to his house and freaked out completely. Because for whatever reason a good portion of her issues seemed to need to be worked out on Gage. She had genuinely hoped that it wouldn't have to be, that she could just forget he existed, but that didn't seem to be happening so all she could really do was follow that particularly fucked-up arrow where it was pointing.

"I did dance with him," Rebecca said. "And I... thought about maybe doing something more. But it wouldn't have happened. Even if Gage hadn't shown up."

"What...what happened with Gage?"

Rebecca's face felt like it was on fire. She squeezed out of the bathroom door and into the little antechamber that separated the small room from the rest of the store. She could lie. She wanted to lie. Her friend was going to think she was a complete psychopath.

But of course she was also acting like an absolute crazy person so a lie was only going to look like a lie. That wouldn't be good. She could feel it. In the way the air between Lane and herself felt brittle.

Lane had been the first real friend she'd made after high school. She'd been so isolated in school, and she'd imagined she always would be. But she'd met Lane after they'd both gotten jobs at the Crab Shanty, and then they'd stayed in each other's circles ever after.

Thanks to Lane, Rebecca had a group of friends.

Rebecca owed Lane so much. But even so, she'd always kept her friend at arm's length. They got together and watched movies. They ate snacks and talked about sexy celebrities. But Lane didn't know that up until last night Rebecca had been a virgin. She hadn't known the name of the man who had caused Rebecca's accident.

So many things that Rebecca kept buried down deep because she didn't know how to have those sorts of conversations without feeling horribly exposed.

Whenever she thought of it, she thought of what it was like when the gauze bandages were removed at the hospital right after her accident. When a nurse had unwound the bandages with Jonathan and her mother in the room.

She didn't know what they'd expected to see. But Jonathan's face had turned to stone, and her mother had burst into shrieking tears that felt like salt on those unresolved wounds.

Exposing them to the air had hurt. Seeing their reactions had been even worse. She had always thought they'd both expected her to look more healed. To be more okay.

But if she turned Lane away now, she would break something in their friendship, and she couldn't risk that. Not when everything was so messed up. Rebecca hated to need anyone. She really hated it.

This wasn't need, but it was a really strong want. And it was going to win over her desire to hide.

"I…" Rebecca's throat felt like it had been packed full of sand. "I went home with him."

"To…see his new knitting pattern? To discuss *War*

and Peace?" Lane's suggestions sounded hopeful and desperate and it made Rebecca feel even worse.

"War and Peace," she said.

"Holy hell, you slept with him."

Rebecca let out a long, hard breath. "I mean, not really. Because I didn't stay the night so we didn't sleep."

"I thought you hated him."

"I do," she insisted. And then felt like she was lying. She wasn't sure she hated him. She wished she could. But she didn't think she did anymore.

"But you slept with him."

"You've never slept with a guy you didn't like?" she asked.

"No," said Lane. "I mean, I have often come to dislike them after the fact. Depending on how things went, sometimes very soon after the fact, but not…during."

"I don't know what I'm doing," she said, feeling helpless. Sounding helpless.

"Obviously you can't do that again."

"Right," she said, even while her stomach turned over at the thought of doing exactly that.

"Rebecca, he's evil. He caused your accident and he's messing with everything."

"And selling you your store."

"I didn't know about the connection," Lane said.

"I know. But I just mean…he's not evil."

"Even if you thought he was evil… Would you have not done it?"

Rebecca didn't like that question, mostly because there wasn't a good answer for it. Well, there was a lie. Which was that she had clearly decided that he was a man of excellent character, and therefore had made an extremely reasonable decision to follow her completely normal attraction to him.

The truth of the matter was there was no logic involved in any of this. She had made absolutely no decisions about the quality of his character. She had just been feeling. She spent so much time doing her very best not to do that, and here she had gone and done it spectacularly.

She had led—if not with her heart—then with her pants. There had been absolutely no reason or logic involved.

"I don't know how to answer that," she said, rather than going for strict honesty.

Lane arched her brows. "You move your lips and you say words. You just don't know how to answer it because you don't know how to have honest conversations."

"Hey! I'm having a conversation with you. Insulting me is not the best way to get me to give up information."

"I'm sorry," Lane said, wrapping an arm around her shoulder. "But, I really don't think it's the best idea for you to get involved in such a complicated relationship."

"It's not a relationship. I just… Look, I guess it's messed up for him to get involved with me, and I know it's messed up that I got involved with him. But I just think it's something that needed to happen. Sex is…a release. And I think there was some pent-up stuff. That needed to release."

Lane looked at her skeptically. "If you're in some kind of hostage situation just blink twice."

"No, I did this to myself. And obviously I'm feeling a little bit messed up about it. But, it happened. And he didn't hurt me."

Lane looked at her out of the corner of her eye. "Was it good?"

"What?"

"The sex."

Rebecca had to seriously consider how to answer that too. "Is sex ever really...bad?"

"Yes. Sometimes it's very bad. If you haven't had that experience, that just makes me mad. So I'm curious. Is having sex with somebody you don't like actually good? I've never done it outside the context of a relationship."

"Really?"

"Really what?"

"You've never had sex with a guy you weren't in a relationship with." She hadn't really considered that. She just sort of assumed that almost everybody else was much more casual about it than she was.

"No. I've never really seen the point."

"Oh. Well, I can honestly say that this was... That... I..."

"That good?"

Rebecca covered her face. "I've never felt so good in my entire life. Followed by being incredibly embarrassed and never feeling quite so bad in my entire life." And then there had been all of that at the hospital. Witnessing the way he cared about his family but didn't quite know how to build bridges between them.

That made her feel things. Things that weren't entirely negative. She had felt… Well, in that moment she had felt almost like she understood him.

"Come on," Lane said, tightening her hold on Rebecca's shoulders. "You need cheese."

She propelled Rebecca out of the small space between the bathroom and the main part of the store, and back toward the entryway. Finn was still there, and Rebecca wanted to melt into the floorboards.

"I didn't see any of this," he said, climbing back up the ladder and fiddling with another light fixture.

"Appreciated," Rebecca mumbled.

"Cheese," Lane said, reaching into the cooler and producing a wooden board with thin slices of meat and some precut cheese, covered by saran wrap. "And a promise of discretion from me too."

"Thank you," she said, her throat tightening.

She felt… She felt tender and exposed, but in some ways she did feel better. She knew more about Lane than she had before. And Lane knew more about her. It was strange, to let somebody in on your secrets. Things that you weren't sure about.

She couldn't say she liked it. But, she felt like it was the right thing to do in the situation.

"I never noticed how quiet you were during our girl-talk sessions," Lane said, her voice low. "Actually, I've been noticing lately."

"Some things just feel too personal to me," she said, not offering any further information.

She could only take so many steps. Could only give away so much. She felt like something had shifted inside of her, as though she were in the middle of an internal sea change. She hated it. All of this. But at least there was cheese.

"Thank you," she said again.

"For what?"

"For letting me tell you all of that. And for not making me feel bad."

Lane smiled slowly, stretching her hand out and putting it over Rebecca's. "That's what friends do, Rebecca. And I'm really sorry if I didn't show you that sooner."

Rebecca was finding it difficult to breathe. "You don't have to be sorry for anything. If I wasn't friends with you, I wouldn't have any friends at all. You were the one that introduced me to Alison and Cassie. You were the first person to really treat me like I wasn't just someone with scars and a sad past."

That was one reason it was so hard to share with Lane. She didn't protect her. Didn't treat her like she had a fragile sticker affixed to her forehead.

"I don't deserve thanks for that. It's the easiest thing in the world to treat you like you're more than a victim. Because you are."

Rebecca's heart turned over. She nodded because she didn't have any words.

Everything inside of her felt jumbled up. Like someone had ransacked her feelings. Pulling them out, riffling through them, turning them upside down and leaving nothing but a mess.

She didn't understand. Didn't understand what was happening inside of her. Didn't understand what had compelled her to kiss Gage in the first place. She didn't really understand what had been driving her actions at all starting last night and ending today with this strange bit of honesty that had passed between herself and Lane.

And that statement about her being more than a victim stuck with her. She held it close, turned it over. Maybe that was why. Maybe that was why she'd kissed Gage. Why she'd done all that with Gage.

To prove she was more. But she'd done it. It was over. She didn't need to touch him again. And she wouldn't.

CHAPTER FOURTEEN

GAGE HAD SPENT the day going over the financial state of the family with Colton. His younger brother had come to his house, and they had sat across the living room from each other, poring over various spreadsheets.

It hadn't been the friendliest interaction, but it hadn't been bristling with animosity either. They hadn't made a whole lot of personal conversation, but he hadn't minded that either.

He didn't really know how to have a personal conversation.

Colton had told him that Sierra and the baby had gone home, and that everything was going well. Which had been good to hear.

Colton had actually seemed to be pretty happy that Gage had decided to come to the hospital. Something he had to give Rebecca credit for.

Just thinking about Rebecca sent a streak of heat through his body. He couldn't remember the last time a woman had affected him so much, couldn't remember the last time sex had damn near blown his head off.

He had spent a lot of years wandering from town to town, but he sure as hell hadn't played the part of chaste monk. Moving around like that made it easy to slip in and out of casual sexual relationships. And it was how he liked it. Women who didn't want to know much more of anything beyond the size of his dick and what he could do with his hands.

Rebecca, on the other hand, was inextricably linked to this place. And just so many different aspects of his life. It made him question his sanity. But it did not make him question his resolve to keep it at a onetime thing.

Still, even while he thought of her, he burned.

She had been a virgin. Because of her scars. Because of him.

Shame lashed over him like the crack of the whip. There was no end to it. No end to the consequences of his mistakes.

Sometimes he felt like there was a boulder resting on his chest threatening to crush him completely.

When he'd been with her, he hadn't felt ashamed. When he'd been with her, it had felt good. Wrong, a little bit dirty, a whole lot like embracing the dark side in him rather than turning away from it. Opening up all that need he normally kept on lockdown and just letting her have it. It made him want more. It had felt so good to just let himself have that. Instead of being with a woman who barely made a ripple inside of him.

He stood from the couch, stretching out his muscles, aching from being sedentary for most of the day. He wasn't used to this. Wasn't used to managing this level of paperwork.

But, it was a convenient thing to bury himself in. To bury the rage and grief he felt over this entire situation in a stack of ink and paper instead of actually having to go and see his dad and try to have a conversation with the old man in his reduced state. Instead of making time to go to the house and visit his mother, who he still hadn't seen.

Dealing with Rebecca was even easier than all of that.

Just thinking her name reminded him of her body. Of how soft she felt to his touch, of how her hair had sifted through his fingers. Of the sounds she had made when he'd made her come. All primal and unrestrained and every damn thing a man could ever want.

He was sick to want her, maybe. But then, he was kind of past concern for his mortal soul. He was damned if he did, damned if he didn't, damned all the way down to hell.

Might as well enjoy the trip.

He looked over at his phone. Rebecca's number was on it. He could call. See what she was doing.

"You're acting like an ass," he said into the silence of the room. Acting like a man who had a right to get in touch with her after sex. Acting like a boyfriend, or a friend, and he was neither of those things.

He was hot for her though. And just the thought of her had left him hard and aching. But, he didn't really think he deserved to have any of that satisfied. It was probably a fitting punishment. To want the last woman he shouldn't want, to know exactly how good it could be to slide inside her. To know just how erotic it was when she came hard around his cock.

To know all that and never be able to have her again.

Not having her was the honorable thing to do. If there

was any honor to be had in this incredibly messed-up situation.

He picked up his phone, and he was already scrolling through the contacts, looking for her name. Because he didn't have any honor. That was the real issue. He had come back here to play the knight in shining armor. Had come back here to fix things, but he just didn't know how. He wasn't good, and acting like a good guy was never going to make him one.

He hated himself. He hated himself as he dialed her number. Hated himself even more when she picked up and answered in a tense, breathless voice that ran across his aching dick like a wet, slick tongue.

"Hi," he said back.

Heavy silence fell between them, stretching the entire distance between his house and hers.

"You're the one that called me," she pointed out when he didn't say anything else.

"I know."

"Is everything all right with Sierra and the baby?"

It touched something in him that she thought that's why he might be calling. It touched something that she had thought of them. She had no reason to. She had no reason to care about any of his family.

"Everything's fine."

"Then why are you calling me?"

"Are you home?"

"Yes," she said, the word simple and so sweet it made him want to bow down and give thanks. But surely no God in heaven had arranged this for him.

"I'm coming over," he said.

He hung up, and strode out the front door to his truck, not bothering with a coat. His hat was sitting on the driver seat, and he put it on, starting the engine before he could have any second thoughts.

He wanted her. That thought, that *certainty*, pounded through him with every mile he drove down the road. He turned off the pavement onto the long, dirt driveway that would lead him to her place, tightening his grip on the steering wheel, clenching his jaw as he drew closer. Restlessness ran through his entire body, a kind of wild heat that burned like a brush fire. Hot and dangerous and just as difficult to contain.

He shouldn't be doing this. He hadn't even stopped to listen to her answer. Didn't even know if she wanted him to come over, but he was coming anyway.

He was a bastard. Such a bastard.

That thought played on repeat as he pulled up to her house, killed the engine and slammed the door shut. As he walked up the front steps of her modest porch.

He was about to knock when the door opened, and Rebecca was standing there, her dark eyes wide. "You came," she said.

"Yeah," he said, his feet still firmly planted on the deck, making no move to come into the house.

"Why?"

He laughed, but the sound didn't have any humor to it. "Baby, you know why."

She shrank back slightly, biting her lower lip. "We said it would just be that one time."

"Yeah."

She closed her eyes, the expression on her face one

of distress and anguish, and he hated himself for hurting her again. For putting her in this position.

Not enough to leave.

"This is… It doesn't make any sense." She opened her eyes again, her emotions blazing there. "Why? Why is it you? Why do I want you? I could want anyone else. I almost hooked up with Finn instead of you. And that made… It made so much more sense. Even if it was only ever sex with him, at least I like him. At least he's a good guy, and he has been here forever, and he runs a ranch with his grandfather. He's like… The salt of the earth. He was in Lane's store today inspecting the wiring. Just because he's a good friend. And what have *you* done?" Her words were furious now, shooting out of her mouth with the velocity of bullets. "What have you ever done for anybody? You cause destruction and pain and then you walk away. You're going to do it with me. I know you are. So, why are you here? And why do I want to invite you in?"

He reached across the threshold, grabbing hold of her, forking his fingers through her hair and curling them into a fist, grabbing her tight, holding her against him.

"I can't promise I'm not going to hurt you," he said, his voice a low growl. "I can't promise I'm going to leave anything other than a burned-out mass of devastation in the end. Oh but, baby—" he slid his thumb across her bottom lip "—I'll make you scream all the way there. I can make it feel good." His throat was prickling, hot with some kind of strange emotion he couldn't name. "This time I'll make it feel good," he said, every word a raw, stripped-down promise that he wasn't sure made any sense.

She was trembling, her dark eyes liquid with unshed tears. And he still didn't release her. He still didn't leave. She was angry, and she was upset, and he was holding her crushed up against his body so that she could feel the raging of his heartbeat, so that she could feel just how hard he was for her. He didn't know what the hell was wrong with him.

He didn't know who the hell he was.

But, he suspected that he hadn't known who the hell he was from the moment he walked out of Copper Ridge. Because the problem was, when he'd been here, he had known exactly who he was. He was the spitting image of Nathan West. The heir to the older man's kingdom. A selfish bastard who had never done anything for anyone but himself.

He was the same. He hadn't changed. Standing here now, he could see that clearly.

He had wanted to be better, but he simply wasn't. He had just moved fast enough that he'd never been put to the test over all these years.

"All right," she said slowly. "Make me feel good. I have felt… So bad for so long. My body has never given me much of anything other than pain. And last night you made me feel so damn good. You're so wrong for me, and I know that it can never be anything but this. And I know that there's something so very, very wrong with us. That we want this. That we're doing this. But I don't care." She stretched up on her tiptoes, pressing her lips lightly to his. "Please, just make me feel good, Gage."

That was all the invitation he needed. He propelled them back over the threshold, using his foot to shut the door tightly behind them without taking his hands off of her. He kissed her then, deep and hard, consuming her mouth, each stroke of his tongue going deeper.

He was desperate for her, for this. Desperate to ease the unbearable tension inside of him. It wasn't all physical. It would be better if it were. But there was an intense, fraught longing between them that went so much deeper than simply sex. If it were sex, it could've been with anyone.

But no.

This felt like some kind of misguided bid for healing on both of their parts. Or maybe, they were both just compelled to keep on causing pain. To themselves. To other people. He didn't know. But he did know that she was with him every step of the way. If he couldn't raise her up out of the pit, he would at least take comfort in the knowledge that she was willingly walking down into hell with him.

This probably *was* hell. It burned like it. But underneath that sweet streak of fire it felt so damn good it was hard to care.

"Where's your bedroom?"

"Down the hall," she said, her words punctuated with harsh breaths.

He slipped his hands down to cup her ass, moving them down further, taking hold of her thighs and lifting her, wrapping her legs around his back.

He walked them both down the narrow, rustic hallway that led to a small bedroom. Her bed was a double, but the kind that was not quite long enough for someone of his height. He didn't care. They weren't going to sleep anyway.

He threw her down onto the middle of the mattress, breathing hard. He forgot to be gentle. Or maybe he just remembered he wasn't.

Her eyes were round like saucers, a sudden shock of fear streaking through them.

"Turn off the light," she said, the words nearly desperate.

He warred with his desire to see her, his desire to shield her from discomfort and his own desire to shield himself. Ultimately, he decided to comply with her demand.

He reached back and flicked off the switch, pledging them both into velvet darkness that didn't do anything to blot out the tension between them. He had a feeling there was nothing in heaven or hell or anyplace in between that could.

He turned back to the bed, his heart setting a dull, slow rhythm, a reminder of the fact that no matter how much he wanted this, he *was* in control.

He'd spent the past few years feeling like he didn't deserve much of anything, but knowing he had needs that had to be met. Doing the bare minimum to take the edge off of hunger—sexual or otherwise.

He was making a choice now, and he was doing it with grim determination. He couldn't justify it later by saying he'd lost his mind, by saying he had been overcome. That was the easy way out. Part of him wished he could take it. But it wouldn't be fair.

It would be giving his scarred, ruined soul a whole lot more credit than it deserved.

He took his hat off and set it at the foot of the bed. Then he grabbed hold of his T-shirt and tugged it up over his head. He could hear Rebecca rustling around on the covers.

"Stop," he said, the word hard-won, forcing it through his tightened throat a serious effort.

"What?"

"Let me do that," he said, instinctively knowing that she had been undressing.

Maybe he was too much of a coward to look at her. Maybe she was too afraid to let him look too. But he was going to touch her, everywhere. Taste her too.

He'd worry about the guilt later.

He stripped off the rest of his clothes, bringing a condom from his wallet over to the bed with him. Seeing as she'd been a virgin until yesterday, he hadn't imagined she would have supplies on hand.

He lay down next to her, curving his arm around her waist, pressing his palm against her back and sliding it up between her shoulder blades. He pressed her body against his, enjoying the soft, lush feel of her.

"This is a very bad idea," she said, her voice trembling slightly.

"I know," he said, chuckling low and soft. "But bad ideas are all I have."

She paused for a moment, fingertips lightly tracing shapes over his chest. "Sometimes I think I don't have any."

He moved his hands over her curves as she spoke. "Why do you think that?"

"I mean, I have some ideas. I have a pretty successful store. But... Not what to do with people. With men. I wanted you. But, I wasn't going to call. This is going to end badly. And that scares me. I'm starting to think maybe a bad idea is better than nothing."

"What would you have done if I hadn't come over?" He asked the question, then angled his head, pressing his lips to the vulnerable skin on the side of her neck. "Tell me. What does a typical night look like for Rebecca Bear?"

It wasn't just an idle question, not the moment the words left his lips. He wanted to know. More than that, he needed to know.

"Well," she said, gasping as his teeth scraped her skin. "Usually I watch TV."

"Movies?"

He felt her shake her head. "No."

He slipped his hands over to her hips, up to her waist. "Why not?"

"Because," she said, "they're too long. I always think that maybe I'll just watch one episode of something. But usually, I end up watching endless reruns on TV, and I sit there for four hours, and a movie would have been shorter." The last word ended on a squeak when he bit down on her shoulder.

"Very interesting," he murmured.

"I don't think you're actually listening to me," she said, groaning as he soothed away the sting of the bite with his tongue.

"I'm very interested in what you have to say," he responded, his words roughened by his arousal.

He moved his hand up, skimming her breasts, gratified when she wiggled against him in obvious pleasure.

"I don't think you are," she returned.

"TV. What else?"

"Well," she said slowly. "I cook."

"Really?" He curled his fingers around the hem of her shirt and tugged it up over her head. "What do you like to cook?"

"I'm very accomplished at making flatbread. By which I mean, I take a tortilla and throw stuff on it and then put it in the oven."

"Gourmet. Anything else?"

"Burritos. Because that's basically a tortilla and you put stuff in it, but you roll it up."

"I can see a common theme." He moved his hands to the clasp on her bra and undid it with practiced fingers. "Let me guess? You're also proficient with soft tacos?"

"I have a pretty good handle on them."

"Where did you learn to cook?"

He kissed her collarbone before she answered, sliding his tongue along the plump curve of her breast, to where her lace bra concealed the rest of her body.

"I used to cook for my brother."

Those words settled hard in him, like they were a little heavier than the rest. "Did you?"

"Yes. He worked. Long hours. More than one job. So, I always tried to make sure there was food for him. And buying a big thing of tortillas was easy."

That made him ache. For the girl she had been.

Alone, taking care of someone when people should have been taking care of her. After everything she'd been through, she needed to be taken care of.

Where did he get off being pissed about that? He hadn't been here either.

"It sounds like you have a lot of ideas, Rebecca," he whispered.

"I'm pretty good at surviving."

He couldn't fix the past, God knew it. But there was this. Tonight, there was this. "Well, tonight you're going to do more than survive."

He let her bra fall free, pulling it away from her arms and tossing it onto the floor. Then, he undid the snap on her jeans, wiggling the stiff denim down her legs, taking her panties with them. He pressed his palm onto her hip, digging his fingertips into her skin. He loved the feel of her. The softness. She was athletic, no question, but she was also just very soft. Very female. Made completely differently to himself.

It captivated him. It shouldn't. A woman was a woman, no matter how she was shaped. He'd been with enough to have seen about every variance. Still, she captivated him. Even in the dark.

He slipped his hand between her thighs, sliding a finger through her slick folds, finding her wet and ready for him. He moved the moisture up over the sensitive bundle of nerves there, rubbing her until she gasped.

He couldn't remember a woman's pleasure ever feeling so essential before. Yes, he had always wanted to leave his lovers feeling satisfied. But this was different. He had given her so much pain. So many bad feelings.

He wanted to make her feel good. Even if it was just for a few minutes, even if there would be nothing but regret later, he wanted her to feel good now.

He pressed the heel of his palm against her clit, pushing his fingers back and slipping two deep inside of her, rocking his hand and establishing a steady, teasing rhythm that made her shake and cry out.

"Oh," she breathed, grabbing hold of his wrist as if she could possibly take control. This was his game. No way in hell. "If I had known it was this good, I probably wouldn't have waited."

He chuckled, but her words made his chest tight. He didn't like the thought of her being with other men. He liked this. Liked the idea that he was the one commanding the response in her body. The only one. If he hadn't known he was sick before, this would've confirmed it.

He was responsible for her lowest physical lows, and he enjoyed the idea of being responsible for her physical highs.

He was a bastard. Through and through. He didn't care. Right now he was a hell of a satisfied one.

He leaned forward, capturing her mouth with his, kissing her deep and hard, trying to pour all of the intensity building in his chest into her. Trying to transfer it to pleasure. Trying to make her feel just a bit of what he was feeling now.

He pressed his hand against her shoulder, flattening her onto her back, withdrawing from between her legs. Then he kissed her neck, that smooth, elegant line of her collarbone, down to her breast, taking one nipple and sucking it deep into his mouth.

She gasped as he settled between her thighs, pressing his cock up against that soft place where she was wet and needy for him. He rocked against her, mimicking the movement his hand had just made, teasing her already sensitized flesh.

She grabbed hold of his shoulders, her fingernails digging into his skin. He gritted his teeth. "Harder," he growled.

"What?" she asked, sounding dazed.

"You can hold on to me harder than that, baby," he said, his voice a stranger's now.

She complied, digging her nails even deeper into his skin, and he took it as his punishment, as his reward. He should be left marked by her. It was only fair. The tattoo wasn't enough. It would never be enough. Nothing ever would be.

This was a start. A finish. It was all he had.

"Gage," she said, "I want you. Please."

He grabbed hold of the plastic packet he'd gotten earlier and opened it, deftly rolling the protection over his hardened arousal. Then, he moved back between her thighs, rocking his hips lightly, the head of his cock teasing her slick entrance.

Teasing them both. He moved lightly, in fractions, promising fulfillment, denying them both.

He didn't stop until she was panting, until he thought he was going to shatter his jaw, he was clenching his teeth so tight with the effort to remain in control. Then he moved forward, pushing in all the way, consumed, enveloped by her heat.

He lowered his head, pressing his forehead against

her shoulder as he lost himself for a moment and the intense pleasure of being inside her body. Then he raised his head, and he could see her eyes, glittering in the darkness.

He didn't know if she was crying, he thought maybe she was. He called himself ten kinds of asshole as he rocked his hips back, then thrust inside her again. He wasn't going to stop. He couldn't stop.

He needed her, needed this. Like a baptism of fire, his only hope of ever being clean.

No, he never would be. There was no question. There was no coming back from the man he'd been, it was all inside him. In his blood. He was his father's son. Through and through. He had proven it over and over.

He was proving it now. Chasing his own pleasure, pretending it was for anyone but himself.

He shut that thought down, bracing his palms on the mattress on either side of her head as he moved deep, then rolled his pelvis forward, pressing hard against her clit before withdrawing and repeating the motion again. She gasped each time, at each measured thrust that brought them both closer to the brink.

"I need… I need…"

He knew exactly what she needed, but he intended to torture them both a little bit more first. He lifted one hand, placing it over her breasts, teasing her nipple with his thumb as he rolled his hips back and forth. He felt her internal muscles tightening around his dick, the first waves of her orgasm beginning to shudder through her.

"Rebecca," he growled, thrusting forward hard, the rhythm broken, the action rough.

"Gage."

And that broke them entirely. The sound of his name on her lips, like a prayer instead of a curse.

Whatever he had been trying to do, whatever game he had been playing with the slow and steady tide that was trying to sweep them up had become a tsunami. There was no control. There was no thought. There was only a frantic, jagged need that sent him hurtling forward, thrusting into her desperately, taking every last ounce of pleasure that he could.

He forgot her. He forgot himself. He forgot everything but what it was like to be inside of her. To feel her small hands sliding over his skin, her nails raking over him, her legs locked around his hips as she arched her hips now to meet his every thrust.

His orgasm crashed through him, beyond his control, beyond his ability to withstand. And he was left shuddering, spending himself inside of her as he lost himself completely in this. In her. She froze beneath him, arching into him, her small breasts pressed into his chest as she rubbed her clit against him, finding her own pleasure, her internal muscles tightening around him like a vise as she surrendered to her release.

When it was done, he rested his head against her chest, slid down her body, grabbing hold of her hips and pressing his cheek between her breasts. He couldn't catch his breath. He couldn't think, hell, he could hardly see straight.

"How many condoms did you bring?"

The breathy, timid question made him laugh. "A few."

"Thank God." She curved her arm around his head, lacing her fingers through his hair. "Thank God."

CHAPTER FIFTEEN

WHEN REBECCA WOKE up the next morning she was aware of the bite in the air touching her face and one shoulder that was above the covers. The fire had obviously gone out in the woodstove overnight, and since it was only just now getting into the fall, she hadn't got out the space heaters she used to keep the bedroom warm on chillier nights.

The second thing she became conscious of was the fact that she wasn't cold. Not really. She was nestled up against a hard, warm body that was acting like her own personal furnace. She turned over, looking at the large man in her very small bed. Pale light was filtering through the curtains, exposing him and the careless expression that erased lines from his face as he slept. Exposing her and her imperfect skin.

But she couldn't quite bring herself to move. She turned over, pressing her fingertips against the broad expanse of his chest, tracing over his muscles lightly, relishing the feel of all that gorgeous masculine hair. She hadn't realized how much she would like that. How enticing she would find those stark reminders that he was very much a man and she was a woman.

His size, his strength, the uncompromising masculinity in every line of his body aroused her on every level.

He aroused her. Inescapably. Against her will.

When he'd called last night and asked if she was home—when he had said he was going to come over—she should have barred the door. Should have locked it. Should have had some sense of self-preservation. But no. Here they were.

She wasn't even all that sorry.

Gage stirred beneath her touch, placing one large, warm hand over hers, pressing her palm more firmly against his chest, until she could feel his heart beating. A low, steady rhythm that seemed to echo inside of her, modulating her own, making it beat in time with his.

She felt dizzy then, overwhelmed with sensation. She blinked hard, then when she opened her eyes, she found herself staring into his.

"Good morning," he said, his voice raspy from disuse.

She tried to force a smile, and she found she couldn't readily find any words. So she just nodded.

"I didn't mean to stay the night," he said.

"I know," she croaked, her own voice completely useless.

"How are you?" She could tell by the expression on his face he really meant it. He lifted his hand, brushing his thumb over her cheekbone, and she shivered.

"Cold?"

"Yeah," she said, because the only other response was no, and that would betray that it was just his touch that made her tremble.

He lifted the blankets up higher, covering her bare shoulder, then turned her body, so that she was pressed against him from breasts to toe. "Better?"

"Better," she responded.

She ached all over, not physically—it was something deep inside, something that she couldn't put a name or a bandage on.

She wondered what it was that drew her so inexplicably to this man. If it was some kind of extension of self-destruction, or just the fact that he loomed so large in her past.

That thought made her frown. Because none of that seemed like it had any place in this moment. She didn't feel angry. She didn't feel outraged or disgusted by him.

She didn't know how that could be. All she knew about him, all she had ever known about him before he had come back into town was that he was the man who had—through his negligence—caused her lifelong injuries. But that wasn't the end of the story, and she knew it. It wasn't the sum total of Gage West any more than it was the sum total of Rebecca Bear.

Maybe it did make her kind of sick, wanting the man whom she blamed for so much. But right now she didn't *want* it to be about that.

Suddenly, she felt hungry to add more details to the picture of him that she had in her mind. Suddenly, it seemed imperative that she make him something else. Because otherwise, she was well and truly fucked in the head.

"Tell me," she said, resting her cheek on his chest,

his warmth spreading through her. "Tell me what you did with all those years."

His fingertips froze on her arm, then began to slide up and down slowly again, his touch heating her down to her blood and bones.

"You want to know everything?" His voice rumbled against her ear.

"Yes," she said, feeling completely certain. "Absolutely everything. You left, and then what?"

"I bought a plane ticket," he said, "and I flew to Texas, because I thought that was as good a place as any. I had experience with horses, and I was able to get a job on a ranch there. All of that led to a little bit of amateur rodeo work."

"Where did the investments come in?"

"I started to earn a little extra pocket money on bets. I got a cut of the winnings when I kicked ass in events. So, I ended up with all this cash in savings. I talked to a guy who used to ride pro, who had made a bunch of money on endorsement deals. He was injured and he couldn't compete anymore, but, he had figured out a way to keep his income rolling in. And I thought that I should look into it. So, I contacted the guy he recommended and everything kind of snowballed from there. I started out with my father's money, it bought me the plane ticket, but after that… It was me on my own."

"So all of the debt you're dealing with now for the West family, that has nothing to do with your personal fortune."

He laughed. "I don't know that I would call it a personal fortune. But, I'm not going to end up out on the street anytime soon."

"So, you started getting money. Why didn't you settle down?"

His muscles went rigid beneath her touch. "I didn't feel like I could. Every time I stayed in one place for too long I felt like a rock was sitting on my chest. Every time I got to know people, every time I lingered, it felt like… Well, kind of felt like a betrayal. It was one thing to walk around and take whatever work I could get, to never settle, and to convince myself that I couldn't. Leaving my family for that… Well, that seemed okay. But if I were to settle somewhere else and really make it home then I guess it was real that I'd left them. That I left for good."

"Then why didn't you come back?"

"I couldn't. I couldn't do that. And it wasn't just because of you, though… I felt so much regret for that. And unable to do much of anything to fix it. But it was also my father. The more I chipped away at who he was, the less I could stand the idea of staying and becoming him. I already knew that he had an illegitimate kid. He told me about Jack Monaghan way before anybody else knew. I knew about him, and I didn't do anything. I'm completely at fault for Jack being disenfranchised from the family, for the fact that he had such a difficult childhood. Because for the longest time I thought that if my father had a reason for doing something it was a good enough reason. Because he was Nathan West, how could he be wrong? But there were so many things. So many little things. All of the money that was being used for God knew what. The secrets that he kept from my mother. And your accident was the last straw."

She froze, her hand still pressed tightly against his chest. "How?"

"He told me not to be an idiot. He told me to let him make it all go away. He wanted to pay you off, make sure that I didn't get in any trouble. He wanted it to be kept a secret so that it wouldn't impact the family. I'm not blameless. I obviously accepted the out. I'm not going to pretend for one second that I'm somehow blameless, or that I'm noble in any way. Because I let him do it. But I just couldn't… I couldn't be a part of that family anymore. I couldn't live there, knowing that I was expected to be everything he was. It's amazing to me, coming back and seeing Colton. He was raised by the same man, and he stayed. And he's turned into a helluva guy."

"Colton certainly hasn't ever gotten in any trouble."

"And I know he blames me for that, more than gives me credit. He's angry that I left, and that I left him with all of that to carry. But they were better off with him. They were always better off with him."

"Why?" She asked, her words hushed.

"Because, in case you hadn't noticed, I'm not a very nice guy."

"Yeah, you're a real terror, Gage. Coming back and trying to make things right."

"You're not going to start giving me credit now, are you? Because the last time we discussed this, you made it pretty clear I didn't deserve any."

She shifted against him. "Well, maybe I don't think that now."

"That's the sex talking."

"I don't think so. I mean, the sex is pretty good, I'll give you that. But I'm not an idiot. And a few orgasms are hardly going to change my thought process."

"You're wrong about that. It changes everyone's. It's why men like my father are somehow able to walk around with their heads held high while they treat every woman in their lives like absolute garbage." He let out a heavy breath. "They think they deserve something better, they think they're above any kind of consequence. They're buried so balls deep in their own bullshit they can't see past it."

"I guarantee you I'm not buried balls deep in anything," she said, keeping her tone deliberately dry.

"I'm just saying, I'm not sure that you're in the best position to absolve me right now."

"I'm not offering you absolution, you idiot. It's not about that. It's not about whether or not I can magically wave a wand and make you good or valuable or worthy, or whatever crap you're thinking. It's just that you're not a bad man. You did a bad thing. For all I know you've done a lot of bad things. But the bottom line is that, when your family needed you, you came back. And you never had to look me up. Ever. You gave me money. You want to make sure that I can retain my business. If you are all bad, you never would have done that. And you know what? I'm a little offended by the characterization. Because that means you think I'm stupid enough to sleep with a very bad man just because he's hot."

He laughed and the sound scraped against her raw nerves. "Oh, honey, why do you think bad men get laid so much?" He leaned in, brushing his thumb over her nipple. "It's because we know how to make this more important than anything else on earth."

She shivered wiggling out of his hold. "Okay, maybe you're not Saint Colton West, but you're not a terrible person. And walking around claiming it like that? That's just a shield. You're using it to protect you, to make it so that if you do mess things up, you can take a step back and shrug your shoulders and say that you made sure everybody knew what an awful person you were so they can't be surprised when you messed it all up. But that's just crap. And it's you being scared."

He tightened his hold on her. "Are you calling me a coward?"

"Yeah, pretty much."

"Baby, I used to ride bulls for money. I'm the furthest thing from a coward you're going to find."

"It's not really all that impressive that a man who is unquestionably self-destructive is willing to throw himself on the back of thousand-pound animal and get thrown around an arena. You're pretty badass physically because you don't care about what happens to you. Not when it comes to that stuff. But, you're afraid to deal with your family. Have been for the past seventeen years. In fact, sometimes I wonder a little bit if the only reason you're dealing with me is that it's a great distraction from them."

He growled, rolling over so that he was on top of her, his hard length pressing against that tender place between her thighs. "Does this feel like a distraction to you?"

"I'm pretty distracted," she said, her voice much more breathless than she would like it to be. She couldn't hide from him. That was a problem. But with his hard body pushing her deep into the mattress, and all the delicious sensations it fired off inside her, she couldn't bring herself to do much about it at the moment.

"You're not just a distraction. You are the reason I decided I needed to change myself."

"Not me," she said, reaching up and touching the deep groove that bracketed his mouth. "The idea of me. But, you didn't know me. I didn't change anything. You were the one that made all the changes, Gage."

"It *was* you," he said, his voice rough.

She shifted, then gasped as the head of his cock came into contact with the sensitive bundle of nerves between her legs. She wanted to get away from him, but she wanted to stay close to him forever at the same time.

"I'm not your monument," she said, "I'm not some wispy, white-clad virgin you can put up on a pedestal and worship. I'm not your patron saint of suffering. I'm not some kind of magical, mystical being. I'm just me. I'm a little bit broken, or maybe a lot. I'm not very nice. I'm a terrible friend. Kind of desperately screwed up. I can't even fix my own life, Gage." She closed her eyes, swallowing hard. "It would make me kind of mad if you thought I had fixed yours, when I hadn't managed to put mine in working order."

"I didn't say I was fixed," he said, his voice gruff. "I said I was changed. Before that accident happened I was headed straight to hell and I was bound and determined to take everyone around me along for the ride. I didn't care who I hurt. Worse, I don't even think I thought for one second that I *might* hurt someone, or that it would matter if I did." He paused, then when he spoke again, his voice was thick. "I remember that night."

"I don't really want to talk about it."

He slid his hands down her shoulders, past her elbows, down to her wrists. He wrapped his fingers around them, then lifted her arms up overhead, pinning them against the soft pillow. "We're going to talk about it."

She closed her eyes, turning her face away from him. Talking about it was always going to be hard. But talking about it like this when there were no walls between them, no clothes between them. Not even any space between them. That seemed impossible. "There's nothing to talk about. I remember it too."

"You hit a tree," he said. "Your side of the car hit a tree. I stopped and I looked inside. And I saw this little girl… You were hurt. You were hurt so bad. And you were crying. I remembered that you weren't supposed to move anybody after an accident." She could feel the heaviness of those words, feel how much they cost him to speak. "You have no idea how much strength it took to call 911 instead of just opening the car up and grabbing hold of you. But I didn't. Because I didn't want to risk hurting you more. At least I knew that much. We waited for the paramedics to arrive, and we lied. We told him that we didn't know what had happened. That we had just come upon the accident. It was such an easy thing to do. To lie about that experience. And then, my father found your mother and offered her money to keep the details quiet. I couldn't forget you, Rebecca. I never did. It's not absolution I'm seeking. It's just a way to get that image out of my mind. You crying like that. Hurt like that. Because of me. I just didn't want to be a man that could do that again. Not anymore. I wanted to change. I couldn't stomach turning into a man like my father, who was so callous about all these things that it was about minimizing scandal and not about taking responsibility."

"But you didn't take responsibility," she said, her tone gentle.

"No," he said, "I ran. Because I figured I wasn't really a good enough man to do anything else."

"I don't remember you," she said, tracing his upper lip with the edge of her thumb. "I don't remember much about that night at all. I remember just before we hit the tree. And everything after that is blank. Everything except waking up in the hospital. And then after that, I was just in pain. My leg, my skin. Every part of me hurt."

"I'm sorry," he said, his throat tight.

"I know. But I don't want to know all of this about you. I want to know the other things. I want to fill in the rest."

"Why?"

She laughed uneasily. "Because I can tell you, sure as anything, that the reason I'm sleeping with you isn't because of what happened that night. It's something else. It's the way that you came back. It's the way that you looked when you came back from seeing Sierra that night in the hospital. The way you look at me. There's not another man in town who wanted me."

"That isn't true. That guy I pulled you away from on the dance floor the other night would have had you a thousand times by now."

"Maybe. But, mostly because he feels sorry for me. Or because he wants to protect me from other guys, because he thinks I'm delicate. That's not the same. It's not the same as what we have. Tell me..." She blinked, trying to keep back the stream of tears that was threatening to come. "Are you with me because you feel sorry for me? Or is it because you want me?"

"I told myself it was because I felt sorry for you. Because you told me you were a virgin and that it was because of me. And that it was my responsibility to put it to rights." It was his turn to laugh. "Any kind of lofty justification a man can apply to getting laid, I guess. But the fact is, I want you. I would never have come over here last night if that weren't the case. If I were stronger than I was. I don't see a future for us. And I don't want to hurt you. But I'm still here. That has nothing to do with pity."

"Did it ever occur to you that maybe this isn't hurting me? That maybe this is exactly what I need?"

"I'm not staying. I can't give you anything other than this."

"I don't want anything other than this. But for someone who's never had it before, you have to understand that it's a pretty big thing. That it's something that makes me feel new. Different. Something that makes me feel like maybe I'm not so damaged after all."

He kissed her then, deep and long. "Rebecca," he said, "of the two of us, you're definitely the least damaged."

"Tell me everything else," she said, sliding her fingers through his hair, studying the hard lines on his face. "After Texas, then what?"

She didn't know what she was doing, building stronger bonds between herself and this man. All she knew was that she was starving for these details, to build a complete image of who he was, of who that night had made him. Of all that had transpired in the ensuing years.

And so, he told her. About leaving Texas and the rodeo behind, about driving a truck for a little while before he decided he hated it. About taking odd jobs on various ranches, and working construction. He had even done logging up in Alaska for a time. Basically, if the work was punishing, Gage West had done it. He was something entirely different than she had imagined him being.

But then, she was something entirely different than he imagined she was too.

IF GAGE HAD had his way he would have spent the entire day in bed with Rebecca. Sadly, there was work to do. Less sadly, since Rebecca was still holding on to the idea that she was working off her perceived debt, she accompanied him back to his barn.

He walked on ahead of her, listening to the sound of

her uneven footsteps in the gravel behind him. Then he turned, and she stopped, shoving her hands deep into the pockets of her jacket, her cheeks turning pink. She was holding back a smile as best she could, and the fact that she had to fight a smile instead of a scowl in his presence did something to his chest.

"What?" she asked.

He lifted a shoulder. "Nothing."

"Then why are you looking at me?" The smile tugged even harder at her lips, the motion pulling at the scar tissue at the corner of her eye. He frowned. And that immediately extinguished her grin.

Dammit.

"Because you're beautiful," he answered, a beat too late.

"Right. That's why your expression contorted with horror for a second there."

"It didn't."

"Yes it did. I know when I smile it makes the scars look worse."

He let out a heavy sigh. "You know that has nothing to do with you. It has nothing to do with how they make you look. But how am I supposed to feel about them? It's kind of a helluva thing. They don't bother me in an aesthetic sense. But it bothers me that I did this to you."

"You see the accident when you look at me."

He nodded, pressing his palm against the side of the barn. "Can you honestly say you don't see it when you look at me?"

"It's getting a little bit more complicated than that. Yes, I think of the accident. I think of everything that happened. And then, I think about last night. And the first time. What happened in the truck… And it all gets confused."

"There's only one thing on earth that ever made me feel like life made sense. That ever made me feel like I made sense."

"Are you going to try to give me a copy of the *Watchtower*?"

The unexpected bite of humor made him laugh. "Let's ride."

They went into the barn and saddled up the horses silently, then they started on the trail they had ridden on the first day she had come to work on the property. They were silent for the first mile or so up the trail then he heard Rebecca's voice come from behind him. "Passing on your left."

She and her horse maneuvered adeptly around him, taking the lead. He watched as she took the uphill portion of the trail with ease, her brown hair shimmering over her shoulders, falling to the middle of her back.

She was beautiful. And he had made a mess of things earlier. Typically, when he did anything other than running away from a problem, he only made it worse. Still, he was here. He wasn't running. He was with her. So he supposed that he should try to make amends.

He urged his horse forward, closing some of the distance between them. "I meant what I said."

"About riding horses being about the only thing that gives clarity? I could agree with you on that. Easily. We lived in the worst house ever. A small little shack kind of in the middle of nowhere. But we had a bit of property. After my mom left, Jonathan got me a horse. He was kind of a wretched little pony, and I was still recovering, so I couldn't just go out and ride. But it was everything that I'd ever wanted. It was the only bit of happiness that I had during that time. Except for Jonathan."

His chest tightened, his limbs suddenly feeling leaden. The picture that she painted of her childhood was so bleak. The gulf between what he'd had growing up and what she'd had was stark and severe. He wondered if anyone had ever told her how beautiful she was. If anyone had ever cherished her, or if the most she'd ever gotten was basic caregiving.

Obviously, her brother cared about her. Cared enough to work long hours, to use the money that he earned to get her a horse because he knew she was lonely and needed something like that in her life.

Still, he wanted to give her more. Because he had that luxury.

"That's not what I meant," he said, his voice rough. "You're beautiful. That is why I was looking at you, whether you want to believe it or not."

"But you still see the scars."

"I could say that I didn't, but it would be a lie. And I can't say that they don't affect me. Like I said, I take the blame for that. I can't help but feel responsible. I can't help but feel angry at myself when I look at them. But at the same time, they speak to your strength. And if I ignored them, it would be to ignore a big part of who you are. They aren't a flaw, and they certainly are a weakness."

"I feel differently about that at the end of the day when my muscles seize up. When the injuries that are just under the surface start to react."

They broke through to the clearing, bringing them back to the vantage point they had gone to on that first day. The first day that pull between them had become impossible to ignore. She didn't dismount, as though she were doing her best to keep distance between them, and as if staying on the back of the horse would accomplish that.

"I know. Can you just let me say something nice to you? I don't actually think you want to have the same fight over and over. I don't actually think that all I am to you is the man that caused the accident. Right now, I think the thing that makes you the most angry is that I'm challenging you."

She laughed, turning to look at him. "You think I feel challenged by you complimenting me?"

He got off of his horse, walking toward her. "I think you're most comfortable when nobody's touching you. And I mean that in more than just the physical sense." He walked up to her, placing his hand on her thigh, looking up at her. "I think you don't want a man to tell you you're beautiful. I think you want him to tell you there is something wrong with you so you can haul off and punch him in the face."

Her entire face paled. Then she scowled. "You think you have me figured out?"

"Not even close. But I have figured a couple things out. You don't want to be told you're beautiful." He let his hand drift from where it was on her thigh, up to her hip. "But you like to be kissed long and deep. You might not want to hear the words, but you don't mind a man showing you."

Her dark eyes looked nearly black, the color rising in her cheeks again. "You don't...you don't know that."

Now he knew that she was just challenging him because she wanted a fight. That was another thing about her he'd figured out. "I do know that," he said, giving her exactly what she wanted. He moved his hand up a little bit further, skimming the underside of her breast with his thumb. "You like that too," he said, his voice getting rough.

She let out a long, ragged breath. "Cheap shot, West. Very cheap."

"Why? Because I'm irresistible?"

That made her smile again, and this time she didn't try to hold it back. When she smiled like that, he had the sense that the sun had broken through the heavy gray mist that hung over the mountains.

"Look, until this week I was a virgin. I'm a pretty easy target."

"Yeah," he said, reaching up and grabbing hold of her chin. "You really have made things so easy on me."

"I just mean, I'm about as hard up as they come. Twenty-eight years without sex is a long time."

"Come here," he said.

She didn't make any move to get down off the horse, so he wrapped his arm around her waist and lifted her down from the horse. Her dark eyes widened and she tried to jerk away from him, but he held her steady. He looked at her, taking hold of her face, sliding his thumbs across her cheek. He traced the line of scar tissue that ran from the outside corner of her left eye down to her mouth.

"Beautiful," he said, his stomach tight now, arousal welling up inside of him like a hot spring. He slid his thumb down, tracing the edge of her lower lip before leaning in and kissing her.

He deliberately kept it slow, every pass of his tongue going a little bit deeper. He cupped the back of her head, letting his fingers sink deep into her glossy, dark hair as he continued to ravish her mouth.

She whimpered, arching against him, and he moved his other hand from her face, letting his fingertips drift down the side of her neck to her shoulder and down her side to the curve of her waist where he flattened his palm and gripped her tight.

He pressed her body against his, the feel of her firm, small breasts against his chest enough to make him groan with pent-up need.

He moved his hand down lower, sliding his fingertips beneath the hem of her shirt, moving them upward, his other arm wrapped tightly around her waist, still holding her to him.

She pulled away suddenly, struggling to get free.

He released his hold on her and she took a step back, curving her arm over the back of her horse, as though she was using him for protection. "What?" he asked, examining her frightened expression.

"We're out in the open." And in the light. The unspoken words were as loud as anything else. She had made him leave the room before she had gotten out of bed this morning. Hadn't allowed him to see any of her body.

"Right," he said, not wanting to push her anymore now.

"I can't... I can't..." She swung her foot up in one of the stirrups, ready to get on the horse again, and he closed the distance between them, curving his hand around her neck, kissing her once more, long and fierce, before releasing her.

She slung her leg over the back of the horse, positioning herself on its back, her cheeks a brilliant pink. Her eyes were glittering and she was staring straight ahead, careful not to look at him.

"Are you mad at me?"

"No," she said, "I'm not mad at you."

"Are you ready to tell me thank-you for saying you're beautiful?"

"No," she said, turning her horse around and taking off at a gallop.

He swore and got on his own horse, taking off after her. She went a different way, taking a wide-open field that led the roundabout way back toward his property.

By the time he made his way back to the barn, she had dismounted and was leading the horse to a trough. He got off his own, tethering her to the side of the barn before following Rebecca over to the end of the barn, near the fence.

He grabbed hold of her arm, and she spluttered, then he pressed her back up against the roughhewn wooden slats, curving his hands around the top rail on either side of her. "Don't run away from me."

"Gage," she said, and he realized how long it had been since she had said his name.

She was begging him for something, with that one word, but he wasn't sure what. To kiss her again, to leave her alone. So he figured he would take the option that he liked best.

He wrapped his arms around her waist, reversing their positions so that he was sitting down on top of the fence now, pulling her up against him, trapping her between his thighs.

He pressed his mouth to hers, keeping it simple, keeping it straightforward. He didn't taste her the way that he wanted to, didn't part her lips and invade her mouth. Instead, he kept it cool, dry, let her set the pace.

She turned her head, pulling away when he had hoped she would deepen it.

"Thank you," she said, her words a rushed whisper.

"There," he said, "that wasn't so bad, was it?"

"Nothing about you is. I keep hoping that you'll confirm my fears at some point and reveal yourself to be a monster." She lifted her hand, tracing the groove by his mouth. "Instead, you keep on being something else entirely. Something that keeps on surprising me."

"What's that?"

"A man. A man that I want."

"Well, at least that's not as scary as a monster."

She shook her head. "Scarier."

"Why is that?"

She lifted a shoulder, the sun breaking through the clouds, casting a halo around her hair. "Because, as long as you're a monster then all of my hiding away was for a good reason." She let her fingertips drift down to the center of his chest. "But I guess you were what I was hiding from all this time."

He knew that she didn't mean him. Not specifically. He hadn't been around for her to hide from. But he suspected that she meant this. Attraction. Relationships. There was a reason that she hadn't been with anyone, and he didn't think it was really because of her scars. At least, not her outward scars.

"I'm pretty scary," he said, to avoid taking the conversation into deeper territory. "I don't blame you for hiding from me one bit."

He rocked his hips forward, letting her feel the evidence of how much he wanted her.

"Gage," she said, "I don't have time. I have to go to work."

"Fair enough. But are you going to come over after work?"

He didn't know quite what he was doing. Quite what they were doing.

"Yes," she said, ducking her head.

"Good," he said, grabbing hold of her chin with his thumb and forefinger and tilting her face back up so he could steal another kiss. "I'll make you dinner."

She blinked rapidly. "You don't have to do that."

"You'll be hungry. And I want to."

She chewed her bottom lip, and he could see that it was giving her serious issues. That she couldn't decide whether or not it was okay for him to cook for her, or if that would be unbalancing their scales even more, as she saw it.

"Stop keeping score," he said, his tone stern.

"I don't know how."

"It's easy. Stop keeping track."

The edict was as much for himself as it was for her. Maybe, while he was here getting all of the stuff with his family sorted out, he could have this too. Maybe, he could leave town with everything fixed for Rebecca and in the meantime... There could be this.

"Dinner will be on at six. Don't be late or I'll eat it all."

"I should help you with the horses."

He shook his head. "You have to go. So go."

He could see that she was relieved to get some distance between them, and that was the main reason she didn't argue about getting out of taking care of the horses' tack.

He watched her turn to leave, watched the gentle sway of her hips and the glossy shimmer of her hair as she shook her head. She was doing something to him. Something he hadn't expected. Something he certainly hadn't been looking for.

He felt stuck to the spot in that moment, as though roots were growing beneath his feet. The kind of roots he had spent seventeen years avoiding.

He gritted his teeth and headed back out to grab hold of his horse. He wasn't staying here. That wasn't an option. No matter how tempting Rebecca Bear made it seem.

CHAPTER SIXTEEN

"So, ARE YOU coming tonight?"

Rebecca stared across the store at Alison, who was standing next to Lane, both of them on their lunch breaks and perusing the shelves for various Christmas items.

Rebecca could have punched her own face. She had forgotten that tonight was their girls' night.

"I'm busy," she said, grabbing a dry rag from by the cash register and working at a bit of imaginary dust on her counter.

"You're busy?" Alison asked, her tone disbelieving.

"I have a life, Alison," Rebecca said.

"Yes, I'm sure you do. It's just that it mostly centers on us."

Lane looked at her askance. "Are you busy with anyone in particular?"

Rebecca felt her face heat up. Dammit. If only she could figure out how to control that particular reaction. "Maybe I'm going home and playing solitaire."

"Or having dinner with Jonathan?" Lane asked. "That's what I would've gone with."

Rebecca scowled. "Fine. You're better at lying than I am."

"What's going on?" Alison asked, looking increasingly annoyed.

"Rebecca has a special friend."

The wave of heat intensified, and Rebecca felt like she might suffocate beneath her embarrassment. "He's not a... Don't call him that."

"A special friend?" Alison raised an eyebrow. "Like a special friend...like a penis friend?"

"Alison!" Rebecca scolded.

"I'm so jealous," Alison said. "Well, I'm not really. Men are douche bags. And they're more trouble than they're worth." She held up a hand. "Not that I'm not thrilled for you."

"It's not like that. It's not a relationship. It's..." Lane made an obscene hand gesture.

"Thank you, Lane," Rebecca said drily, "that's what it is."

"That's ideal," Alison said.

"Anyway, that's why I'm busy."

"I suppose I should be offended because sisterhood and chicks before dicks and stuff, but God knows if I had a chance at getting laid tonight that's where I would be too," Lane said.

"He's making dinner or I would do the girl thing first," Rebecca said, feeling defensive at the idea that she might be abandoning her friends for a man. Of course, she had never had occasion to be accused of such a thing.

"He's making dinner?" Lane asked, her tone altering.

"Yes. He does eat and he therefore cooks."

"Yes, but he's cooking for you. Which is different. Also, it's more than just sex."

"It's sex and food. Which I have to say, are both good." She tried to sound casual as she said that. "So, don't ask me to look quite as worried about it as you do."

"I just think you should be careful with this guy."

"What guy is it?" This question came from Alison, and that was when Rebecca realized that Lane had not filled their other friend in on any of the details.

"A guy. That owns my building and caused my accident. That guy."

"Who is also Gage West," Lane said, clearly unable to hold back information any longer. "Of the increasingly disgraced Wests. And he's easily the worst, not even solely because of Rebecca's accident. But he ran off years ago and nobody knew what happened to him. He just kind of left the whole family—which, given what a mess they are, kind of makes sense now—but still makes him seem a little bit like a flight risk.

"Another risk," Lane continued, "quite frankly, is that he seems like an extremely dangerous choice. Which, I guess probably makes it fun?"

Rebecca frowned. She didn't exactly like the idea of Gage being some kind of strange response to her spending so many years being sheltered. Though, she imagined whatever sexual relationship she chose to embark on would be that to a degree. Because it was taking a step. Breaking through years of habit and self-protection and allowing herself to be, if not completely vulnerable with somebody, then naked in the literal sense at least.

Of course, you haven't let him see you yet.

But, he wasn't pushing for it either. She wasn't going to lead that charge. The idea of him seeing her body, the scars, where the skin grafts were… She didn't like that at all.

"So how did you get to having sex with that guy from wanting to kill him not that long ago?" Alison asked, looking genuinely perplexed.

Lane gave her a bland look. "Sometimes attraction doesn't make sense."

"I'm familiar with going from love to hate. This… I guess it's been so long for me that I forgot. On second thought, maybe I don't miss it as much as I thought I did."

"Well, as much fun as this has been, I think you ladies have jobs to get back to," Rebecca said.

"That's nice," Lane said, her tone dry. "Look how quickly we've been replaced."

"You haven't been replaced. It's just that I'm not going to stand here and discuss the nature of my… dalliances."

"Is there more than one dalliance?" Alison asked, her eyebrows raised.

Rebecca noticed that Lane looked slightly concerned. "No there isn't," she said, her tone emphatic. "Gage is quite enough on his own."

Too much.

"Okay," Lane said, "you have a point. I should get back to work. But, give me a call if you need anything. We'll be traveling in a pack tonight."

"I'll keep that in mind."

Alison held up her finger, signifying that she needed

another minute, and Lane nodded before walking out of the store. The petite redhead moved closer to the counter, her expression full of concern. "Is everything okay?"

"It is. I promise. I know it's weird, but he didn't force me into anything. I get that from the outside looking in it seems incredibly unhealthy and maybe it even is. But I think it's something I need."

That made Alison's expression get even more concerned. "The minute you feel like you need him, it's trouble."

"That isn't what I meant. I know that you are on hyperalert for this kind of thing, and I don't blame you. But he isn't like your ex-husband. I wouldn't say he's a nice guy, but he doesn't pretend to be either. He's definitely not Prince Charming. He's not even the huntsman. He might be the beast. But I'm not holding out hope I'm going to find the man underneath all that. That isn't the point. This is for me, it isn't for him."

But the moment that she said it, she realized that he was getting something out of this too. That as selfish as she intended for it to be, he needed it for some reason just as badly as she did. And she cared about that. She was starting to care about him.

"What happened…" She took a deep breath. "It happened. But it doesn't define me, and it shouldn't define him either."

"Okay. I trust you. But I don't trust him. And if anything happens… If he hurts you any more than he already has, I'm going to shank him with the sharp end of my pie server."

Rebecca took a deep breath, trying to ease the tension in her chest. Battling with the strange emotions that were bubbling to the surface. There was something about this relationship that was forcing honesty. Between herself and Gage, between herself and her friends. Within herself.

And she had never felt more grateful for Alison, Lane and Cassie than she did now. That she had backup if she needed it. That she could have this conversation with them. And that they would have her back regardless of what was happening.

She rounded to the front of the counter and wrapped her arms around Alison, pulling her friend in close. "Thank you," she said, releasing her almost as quickly as she'd taken hold of her.

She wasn't a big one for touch. Mostly because it hadn't been on offer. Her mother had been distant at best, and then absent after that. Jonathan wasn't demonstrative. He'd grown up in the same environment she had, if not slightly worse. From what she had been told, his father had been a horrible bastard who had only touched anyone with his fists.

Rebecca's father was just gone. That, she imagined was preferable. Still, she was starting to think that maybe she needed a little more than she had previously imagined. That she needed the people in her life to be a little bit closer than she had always kept them.

"You're welcome," Alison said, her eyes looking suspiciously bright. "I'm always here for you. You know that."

Rebecca nodded and smiled, doing her best not to get stupid emotional.

After Alison left she spent the rest of the day in a kind of strange suspended state, held between anticipation and dread. Now she was thinking that the dinner thing was a bigger deal than she had originally given it credit for being, thanks to the overreaction of her dear friends.

By the time she pulled into Gage's driveway she was nearly trembling with a strange adrenaline-fueled anticipation that made her limbs feel weak and her stomach clench tight. She took her hands off the steering wheel and shook them, as if she could release the nervous energy through the ends of her fingers.

A little shiver ran through her and she got out of the truck, taking every step a little bit harder than necessary, as though it might ground her a little bit.

She took a deep breath before knocking on the door, and then she waited. She didn't hear anything. No footsteps, no sounds of clattering pans. Great. He was probably hiding. He had probably found some nice sexually experienced girl to do some real acrobatics with.

She was being intentionally dramatic, but even still the very thought made her feel like she was on the verge of a nervous breakdown.

The door opened and she jumped, then her focus went straight to his bare chest, which was right at her eye level. Her mouth dried and she let herself slowly, very slowly, take in the view before her. Gage was shirtless, and he was wearing a pair of very low-slung jeans that showed off his hard-cut abs and a matching pair of glorious indents that seem to make an arrow that disappeared beneath the denim, drawing her eye right down to the bulge at the apex of his thighs.

Well, this was what she gave up, making love to him in the dark. She had only thought of herself, of protecting her dignity and all of that. She hadn't really appreciated what all she was missing by denying herself the sight of his body.

"I'm pretty sure you're violating a health code," she said, her words scratchy as she tried to force them through her terminally dry throat. "Wandering around the kitchen half-dressed."

She looked up at his face then, at the extremely self-satisfied and unapologetic look in his eyes. "But you like it," he said.

She couldn't really argue with that, but still, she tried to keep her expression stoic. She breezed past him and walking into the house. "I want to make sure my food's preparation is up to standard."

He reached out, grabbing hold of her wrists and drawing her hands forward, pressing her palms against his bare chest. "You like me like this."

"Sure," she said, going up on her tiptoes and kissing his lips, a rush of pleasure and regret racing through her as soon as she finished. It was a little bit too telling, both to him and herself for her to start acting all affectionate. But she was desperate to taste him. So maybe that was more sexual than it was affectionate.

She needed lines. Unfortunately, every available line seemed to be blurry. Because sex felt good, and made her want to feel good more often. Heaven knew she had too little of it in her life. Then there was the fact that every inch of him pressed against every inch of her made her feel warm all over, made her feel like curling her toes just thinking about it. Which made her want to touch him, in some capacity, in any capacity, every time she saw him.

Which started to feel a lot more like closeness than simple physicality. Blurry damn lines.

"I don't want to brag, but I'm actually a pretty good cook. It comes from years of being on the road and making do with incredibly Spartan situations. I'm the MacGyver of cooking."

"Does that mean you made a tortilla out of a paperclip?"

He laughed. "Not quite. But, if it exists I've probably cooked it on a camp stove. So what I made for you tonight is skillet macaroni and cheese with bacon, a salad, just so we don't feel guilty, and I bought a pie from your friend Alison."

"Oh," she said, not quite sure how she felt about him getting in the middle of her life like that. Her real life. It was easy, up here at the lake, to feel separate from everything that happened in town. That her store, her friends, all of that was somehow a different life. Even the Gage she dealt with in the professional capacity could be a different one than her lover. But not if he was going to keep blurring all the lines.

Again with the blurry lines.

"I suggest you start with the macaroni and cheese, skip the salad and go straight to the pie."

"Then why did you make the salad?"

"The appearance of virtue."

She laughed, in spite of herself, in spite of all the jumbled-up messed-up feelings rolling around inside of her. "As far as I can tell, you never really bother with appearing virtuous, why start now?"

"Because you do."

She frowned. "I do?"

He reached out, wrapping his arm around her waist and pulling her up against him so that her back was resting against his chest, his hand splayed over her stomach. "Yes," he said, his breath hot on her neck. "You're such a prickly little thing. Like a sea urchin."

She scowled, whipping her head around and looking up so that she could see him. "That is the most unflattering comparison I have ever heard."

He ignored her. "Prickly, near impossible to get to the center of. Yeah, hate to break it to you, baby, but that's you."

"A virtuous sea urchin?"

He chuckled, low and soft in her ear and her knees forgot their function, buckling beneath her, only his strong hold keeping her from crumpling into a Rebecca-shaped heap on the floor. "I didn't say you were virtuous, I said you gave the appearance of being virtuous. It's all a part of that untouchable vibe you have going on."

She struggled to get out of his hold, pushing her hair off of her face and turning to face him when she succeeded. "I'll tell you what. Why don't you skip the psychoanalyzing, and just feed me bacon."

"If you prefer."

"Who doesn't prefer bacon over self-examination?"

"Well-adjusted vegetarians?"

She snorted. "Well, I hate to break it to you, but the two of us are neither of those things."

She took a seat on the couch with a glass of wine provided by Gage, and continued to watch him wander around the kitchen looking like some strange fantasy she hadn't even realized she had. But oh boy, did it ever work for her.

His muscles shifted and punched with his every move as he efficiently prepared their plates. And every time he bent down for something she hoped that his jeans would slip a little bit more. They never did. They were some kind of magical, infuriating cut designed to drive women crazy.

She couldn't remember ever being taken care of this way before. Jonathan had cared for her every practical need, and she couldn't fault him. He had been a kid, doing his very best to take care of a kid. But no one had ever done this. This felt luxurious, lavish.

Dinner tasted amazing, the kind of rich comfort food she had never indulged in growing up, because it was too complicated for her to make and too expensive to buy. They talked about their days. He about the progress he'd made with the Main Street buildings, and she about the incredibly loud tour group that had nearly rattled her ceramic birds off their perches with their noise, and about the loose floorboard she kept stubbing her toe on, even though she knew it was there.

And then, when it was all finished, he did the cleaning up while she lay down on the couch, listening to music that he played from his phone to a wireless speaker.

She closed her eyes, humming along until she must have fallen asleep, because the next thing she remembered was being picked up, held against Gage's chest and carried to the bedroom. When he tried to set her down, she clung to him even harder, reluctant to lose this feeling. Of being small, of being light and easy to hold on to. Of being completely and utterly sheltered in the strength of his hold.

Of being safe.

"I'm just going to set you down on the bed," he whispered, his words as rough as the stubble that scraped against her cheek when he spoke. "I'm not going to leave you."

She let him set her down, and she felt the mattress depress behind her, felt him stretch out alongside her, curving his hand around her body, holding on to her protectively. He seemed to remake himself to fit around her, something she would have thought impossible for such a hard man to do, and yet, he did it.

Her last thought before drifting off with him was that it should be unsettling to fall asleep with someone like this. But it wasn't, not with him. Hadn't been even the first time. Somehow, being with him, though in a strange bed, made her feel an awful lot like she was home.

CHAPTER SEVENTEEN

"WHAT ARE YOU doing here?"

Gage ignored Rebecca's evil glare as he walked over the threshold into her shop. "I came to fix your floorboard."

"This is real life, Gage. This is not porn. So, whatever you were thinking was going to happen here…"

He laughed, because even though she was playing prickly with him, she was also teasing him, and that was a welcome change. "No, I came to literally fix your literal floorboard. The one that you said you keep stubbing your toe on."

Her eyes went wide, and her mouth dropped open into a perfect O.

"What? I can be nice. See, I'm being nice. Also, I listen."

"You do," she said, looking slightly surprised that she agreed with his statement.

She looked a little bit worried when he walked toward the back of the store, eyeballing all of the boards as he went.

"It's over here," she said, gesturing to a spot behind the counter. "But…"

"You're afraid somebody's going to see me here and start asking questions."

"Yes. Absolutely, that yes."

"I own the building. Also, that's not very good for my ego."

"What?" she spluttered.

"The fact that you are desperately ashamed of us being involved."

She crossed her arms, then began to pace as he made his way to the offending board and knelt down. "I'm not ashamed. It's just that we are not really involved. Not on a permanent or even semipermanent basis. We are only doing this until you leave."

"Yeah, I know."

"Also," she said, "I do know how to fix a loose board. I just hadn't gotten around to it."

Of course she would know how to fix her own board. Rebecca did not strike him as the damsel in distress. In fact, she was aggressively independent. "Maybe that is the point. Maybe the point is that you just need to learn to let someone do something nice for you once in a while. Even if you're capable of doing it yourself, sometimes you have to let someone do it for you."

"I disagree. Because then you start needing people."

Her words made his stomach seize up tight. How long had it been since he'd needed somebody? He couldn't remember. It was a fine thing for him to lecture her on taking help when he had been no less solitary for all these years.

But he wasn't the point. She was. And he was fixing the damn board.

He heard the bell over her entry door go off, and he

turned just in time to see a very large man who looked to be in his early thirties walk in. "Rebecca?" he asked.

It did not take long for Gage to connect what the relationship was between this man and Rebecca. His skin was darker, his hair a glossy black, but the hard expression in those dark eyes were definitely a Bear family trait. The biggest difference was that he was large enough to kill Gage with one fist.

"Hi," Rebecca said, too quickly. "Jonathan, what are you doing here?"

"I came to see you. Because I've been busy. So I felt bad because we hadn't managed to connect in a few days. Also, you need to start answering your texts, brat."

Gage stood up from his position behind the counter, and he immediately caught Jonathan's attention. He probably could have smoothed the situation over easily, but Rebecca's face turned bright red, her expression registering intense distress.

Jonathan's dark eyebrows locked together, and then, he looked over at Gage, studying him intently. "You wouldn't happen to be Gage West, would you?"

Gage had a feeling that was his polite way of asking if Gage wanted to die today.

"I am," he said, crossing his arms over his chest.

He wasn't going to back down, not now. Of course, he imagined Rebecca would rather that he and Jonathan didn't have a bar brawl in the middle of her knickknack store, but Gage wasn't going to start it. He'd damn well finish it if he had to—that was the conclusion he came to then and there.

"What the hell are you doing in my sister's store?"

"She had a loose floorboard. I came by to fix it."

"I see, and how do you know about the floorboard?" Jonathan took a step toward him.

"She told me. I didn't break into the place late at night and start testing for weak spots."

"Gage," she said, her voice hushed, "stop."

Jonathan's dark eyes narrowed. "Why didn't you throw him out?"

"Jonathan," she said, "maybe we should talk somewhere else."

"What the fuck is going on?"

"I'm just fixing the floor," Gage said, because the last thing he wanted to do was cause more trouble for Rebecca.

"No, you're not just fixing the floor," she said, then she turned her furious gaze onto Jonathan. "He's not just fixing the floor. He's... I'm...we... We're not exactly dating..."

And that was when Gage found himself being hauled over by the front of his shirt. "Are you fucking my sister? I would've thought you'd done that enough."

"Stop it!" Rebecca got between the two of them, putting her hands over her brother's, trying to break his hold on Gage's shirt.

Jonathan released him, Gage suspected only because he was concerned about hurting Rebecca. "Did he hurt you?" he asked her.

Rebecca scrubbed her arm over her eyes. "No. This is not a hostage situation. Why would I have told you if I was ashamed? Or if I was upset?"

"I figured you told me because you wanted me to kill him."

"No. I don't want you to kill him, but I'm not going to sneak around, and I'm not going to lie to you. Jonathan, we've been through too much together for me to lie to your face. Yes, I was going to avoid having this discussion if I could. But, I guess we can't avoid it."

Jonathan turned to face Rebecca, acting as though Gage wasn't even there. He reached out, sliding his thumb across her scar-roughened cheek. "He did this to you. It's his fault. How could you ever let him touch you again?"

"Because we both deserve to be more than those scars."

He had a feeling she might mean Jonathan just as well as she meant him. Jonathan stiffened, drawing away from her. "It wasn't just you. And it isn't just the injuries."

"I know," she said, her voice thick.

"And you're still with him?"

She nodded silently, and he treated her to a long, hard look. Gage expected him to haul off and punch him next. But he didn't. Instead, he turned around and walked out of the store, slamming the door so hard behind him that the bell screamed and a small ceramic ornament fell from the top of one of the armoires, smashing onto the floor.

Rebecca put her hands over her mouth, like she was holding back a scream. Gage closed the space between them, wrapping his arms around her, holding her against his chest. "You didn't have to tell him," he said, his voice rough.

"I know," she said, her words muffled.

"Why did you?"

"I just want… I just want to have this. And I don't want to feel bad about it. And I was hoping that maybe he would help. But he's not going to." She took a deep, shaking breath. "I guess that's important too. He disapproves. I knew that he would. But, I'm going to do this anyway."

She pulled away from him, picking at some imaginary dirt beneath her fingernail. "This is the other thing I do, you know. I don't put a foot out of line. I've never fought with Jonathan. How could I? How could I when he gave everything to take care of me."

"That's what he meant. About it not just being the accident. He blames me for your mother leaving."

"Sometimes I think he blames me," she said.

And then she went down onto her knees.

REBECCA FELT LIKE she was going crazy. Like she was breaking apart inside. She had no idea what she had been thinking, telling Jonathan that she was sleeping with Gage. She had no idea what she was thinking confessing that deep, betraying thought that she had always carried so close to her chest.

Maybe this was the thing. Maybe it was circular. Maybe it always had to be him. Maybe he had needed to be brought out into the light, revealed to be nothing more than a man so that she could finally face the real monster. The one that lived inside of her.

The one that was afraid she was the reason her mother had left. She had become too much, she had become too much to handle and so her mother had left her, left her as a burden for Jonathan, and he had done the right thing, the strong thing, but even he probably resented her. And she had no doubt that he knew she was the real reason their mother wasn't there.

Their mother, who had barely been strong enough to raise two children on her own as it was, was never going to be strong enough to care for an invalid daughter who had endless health issues. And that was the real problem. It always had been. She had been the tipping point. Her.

In that moment the bandage had been removed. The moment she had been exposed. That was when she had lost her mother.

Sure, the accident had been the catalyst. Nathan West had provided the getaway cash.

But she was the culprit.

And so she had spent the past seventeen years trying to do her very best to avoid being left again. To hold people at a far enough distance that she would be able to handle it if she lost them. To make herself palatable enough that maybe people wouldn't want to leave.

She was doing a terrible job of it now. She had just alienated her brother in a huge way, and now she was breaking into tiny pieces in front of the only man she had ever allowed to touch her. He was seeing her naked now, even though he had never seen her naked in the physical sense. She was completely bare to him.

And she was too caught up in her misery, in her brokenness to care.

Gage was holding her now, and that made it feel better too. Just like he had done last night, he made a shelter for her out of his arms; his broad chest and shoulders were more than enough to shield her from almost anything that came from the outside. But he couldn't help her with this. He couldn't stop it. The storm was inside. There was no hiding from it. There was no escaping it.

"It wasn't your fault," he said, mostly because she imagined it was what any decent person would say in this situation. But it didn't make it true. It had been the thing that pushed her mother away once and for all.

Even if it wasn't fair it was true.

Fair didn't have any place in life.

At least, not in hers.

She nodded, feeling that his shirt was wet beneath her cheek. Great, she was crying on him. She was too miserable to care. "I want to go home," she said.

"Your home or mine?"

"It doesn't matter. As long as you come with me."

WHEN THEY GOT back to her house it was cold inside. The fire in the woodstove had gone out and Rebecca wrapped her arms around herself to keep from shivering. She felt like the cold was coming from inside of her. She doubted a fire would help.

Still, Gage set about warming the interior of the house. She supposed the rest of it was up to her. Figuring out how to deal with her own self. How to get a handle on the emotions that were rioting through her.

She wasn't sure she wanted to get a handle on them. She never let them break through. Never let these thoughts form all the way. They just sort of hovered in the back of her mind, a vague kind of dread that she never allowed herself to truly look at. Never allowed herself to understand. She could see it all now. All of that vague, often overwhelming anxiety now taking its full form.

For some reason that realization, the full understanding of exactly what she was afraid of made everything feel so tenuous. Like Jonathan really might pull away from her completely. Like her friends would all desert her.

Made her feel as if even this, this connection that she had with Gage, was a kind of thin, fragile line.

She watched him as he put pieces of wood into the woodstove, moving them around with his bare hands, trying to get them to ignite. She watched the tattoo, that thick black band that signified their shared past, shift and ripple over his muscles, and a shiver ran down her spine.

She was the only one that knew. The only one that knew the entire story. Other than his father, at least. But not even his father had the full picture. The years that had passed in between the time he had left Copper Ridge and when he had come back. Rebecca knew. She was the keeper of Gage's story.

And he was the keeper of hers.

Somehow, this relationship had shifted, changed. They had become each other's confidants. They kept each other's worst secrets, had done so for years. Not to protect each other, but initially to protect themselves. Everything seemed like it was turned on its head now.

Somehow, that thread that had connected them for so long had wound around them both, drawing them together inextricably.

Nobody, not a single person, knew more about her than Gage West. And she had a feeling that nobody knew more about him than she did. Still, she was hiding her body from him. Protecting them both. It was their very last secret.

The one that let them hide. The one that separated their being lovers from the past. Oh, they talked about it, but when it came time for sex, they both shoved it to the side.

She didn't want that anymore. She wanted it all. She wanted all of him.

And whatever the cost, she didn't want to live in the dark anymore.

She took a deep breath, grabbed the hem of her top and pulled it up over her head. Then she reached behind her back, grabbing hold of the clasp on her bra and releasing it, shimmying her shoulders and letting it fall to the floor.

She closed her eyes, taking a deep breath and releasing it slowly. When she opened them, Gage was looking at her from his position down on the floor, his dark eyes intense. He was unmoving, unflinching. Completely unreadable.

She might know more of his secrets than anyone else did, but she didn't know all of them. She never would.

That thought made her unaccountably sad. She

shouldn't care whether or not she knew all of his secrets. Whether or not they had infinite time together or severely limited time. It was never about the two of them. It was about purging all of the ugliness inside of them both. Finding a safe place for it to land. So it didn't have to live inside of them, poisoning them, trapping them.

She gritted her teeth, straightening her shoulders and staring him down. "I don't see any point in hiding this anymore," she said.

He pushed up from the floor, moving into a standing position, keeping a healthy space between them. His breathing was harsh, hard, his teeth clenched together. A muscle in his jaw twitched as he continued his distant visual perusal of her body.

He moved to her slowly, not saying anything, and then he dropped to his knees again, right in front of her. He put his hand on her stomach, tracing along the line left by the accident, or subsequent surgeries. They were a part of her she couldn't escape. A part she took on with grim acceptance.

But when he touched her, she saw something different. She saw his regret, his shame. And when she saw it in his eyes, she could see how unfair it was to have such a limited perspective. To look at her own body and hate it the way that she did.

Yes, the accident had changed her. It had changed them. But just as she had said to Jonathan, they were both more than this one mistake. Than this one moment in time.

All of the pain, all of the fear, all of the shame was

tied to a day that was well behind them now. It seemed like such a shame, such a waste, to sacrifice every year that came after it on the altar of that one day. That one moment.

It was impossible not to be changed by it. But it was tragic to be destroyed by it.

She reached down, moving her thumb along the edge of his jaw, tracing that square line to the center of his chin. Then, she tilted his face upward.

The stark, raw regret in his eyes almost made her want to turn away. To let them both hide in the dark. It was easier. It let them both hold their pain close while they sought pleasure in each other's bodies. This forced them to open the vein, share it. It wasn't only her being exposed by this. Not only her scars, but his.

It cost her deeply to admit that. To acknowledge that he had been hurt by this too. That his mistakes had caused him pain. She had wanted to claim every last bit of it. Had wanted to make it all about her. Had wanted so badly for him to be a one-dimensional villain.

But now she just saw them for what they were. Two people who were wounded. Who had been wounded long before her car had hit that tree.

He wrapped his arms around her, his hands pressed against her lower back. He turned his face into her, his stubble-roughened cheek scraping against the tender skin on her stomach. She wrapped her arms around him, holding him there, holding them both together for just a moment.

She wanted to hold on to him forever. This man, this man whom she had long believed to be the source of all of her pain. This man who was—in this moment—the source of all of her comfort. Right now, everything outside of this room seemed completely uncertain. But there was this. There was him.

They stayed like that for a long moment, their ragged breathing the only sound in the otherwise silent room.

He was the first one to move, unsnapping the button on her jeans, drawing the zipper down slowly.

She closed her eyes while he undressed her, the shifting fabric against her skin sending little jolts of electricity through her. It felt amazing. Like it always did when they were together. Like it always did when he touched her. But there was something more to this too. Something deeper. That terrified her. But not enough to stop.

He placed his hands on her bare hips, then let his fingertips drift down her legs, back to her thigh, then back up to the part of her midsection where she had been left most scarred from the skin graft.

He closed his eyes, leaning in, his face against the ruined skin something she found she couldn't feel. Her throat tightened, tears blurring her vision. She kept on watching him, even as the first tear fell, then the second. When he moved away from the scar, she could feel the heat from his mouth, the pressure of his lips.

Then they drifted back to the very worst scar, and she lost the sensation again. She took a deep breath, one that turned into a sob.

He stopped, looking back up at her, concern lighting his blue eyes.

"I can't feel that," she said, her throat so tight she could hardly force the words through it.

He released his hold on her, clenching his hands into fists, pressing them down against the hard floor, the muscles in his shoulders and arms tight. He lowered his head for a second, then raised it back up.

"I'm so sorry," he said. "I'm so sorry for everything that I took from you."

For the second time that day, she felt her knees give way. It was her turn to join him down on the floor. He pulled her over onto his lap, holding her naked body up against his clothed one.

She couldn't tell him that it was okay. That she didn't need the apology. That he didn't have to say it. Because she *did* need it. She let it wash over her like a wave. But when it ended, nothing had changed. The scars were still there. And so was his tattoo.

She reached down, pressing one fingertip down against the dark ink on his forearm. She stared at the mark while she moved her fingertips over it, following the line around his entire arm.

"I'm sorry that you were my lesson," he said. "It's not fair. Not a damn thing about it is fair."

She looked up at him, her eyes never leaving his.

"Well, my scars and your tattoo aren't going anywhere, are they?" She pressed her palm over the mark on his skin. "All the regret, all the blame, all the anger and all the apologies in the world won't make them go away."

"I chose to put the tattoo on."

"And I chose to let my scars define me. We make choices. Sometimes we make choices that just make us miserable."

"I don't deserve for you to sit here and try to make me feel better." He lowered his head, kissing her shoulder. "I don't deserve any of this. I don't deserve to touch you."

"But I want you to."

He grabbed hold of the back of her head, pulling her face down and kissing her intensely. She shifted, parting her thighs so that his denim-covered arousal was pressed tightly against her aroused flesh. Even with all of this, all of the pain, all of the difficult truth between them, she wanted him.

"It doesn't make a damn bit of sense, baby," he said, pulling away for a second, more questions than answers in his dark eyes.

"Sometimes I think I don't make any sense. That everything inside me is just too messed up. Maybe I need a guy who's just as messed up as I am to finally help me put things in order."

He growled, wrapping one arm around her waist and reversing their position so that she was lying down on the floor, her body cushioned by a small, braided rug. He took his clothes off quickly, giving her a perfect view of his incredible body.

Impossibly, she felt a smile curve her lips.

"What?" he asked.

"I remember the first time I saw you without a shirt. I thought it wasn't fair. How perfect your skin was. Now, I kinda think maybe it's fair enough. You being so beautiful for me. And me…"

He took hold of one wrist, then another, drawing her arms up over her head and pinning them to the floor. "I want you," he said, his voice rough. "Don't you dare try to tell me that you're what I deserve because you aren't beautiful." He swallowed hard. "I don't know how I can say the scars are beautiful. Not when I put them there."

"You didn't. A tree did." Her throat burned, another piece of her carefully cultivated armor falling away. "It was an accident, Gage. Even if you did something wrong, you didn't mean to hurt me."

"It doesn't matter."

"Yes, it does. Because if you had taken your hands and put them on me and hurt me on purpose, then we wouldn't be here now. There would be no coming back from that." She pulled against his hold, firm, but not uncomfortable on her wrists. "But look at us now. I trust you to do this. What you mean to do matters. It changes it. It changed what's possible for the future. You didn't intend to hurt me. It was an accident."

Saying it, believing it, was just another challenge for her. It stole more of her anger, more of that righteous fury that she had chosen to direct at him for so long.

She had said so many times that she couldn't absolve him. That it wasn't her job. That it wouldn't change anything or fix anything.

But just then, something broke loose inside of her, and she realized that it would change everything. That she had to do it. Until she did, she was still holding on to the anger, she was still blaming him. Still punishing him.

"I forgive you," she whispered.

She felt his body shudder against hers, and he released his hold on her wrists, grabbing hold of her face, sliding his thumbs over her cheekbones, over the tears that were falling there on her face, tears she had barely been aware she had shed. And then, he kissed her. It was more than a kiss. He was consuming her. As though he were bent on taking every ounce of absolution from her lips, from her very soul.

Like a man possessed he kissed her, his tongue thrusting deep, his muscles trembling. And when he finished, they were both shaking. Then, he moved away from her, going for his discarded pants, grabbing his wallet out of the back pocket and taking a condom out of it.

"I need you," he said, his every word tortured.

In that moment, she wanted to be there for him. Wanted this to be something that healed them both. For the first time, she really did care about what this did for him.

She didn't know if it would heal them. Or if it would break them. Maybe it would do both. Maybe both needed to happen. The thought didn't really make sense, but her thoughts were muddled, by emotion, by desire. She supposed it didn't matter either way.

She wasn't turning him away, regardless.

He came down over her, between her spread thighs, kissing her again before he pressed his fingertips against her collarbone, drawing them down over her breast, over the tightened, sensitized nipple there. He pinched her gently before continuing. His fingers skimming over a web of scars on her stomach before moving to her thigh. He gripped her tight, pulling her up into a sitting position, then he lifted them both from the ground, taking them to the armchair that was by the fire. He sat down, bringing her down over him, so that she was straddling him, the damp entrance of her body open to the thick, blunt tip of his cock.

He flexed his hips, teasing them both with near penetration. She held on to his shoulders, boldly meeting his gaze as he slipped inside her about an inch, then pulled out again, the ridge on the head his arousal creating a slick, delicious friction inside of her.

"Gage," she gasped. "I need you."

IT WAS THE simple admission that did him in. Utterly, completely. That simple, perfect admission of need. It was when he lost his control. When he couldn't hold himself back any longer.

Gage flexed his hips, pushing his cock deep inside of her, gritting his teeth, trying to keep himself in check as her tight warmth closed around him.

She slid her hands down his chest, that wonderful, unpracticed touch testing his resolve in a way he couldn't have taught her. He didn't want it to end like this. Didn't want it to end too fast. He owed her better than that.

He grabbed hold of her wrists again, this time pinning her arms behind her back with one of his hands, taking the other and gripping her chin with his thumb and forefinger, drawing her down for a kiss while he pushed up deeper inside of her.

He swallowed the raw sound that rose up in her throat as he pushed himself in and out of her, still holding her fast, holding her captive.

He released his hold on her chin, moving his hand

down to cup her breast, teasing her tight nipple with his thumb until the color deepened, until she was gasping for more. Until she claimed his mouth with her own, kissing him as he continued to move inside of her, kept on teasing her aroused body.

She struggled against his hold, and he held on to her more tightly. "Let me," he said, skimming his lips over her cheek, along the line of her jaw and down her neck, sliding his tongue over her collarbone. "Let me," he repeated.

He fastened his lips over the center of her breast, sucking her in deep. Then, he released his hold on her wrists, grabbing hold of her hips, strengthening the force of his thrusts, pulling her down against him as he moved up, increasing the friction, increasing the intensity in each clash of their bodies.

He was lost in this, in this moment, watching her dark eyes glaze with pleasure every time he came into contact with her sweet clit, every time he went deep. And when she finally came, as her internal muscles tightened around him, her release coming from deep inside of her, he watched her face. Watched her expression as she gave herself up to pleasure.

It felt like absolution for his soul. It felt like every bit of forgiveness he had ever needed.

He surrendered himself to it. Let all of his defenses drop. He had no control here, no more to offer her. All he could do was take. Take each and every bit of that redemption that was on offer. Like it was his last breath, his last chance. Like it was the only thing that could ever save him.

He gave it all up. Gave himself up in a release that was enough to shatter his bones.

He grabbed hold of her hair, tugging her head backward, pressing his lips to her throat, holding her like that until the storm in him subsided.

When it passed, he picked her up, laying them both down across the couch, resting his head on her stomach. Her arms came up around him, holding him against her, her fingers laced through his hair.

It was hard to remember the last time he'd been happy. He wasn't sure this was happiness. But he was lighter than he'd been for a long time. Still, he didn't remember happiness hurting quite like this. Maybe it was impossible to feel anything without a little bit of pain when you knew how heavy the world could be. When you knew the cost of everything.

When he'd been young, he hadn't imagined the cost. His daddy had paid for everything, so as far as he had seen, it was all free. It was what his father was still doing. Paying for everything, trying to cover things that money would never be sufficient for.

He smiled, just a little bit, and he felt a piece of glass shift inside his chest, cutting him a little bit deeper while he let the moment roll over him. While he let this, *her*, mean something. It felt good, and it felt bad too. But he'd had a lot of years of just bad; he imagined she had too.

Right now, there was forgiveness, and she was holding him. So he would just focus on that. And let the rest take care of itself.

For a little while, at least.

CHAPTER EIGHTEEN

REBECCA WOKE UP with a start. She opened her eyes, and found herself staring at her living room ceiling. She was lying on her couch, an unfamiliar weight resting on her stomach. Gage. She was holding on to his shoulders, resting in exactly the same position she had been since they'd finished making love.

It was getting dark outside, which meant they must have been sleeping for at least an hour. It got dark early this time of year, so she doubted it was very late. She never left her store early, but today she had. Today she had had a complete nervous breakdown on the floor then come back and got naked in front of Gage with the light on.

"Gage?" she asked, moving her hand down his back.

He stirred beneath her touch, shifting and looking up at her, a wicked half smile on his face. Her heart fluttered, her stomach turning over. She felt… She felt tender and new. She felt exposed, and she wasn't entirely sure if it was good or bad.

She didn't want to run away though. She didn't want to have a fight. She supposed maybe that was a good thing.

"I'm awake," he said.

His brown hair was rumpled, his eyes sleepy. This was so intimate. Waking up with him like this. Looking at him. She wasn't covered by a blanket, wasn't covered by anything. For once, she wasn't covered up at all.

"Yeah, you look awake," she said, lifting her hand and brushing a lock of hair out of his face.

Her heart ached. Looking at him like this, a little bit mischievous, a little bit boyish and a bit less tortured… It made her feel a bit tortured, and she couldn't quite say why.

"Are you hungry?" he asked, his voice gravelly.

"Starving. But it's my turn to cook for you."

She wiggled out from under him, standing up, searching the room for clothes.

"Do you need clothes?" he asked, reading her mind.

"We went over this. Potential health code violations and everything…"

"I solemnly swear not to report your food handling violations to the state of Oregon."

She shot him a stern glare, then moved across the small room and into the kitchen. "I am going to make you a Bear family special."

"I can't wait. I imagine it's tortilla based?"

"Yes. Because even now that is essentially the extent of my skills." She took a large stack of flour tortillas out of the fridge and a bag of preshredded cheese. Then, she fished around until she found her sandwich grill.

She set about making the world's most basic quesadillas, which the two of them ended up eating naked on the couch.

"I've been mad at you for a long time," she said, chewing thoughtfully.

"I've been mad at me too."

She nodded. "I'm not now. When I said I forgive you, I meant it." She did—that was the most amazing thing. She actually felt lighter, as though the weight were more than simply metaphorical, but as if there had been a literal ton of bricks sitting on her chest for the past seventeen years and finally releasing it made her breathe easier. Made everything seem different.

"It was never the scars," she said, the words costing her. "I mean, yes, I don't love them. And, it did impact my self-esteem, I'm not going to lie about that. But men are men, and plenty of them made it very clear that they would sleep with me if I wanted to. Some of them were jerks. Some of them acted like I should be grateful for the attention. But some of them were fine. I was the one that made the scars a big deal." She swallowed hard. "They've been the best suit of armor I ever could've asked for."

"Rebecca…"

"No, let me finish. Maybe this is uncomfortable for you to hear. It's kind of uncomfortable for me to say. But it doesn't make it any less true. They weren't…not an issue. But they weren't the issue that I pretended they were. They're not the reason that I was never with a guy. They're not the reason that I had trouble making friends. But it's the reason I gave to people. The reason that I gave to myself."

"I don't need to be let off the hook," he said. "Not to this degree."

"That's not why I'm doing it. Trust me. I have no problem making you suffer, you know that."

He laughed. "Yeah, I feel like things are changing though." She knew what he meant by that. That he thought maybe her judgment was clouded because she was getting attached to him. Because of the sex. Well, she couldn't exactly dispute that. But that didn't make this revelation any less real.

Now that she had moved the rest of the junk out of the way. The anger, all of the blame that she directed his way... She could see inside of herself a little bit clearer. The break in the wall that had begun back in the store earlier with Jonathan was continuing now.

"It doesn't matter," she said. "I mean, the way that I feel about you... What's happening between us... It doesn't change this. It doesn't change the truth. There are a lot of things in life we don't choose. I didn't choose these scars. But I definitely have chosen how to use them. I'm smart about it. Aren't we all? Like wounded animals. We figure out how to guard our pain."

She swallowed hard. "Nothing ever hurt worse than my mother leaving," she continued. "Nothing. But it was a lot easier to make you the villain there too. And I did. For a long time. I think Jonathan still does. Because if he doesn't, then maybe it's me, and I know he doesn't want that. And if I don't, then maybe it's me too."

"It was her," he said, his voice rough. "It was always her."

Those words settled uncomfortably inside of her. Because it was so easy for her to give her mother a pass. Because she had always let herself believe that maybe things were just harder for her. That maybe Jonathan was made of stronger stuff, that maybe Rebecca was too.

She had thought for a long time that it was because she was protecting her mother. Now, she thought it was just because she was protecting herself. Because behind all of that denial was a wall of rage so intense it might consume her completely.

"She left me," Rebecca said. "She left me. When I needed her the most. It was never your job to stay," she said, looking at Gage. "It was her job to stay with me no matter what. Because I was her daughter." It took all of her strength then, not to double over and howl in pain. This was why she had shielded herself from the reality for all of this time.

But from the moment Gage had walked into town layers had started stripping away. Like an old house being stripped down to the studs, to what created it, to what really made it. Without all of the excuses and the renovations to hide the truth.

And now, finally, she felt like they were at the center of it. At the heart of it.

"I think I hate her," Rebecca whispered, a tear sliding down her cheek.

Strong arms came around her, pulling her against his body. He stroked her hair, and the tender gesture only made her cry harder.

"I know I do," he said, his voice husky.

"It felt good to say it," she said, her voice muffled. "It doesn't fix anything though."

"Well, that doesn't really matter. What matters is

that it felt good, right?" He tightened his hold on her. "It's nice if you can feel good for at least a little while."

"Is that what you've been doing? All those years on the road? Trying to feel good just for a little while."

"I told myself that I was punishing myself. It sounded a lot more gallant than running away. Like I was denying myself something by being away from my family. But, you're probably closer to the truth."

"I was running away too. Just in place."

The moment she said it, she knew it was true. She thought back to all the little birds that decorated her shop. How much she liked them. How much she had always identified with them. They could go wherever they wanted but they always stayed in the same place.

She realized that's what she was doing. She was hiding right there in Copper Ridge, using it as an excuse too.

"You know what? It would've made more sense for me to leave."

"You think so?" he asked.

"Of course. I've always talked about how everyone here feels sorry for me, treats me like I'm special—or broken—because of my scars. All the men here know me. And that makes it hard. So I could go somewhere and make myself a stranger. A place that doesn't have my history. But then… How could I use it?" She laughed. "My family doesn't have any kind of great reputation, and I still stayed. Being a stranger somewhere would be an asset to me. I wouldn't be the abandoned, scarred daughter of a single mother. But, out there on the road you're not Nathan West's son. That doesn't help you at all."

He stiffened. "Well, that was part of it. I didn't want to be Nathan West's son. Not anymore. Not when I realized what all that meant."

She swallowed hard. "I would have been tempted."

"Tempted to do what?"

"To stay. To use all of the power. It's a 'get out of jail free' card. I've never had one of those. I mean, aside from my scars, which I used as best I could. That's what most of us do. We take the hard stuff, and we use it to our advantage. I know that your dad isn't great, but you could have used that."

"That's the problem," he said. "That's exactly what I would've done if I had stayed."

He leaned in, kissing her, hard and rough, cutting off the thread of the conversation. She had a feeling he did that on purpose.

But the kiss was hot, and sure, and it filled her with the kind of deep, sweet warmth that touched her in hidden, freezing places inside of her that had been cold for so long she had forgotten they could be anything else.

So she let him change the subject. Because she liked this one so much.

When they parted, they were breathing hard. He pressed his forehead against hers, looking at her, his dark eyes intent on hers.

She lifted her hand, tracing the deep grooves by his mouth. This man, her monster, was quickly becoming her very favorite thing and she wasn't sure what to do with that. It terrified her. Though, at least now she had an idea why.

It was the losing him, that was the thing that would hurt.

But she'd spent the greater part of the past seventeen years dwelling on pain in order to prevent herself from experiencing any more. She was going to let that rest. At least just for a little while. Something was happening. Something was changing.

He was changing her.

She wanted that too much to stop now. No matter how bad the impact of losing him might feel.

She supposed that should be terrifying. To the Rebecca she had been a few hours ago, it would have been. Depending on someone, admitting that she needed him in any capacity, would have been devastating.

She wasn't afraid of it now, and she couldn't quite pinpoint why.

"Are you going to stay tonight?" She tried to phrase the question casually, even though there was nothing casual about the way she felt. Her heart was rambling around her chest like a frightened mouse.

"Your bed is a little bit short for me."

"Actually, I think you're a little bit tall for my bed. Mattresses are a pretty standard size, Gage. You're the one that exceeds normal parameters."

"Was that a compliment?"

"Probably," she said, a smile tugging at her lips in spite of the fact that part of her was pretty sure he was just trying to make excuses to put some distance between them.

She didn't really think he was more distant now than he had been before. She was the one who was drawing a little bit closer. She was the one who had a little bit less armor than she had in the beginning. That was why she felt it now.

She was the one who had changed. It wasn't him. So, she could hardly take it personally now. That was what she told herself.

"I should probably go home," he said.

She waited for him to issue an invitation for her to come with him, but he didn't. She let the silence hang, for just a little bit longer than was natural. She was kind of pathetic.

"Okay," she said, trying not to reveal any disappointment.

He got dressed, and once he was completely covered up she felt silly sitting there naked. Like suddenly she fully realized that she'd been naked when before it had just felt right. A full, Garden of Eden situation happening right in her living room.

"Okay… I guess… I'll see you tomorrow when I come by to check on the horses."

He reached down, plucking her up off the couch and pulling her against him, kissing her. A wave of relief rolled through her. "See you tomorrow."

It wasn't exactly what she had wanted, but it was better than she'd thought she was going to get.

"Okay," she said, "tomorrow."

After he left, she settled onto the couch, and she felt a little bit happy that he had left. It was probably a good thing that she had a few moments to spend alone with her thoughts. It had been a hell of a weird-ass day.

She took a deep breath and got up, pouring herself a glass of wine, then pacing the length of the room.

She just walked for a moment, going over everything that had happened. She had forgiven him. She really had. It had released something inside of her. Had allowed her to let go of something she had been holding firmly in place for more years than she should have.

It made her think about her mother, about that wound inside of her that had been left behind when she had left. It was the big one, the one that she had never wanted to look closely at. The one she had never even wanted to take steps to heal because that would mean acknowledging that it was there in the first place. She didn't want to do that. It was too difficult.

But, now she knew it was what she had to do.

She looked over at her phone, chewing on her lip. It was probably a bit soon to call Jonathan. It wasn't like she was going to spend the rest of her life not speaking to him. But he might not answer. This might have been the last straw. Maybe it was the excuse he needed to finally cut ties with his needy younger sister.

Along with the acknowledgment that she was afraid of being left came some more crystallized thoughts about fear of abandonment than she would like.

She took a long swallow of wine, then picked the phone up. She opened her call list, and found Jonathan easily. He was the last person who had called her.

She sighed heavily. He had never done anything to deserve all of her fear and distrust. He had always been there. Even if he was surly, even if he showed his affection in his own way, he loved her.

She pressed the number, waiting as the phone connected then began to ring. She closed her eyes, anxiety building inside of her while she waited for him to pick up.

"Hello?" He answered. And she knew that he knew it was her. Because he sounded too grumpy to be responding to a stranger.

"Hi. I know you're still mad at me."

"Yep."

"That's fine. I just want to know... Do you know where our mother is?"

CHAPTER NINETEEN

WHEN REBECCA BEAR showed up on his doorstep bright and early, bundled up against the December chill—her dark hair hidden beneath a knit cap, her cheeks rosy from the wind, the tip of her nose bright red—Gage felt like he had been gut punched. He had been expecting her to come to the property, but he hadn't expected her to show up at his door.

Apparently, he needed adequate warning before he came into contact with her. He had most definitely needed a warning for last night. For how it would make him feel, for the distance he would need afterward.

It was a strange thing, to come into possession of something he had told himself he'd wanted for a long time.

To know she was okay. To find some form of forgiveness for his transgressions.

But he had it now. And he found there was still something missing.

Damned if he could figure out what it was.

He wasn't sure he wanted to.

"Good morning," he said. "You're up early. And you're wearing mittens."

"It's cold."

He had never thought of mittens as being erotic. Suddenly, he wanted her to press her mittened hands against his chest. That was just weird. But, that feeling, at least, he had a name for, and had a handle on. He could deal with being horny for her. It was the rest that concerned him.

"What's up? You look impish."

She crossed her arms and bounced slightly. "Aren't you going to let me in?"

He reflected on some of the other times she had come to the door. On how tense things had been. The aura of anger that usually wrapped itself around her. It wasn't there. Not now. She seemed different. Easy. And it wasn't just down to this specific interaction with him.

It was something that went deeper.

"You can come in. But you do have to give me a kiss first."

He expected her face to contort in irritation. Expected her to scoff at him. Instead, she leaned in easily, as though closing the distance between them were the most natural thing. Then, she put those mittened hands on his face—and damned if he wasn't right, that was erotic as hell—and pressed her lips to his.

When she parted from him, her cheeks were even redder, and this time he knew it wasn't from the cold. "Now can I come in?"

"Okay."

He moved to the side, and she brushed past him, removing her hat, scarf and gloves quickly. "I talked to my brother last night."

"You did?"

"He's still mad at me. It wasn't about us." She said that casually too. As if the two of them being an us was natural. "But I asked him if he knew where our mother is. He does."

"I thought she'd... Disappeared or something."

"She left us. And she doesn't see us. But, I'm not all that surprised that Jonathan kept tabs on her. I just never wanted to know. I spent a long time kind of pushing all of that to the back of my mind. I spent a long time making you the bad guy because it was easy. But I'm not doing that anymore. I'm kind of confronting things. And I want to keep doing it."

Something shifted inside him when she said that. He supposed forgiveness meant he wasn't the villain anymore. And that was even harder to wrap his head around. "Go on."

"If you aren't busy today... I want to drive down to Coos Bay and see my mom."

"Are you going to...call first?"

She shook her head, her dark hair swirling around her face. "No. I just thought I would go. But, I want you to come with me."

She was willing to drive a couple of hours south to go and see her mother, and he hadn't even physically gone to see his father since coming into Copper Ridge. Hadn't seen his mother. It galled him. And, something else that she said scraped against something inside of him that he was trying to ignore. The fact that he was throwing a whole bunch of things in front of issues he didn't want to deal with either.

"I can go down with you. Is the shop closed today?"

"I have a couple of teenagers that come and run it for me a few days a week. I asked one of them to fill in today. I just don't want to wait. I want to do this, or I'm going to lose my nerve."

"What are you going to... Say to her?"

"I'm going to ask her why she left."

She was bright eyed and hopeful, looking at him just then. It killed him to see her like that. At least that sharp-eyed, angry Rebecca he'd met when he arrived in Copper Ridge was insulated against hurt. This one? She was opening herself up to it. It made him want to grab her, shake her, ask if she was crazy. "Rebecca, you might not want the answer to that question."

"I know I don't. Because there isn't a good one. There just isn't. There isn't an excuse for leaving your children like that. But I need to know. I just need to do this. I'm spring cleaning my soul."

"It's December," he pointed out.

"It's metaphorical."

"And you think this is the best way to what... To change things? To heal things?"

"I can never heal the scars on the outside. But it may not be too late for the ones inside."

He looked down at her, at the hope in her eyes, and he hoped like hell that what she was saying was true. For her. Because he knew it was too late for him. Knew that it was too late to do any real redemption. Maybe that's what was bothering him. He had her forgiveness, and while it mattered, while it meant something, it didn't come with the fix that he had always hoped it might.

It was just one more piece of evidence that Gage West was damaged beyond repair.

He should walk away from her. Hell, he never should have walked into her life in the first place. Now, for some perverse reason, he agreed with the Rebecca he'd first met, who felt like he had no right to be in her life shaking things up.

But if he could fix this for her, if he had any part in doing something good for her, then he supposed it was worth it.

She was a better woman, a better person than he would ever be. And if he had never damaged her, he wondered what she might've become. Where she would be now.

She doesn't blame you, so maybe it's time you stopped blaming yourself.

He didn't like that. He didn't like it at all.

Maybe that was the other problem with accepting her forgiveness. He would have to give some to himself. And God knew where that might lead.

"Okay, I'll go with you. Do you want me to drive?"

"Please," she said. "I'm too nervous."

"I can hardly imagine you being nervous."

"The man who took my virginity while I trembled can't imagine me being nervous?"

Her words were like a direct kick from a horse, straight to the gut. "We both know you were only trembling because you wanted me so much."

That made her smile, and it resonated inside of him. Another bit of warmth, an unexpected bit of happiness. Another cut on his soul. "Okay, it was a little bit of that," she said.

He put coffee in a thermos and they got into his truck, starting the drive down the coastal highway to the small town of Coos Bay, Oregon.

Rebecca filled the silence with chatter, which was funny, because he had never taken her for much of a chatterer, but apparently when she was nervous she did a bit of it.

She told him about her first horse, and her second, about learning to ride and doing it even when her injuries hurt because it was the only thing that had brought her some comfort in the months and years after their mother had left. In the large amount of time she had learned to spend alone while her brother worked and she rattled around a small, empty house. It was why she had preferred the outdoors.

That made him wonder about something. He couldn't remember the last time he had wondered about another person, but he wondered about her endlessly.

"You love the outdoors, so why do you run a shop on Main Street? It seems to me like it's a pretty claustrophobic choice for somebody who spends all of her free time rambling around in the mountains."

She paused for a moment, a stretch of silence and road passing before she spoke again. "Because it's like a home. It's every great holiday, warmth and spice. I had a friend for a little while when I was growing up, and her mom used to put spices on the stove, not for any practical reason, just to make the house smell good. She decorated for every holiday. I mean, meticulously.

She kept it perfect. And it was so warm. To me, that was what home should be like. I had a house. Which, trust me I knew was lucky. Because if Jonathan wasn't willing to work as hard as he did I wouldn't have had that. But to have a home like that... I aspired to it. So, I guess I work in that home. My store is that slice of happiness I never had. And I want to give people a little piece of it. People who maybe don't have it. Or people who want to." She took a deep breath. "Other than the outdoors, it's pretty much the perfect place as far as I'm concerned."

"Why doesn't your house look like that then?"

He had a feeling it wasn't something he should ask. Had a feeling that he shouldn't take things deeper like this, not when it was so difficult for him to give anything else in return.

"I don't know. It just never seemed like I could."

Silence lingered between them for a moment before Gage spoke. "Sometimes I wonder which one of us is really punishing themselves, Rebecca."

It was the last thing either of them said before he pulled the car onto a narrow, two-lane road that turned into dirt, leading to a small trailer park just out of town. "According to the directions you gave me, it should be here," he said.

He watched as Rebecca clasped her hands in her lap, twisting at them nervously.

"Maybe nobody's home," he said.

She nodded slowly. "Maybe. Okay," she said, taking a deep breath, putting her fingers on the passenger side handle. "Will you come with me?"

An unexpected slug of emotion hit him in the chest. She had gone with him when he'd gone to the hospital to see his sister, and he had been happier about that than he would like to admit. All things considered, he supposed he needed to be with her now.

"Of course."

They got out of the truck and the two of them walked up to the small, faded yellow house with metal siding that was peeling up and a porch that seemed like it might collapse beneath the weight of the two of them.

She took a deep breath, raising her fist and knocking on the tin door, the sound hollow and unsatisfying.

Then the door opened, and Rebecca took a step back, leaning against his chest as though he were the only thing keeping her on her feet.

FOR THE SECOND time in the space of a few weeks Rebecca was staring down a person she had built up to be much larger in her mind that she was in reality. Much like Gage, her mother had become something of a legend in her imagination. Not a real person anymore, not an accurate memory.

The woman standing in front of her was, undoubtedly, her mother.

But she was faded, shrunken. As if the years had taken pieces off of her, reducing her to something much less than she'd been. Roundness becoming hollows. The color had leached from her hair, all of the rich black faded into a tarnished silver. Her brown skin had the look of rawhide about it, her lips like wrinkled paper. A smile would tear them, Rebecca was almost certain.

But the other woman didn't smile anyway. Perhaps it was for the best.

"Can I help you?" she asked, her voice as thin and fragile as the rest of her.

"I think so. I'm looking for Jessica Bear."

The older woman looked at her, her brown eyes cold, flatter than Rebecca remembered. "If you're going to serve me papers, I'm not going to take them."

"I'm not here to serve you papers," Rebecca said, her heart twisting gently. "I just wanted to see you." Wind whipped across the porch, blowing through brittle coastal grass making a sound a lot like broken glass. "I'm Rebecca."

What little color was in her mother's face drained away, but the hard, stoic expression remained. "If you're here for money, I don't have any of that anymore either. I would think that was pretty obvious."

From the perspective of the child, Nathan West had given Jessica enough money to make a new start. As an adult, Rebecca could better understand how all of that could drain away in seventeen years. Though, the situation was a bit more dire than she had expected it to be.

"I'm not here for money either. I really did just want to see you."

"Why?"

If Rebecca knew the answer to that, she would give it. But, she wasn't sure she possessed anything quite like deep insight at the moment.

"Just to see you," she said.

"Well," Jessica said, "you can come in if you like."

She moved away from the door, granting them admittance into a threadbare room that smelled like old smoke and firewood.

Her mother lit a cigarette and took a seat on the green couch in the corner. Rebecca opted to stay standing. Gage stood behind her, a wall of strength that she was grateful for since she felt at the moment she didn't have much of her own.

She looked around at the fake wood paneling that seemed to close in around them, and the heavy curtains covering each window as a rebellion against any kind of light.

Rebecca didn't know what to say. There was too much to say, and really, not enough to say. She didn't want to yell at her mother. Not now. Not because she felt sorry for her, not because life had clearly turned out nothing like she had imagined it would when she had run away from her children, from her bleak life, with the money that she had been meant to use to care for them. No, she didn't feel sorry for her because of that. That, in Rebecca's estimation was nothing short of karma.

She just wasn't angry. And she couldn't hate her.

Standing there, looking at the woman who seemed so reduced, so dry, Rebecca couldn't feel much regret that she had gone. And she couldn't feel at fault either.

Jessica Bear was immovable. As immovable now as ever. Stubborn. Tragic. Rebecca couldn't have made her leave any more than she could have made her stay.

"You doing all right?" Rebecca found herself asking, a question that her own mother hadn't bothered to pose.

But, she wasn't really Rebecca's mother. Not in any way that mattered. She had given birth to her, but Jonathan was the one who had stayed. He was the one who cared. Then there was Lane, and there was Alison and Cassie, Finn—who had been gallant, even while he was being a little bit of a cad.

There was Gage.

There were people in her life who mattered, who deserved to have more of her than this woman. This woman who had occupied so much of Rebecca's soul for so long.

Whose abandonment had dictated Rebecca's every action and emotion. For too long. For far too long. She didn't deserve it. And Rebecca was tired of giving it to her.

There was no angry outburst, no grand reckoning that would ever restore what was gone. There was only moving forward.

Realizing that the monsters were only monsters in her head.

"I don't need charity," her mother responded, "if that's what you're asking."

"I run a store on Main Street, in Copper Ridge," Rebecca found herself saying. "Jonathan owns a construction company. He does very well for himself."

The words seemed to bounce off of her mother, like rain against hard ground. Too dry to absorb anything. To let anything in.

"That so?" she asked, finally, no indication of whether or not she cared was reflected in that flat voice.

"Yes. He did a great job of taking care of me."

"This your boyfriend?" Her mother asked, gesturing to Gage.

Rebecca didn't quite know how to answer that. He wasn't her boyfriend, not really. And even if he were, that word wouldn't seem like quite enough.

"He's a friend," she decided to say.

Because she was discovering what all her friendships meant to her. How much they had saved her. The degree to which they had supported her over all these years, even when she hadn't given equally in return.

Calling him a friend didn't minimize him at all.

Her mother nodded, taking a drag on her cigarette. "Yeah, I had a lot of those friends."

Rebecca gritted her teeth. "He drove me here to see you. To support me. I don't know if you have any friends quite like that."

Her mother laughed. "Did you come here to make up?"

"I can't do that on my own," Rebecca said.

Her mother said nothing, crossing her leg over the other, jiggling her foot, rocking back and forth as she put the cigarette into her mouth again. "Guess not," she said, talking around it.

"I wanted to say that I forgive you. And I think I can do that without an emotional reunion. It's not really about you. It's just about what I want to hold on to now, and what I don't."

Jessica Bear shrugged her bony shoulders. "You can't forgive things like that," she said, drawing more tightly in on herself. "I never forgave your father for leaving us. There's no reason for you to forgive me."

"No, there isn't," Rebecca said. "But I'm doing it all the same."

"I don't want you to." Those words were full of spite, confusion.

As if Jessica Bear needed her daughter to be angry at her.

"I didn't ask," Rebecca said. "I need to do it for me. This has nothing to do with you. But I needed to come here. I needed to let it go. So I'm doing that. My store is called the Trading Post. If you ever want to come see me, you can."

Then she turned, walking out of the trailer, the first breath of cold, fresh air like breaking the surface of the water after too long under the surface.

She could feel Gage following behind her. She got into the truck, buckling herself, leaning her head against the cold window, willing herself not to cry. She wasn't going to shed any more tears. Wasn't going to let any more anger build inside of her.

Gage got into the truck then, starting the engine. "Do you want me to wait a second?"

"Just in case," Rebecca said. They waited, but her mother didn't come out of the trailer. Finally, Rebecca took a deep breath. "We can go."

"I'm sorry," he said.

Rebecca laughed. "I don't know what I expected. You can't really expect a woman who abandoned her children to receive one of them with open arms after seventeen years, can you?"

"I don't know. I mean, my own family didn't exactly open their arms to me, but it wasn't like that."

"Yeah, but you're the one that did the leaving. Not them. I know she doesn't feel things quite the same way other people do. Or maybe she does, and she just doesn't know what to do with it. I'll tell you one thing—I think she's angrier at herself than I've ever been at her."

He nodded slowly. "Accepting forgiveness when you know you don't deserve it isn't easy."

"If you're talking about yourself again…don't. You do deserve it. We both deserve to move forward."

"I do accept it. If only because I just saw what rejecting it looks like. And how little it helps."

"Thank you."

"So," he said, his tone lighter, like he was trying to put a Band-Aid on the situation. For some reason that bothered her, and she couldn't pinpoint why. "You want to go see a movie? They have a movie theater here."

She laughed, reluctantly. "I'm not exactly in a theatergoing mood."

"Fish and chips?"

"That I would take."

This hadn't gone quite the same as forgiving Gage had. She didn't feel free or light, not immediately. But she felt like something was changing. Like something important had just taken place. Even if it hadn't been a magic fix.

She looked to the side, at the man she was sharing the truck with. The man who had driven her all the way down here, who had stood there and witnessed all of that. It hadn't occurred to her to be embarrassed to expose that moment to him.

He was the keeper of all her secrets, after all. She just wished that he would give her more of his. Pointless maybe, but something that was starting to make her ache.

"Thank you," she said, "for coming with me."

He shrugged a shoulder. "I figured it was time I started giving more than I took."

CHAPTER TWENTY

SOMETHING ABOUT THE words that Gage had spoken in the truck dug at her all through dinner, and all through the ride back to Copper Ridge.

She wondered if she was just feeling unsettled because of what had happened with her mother. There really was no guidebook for how to deal with that. A strange, unsettling reunion that had put so many fragmented pieces back into place, but had solidified the fact that there would probably never be a magical reconciliation.

But it was more than that.

I figured it was time I started giving more than I took.

She turned those words over until they pulled into Gage's driveway. It was unspoken that they would have sex again. The only question had been which house he would choose to go to. She imagined the fact he had chosen his made it less ambiguous. Made it clear that she was supposed to come in and stay a while.

She wondered if he would want her to stay the night. In which case, she should probably get some things from her house. But, she didn't want to broach that subject. She didn't want to seem needy.

Her thoughts kept on spinning like that as she walked up the steps and into the house. As soon as they closed the front door behind them, he turned, drawing her into his arms, up against his chest.

"Let me fix it," he said, kissing her on the neck.

And suddenly, everything clicked into place. Exactly why those words he had spoken in the truck hit her wrong. Exactly what was wrong with all of this.

"That's all you've done. From the moment you came back to town. Fix things. Whether I wanted you to or not."

He released his hold on her slowly, taking a step back. "I came with you today because you asked me. Are you really going to start pretending like you didn't want any of that?"

"Of course I did. I asked for it. But, then you go into this self-loathing space where you start talking about breaking things. About how you've broken me. I don't know why you do it."

"It's called owning up to my mistakes."

"No," she said, slow realization dawning over her. "I don't think that's it."

"You think you know me? You think you know what I'm doing and why better than I do?"

"I can't answer that. You might know what you're doing. You might even know why you're doing it. But you're not being honest with me. I would bet you aren't being honest with yourself either."

"Is that what we're going to do now? We're going to have a therapy session? Because I was hoping that we could just fuck."

The words hit her like a stark slap. And as much as she wished that she could be angry about them, as much as she expected to be, she wasn't. She couldn't be. She realized then that this was what had to happen. He had walked back into her life playing the part of benevolent benefactor.

The contrite and tragic figure that had ruined her life, come to set things to rights. He had cast her in the role of angel, put up on a pedestal, beautiful and tragic. And he had cast himself in the role of villain seeking absolution. But there was no nuance to that. No reality. And it helped no one.

He was comfortable this way. Giving, and giving while taking nothing in return. Calling himself terrible at every turn while never once proving it to her.

"Is that what you need?" she asked.

She cared. She found that she cared desperately. She was on a mission. A mission to exorcise every demon inside of her. And he was keeping his locked up tight inside of him. It hadn't gotten better since she'd told him that she'd forgiven him. It hadn't changed anything for him. It had changed everything for her.

But she couldn't reach him. He made it impossible. She could see that now. That he was somewhere deep inside of himself, behind the walls that he had built up around his soul. That he was more deeply protected than she had ever been. He was willing to come in and call himself all kinds of terrible things. Willing to take the brunt of everything.

But he wouldn't open up. He wouldn't let anyone in.

Least of all her. Suddenly, she felt desperate. Desperate to break him open. Desperate to reach him.

"Don't ask me what I need," he said, obviously angry that she was.

"Why not? Why shouldn't I ask you what you need? You've spent all this time taking care of me, coddling me like I was a baby bird."

"Right. I treated you so gently all the times I forced my lust on you."

"Right. All of that horrible oral sex and endless orgasms. You really are a monster."

"Don't wilfully misunderstand. You know what I mean."

"Yes, I do know what you mean. Better than you do."

"Stop it, Rebecca. I didn't want to have a fight with you. Especially not after what you went through today…"

"Don't make it about me." She was filled with anger now, fury, because she was starting to realize just what an illusion their time together had been. She felt like they had been opening themselves up to each other. She had felt like, because she knew so many of his secrets, she knew him too. But she had never reached him. Had never seen him. He was hiding behind his mission—this supposed mission to care for her—to atone for his sins.

He had walked into her life and changed everything. And he was determined to walk back out again exactly the same as he had appeared.

She didn't want that. She wanted him just as destroyed and altered as she was. She wanted him to be irrevocably and completely changed by this. To be healed.

But she could see, even now, in the flat darkness of his eyes that he wasn't going to accept it.

"You wanted to give me the store. You wanted to give me pleasure. You made me dinner. You went with me to see my mother. And still, you act like you have more to atone for. But I can't continually offer you that without you giving me anything in return. It doesn't work. One person can't change while the other one stands there. One person can't give endlessly."

"Maybe in a relationship, but this isn't really a relationship."

His words hurt. They cut deep, even though they were true. Even though it was nothing more than what they had talked about.

"Well, you want to fix things. You want to make me happy. What if I told you I wanted more?"

"That won't fix anything for you."

"Right. Because you're only going to do exactly what fits within your idea of how fixing me works. Only you can do it, and only for a limited time, because then you have to walk away. Because you're so terrible."

She was digging at him now, pressing against the wound, because it was the only way she was going to get a reaction out of him. She knew it.

"Rebecca…"

"Show me. You keep telling me what a terrible man you are, all while fixing me dinner and giving me amazing sex. Maybe it's time you show me. Stop talking about how awful you are and give me some of it."

"You don't want that."

"No," she said, "you don't want that. Because that

would mean showing me something of yourself and you're too afraid to do that. I'm not afraid of how terrible you are. You're the one that's afraid of it. I can handle it. I'm not weak. I never have been. And I'm tired of people treating me like I am. You were the one person that I thought understood. But now, I think you're going out of your way to not understand. If I'm not the victim, where does that leave you?"

She found herself being hauled up against him, his hold hard, punishing. Borderline bruising. "This is what you want? You want to see me being terrible?"

"If it's honest."

"I don't think you want my honesty, Rebecca."

"Stop telling me what I want, Gage. I have never been the tragic waif sitting around waiting for you to come back and redeem her. Never. I had a life, and I had to live it the best way that I could. I've admitted that it wasn't actually all that functional. But that had nothing to do with you either. That was all me. So I don't need you to come in here and clean up all of my messes so you can ride out into the sunset feeling good about yourself, or bad about yourself still, or whatever it is you're trying to do."

She reached up, grabbing hold of his chin, holding his face steady. "Show me what a selfish bastard you are."

Show me what a selfish bastard you are.

Those words ignited something inside of him. Something that he had tried to keep repressed since he had first seen Rebecca. Hell, it was something he'd tried to keep repressed for the last seventeen years.

She was pushing. Because she thought that if she pushed hard enough she would find something good down underneath all that. She was pushing because she thought that she could heal him.

Everything in him rebelled at that thought. She was wrong. And if she wanted him to prove that, then he would.

"Don't you dare ask me if I'm sure," she said, her dark eyes burning into his. "Don't you dare treat me like I'm broken. I'm not broken. I think I've proven that."

She might not be broken now, but maybe she would be broken after this. Maybe they both would be. That thought made his chest tighten up, made him feel like someone had reached inside of him and grabbed hold of his heart.

"What's wrong?" she asked, her tone goading. "Do I scare you, Gage?" She slid her hands down his chest, her fingernails raking across the thin material of his T-shirt. "You're such a big, bad man, but I'm the one that scares you."

He grabbed hold of her wrist, holding her steady, staring her down. He said nothing, taking his other hand and working at his belt, then flicking open the button on his jeans, before tugging the zipper down.

"You want me to be selfish?" he asked. "You want to know what I want? The kind of thing that I fantasize about, that I want only for me? I want you down on your knees in front of me. I want to watch you take me into your pretty mouth before you suck me hard."

The words hit him hard as iron, even while he felt

sick in the pit of his stomach over what this had brought him to. Over what she had brought him to.

Her breath quickened, her breasts rising and falling with the movement, color high in her cheeks.

Tell me to go to hell, he pleaded silently.

If she walked out the door, away from this, away from him, it would give him time to get a hold of himself. To get a grip on his control. Right now, if she stayed, there would be no going back. He couldn't treat her the way that he wanted to, he couldn't treat her the way that he needed to.

But she didn't.

Slowly, Rebecca sank down to her knees in front of him. She leaned forward, her chestnut hair cascading over her face in a glossy curtain, hiding her from him. Then, her delicate fingers found him inside of his underwear, wrapping around his aching cock, squeezing him tight.

Sweet, slick heat consumed him as she flicked the edge of her tongue along the hard ridge of his shaft.

He grabbed hold of her hair, using it as an anchor, pulling it away from her face so that he could watch exactly what she was doing. She looked up at him, a challenge visible deep in those dark eyes.

She tasted him slowly, without skill, moving her tongue from the head of his dick all the way down to the base, then back up again.

"Stop," he said, the word a hard command.

She did, her gaze watchful, waiting for the next order.

"If this is for me," he said, "then take your top off. Let me see you."

He let go of her hair for a moment, waiting for her to make the next move. She rocked back slightly, grabbing hold of her T-shirt and yanking it over her head, then unhooking her bra and sending it flying across the room.

She placed her hands in her lap, sitting in front of him wearing her jeans and nothing else. He was completely transfixed by the sight of her. By her perfectly formed breasts, that beautiful golden skin.

Selfish. She wanted him to be selfish? She wanted him to be terrible? It would never end. It was a well inside of him, deep and yawning, never satisfied because he never allowed himself to replenish it.

Never allowed himself to admit just how much he needed something like this. How much he needed another person.

For seventeen years he had walked through life without forging any deep connections. Staying one step ahead of the howling demon inside of him that was so desperate, so lonely, if he ever let it catch up to him it would consume him completely.

It had caught up to him now in a raging torrent of need, a dark beast that had sunk its teeth deep into his throat, shaking hard.

He reached out, wrapping her long hair around his fist, drawing her face back forward toward him.

She pressed her hands against his thighs, parting her lips and taking him in, a sweet, shallow tasting that was reflective of her inexperience.

The best part about a blow job in Gage's estimation was the anonymity. It was easy to close his eyes and feel. It allowed him to detach completely from what was happening. At least, that was how it had been in every other situation.

It was impossible to pretend that this was anyone other than Rebecca. And he didn't even want to. He wanted it to be her, down on her knees in front of him, making him feel like this. Need burned inside of him, hot and reckless. And he couldn't see an end to it. He wanted more. More and more, and he didn't think it could ever be satisfied. The deeper she took him, the slicker the slide of her hot, unpracticed tongue, the more that he wanted.

He laced his fingers through her hair, holding her tightly as she continued to torture him. He could stay like this forever. It still wouldn't be enough.

Need consumed him, suffused him. He couldn't remember the last time he had been desperate for another person. Not just for their touch, not just for sexual completion, but for them. Never. It had never happened.

But he was desperate for her, needed her, the wall of stone he had placed in front of his soul cracking open, dark, messy need pouring out all around them.

She wrapped her hand around the base of him, sliding her tongue up his length, her eyes meeting his, a shot of heat and pleasure shooting down his spine, gathering at the base, tension gathering low and hard inside of him.

"No," he said, his voice rough. "Rebecca, not like that."

"Why?" she asked, her face flushed, her eyes glittering with pleasure. "Because then you'll have to admit that I get pleasure just from being with you. Not your hands, not your… Not your cock, not your mouth. Just you? That you're the one that turns me on? That you're the one I want?"

Her words washed over him like a wave, leaving devastation in their wake. Every soft, delicate truth that spilled from her tongue moving mountains inside of him.

Right now, she was more than a woman. She contained a tsunami, and she possessed the ability to destroy everything that he was.

Still, he didn't pull away.

"No," he said, his voice rough, hauling her up to her feet. "Because then I wouldn't be inside you when I came."

Her mouth dropped open, the color in her cheeks higher, shock, desire darkening her eyes. "Did I shock you?" he asked. "Does it surprise you to know how much I want to be buried in you? To feel you all around me?" He turned his head, pressing his face to the curve of her neck, inhaling deeply, the soft scent of hay, soap and Rebecca. "Do you want me? Do you really?"

It had started out as a game. A game to see if he could make her cheeks turn a brighter color, to see if he could shock her. But now, now he just needed her to say it. He needed it more than he needed his next breath.

The challenge of her last words echoed through him. She was right. He was afraid to admit it. But he needed to hear it. That she wanted him. That she wanted this.

More than that, that she needed this.

That he was more than an antivenin. More than just

an antibody of the same poison that had brought about her wounds in the first place.

That this woman, this strong, beautiful woman wanted him. That when he left here, she would still think of him. That she would burn for him. That part of her would always wait for him to come back.

You bastard, that's the last thing you should want. You should want her to forget you.

Why?

It was the first time he had ever questioned why. Why he felt like he had to leave. Why he was so comfortable being the villain.

If I'm not the victim, where does that leave you?

He pushed all of that out of his mind, picking Rebecca up and carrying her up the stairs, holding her so close that he knew she could feel his raging heartbeat.

He deposited her onto the center of the bed, his blood a slow burn that he knew would catch fire the moment he touched her again. He stood back, pulling his shirt up over his head, standing before her with his jeans open, the evidence of how much he wanted her obvious, thanks to the steel jut of his cock, begging for her touch again.

He was so hard it hurt. That need, that specific, all-consuming need nearly undoing him completely. "Tell me you want me," he said, the words coming out low and rough, completely without his permission.

It was Rebecca's turn to take off her remaining clothes, to lay down on the bed and spread herself before him like a carnal buffet. "You first," she said, soft words shot through with iron.

"I want you," he said, shoving his jeans and underwear down and leaving them on the floor.

He moved to the bed, kneeling in front of her, his hands shaking as he placed his palms against her thighs, stroking her up to her hips, holding her tight as he looked into her eyes. "You. I want you."

"Why?" she asked.

Because I need you.

But he didn't say that. "Because you're beautiful."

"No. If it was all about being beautiful, then you would have someone else. Why do you want me?"

A shiver worked its way down his spine, evidence of frustrated desire, he told himself. Because he didn't want to know what else it could be. "Because you're strong. Because you can take me, and I don't think anyone else can."

Those words came from deeper in his soul than he would've liked, cut closer to the bone than he had intended.

"Then give it all to me," she said, grabbing hold of his shoulders, urging him up. "Give it to me."

He moved, pressing his hands into the mattress on either side of her face, leaning down so that his lips were a breath away from hers. "Tell me you want this."

"I don't want this," she said.

The spike of pain that stabbed his chest took his breath away. Then Rebecca grabbed hold of his chin, holding his face steady. "I don't want sex or experience, I don't want the orgasms I was deprived of over the years. I want you. I want you, Gage West. So deep inside of me I can barely breathe."

He growled, reaching over to the nightstand, quickly procuring a condom and rolling it onto his length. Then he pressed against her slick, tight entrance, his muscles tensing as he thrust home, desperate to be inside of her. Surrounded by her. To give her what she said she wanted.

To give himself what he knew he needed.

He let every word, every worry, every truth, burn into bright light. Nothing in his mind but the white-hot burn of pleasure. He pushed it all away, held it at bay. Because as close as he had been to losing it before he had joined his body to hers, it would send him over the edge now.

So he let this consume him. The feel of her, the scent of her. Delicate fingertip sliding down his back, soft, feminine sounds of pleasure, the way that her thighs parted just for him. The way that he fit there, not comfortably. Nothing about this could ever be called comfortable. It was too much. Too hot, too tight. But it was the only thing he wanted.

She was the only thing he wanted.

It wasn't perfect, sweet satisfaction and it never would be. It cut too deep for that. It hurt too much.

Fingernails dug into his skin, her internal muscles tightening around him as she found her own release. And he was powerless to fight against that. He could do nothing but surrender. The sharp edge of his orgasm stabbed deep like a knife, stealing his breath, making it impossible for him to do anything but hold on to her while a bomb burst inside of him.

It left everything in him ruined, devastated, the jagged bits of his release biting into him, leaving their mark, burying themselves so deep he knew they would be there forever.

He would never be the same. Rebecca Bear had left scars on his soul that would never go away.

He pressed his head down, resting his forehead on her shoulder. She stroked his face, his back, his arms, touching him everywhere she could reach. As if, even after that she wasn't satisfied.

He felt the same thing. The dark, devastating sense of dissatisfaction even as he lay there replete, barely able to move. It was terrifying. Overwhelming. Enough to make a grown man want to turn tail and run.

"Gage," she said, the word splintered. "Gage, I love you."

CHAPTER TWENTY-ONE

REBECCA COULDN'T QUITE believe that she had spoken the words out loud. She couldn't quite believe that they were true. And yet she had, and they were.

She was still digesting that when Gage moved away from her, like she was a snake who had just struck at him.

"I'm going to ignore that," he said, his voice rough. He started hunting around, for his clothes presumably. As though he were desperate to put some layers between them.

And after all that, she wasn't particularly surprised. That was the most open he'd been. The most honest. It was there, not just in his words, but in the way his hands shook when he had touched her.

When she had stripped away all of his excuses. That layer that he put up between himself and the world, the one that provided every excuse for why he did what he did, and why it was for other people and never for him, had begun to unravel.

And it was continuing now.

"You're going to ignore it, and then you're going to run away?"

He froze. "It would be better for you if I did."

"Bullshit. Absolute bullshit. It would be better for *you* if you did. That's what this has all been about. From the beginning." Anger poured through her, a different kind than she could remember feeling before where he was concerned. This wasn't for herself. It was for him. For everything that he denied himself underneath the guise of being undeserving.

For every lie that he told himself as he let himself walk down a darker, lonelier road. For what? She couldn't figure it out.

She wanted to grab hold of him, wrench him open, force him to show her exactly what was hidden inside of him. She knew he was hiding. She knew it. She just didn't know what.

She looked up at him, at the beautiful, blank wall that was Gage, and she wanted to fold in on herself with pain, anger and frustration. But she was done with that. Done with hiding.

She would be damned if she would let him carry on.

"Why? You still didn't show me why I should hate you. Why I should be afraid of you. Why you're self-ish. You think that I'm going to be impressed by you making me get on my knees and do something I wanted to do anyway?"

"Rebecca," he growled.

"Gage," she said, planting her hands on her hips, staring him down. She was naked, and she was not ashamed. She didn't feel damaged, she didn't feel disadvantaged. She felt strong.

It was a different kind of strength than the one she'd been convinced that she had when this man had first walked back into town, back into her life. It wasn't brittle. The foundation wasn't bitterness, a root that ran deep but was poison for all concerned.

No, this was different.

She had spent the past seventeen years being broken. Believing she was broken beyond repair and reveling in that pain. Using it to keep people at a distance, using it to give herself excuse after excuse not to risk herself. Not to try.

And here she was, risking herself in the deepest, most profound way she ever had. With this man. The man she had spent so many years blaming for all of her pain.

But that wasn't who he was, any more than the scars were who she was.

She didn't think he believed that was all he was either. But he was going to stick to that story. Was going to continue to use it, just as she had done.

"You're just as much of a liar as I am," she said, the words void of anger. "You took this thing that happened, this terrible thing, and you let it define you. You used it as your protection. As your excuse to leave. But I want to know what really happened. I want to know what's happening inside of you now. I want to know why you don't think you deserve to be happy. And please don't tell me it's because you left me with a few scars."

"And a limp. And all of the other hidden things that cause you pain every day," he said, his voice rough.

"I believe that you feel guilty about that, Gage. And I'm sure that there isn't much I can do to change that. So, I'm going to need you not to pity me if we're going to spend more time together. Because I can be a person you care about. I can be a woman that you want. I'd really like to be the woman that you love. But I can't be a woman that you pity. Whether you mean it to be or not, you living like this holds both of us back. You're forcing me to continue to dwell in it, and I don't want that. So if you care about me at all, if your guilt is really about me and not about you, then you need to change the way that you deal with things."

"Of course it's about you," he said, his voice like gravel.

"No," she said, new certainty infusing her tone. "It isn't. It never was."

"You don't think I feel bad about this? You think I'm some kind of monster? I thought we were past that."

"Don't you dare turn this on me, Gage West. I do think you feel bad. I said as much. But I don't think it's the thing that kept you running for seventeen years. If this is really all about becoming your father, if this was really all about you being angry because he didn't face up to his own mistakes, then you would have done something differently."

"You don't understand," he said, raging suddenly. He took a step toward her, then another. She took a step back, until her shoulder blades butted up against the wall. He pressed his hands to the smooth surface, on either side of her face. "It was so easy to let him fix it. So easy to take that out. And I could see myself sliding down the slippery slope. Being the kind of man who would end up just like that."

She looked up at him, at those dark eyes that were

so close to hers, and yet, not looking at her. "I don't be-lieve you," she said softly.

He pushed away from her, forking his fingers through his dark hair. "You're going to tell me what I feel now?"

"Why not? It's what you've been trying to do to me since you came back. Telling me what I should accept, telling me how I should think of you. Well, let me tell you something. I've decided how I feel about you. I've decided who you are based on what I've seen, not what you've told me. You're the man who took so much care with my body when you took my virginity. The man who went to see his sister after she gave birth, even though it wasn't easy. The man who came back to deal with his family's issues after so many years detached from it, because when push comes to shove, you're the kind of man who will be there. You don't let people go, Gage. You're not sliding down any slippery slope, and you never have been." She swallowed hard, conviction burning in her chest. "You care too much. Too much for other people who aren't you. Nothing about being back here benefits you, not really. This isn't for you."

"Oh, you have no idea how much this was for me," he said. "How much all of this was for me. From com-ing back here in the first place to the first moment I put my hands on you. That's the only thing I know how to do, Rebecca. And no matter how far I run, it stays the same. I know how to please me. I know how to serve me. That's it. Doesn't matter what I say I want to do, doesn't matter what I try to do, the end result is always the same." He shook his head, pacing the length of the room. "You know why?"

"I'm sure you think you do," she said, crossing her arms, trying to brace herself for what he might say next. He was on a warpath, and she knew it had nothing to do with her, but with him. He was bound and determined to blow this up. She could sense it. Could sense that the blow was coming, but it didn't mean that it would make it easy to take.

"Because I am a selfish bastard. You might not believe it because you had a short amount of time with me, but trust me, I've had more than thirty years inside this body, and I know me. Do you want to know the absolute truth, Rebecca?"

"You're going to tell me whether I want you to or not. In fact, I think if I don't want you to, you're even more likely to tell me. Because you're blowing this up, aren't you? The last thing you want to hear is that I love you. It scares you. You're going to ruin this."

He laughed, the sound cruel, unkind. "It was never supposed to be something that could be saved. It was ruined from the start."

"Because of you?"

"Hell yes. Why do you think I behaved the way that I did growing up? Because all I cared about was myself. Satisfying myself. There was always this thing inside of me, this hungry beast that wanted to be satisfied, and nothing has ever proven to be enough for me. Not alcohol, not women, not driving too fast on two-lane roads in the dark." He took a deep breath. "It was a relief."

"What was?" she asked.

"Finally doing something bad enough that I couldn't come back from it. Do you understand? That accident was the best thing that ever happened to me. Because finally I could look my father in the face and tell him what I thought. Finally, I could leave. I could walk away from this place, from everything in it. All of the dissatisfaction, all of the…"

"What? Are you still going to tell me it let you walk away from becoming your father?" She felt like she had been slapped. Felt raw and wounded. Just as she imagined he wanted her to feel. But even though she knew that was what this was, it was impossible for her not to have an emotional reaction.

But this, she had a feeling was actually honest. It was unfiltered, because he wasn't trying to spare her, but it was real. She had wanted reality. Had wanted to know what was going on inside of him, what tortured him, what made him feel like he couldn't come back. What made him so desperate to cling to the fiction he had created. So now, it was beginning to come out, and no matter how much it hurt, she couldn't reject him because of it.

She couldn't.

So she steeled herself, not with the shield of false strength she had used all of this time, that angry victimhood that had defined her for so long, but with love.

Love was stronger. Stronger than the past. Stronger than old wounds. Strong enough to take on a few more.

At least, she hoped it was.

"No," he said, his voice rough. "Because you're right, if I had really cared about that, I would have stayed. I just wanted relief. From myself. A chance to get away from this family and everything about it that hurt."

"What hurt you so much?"

"No, we're not going to do this," he said.

"Why?"

"Because there's no point to this. Because I'm going to walk away from you in the end, and if you really want me to leave you worse off than when I came, we can keep going down this road, but I don't think you actually want that. Because I'm going to leave you alone. Just like I promised I would in the beginning. Just like you said you wanted. Don't go changing the rules now because I'm not going to adapt to this new plan of yours."

"It's not a plan. I'm just in love with you. And in the beginning I wanted you to walk away because I was angry with you. And because I was afraid to need somebody." She looked at him, clarity rolling over her like a wave. "And so are you. You're afraid to want somebody. You're afraid to need them. Is that why you spent all of this time walking through your life alone? Because God forbid you accept any help? God forbid you accept any love? What happened to make you so afraid of this, Gage?"

"What do you think love is, Rebecca? I'm asking you honestly."

She thought back to the ways her life had changed since he had come into it. The way that he had filled all of those empty spaces inside of her. He had taken care of her, and she had let him. Hadn't felt hard, or terrifying. There was peace in it. A kind of completion that she hadn't known she could have.

He had taken all of the sharp, restless feelings that lived inside of her and wrapped them up in his arms, held her close to him even when those jagged pieces of herself cut into him. He had withstood. He had allowed her to rail against him with her words, with her fists.

"Mostly, I think that love is strong. Strong enough to get in there and fill the empty spaces, to reinforce somebody that's about to crack apart. At least, that's what it's been for me."

"That's never been what it is for me. Love for me has been nothing but disappointment, fear and a whole lot of unfulfilled expectations."

"Is that what we are?"

"It's what we would be if I loved you." His eyes were black, blank, his words cutting her down to the bone.

"What am I then, Gage? If I'm not someone you love... What am I to you?" She swallowed hard. "Am I anything other than your escape route? Is that what I am now too? The excuse for you to get out of town quickly?" Suddenly, she was suffused with terror. A kind of fear she hadn't felt since she'd woken up to discover that her mother was gone and she was never coming back. "Am I really that much of a fool, Gage?" Her throat tightened, the rest of her words escaping as a horrified whisper. "Did you let me make that much of a fool of myself?"

"I didn't let you do anything, baby, and you know that. I was honest with you from the beginning. More or less."

Something about him using that endearment, an endearment he had used in intimate moments, cut almost deeper than anything else. "You said a lot of things, but you showed me different things. So don't stand there acting like you're completely absolved of any of the fallout from this. That's one thing I was never going to be, one thing I can never be. Your absolution."

"Too bad for you, you said you forgave me."

She swallowed hard. "I did. But it didn't change the way you felt about yourself, did it? Not really. Because you still can't handle this. You still can't give me honesty." Her heart was thundering hard at the base of her throat, echoing in her head. She was being bold, accusing him of lying when he might well be telling her the truth for the first time. But she had to believe that this wasn't the truth. There was still more. That if she dug down deep beneath the layers there was still something else there.

She didn't believe that Gage was beyond redemption. She didn't believe that he was cruel. Most of all, she didn't believe that this was the end.

She couldn't.

"This is all I've got. You don't want me to uncover the rest."

"I do. That's what scares you."

"I'm not the one who should be afraid."

She took a step toward him. "Is this the part where you try to prove to me that you're a monster? Because I've been waiting for that."

Suddenly, she found herself being hauled up against his chest, his mouth hot and firm over hers. If it had happened at any other moment, she would have called it a kiss of possession. But now, she had a feeling it was just goodbye.

So she gave it everything. All of her rage, all of her tears. All of the love that she had inside of her body for Gage West. The love that overflowed her, filled her, replaced every ounce of hatred she had ever thought she possessed for this man, transformed into the kind of love that could never be simple, could never be quiet or tame.

It was the only kind of love people like them would ever be able to have. Because she wasn't quiet, because she wasn't tame. And neither was he.

It was the kind of love that would never allow distance, the kind of love that wouldn't allow them to hide behind walls they built up to keep other people out. She was ready to do it. Ready to open herself up and take this.

Her kiss was a plea for him to do the same.

She kissed him deep, because if this was his last chance, their last chance, then she wasn't giving him any excuse not to take it.

When they parted, he was breathing hard, and so was she. But he just stood there, looking at her like he was a wild animal, ready to attack or run if she took another step toward him.

"Don't you understand? I would use you like this. All the time. Without giving a damn that it was costing you. That it was killing you. I would take from you until there was nothing left. And you would let me. Because you think that's love. So don't cry when I leave you, Rebecca. I'm doing you a kindness, even if you can't see it."

"No. Don't do that. Don't you dare. From the moment you came back to Copper Ridge this is what you've been doing. Telling me what's good for me, telling me what I should think about you, what I should think about myself. I'm done with that. You can walk away, Gage West. Walk off into the sunset if that's what you need to do. I'm never going to be able to keep you here if you don't want to stay. But by God, do not tell me that I'm better off. Don't tell me what I should feel. Don't tell me what I should think. And do not tell me that you're doing it for me when we both know you're doing it for you. Stop it. Stop making me a victim so that you can feel benevolent. If you think you're a monster, then you own it. Then you walk away knowing that you hurt me. That you destroyed this. That we had something you refused to let us keep."

"Does that make it better for you? Then all right. This is for me. I'm leaving because I want to. Goodbye, Rebecca. I think it would be better if we didn't see each other after this."

"But what about…" She looked around the room, scanning to see if she could find her clothes. They were there, evidence of just how much she had changed because of him. That she didn't feel the need to grab them now. That she was angry she would have to get dressed, and pretend none of this had ever happened. That they would have to go back to being something different than they were before. That she was going to have to hide again. "What about the store?"

"It's yours. That's how it was always going to end."

"With you getting exactly what you wanted me getting—nothing?"

"You are the one who decided that maybe I could be Prince Charming, Rebecca. I never pretended to be anything of the sort. Anyway, you're getting the store. You aren't getting nothing."

"Wow," she said, deadpan, collecting her top and her pants. "Lucky me."

"I want to tell you something," she said, pulling on her clothes, tugging her shirt over her head.

"Go right ahead," he said.

"I love you. And when you're wandering the earth again, self-flagellating, pretending that you're beyond redemption, I want you to know that somebody back here in Copper Ridge loves you. And she would have given you a chance. You are the one who wouldn't take it. You're the reason you can't have love. Nothing else. Just your choices. If you made a different one... Your whole life could be different but you won't. Because you're afraid."

"Only an idiot isn't afraid of something that can destroy them."

"I guess I'm an idiot."

And then Rebecca walked out of his bedroom, taking the stairs down to the entryway two at a time. She flung open the door, taking a deep breath of sharp, night air, not caring that she had forgotten her coat, that she had nothing to protect her against the elements.

She was raw and exposed anyway, it might as well extend to this.

She wrapped her arms around herself, walking down Gage's driveway and heading back toward her house. It felt like a lifetime had passed since this morning. Since she had first come to his door and asked him to help her with her mother.

She felt like an entirely different person.

She looked up at the sky, uncharacteristically clear, blue velvet and shot through with fragments of light. Too many to number.

She supposed that was a good reminder. That even now, in the middle of the darkness, there was hope. That there was light.

Right now though, all she could focus on was the darkness.

She couldn't remember anything hurting this bad since she was a child. Since her mother had abandoned her. This was what she had been protecting herself from. It made sense. She couldn't call herself a coward, not when this pain felt terminal.

She had been smart to protect herself.

She huffed out a laugh, her breath visible in the frigid air.

The sad truth was she simply had let herself care enough about anything to feel this kind of pain. This was the other side of joy. The other side of happiness. Of love. You couldn't have the beauty without the pain.

Couldn't have the stars without the darkness.

And she had stars.

She had Lane and Alison and Cassie. She had Jonathan. She had this town, this wonderful, beautiful town and her shop that was like the home she had always wanted.

But Gage… Gage was the one who had shown her the way.

She swallowed hard, fighting back tears, fighting against the terrible, overwhelming pain that was threatening to swamp her. She looked up at the sky again, at the smattering of lights in the darkness.

She tried very hard not to think about how she feared that, while her sky had any number of beautiful stars, her north star was gone.

And without him, she might not be able to find the way forward.

CHAPTER TWENTY-TWO

GAGE WEST STARED out at the lake, his hands resting on the deck railing, the chill from the wood biting into his skin. He didn't care. If he could change anything, it was that it would hurt worse.

That it would be something other than this dragging, yawning ache inside of him that was threatening to undo him completely. This was too familiar. This was too much like what he had left behind in the first place.

She was right.

He was running, but not from what he had told himself he was running from for all of these years. He was running, but not from becoming his father.

He was running from how much he loved his father. From how much he wanted to be accepted by him. From the fact that his love had never been returned no matter what he did—right or wrong.

A deep, dark pit that was there long before he had met Rebecca. Exposed now. Deepened.

Running and running, because he knew that there would never be an end to it. Because he had seen it. He had seen it every day in his mother's eyes.

He was the same. He knew he was.

Had known it for certain from the moment he had

found out about Jack, his half brother. His father had told him. Because, it had been essential that Gage know, since he was going to eventually take over the West empire. There could be no secrets.

I've made mistakes, Gage, his father had said. *But the important thing is that I've handled them. So that you and your siblings, your mother, will never feel the consequences of those actions.*

His words had echoed through Gage as he had wandered the halls of the house, sixteen years old and the keeper of his father's darkest secrets. He had a half brother. One that was his younger brother Colton's age. A brother who was not allowed to be a part of the family because Nathan West needed so badly to protect the West name.

Does he know?

Not who I am, no. But I imagine there will come a time when I'll have to deal with that too.

He's your son, Gage had said, feeling both loyalty and jealousy in that moment directed at a boy he didn't even know.

But not like you are. Not like Colton.

Why?

Because he isn't legitimate.

Not because he loved them.

That matters?

It matters to our reputation, and reputation is everything. I'm trusting you with mine, Gage. And someday you'll likely trust me with yours. I hope you'll remember this when you do. We look out for each other, the

Wests do. Because we must protect each other. We must protect our name.

He had been reeling, dazed. And then he had run into his mother.

Did you have a good talk with your father? As always, she seemed brittle. She smelled faintly of expensive floral perfume and alcohol.

Yes, he had said. Lying.

He could sense something then. That she might know. That she suspected he knew something he wasn't telling her. And he wondered what his responsibility was. But he felt destroyed inside, finding out that his idol was nothing like what he had imagined he was. And he couldn't bear to expose him further. It had nothing to do with protecting his mother's feelings. And everything to do with the fact that he didn't want to expose his father. That man who he had wanted so badly to pattern himself after.

She had known he was lying. He could tell. Could tell in the way her shoulders had folded in slightly. In the way her lips pinched tight. And yet, she didn't say anything either. Both of them protecting a man who didn't deserve it. Out of love. Out of loyalty.

But he hadn't reached out to help her. And she had not reached out to him. To do so would be a betrayal of Nathan. And neither of them would do it.

They were too desperate to do the right thing. To earn the love of the man who withheld it with such ease.

He had always seen his mother as being a faded figure. She had never been deeply involved in her children's lives. Everything she had ever done had been in the service of her husband. Gage had always felt a little bit disconnected from her. Had seen her as weak and frail if anything. But suddenly, in that moment, he had realized that the two of them had a lot more in common than he had seen before.

It had been something he was unable to shake.

It had lingered with him, even as he had continued to do everything his father asked him to do, continued on the path to become the son his father needed him to be. He had managed to twist it all inside of him. To believe his father's version of the truth. That being a West, that protecting that name was the most important thing.

They were pillars of the community, after all. Those pillars had to be upheld, no matter what.

Deeper, though, something about that interaction with his father had shaken him to his core. And he had felt the need to push back. To create a situation in which his father would have to prove that loyalty he'd spoken of. And he had. He had done it, and he had swept Rebecca up in it too.

When he had stood before his father, the reality of what had happened laid out before them, he had waited for something. Some warmth. Some sign that his father did any of this out of love. And he realized then that the older man didn't.

That was when it had all become clear to him. He wasn't his father. He was his mother. The two of them would destroy themselves for love. For people who would never love them in return. And it wasn't only themselves they would destroy, it was everyone around them.

That night was the first night he had dared to ask her

about it directly. Dared to broach the subject, to even imply that Nathan West was anything short of perfect. He was bruised, he was broken inside and out. There was a girl in the hospital because of him, his father offering to make it go away, not out of love, but of loyalty.

"Why does he do it? Does it have anything to do with loving us?"

She had looked at him, and right in that moment Gage had realized how infrequently she did that. "He has too many things to care for to worry about loving people too much. That's why he needs us to support him. But," she said, her expression changing, sympathy in her pale blue eyes. "You have to be careful. Because people like you and me, we'll give and give until it takes everything from us. We care more than other people, Gage. And it's the kind of weakness that can ruin a person. And then when there's nothing left in us, it starts taking from the people around us."

He realized that that was exactly what he was doing. Already. The revelation about Jack had caused his rebellion, had caused him to act out the way that he did. And he had already started hurting people.

Rebecca had been the first casualty. All for what? To gain the attention of his father? To gain love that very likely wasn't there?

He saw in his mother that endless forgiveness, that endless ability to put up with anything, and he saw how destructive it was. Because there was no end. His father could never satisfy her, she could never be satisfied. Anyone who was with him would end up in the same position.

And he was an unholy mix of the two of them. His destruction was bigger than his mother's could ever be. He had all the selfishness, all the inclination to protect himself that his father had. And all of that need that came from his mother.

The terrible thing was, he had run to avoid doing more damage. That much was true.

But he had done more this way. So it hadn't been the only reason. It hadn't been for them. It had been for himself.

If I'm not the victim, where does that leave you?

A coward. He was left facing the fact that he was a coward.

It was why her forgiveness had been more of a burden than a relief. Why he had felt stripped down afterward.

In some ways, he could understand why her mother had been so desperate to deny that same forgiveness. It was just like she'd said to him earlier. He was walking away. He was the one leaving when someone was waiting for him with open arms.

Leaving was so much easier when you could leave with a cloud of sulfur behind you. Knowing that everyone hated you. That you had broken things beyond repair.

That you at least deserved to not be loved now.

That was what he'd done. That was why he was so dedicated to believing he was a villain. Because maybe if he didn't deserve love he wouldn't…crave it so much anymore.

But Rebecca wasn't allowing that. Wasn't allowing

him to burn the bridge. She was making sure he knew it was still there. And he liked to burn bridges. It was the only way he knew to manage that yawning canyon inside of him. To make sure he placed it between himself and the person he needed to escape from.

Rebecca didn't do that. She was brave. She faced down everyone. Her mother, him. She had stood between himself and Jonathan, defending him. She hadn't hidden. That woman didn't have an ounce of skittish in her.

No, he was the one on the run.

And now that all of his excuses had been taken away, it was impossible to justify.

He took a deep breath, squinting out toward the lake at the full moon reflecting across the surface. Rebecca's house was there. Rebecca was there. He ached for her, to hold her in his arms. He ached with the need that wouldn't end, he knew it wouldn't. Because that was how he loved.

Deep, destructive. He didn't know another way. He was still too broken to drag her down into it. Into him.

How could he ask for a love like that? When his own mother looked through him and his own father had barely ever seen him.

He was too broken for such a thing.

"So, fix yourself." He said those words out loud, his breath visible in the dark air.

He knew what he had to do. He knew it wasn't because he was too busy that he had been avoiding his father. Knew it wasn't because he had been caught up in everything else. No, he was avoiding his father because that was what he did.

In that, Rebecca was right. Initially, he had been using her. To put distance between himself and his family. Because she had never been the reason he left. It had always been them, always been him.

He laughed, the sound swallowed up by the thick pine trees and the dense night. He had come back to town bound and determined to fix Rebecca Bear, and he had found that she wasn't broken. Instead, she had shown him the million different ways he was splintered into unfixable pieces.

Maybe it was time he went and fixed one. He didn't know if he could ever be what she needed. Didn't know if he could ever justify trying to make a future with her.

Hell, he didn't know if he had the balls to give himself over to the kind of love he felt like he could have for that woman.

But he did know that if she could stand on her own two feet and face all of her monsters, then he could damn well go face a few of his own.

REBECCA WOKE UP to pounding on her door. Her heart slammed against her chest, mimicking the rhythm. She scrambled out of bed, padding down the hall and wrenching the door open, her heart freezing completely when, for one moment, she thought it might be Gage.

But no, it was Jonathan. His arms were crossed across his broad chest, his expression matching the steel-gray clouds outside. "Good morning," he said.

"Good morning," she mumbled, taking a step back and gesturing for him to come inside.

"It's ten thirty. I didn't think you would still be asleep."

"I had a rough night."

"Did you go see her?" Jonathan looked like he hadn't slept last night. It was strange to see him looking like this. Careworn and concerned, when normally he was impenetrable, at least from her point of view.

It took her a moment to realize that he was concerned about their mother, not about anything to do with Gage. Of course. Then, yesterday came back into focus. The fact that she had gone to see her mother. That Gage had gone with her. And then…

Well, she didn't want to think about the rest.

"Yes," she said.

"Are you okay?"

"Yes," she said. "She lives in a trailer park, but I imagine you knew that, since you knew the address. Obviously she didn't manage that money very well after she took off."

"I know. I make sure that she doesn't go hungry."

"How? She didn't seem like she wanted any help from me."

"Oh, I get it to her in a variety of ways. But, she doesn't know it's from me." He looked around, his expression stern. "Is he here?"

"The milkman?"

"It's not 1950, so no, that isn't what I meant. I meant West."

"No," she said, battling against the sharp slice of

pain that went through her when she gave him that answer. She wondered how long it would be before it stopped hurting.

"Okay," he said, clearly not quite sure what to do. She wondered if he had been intent on dragging Gage out of her bed and giving him a pummeling.

He turned as if he were going to go. "Jonathan," she said, her voice stopping him in his tracks. "Can I ask you something?"

He turned back toward her. "Sure. It doesn't mean I'll answer it."

She smiled. She could always count on Jonathan to be a little bit taciturn. "Have you ever wanted to rebuild things with Mom?"

"No," he said. The word was so firm, so sure. It surprised her. Because she didn't really know what she wanted from her mother. Hadn't until she had gone to that house and realized that she didn't need anything from the older woman, she only needed to change something in herself.

"Not at all?"

"Rebecca," he said, his voice rough. "She left you when you needed her most. I'm never going to forgive her for that. I'm never going to want to rebuild that bridge. And if she tried I would be the first one to light it on fire so that she couldn't cross it."

The conviction in his voice, the vehemence, surprised her. She didn't know why it should. Jonathan had always been there for her. And she had kept him at a distance. Sure, he wasn't the most demonstrative person alive, but she had never made a move toward having it be any different.

"I… I thought…" Her throat started to close. "I just thought that… Jonathan, I have spent a long time being afraid that everyone in my life would leave me eventually because I was so much trouble. Because I needed too much."

Her words were cut off as Jonathan pulled her into a hard, strong hug. She knew it came from somewhere deep inside of him. Knew that it cost him, because he never did things like that. Ever.

She pressed her face against his shirt, and she let the tears that had gone unshed in her sleep fall.

"If you are afraid of that, then I didn't do a very good job with you," he said.

She shook her head, sniffing as she did. Then she pulled away from him. "No," she said, "it wasn't you. You never gave me a reason to feel that way. You were there, day in and day out. It hurt me the way that she left. But I know that what she left you with… As unfair as it was for her to leave me, leaving you with all of that responsibility was even worse. She's just lucky that you're you. That in spite of the way she was, the way that your father was, you were willing to stay and take care of me."

"It wasn't even a hardship, Rebecca. I'd give up my life for you without even hesitating. It's one reason it killed me to see you with West. I don't understand how you could do that. I don't understand how you can want to do anything but kill him slowly and painfully for what he put you through."

"I don't know if I can explain it," she said, knowing even now that it wasn't that easy. That it would take hours and recounting all of the things Gage had done since he'd come into her life, large and small, in order to make Jonathan even begin to understand. "I definitely wasn't looking for it. But he's the reason... He's the reason that I realized that I'd been hiding. Afraid that people would leave me. Holding on to the past so I didn't have to deal with the future. So I didn't have to let people close. But he...he made me want someone close. He made me think maybe I could have that."

"So it took that bastard coming back into your life to make you realize that? I've been here the whole time, and you didn't pick that up from me?"

His words gouged at her soul, guilt pouring through her. "My only excuse is that it took someone coming in from outside. To show me, to shake me. You were like a foundation I didn't know I was standing on, Jonathan. But trust me, I'm realizing it now, and I'm grateful for it. We... Gage and I broke up."

Broke up seemed an insipid term for what had happened last night. For actively having your chest ripped open and your heart torn out. But then, *boyfriend* had always seemed an inadequate name for him too, so it stood to reason that this didn't really fit either.

"Do you want me to go kill him? Because my offer still stands."

She laughed, watery and shaky. "I don't doubt that, not for a moment. But, I don't actually want him to die. I love him."

"Damn," Jonathan breathed. "I really don't understand that."

"Hating him never helped me, Jonathan. Not one bit. But loving him…" A tear slid down her cheek. "It healed me. It changed me in ways that I didn't know needed changing. And right now, even though part of me—a different part of me than before—feels a little bit broken, I feel fixed too. That makes about as much sense as any of it, I guess. But it's true."

She looked around the house, her house, the one that she was so proud of, and yet had never brought a single bit of those seasonal decorations into, those things that she felt so strongly made a home. She had kept them from herself. Because, somehow she had felt she hadn't deserved them. Because she had felt like her mother's abandonment was her fault, because she had forced her brother to live a life he shouldn't have had to live.

But things had changed now. Gage West had changed her.

"I think I'm going to redecorate," she said.

"That's…random, but if you need help… You know I'll help you. Whatever you need. Hell, having a brother who works in construction has to be useful somehow, doesn't it?"

"It's not really that random," she said, taking a deep breath. "It's actually been a long time coming."

CHAPTER TWENTY-THREE

WHEN GAGE ARRIVED at the rehabilitation facility the next morning he felt...nervous. He couldn't remember the last time he had felt anything that he would characterize as nerves. But he had been putting off seeing his father for a long time. For so many reasons. Reasons tangled up in other reasons that were difficult to find the end of.

A nurse ushered him into his father's room, and when he got there, he saw his mother, holding vigil by the side of the bed, his father sitting up with the aid of the hospital bed.

He suddenly felt too large for the space, too large for the town. Standing there, encroaching on this moment. His mother looked so brittle it caused an answering crack to run through his own heart. There she was, still sitting by this man's bed. This man who had never given her a damn thing in return.

Her hand was resting over his, and he wondered if his father had any idea just how fortunate he was to have that hand there.

"I can come back at another time," he said.

Both of his parents turned and looked at him, his

mother quickly, his father slowly, age and ill health altering his movements.

"Gage," his mother said, sounding shocked.

Nathan West said nothing. His expression was immobile, and Gage wasn't certain if that was just the old man or if it had something to do with his stroke. Either way, it made his chest twist.

"I'm so sorry that I didn't come sooner," he said, and he was surprised to discover that he meant it.

"I know you've been handling all of the financial things," his mother said, her voice thready.

"I'm sure that Colton talked to you about it."

"Madison," his mother said. "Madison told me that you were back and that you are taking care of everything."

Of course Madison had. His unlikely little ally. His younger sister he hadn't seen nearly enough of. He was overwhelmed with a sense of need then. A need to change.

"Would it be all right if I talked to Dad alone?" He posed the question to his mother.

"Of course," she said, standing quickly and moving out of the way.

He had a feeling that someone else, in this very same situation, would be slightly offended at being asked to leave. But not his mother. Because of course, she would accommodate whatever was necessary for those in her life. Of course, she would bend and stretch, break even to make things better for a husband who had never done half of that for her.

She moved past him and he reached out, taking hold

of her hand and squeezing it. She looked up at him, confusion and fragility and a need that mirrored his own visible there.

"I should've been there for you," he said, the words coming from deep inside of him, regret tugging at his soul.

They could have been there for each other.

"Don't be silly," she said, "I had your father."

He released his hold on her, letting her walk out of the room, aware that she wasn't going to be able to come to the same place he was. In her mind, it was too late to fix the relationship she had with her children, with him. Too late to change her marriage to Nathan.

Gage wasn't going to let it be too late.

He walked across the room, sitting heavily next to his father's bed. "It's been a while," he said.

Nathan West treated him to a baleful look. "You could say that."

"I'm sorry," he responded.

"For what?"

"For leaving. I... I imagine that it hurt you and I... I'm sorry."

"It didn't hurt me. It forced me to prepare your brother for the position that you refused to take on, but Colton is a good man. It hasn't been difficult."

"Well," he said, an unsettled feeling in the pit of his stomach. "I'm glad to hear that."

"And you came back now. When we needed you. That's what matters. I knew that if I kept your name on all the legal paperwork you would be the one to come through."

His father's quiet confidence was void of any warmth. So close to his old man being proud. So close to him caring. But not quite.

Mostly, it came across as the arrogance of a man who no one had ever dared oppose. It had never occurred to him that Gage wouldn't come through, because everyone came through for Nathan West. And he took it as his due, he didn't understand. Didn't understand that he was married to a woman who had given him everything, her trust when he didn't deserve it, her fidelity when he had not given his own.

Didn't understand that his sons had come into the world worshipping the ground he walked on. That no manipulation had ever been required.

There had been an endless supply of people desperate to give his father their love, and he seemed unmoved by it, untouched. He continually manipulated, continually used his money, his power and his influence when all he'd ever needed to do was give a soft word. Give assurance.

All he'd ever had to do was show his family that he cared for them even a little bit, and he could have earned loyalty that way.

The thought hit Gage in an uncomfortable way. Because in that, he had to wonder if he was any different. He had come determined to fix things, not for himself the way that his father did, but it was still all manipulation.

And it allowed him to give nothing of himself.

It was so clear to him on the other side of it that his father had only ever had to give that and never had.

He didn't think his father did it out of fear, but maybe Gage was wrong.

After all, the old man was hardly the formidable figure that had lived in his mind's eye for the past seventeen years. He was just a man.

He and Rebecca had talked a lot about monsters. So far, the only monsters they'd found were inside of them.

It was a funny thing, that because Gage was so much like his mother he had begun to treat the world the way his father did. But, he supposed in a really dumbass way it made sense.

His mother had always seemed easily broken to him. Brittle. While his father had been a rock. Of course he had wanted to fashion himself into the image of the rock.

But now, all that was left was that hardness, leached of all color, left gray and crumbling. And Gage could see it for what it was.

All of that, that self-protection, was born out of fear. It was. He had no doubt of it then. And whatever his mother did, that was the same.

But love wasn't the same as being afraid. It didn't hide.

Love didn't run.

It was more than time for him to stop. That much was clear as he looked down at his father, hoping yet again for something that he knew he would never get. Someone had to break the cycle.

He supposed it might as well be him.

"I didn't come back because of the West name," Gage

said. "I didn't come back because of duty. I came back because I love you."

His father looked at him, his blue eyes filled with a sharp, shocked light. Blue eyes that were so like his own. Like Jack Monaghan's. Telltale signs of his sins and shortcomings. But that wasn't the point. He wasn't going to hold on to the bitterness. He wasn't going to use it.

Love was a lot like forgiveness. It wasn't about what you deserved. Wasn't about what you got in return. Sometimes you just had to give it, because it was good for you.

And yeah, it meant there was a risk. That you couldn't protect yourself.

But protecting himself hadn't done anyone a damn lot of good. So maybe, just maybe, this would.

"What is it you want?" his father asked.

"Nothing."

"You don't come out with something like that expecting nothing in return," Nathan said, sounding hard, indignant.

"Usually, Dad, what you're looking for is for someone to say they love you back." Finally, he had given voice to it. Finally, he was facing down the one thing he'd always been afraid of. And he found it wasn't all that scary.

"You're my son," he said.

"That's supposed to mean something to me? Because I don't think it meant much of anything to Jack Monaghan."

"That was different," Nathan said.

"Is it?" He looked at his father, searching the lines on his weathered face. Whatever the truth was, he knew that his father had to believe this was the truth.

"I'm *frail*," Nathan said, not sounding anything near frail. "I need a rest."

"This is the first time we've seen each other in seventeen years."

"Yes," Nathan said, clearing his throat. "But you know I'm glad you're home."

Gage's chest tightened, and he reached out, placing his hand over his father's, just as his mother had been doing when he had come in earlier. "I'm glad to be home."

He was surprised to discover he actually meant it.

BECAUSE IT SEEMED like the kind of day to try and deal with family, Gage went to see Colton after finishing with his parents.

He walked up the expansive porch, knocking on the door, settling back on his heels and waiting for his brother to answer.

Colton answered, looking surprised to see him there. Which he supposed was fair, since there had been a whole seventeen years when people had come to Colton's door and only once had it been Gage.

"Hi."

"So," Colton said, "you're just here now?"

"Yeah," he said. "Can I come in?"

Much to his surprise, Colton let him in, and even invited him to sit down in the living room. His younger brother sat across from him, staring at him, his manner steady and calm. Colton was surprisingly unaffected by all of the craziness that happened in the family. He had never rebelled in any way that Gage could see. Had never run off into the hills to lick his wounds and hide from his pain.

He even had a healthy and functional marriage.

"You're the best of us," he found himself saying. "You know that, right?"

"Of the two of us? Yeah," Colton said. "Of all of us? I don't think so. Sierra is brave, and she leads with her heart, even though it might hurt. Maddy is fearless, and she leads with her tongue, without any fear of backlash. They're pretty great. It's a shame that you haven't really gotten to know them."

"I plan to change that. I'm done running."

"Are you ever going to tell me why you started in the first place?"

"Well, I can tell you what I told myself. And then, I suppose I could tell you the truth."

And he did. Starting with Rebecca and making his way to the revelation of Jack's existence. Of how he used the accident as an excuse.

Colton looked up at him then, understanding in his eyes. "I think I can relate a little bit better than you might think. I pretty grandly took the burden that you left behind. And I built up a lot of excuses for why I had to do things a certain way. Hell, I nearly married the wrong woman, the safe woman, because I was so committed to doing the right thing. Which was actually just the easy thing."

"Obviously you didn't marry the wrong woman," he said, talking about Lydia, Colton's wife.

"No. Thank God. She was instrumental in helping me realize all the different ways in which I was messed up. Which was kind of good, since it was the only way I could even start to fix it."

"Is there any fixing this?" he asked.

"Our family?"

"Eventually. But I'd like to start with you and me. You don't have any reason to forgive me, Colton. What I did was all in my own best interests. Actually, it wasn't even in my best interest, it's just that it was the easy thing. I'll do whatever I have to do. I'm going to stay here. I'm going to prove that I can stay. I don't expect you to forgive me now. I don't expect you to let go of the past seventeen years right now. I just want to know that there's hope."

Colton leaned forward, pressing his hands together, staring straight ahead. "I don't suppose I have to let it go in order to know that you're my brother and I love you." He looked at him then. "The rest we can work on, right?"

Gage ran his hands over his face. "I tell you what, it's a lot easier to walk off into the sunset than it is to stick around and try to figure out how to do this."

"Do what? Say you're sorry?"

"No, that's easy for me. Calling myself every name in the book, that's easy. Just accepting that I'm a bastard, that's easy. The prospect of coming here and fixing things for you, for Rebecca, that was easy. But only when I thought that at the end I would leave. If I stay, eventually I'm going to have to figure out real connections. I've been avoiding that for a long time."

Colton cleared his throat. "I know I'm your younger brother. And I know we don't know each other very well. Take it from somebody who ran in place for a long time. Eventually, you have to start giving pieces of yourself. Because if you don't do that, you'll look around and see that there's no one there that really matters. You have to give something real to get something in return."

He thought of Rebecca, and his heart nearly cracked in two. She had given him all of her, every piece. From her scarred, beautiful body to her scarred, perfect soul. She had trusted him with those things.

And he had given nothing in return. He had come into her life and begun to manipulate it, but there had been no sacrifice behind it. Nothing genuine. Nothing real.

"How do you do that? How do you do that when you know it might end up draining you dry? When you know that you might never get what you want in return?"

"You do it anyway, knowing that it might cost you. If it's free, it's probably not something you want. Expensive things, those are the things that have value, right? It's the same with emotions. It's the same with people."

"Well," Gage said. "I think that's bullshit."

"Oh," Colton said. "It is. It's also the most important thing I can think of. Lydia changed me. If you had come back into town before I had her in my life, I probably would have punched you in the face and sent you on your way. But she taught me that there are things that are more important than pride. Than duty. If you lead with love, the rest tends to fall into place." He cleared his throat. "And that is it for me on the advice."

Gage thought about telling Colton about Rebecca. But he didn't know what to say. And he realized there was only one person in the world he should talk to about Rebecca. And that was the woman herself.

If she would talk to him.

He didn't deserve it. That was for sure.

But he was ready to try. He was ready to strip himself bare, he was ready to open himself up. Even if it meant pouring himself out until he was dry.

He supposed that was the other side of the coin. The other part that you needed to make love mean anything.

You couldn't hold anything in reserve. You just had to trust that the other person would give back what they took.

It was a big risk. One he had spent the better part of his life avoiding. Because...well he'd never seen it. Never experienced it. For all he knew, what he wanted didn't exist.

But he looked at Colton and Sierra...the happiness they had with the people in their lives and it made him hope.

And Rebecca felt worth it.

Hell, Rebecca didn't even feel like a risk.

If she could only forgive him for everything he'd done. That was a risk. But it was one he was willing to take.

CHAPTER TWENTY-FOUR

REBECCA WAS JUST about to close the shop for the night when she heard the bell above the door. She let out a long, exasperated side. She really wasn't in the mood to deal with seeing anyone. She just wanted to go home and crawl under a blanket.

In the overall scheme of things, she supposed she was doing well. She had ordered a bunch of things for her house that she had put in her store, and it was starting to come along nicely. Operation "turn her house into a home" was a step in the right direction.

In the small, personal scheme of things that had to do with the state of her heart and whether or not it was broken into a million tiny pieces, she was doing pretty badly.

Someday, she would emerge from this stronger. She was confident of that. Mostly, she wanted to lie on the ground and howl. This was heartbreak. And it was terrible.

She looked up, ready to snarl at her customer and let them know she was about to close. Okay, maybe she wouldn't snarl. She would keep her feral on the inside.

Then, she realized it was Gage. Her breath caught, her heart slamming against her breastbone. What was he doing here? It was too mean. It was way too cruel. She couldn't see him again. She just couldn't.

"I thought you were going to give me papers to this place and get out."

He pushed his hat back with his knuckle, then shoved his hands into his pockets. "And I thought you didn't want them."

"I don't," she said, busying herself with an imaginary task. "But since when have you ever given a damn about what I want?"

Gage started to move toward her, his blue eyes intense, his beautiful, sensual mouth set into a firm line. She still wanted to touch him, to put her hands on his face, feel his rough stubble beneath her palms. She wanted to melt into him.

It wasn't fair. It wasn't fair that he could say all those things, all of those terrible things, and she could still want him like this.

And then, even more unfair, he wrapped his arms around her and pulled her toward him. Then, he put his hands on her cheeks, held her still, studying her face. "I care," he said, his voice rough.

"Maybe you would care if you loved me," she said, shooting his words from yesterday back at him.

"You know what, Rebecca, I am damn glad I didn't tell you that I love you yesterday."

She wiggled out of his hold. "Really, asshole? Did you really come to add insult to injury? Just because you don't have a heart, because you can't feel love and pain doesn't mean that I can't. I feel it. You broke me." A tear slid down her cheek and she did nothing to wipe it away. "So if you came back for more, you're too late. And, you're terrible. Just terrible."

He tightened his jaw, a muscle there twitching, his face looking tortured. He reached out for her again, cupping her chin, sliding his thumb over her cheek, wiping the tear away.

"It's a good thing I didn't tell you I love you yesterday because I didn't know what it meant." Those words sounded pulled from him, like they had come hard won from the very depths of his soul. "I've spent years running so that I never had to ask myself any questions. So that I never had to love anyone, answer to anyone. So that I never had to spend more than one night with a woman. So that I never had to make a friend that was close enough to count on me. So that I never had anyone that I counted on. It was easier. Easier than hanging around my family home being everything my father wanted me to be, then desperately acting like everything he didn't want me to be, hoping to get some sign that he loved me."

"If you wanted your father's love, then you had some idea of what love was," she said, knowing that her words were unkind, not really caring.

"No," he said, "I didn't. Because I thought that love drained you. I thought that it left you empty and hollow and broken. Just like my mother. That's what I thought I was. Not my father. But somebody who would let themselves be consumed by this thing that seemed more like a curse than a blessing to me. But that wasn't love. It never was."

He continued. "You asked me what I was if you weren't a victim. I didn't have an answer for you. But I have a few now. If you weren't a victim, then I wasn't a villain. If I wasn't a villain maybe…maybe I didn't need to run. Maybe I needed to stay. I thought if I told myself I deserved to be punished, I deserved to walk around aching and wanting and never finding satisfaction. I thought maybe if I believed that, I could learn to live with it." He cleared his throat. "But even more than that, if you weren't a victim, then I might have to give you something more than just a Band-Aid for your life before I left town again. If you're more than that… Then I have to be more than that. I have to give more than that. I have to give you some of myself, and it's been so long since I've done that I'm not even sure I know who I am." He took a deep, ragged breath. "Unless it's the person I am when I'm with you, I'm not sure he's worth knowing."

"Gage," she said, tracing the lines on either side of his mouth, giving in to her need to touch him. "I know who you are."

"Tell me." He said the words unsteadily.

"You're the man who came into my life when I wanted him least. The man who pushed me to challenge everything about myself. You're the only man who has ever seen me naked. You are the only person to hold me that I can even remember. You're overbearing sometimes, and stubborn as hell, but that's okay because I am too. And you…you want love, don't you? More than anything. But you've been standing on the outside of your own life looking in for so many years that you don't know how to take a step inside. So you fix things. You fix things because it's the only thing you know how to give."

She blinked back tears, a heavy weight in her chest. "You helped me, Gage. You helped me get rid of so many terrible burdens. Please, please let me have yours."

She put her hands on his shoulders, then ran them down his back, felt him shudder underneath her touch. "Let me," she said. "Let me in."

He was an impenetrable rock wall, even now as he shook beneath her touch, it was like they were miles away from each other. And then, he looked up, his eyes locking with hers, and she saw it. Fear. Fear that went down so deep she didn't know if there was an end to it.

"I lived my whole life wanting love, wanting something neither of my parents could give me. And it was much easier to go live a life where I wasn't even tempted anymore. To put myself in a different category, the kind of person who couldn't have it. I had no connections with anyone, so how could I miss what wasn't close? When it was right there… That was when it was hard. When my mom was there, but wouldn't look my direction. When my father was within arm's reach but would never give me a word of reassurance. And it is the most wussy-ass thing…"

"How?" she asked. "Nobody goes through life alone. We aren't meant to. If we were, why would we live like we do? Why would we give our lives for our families? Why would we make vows to one person, pledging ourselves to them until we die? We aren't meant to live alone. The people that are around us mean everything. To have them right there and to feel like you don't have their love? That isn't a small thing. Was it a small thing that my mother left me?"

"Of course not."

"But it's wrong for you to feel bad? That doesn't make any sense. Those things leave scars deeper than any car crash ever could. I know. I know, because I have the ones to match."

She let her fingertips drift from his back, up his neck and to his jaw where she moved on to trace his familiar features. "Don't hide it. And don't pretend it isn't there. That's how we make monsters, Gage. By hiding ordinary things in the closet and letting them feed off the darkness."

"I've always been afraid that no one could ever love me," he said, his voice a rasp now. She could tell that it cost him to admit that, that his whole body was alive with shame.

And so, she kept on touching him, kept on moving her hands over every inch of him. She looked back down at the tattoo on his forearm, the one that had made her so angry at first. "I did a little bit of reading on tattoos. A black band is usually to remember somebody that died." She looked up at him. "Nobody died in that accident, Gage. We're both alive. And we both deserve to live. Really live." She wrapped her fingers around his forearm, drawing them down to his wrist, rubbing her thumbs over the tattoo.

"I know what I want it to symbolize," he said, his blue eyes blazing into hers. "I want it to be about death. The way that I lived. The way that I was. The fear. It doesn't have a place in this. With us." He pulled away from her hold, wrapping his hands around her wrists, pulling her forward. "I love you, Rebecca." The words weren't easy, they sounded as tortured as the rest of them had. As the rest of him was.

But she didn't mind. Because choosing to love Gage West wasn't convenient. He was the last man on earth it made sense for her to be with. But he was the only man alive that she wanted.

He closed the distance between them, kissing her hard, a physical affirmation of everything he'd just said.

When he finally pulled away, she laced her fingers through his hair, never letting her eyes leave his face. "I love you," she said.

"I've always thought that I would destroy somebody with all this need inside of me. That it would destroy me." He took her hand, placed it on his chest. "When I say I love you, it's with all of me. And I don't know if that's too much to ask one person to take."

"Maybe. Maybe if I were a normal everyday woman who hadn't been to hell and back, the kind of woman who wouldn't threaten to shoot you the first time you showed up in her store. Maybe then, I wouldn't be strong enough to handle you. Maybe then, you would be too much for me to take. But Gage, I've already walked through hell, and when that happened I felt like I was alone. Now, I want the chance to walk through life with the man I love. With you."

"Is that a challenge, Rebecca?"

She smiled, her chest swelling with emotion, her stomach tightening with desire. "Hell yeah, cowboy."

He wrapped his arms around her, taking a step back,

knocking her into a display of Christmas decorations. She didn't care.

Rebecca Bear was perfectly happy to be set up on top of one of the holiday displays laid out on her antique armoire, since she was being kissed—and kissed well—by the man she loved more than anything.

She moved her hand, bracing herself on the furniture, brushing her fingertips against something. She broke the kiss, looking down at the object. A ceramic bird.

She stared at it for a moment, and then a smile curved her lips.

She had always liked birds. They could fly anywhere, but they always came back home.

All this time, that was why she'd stayed. All this time, part of her had known she was waiting for him.

She looked up at Gage, then pressed a kiss to his lips. "I'm so glad you came back home."

EPILOGUE

"I NEVER THOUGHT I would see Ace Thompson pouring drinks while holding a baby."

"Lily is hardly a baby anymore. She's mobile now," Rebecca said, looking up at Gage and smiling. Still, even after two years, his heart felt like it got bigger every time she looked at him like that.

And she did it a lot.

"That's why he's holding her, I think," he said, looking over at his brother-in-law who was pretty expertly balancing work and fatherhood as he dispensed refreshments to the guests at the annual Fourth of July barbecue.

The entire town had turned out for the event, held on the Garrett Ranch every year. This was the second time Gage had attended. He could see why it had become such a popular tradition.

Sheriff Eli Garrett and his wife, Sadie, were running around making sure every plate was filled and that people were having fun. Connor and Liss Garrett were standing off to the side, Connor gazing intently at his wife, who was smiling up at him. Like they weren't aware they had a ranch full of guests.

"Hopefully Ace will get a chance to sit down with

us for a while," Rebecca said, moving over to the West family's patch of grass, which had been claimed earlier in the day.

Sierra was already sitting there along with Colton, who was watching as his wife, Lydia, did the rounds. Since she was mayor of Copper Ridge, it was difficult for her to get a moment when she wasn't being bombarded by people.

"I thought the Wests were supposed to be the pillars of the community," Gage said, sitting down on the blanket next to his siblings. "You both married people that outshine us."

"How about you?" Colton asked. "Rebecca is way more popular than you are."

"That's true," he said, wrapping his arm around her shoulders. "But, I haven't married her yet."

"You only have a week left before that stops being true," Rebecca said.

"I can't wait for the week to be over. Then you'll be my wife and your brother will stop asking you if you're ever going to make an honest man out of me."

"I'm like the wind," she said. "I cannot be tamed. But, for you, I will concede to being tied down for life. Because that's love."

"If Maddy were here, there would be a rude comment about Gage tying you up," Sierra said.

"Where is Maddy?" Gage asked. "Are they coming?"

"I just checked my texts," Sierra said. "She said they're running late because they got distracted. I don't want to know."

Gage looked around, still sometimes unable to believe that he was surrounded by family. That he was surrounded by love.

"Jack and Kate said they would stop by the blanket," Colton said. "They want to bring Jasper over to say hi to his cousin. And his aunts and uncles, presumably."

Even stranger was the fact that they had managed to build a relationship with Jack over the past couple of years. That relationship had not extended between Jack and their father, but he had definitely become one of them as far as the siblings were concerned.

It was most definitely a testament to forgiveness on Jack's part. And love. A whole lot of that.

As the day wore on, they all ate too much and talked too much. Later, Rebecca lay across his lap, looking up at the sky, waiting for the fireworks.

He touched the ring on her left hand, always happy to be reminded of that outward symbol that showed the world, and him, that she was his.

The first firework went off in a blaze of brilliant color, bathing the crowd below in bright light. He looked down at Rebecca and realized that she wasn't watching the sky. She was watching him.

"What?" he asked.

She reached up, drawing his head down, kissing him gently on the lips. "I just wanted to let you know that I love you," she said. "And that I'm so thankful I found a man who loves big enough that he can make up for all those years I felt like I didn't get enough."

Gage kissed her back, his throat tight. "I feel the same way."

Then, he drew her up against his chest, and they settled back with the rest of the town to watch the show.

Gage West was home, and there was nowhere else on earth he would rather be.

* * * * *

New York Times bestselling author

MAISEY YATES

**introduces you to her sexy and heartfelt
Copper Ridge series set in a small town
in Oregon.**

 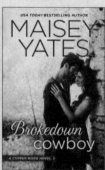 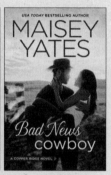

**Can these cowboys find the love they
didn't know they needed?**

"This is a book that deserves to be savored to the very
end, and will surely win Yates—and her Copper Ridge
characters—a devoted following."
—*RT Book Reviews* on *Part Time Cowboy*

Pick up your copies today!

www.MaiseyYates.com

www.HQNBooks.com

PHMYCRS15R2

USA TODAY bestselling author

DELORES FOSSEN

introduces the ***McCord Brothers***,
the most eligible bachelors in Spring Hill,
Texas. Join these cowboys as they get
wrangled by the love of some very unique
women—the kind who can melt hearts
and lay it all on the line.

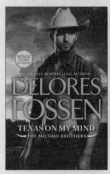

Available September 27!

Get your copies today!

"Clear off a space on your keeper shelf, Fossen has
arrived."—*New York Times* bestselling author Lori Wilde

www.HQNBooks.com

PHDFTMBS

New York Times bestselling author

B.J. DANIELS

**introduces *The Montana Hamiltons*,
a gripping new series that will leave you
on the edge of your seat...**

Available October 18!

"Daniels has succeeded in joining the ranks of
mystery masters." —*Fresh Fiction*

Pick up your copies today!

www.HQNBooks.com

PHBJDTMHSR3

USA TODAY bestselling author

SARAH MORGAN

**introduces *From Manhattan with Love*,
a sparkling new trilogy about three
best friends embracing
life—and love—in New York!**

 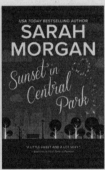 

Order your copies today!

"Morgan's brilliant talent never ceases to amaze."
—*RT Book Reviews*

www.HQNBooks.com

PHSMFMWL

REQUEST YOUR FREE BOOKS!

2 FREE NOVELS
FROM THE ROMANCE COLLECTION,
PLUS 2 FREE GIFTS!

YES! Please send me 2 FREE novels from the Romance Collection and my 2 FREE gifts (gifts are worth about $10). After receiving them, if I don't wish to receive any more books, I can return the shipping statement marked "cancel." If I don't cancel, I will receive 4 brand-new novels every month and be billed just $6.49 per book in the U.S. or $6.99 per book in Canada. That's a savings of at least 18% off the cover price. It's quite a bargain! Shipping and handling is just 50¢ per book in the U.S. and 75¢ per book in Canada.* I understand that accepting the 2 free books and gifts places me under no obligation to buy anything. I can always return a shipment and cancel at any time. Even if I never buy another book, the two free books and gifts are mine to keep forever.

194/394 MDN GH4D

Name	(PLEASE PRINT)	

Address		Apt. #

City	State/Prov.	Zip/Postal Code

Signature (if under 18, a parent or guardian must sign)

Mail to the **Reader Service:**
IN U.S.A.: P.O. Box 1867, Buffalo, NY 14240-1867
IN CANADA: P.O. Box 609, Fort Erie, Ontario L2A 5X3

Want to try 2 free books from another line?
Call 1-800-873-8635 or visit www.ReaderService.com.

*Terms and prices subject to change without notice. Prices do not include applicable taxes. Sales tax applicable in N.Y. Canadian residents will be charged applicable taxes. Offer not valid in Quebec. This offer is limited to one order per household. Not valid for current subscribers to the Romance Collection or the Romance/Suspense Collection. All orders subject to credit approval. Credit or debit balances in a customer's account(s) may be offset by any other outstanding balance owed by or to the customer. Please allow 4 to 6 weeks for delivery. Offer available while quantities last.

Your Privacy—The Reader Service is committed to protecting your privacy. Our Privacy Policy is available online at www.ReaderService.com or upon request from the Reader Service.

We make a portion of our mailing list available to reputable third parties that offer products we believe may interest you. If you prefer that we not exchange your name with third parties, or if you wish to clarify or modify your communication preferences, please visit us at www.ReaderService.com/consumerschoice or write to us at Reader Service Preference Service, P.O. Box 9062, Buffalo, NY 14240-9062. Include your complete name and address.

Turn your love of reading into rewards you'll love with
Harlequin My Rewards

Join for FREE today at
www.HarlequinMyRewards.com

Earn **FREE BOOKS** of your choice.

Experience **EXCLUSIVE OFFERS** and contests.

Enjoy **BOOK RECOMMENDATIONS** selected just for you.

PLUS! Sign up now and get **500** points right away!

Earn **FREE REWARDS** HarlequinMyRewards.com Join Today!

MYR16R

MAISEY YATES

78853	BAD NEWS COWBOY	___ $7.99 U.S.	___ $8.99 CAN.
78965	ONE NIGHT CHARMER	___ $7.99 U.S.	___ $9.99 CAN.
78981	TOUGH LUCK HERO	___ $7.99 U.S.	___ $9.99 CAN.

(limited quantities available)

TOTAL AMOUNT $ _____
POSTAGE & HANDLING $ _____
($1.00 FOR 1 BOOK, 50¢ for each additional)
APPLICABLE TAXES* $ _____
TOTAL PAYABLE $ _____

(check or money order—please do not send cash)

To order, complete this form and send it, along with a check or money order for the total above, payable to HQN Books, to: **In the U.S.:** 3010 Walden Avenue, P.O. Box 9077, Buffalo, NY 14269-9077; **In Canada:** P.O. Box 636, Fort Erie, Ontario, L2A 5X3.

Name: _____
Address: _____ City: _____
State/Prov.: _____ Zip/Postal Code: _____
Account Number (if applicable): _____
075 CSAS

*New York residents remit applicable sales taxes.
*Canadian residents remit applicable GST and provincial taxes.

HQN™

www.HQNBooks.com

PHMY0716BL